3/15/80

chapel shell

EARTH IS DOOMED

There is a mysterious explosion at the galaxy's core, thirty thousand light-years away; and mankind is warned by the Kyyra, an ancient race from the central suns who have a "deal" to propose...

EARTH IS CONSUMED

Torn from its sun by the Kyyra drive, a planet dies—and mankind faces landslides, tidal waves, revolution, and the decades-long terror of the interstellar night.

EARTH IS TRANSFORMED

Life itself is but a memory, a legend, to the remaining humans and Kyyra burrowed in the planet's empty shell, as an unknown star looms larger in the sky ahead...

LIFEBOAT EARTH!

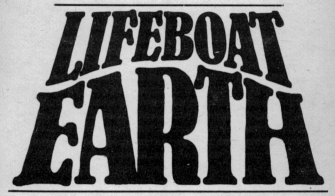

LIFEBOAT EARTH

Stanley Schmidt

A BERKLEY BOOK
published by
BERKLEY PUBLISHING CORPORATION

Berkley Publishing Corporation
200 Madison Avenue
New York, N.Y. 10016

SBN 425-03820-3

*BERKLEY MEDALLION BOOKS are published by
Berkley Publishing Corporation
200 Madison Avenue
New York, N. Y. 10016*

BERKLEY MEDALLION BOOK® TM 757, 375

Printed in the United States of America

Berkley Edition, NOVEMBER, 1978

To Ben Bova

for reasons too numerous to mention

Contents

Prologue

It seemed to Sandy that Scott's face, on the tiny black and white screen, looked much too haggard for somebody not yet thirty—even for one who had been through what he had. She had never seen him looking quite this bad before. And she had never before heard him come right out and ask, in a voice laden with bitterness, "Do you really think it's all been worth it?"

She was shocked. All the more, she confessed to herself, because of the answer she had to give him. "I hope so," she said. "I...think so." She paused. "We'll soon know."

"Three months." Scott shrugged. "At least. I guess you could call that soon." She struggled to see his face on the little screen. He was so close she was almost tempted to go to see him personally. But things were delicate now. It was best to keep doors shut tight and people out of the tunnels whenever possible, and she had to be here in case anything came up while Jonel was out.

"It's soon," she said firmly. "Relatively, it's now." *But it seems forever*, she thought. *I used to feel like this on Christmas Eve. Well...something like this....*

"The Kyyra themselves admit they've never done anything quite like it before," Scott blurted suddenly. "What they have to do at the end, I mean. It's...scary. What if they fail?"

So that's what's bothering him. Sandy wanted to reach out and gently, soothingly, rub his head and shoulders as she'd done when he was small. But of course that was impossible. All she had for him now was words. "They've got us this far," she pointed out.

"Some of us," he said sourly. "I can't help thinking, sometimes, maybe it would have been better not to start. If things were as good Before as you and Dad say they were...we all could have had some happiness then. Even me...and Alycia, or whoever I might've met instead."

"Yes. And we'd all be dead fifteen years now. You'd have been all of thirteen or fourteen when it happened. Isn't this better? Isn't a chance better than certain death?"

"Maybe."

"It wouldn't have been all that happy, either. As the end got near, we'd have *known* we'd be dead."

"Alycia's dead," said Scott. "And...."

He didn't finish the sentence, but Sandy knew what he was thinking. "But you do have Karen," she said. For many silent seconds his eyes and hers locked on each other through the picture-phone system. Finally she said earnestly, "We're going to make it, Scott. And then all this'll be over. You'll see what Jonel and I were talking about."

He looked at her a few seconds longer, then managed a smile, of sorts, for her benefit. But it faded quickly as he said, "I hope you're right."

Then he faded from the screen.

I hope I'm right, too, Sandy thought as she turned away from the phone. Privately, she had even more reason to doubt than Scott. She and Jonel knew more about the conspiracies brewing under the cities, the recently emerging disagreements between humans and Kyyra about how the new planet should be treated, the threat of a popular movement to withhold help from the Kyyra because of what their ancestors had done so long ago.

Partly to take her mind off the worries, she climbed up the sloping floor—which once she would have called the north wall—and began furiously working out on the exerciser mounted there. More important now than ever to keep that up, she thought as she grasped the handles. Her body still felt fine, heart muscles strong and supple, especially for a woman nearing sixty. But how much of that was real and how much was comforting illusion brought on by the present weakness of the effective gravity? She wanted to be sure she was ready when she finally felt again the solid pull of real gravity against horizontal ground under an open sky.

That thought brought back a little of the Christmas Eve feeling, now somewhat less tainted with the bitterness and uncertainty she had caught from Scott. She finished working up a good sweat, then sat back down in front of the phone-screen and dialed the comnet channel that now carried a continuous picture of their destination. She leaned close to stare at it—still just a star, but now a star blazing at minus fifteenth magnitude against a background of brand-new constellations. It wasn't visible on the screen yet, but the Kyyra scout ships said there was a planet there, hospitable and available. A real, living planet, not a battle-scarred corpse like this.

Three months! Sandy thought with a surge of anticipation, a smile blossoming on her face. *Can I wait that long? Or longer? Beldan said that was a lower limit....* Her smile changed to one of ironic amusement at herself. *Of course I can. I've waited over thirty years. What's another three months?*

What was a few hours before Christmas when she was three years old?

An eternity. Could a three-year-old be sure Christmas morning would come, with all it promised?

Could anybody be sure what waited at journey's end?

Abruptly, the doubts crashed back onto her—not only the ones Scott had expressed, but the ones she had not cared to tell him about. Involuntarily, she found herself thinking, *What if we don't make it? Could Scott be right?*

"*If things were as good Before as you and Dad say they were...*" Scott had said. They had been. Usually Sandy and Jonel avoided dwelling on the fact, but now she let herself remember. She remembered when they had lived above ground here, when there had been breezes and clouds and palm trees and sunshine and surf and salt smell where now there was not even air. And the trips north to her stone cottage in the Tennessee mountains, now just a lifeless pile of rubble—not just the cottage, but the mountains themselves. Hiking there with Jonel among rhododendron and laurel blooms in June, rolling expanses of colored fluff in October, snow and icicles in December. . . .

It had been good. Good enough that maybe they *had* been cheated by the migration. Maybe it would have been better to stay and get all they could out of that and accept the end gracefully when it came.

Stop that! she told herself sternly. *You've been through all this before. Sure, it was good. It was good enough to gamble for a chance to have it again, permanently, for Jonel and me, and Scott and Karen and all the generations to come. And we still have a chance.*

And that was what she and everyone else must concentrate on now. For just a moment longer she let the memory linger of what they had had.

It had ended so suddenly, once Clark had nerved himself to make the decision nobody else would make. . . .

A Thrust of Greatness

The world was coming apart at the seams.

That was where it was worst. Tremors were felt all over the Earth, beginning in the south and sweeping north in a globe-girdling wave. Mostly, the ground shuddered a little, quivered, settled, and that was all. But along the Ring of Fire which encircled the Pacific, they were more than tremors. Up the coast of the Americas on one side and Australia and Asia on the other, the plates grated against each other and those who lived along the edges felt the friction. In mere moments, whole villages slid off high perches in the Andes. Great cities like Santiago and Auckland, Lima and Tokyo, San Francisco and even Anchorage fell in one brief convulsion into fields of rubble interspersed with survivors sturdier or luckier than their neighbors. Homeless, frantic survivors roamed the ruins, calling out after missing loved ones—plaintive cries in Spanish and English under morning skies, in Japanese and a multitude of island dialects in the dark of night. Here and there a new volcano coughed tentatively, but there were few of those, and none in major population centers.

But there was a more insidious threat that did not end with the quakes and was not limited to the Ring. Everywhere the ground was tilting—so slightly as to be imperceptible to the eye or inner ear, but enough for air and water to begin flowing south. Unexpected currents caught primitive dugouts and majestic thousand-foot liners unawares and swept them off course to the south, some beyond hope of retrieval. And for those on land, they threatened flooding which nothing could stop.

Meanwhile the breezes rose somewhere in the north and blew south, smashing established weather patterns to start new ones such as no meteorologist had seen. Gradually, relentlessly, the currents of water and air swept southward, even as a spreading gray cloud forced its way northward against them.

And that was just the beginning.

After he committed the world to the end of all it had ever known, Henry Clark had little time to reflect on what he had done before he had to begin facing its consequences. Already, here in this room, he had felt the first tremors that marked the launching. He had told the first fellow members of his species what he had done, and he had finally learned why the Kyyra had offered what they had offered.

Now he stood alone, both drained and relieved, at the window of the office where all that had happened. Beldan, the Kyyra "ambassador," and Jonel and Sandy Turabian had gone out silently, leaving Clark to wonder what was in their minds. Joe Sanchez, strapped in his chair, remained like a silent specter. Clark knew what was in *his* mind, but tried not to think about it. He had trusted and respected his former-counselor-turned-conspirator, once, but that was in the past. It must not be allowed to intrude on the present.

For several minutes Clark stood staring out the window at the expanses of concrete and swamp and seashore that were Kennedy Spaceport. He wasn't really looking at anything. The familiar Florida landscape, not quite focused, was merely a backdrop against which to project his thoughts and let them smooth themselves out. He had to be careful not to let the images of what was going on around the world intrude. It was too easy to become emotional about them.

And there was too much to do to allow himself to become emotional.

Presently he felt composed enough to begin turning his mind toward concrete actions. Then he turned briskly to leave this room for his own apartment.

The first two things, he thought as he meditatively chewed a solitary lunch of beef stew, were obvious. A serious talk with Beldan, to pin down the specifics. And then another—rather more intimidating—with Franz Gerber, to see that the required actions were taken.

He did not have to wait long for either. The knock on his door came only halfway through the stew. In a way he was grateful for the interruption. He had been half-watching the noon news on television, turned on low. He felt a moral obligation to do so—but the unprecedented listing of earthquakes and destruction and human suffering gnawed at his already sore conscience, keeping the tormenting images bright and vivid.

So it was with a certain relief that he got up and walked slowly to open the door. He had to look up to see the waiting faces—the frame was filled and more by the majestic seven-foot forms of Beldan and another of his kind. Clark didn't know the other, and to human eyes there wasn't much to distinguish them. Both had oval, hairless heads with faces strikingly humanoid despite the big, round, red eyes and the pointed ears and the lack of an external nose where a man would have had one. And both were almost completely wrapped in flowing robes of dazzling metallic iridescence and swirling colors, with two slender, two-thumbed hands emerging at angles that required two elbows per arm. Beldan's face had a slightly different color cast and a slightly rougher complexion that made him look older—and from what Clark knew or suspected of his background, that was probably the case.

That was all there was to distinguish them—except for the difference in facial expressions. Beldan's seemed to register a peculiar blend of concern and urgency and guilt. The other's was completely alien and utterly unreadable. It reminded Clark of the one time—just this morning, he reminded himself, struggling to keep his time-sense anchored—when he had seen Beldan so unnerved that he forgot to maintain human facial expressions.

3

"We must talk," Beldan said simply, in his soft, rather high voice. "May we come in?" His English pronunciation was impeccable, except for the oddly singsong intonation that carried over from the absolutely tonal Kyyra language.

With some trepidation, overridden by a firm sense of self-discipline, Clark nodded. "Certainly. Do you mind if I finish eating?"

"Not at all," said Beldan as he and the other followed Clark back into the single big room. "You will need your strength." Clark turned off the television and returned to the table in the dining nook. He scooped up another bite of stew, using his left hand since his right shoulder was still bandaged and somewhat painful. The two aliens, products of a planet that had started out somewhere near the burning galactic core, occupied the couch.

"This is Zhalāū," Beldan told Clark, with a slight gesture at his companion. "She is direct coordinator of the engineer fleet. She will be in charge—if that is the word—of arranging technical procedures for the entire trip. And coordinating them with your people's efforts."

Clark, chewing slowly, nodded slightly toward Zhalāū. "I'm pleased to meet you," he said formally, wondering privately what word would suit him better than "pleased." He would never have guessed that she was female. He mused idly on how the Kyyra distinguished—but he didn't waste much thought on it. "So you lit the match, huh?"

Zhalāū, her face still inscrutable, said stiffly, "Pleased. Yes, my fleet did that, if I understand rightly your idiom. Forgive my English, Mr. Clark. It needs practice."

"It's fine," Clark assured her. "Shall we get to the point?"

"Surely." Beldan took out his music-pipe and began to play softly, improvising a quietly spine-tingling melody. But he was obviously still listening attentively as Zhalāū began, "Now that we are underway, preparations are urgently necessary to insure the survival of as many of the Earth's inhabitants as possible. Some, of course, we Kyyra engineers must do. To do them right, we need to know everything about the planet we are moving. The things you call geology, meteorology, oceanography . . . we have had little time to study these things for ourselves. We will need access to all the information about them your scientists have been able to accumulate. A good selection of books and articles would be helpful initially. A group of experts in these

4

fields, continually available for consultation, will probably prove even more so. Certainly they will be essential."

"I'll see what I can do," said Clark.

"Essential," Zhalāū repeated. "I cannot overemphasize that. Essential that we have them; essential that we have them *now*. Already there has been destruction and loss of life in some parts of your planet in excess of anything we intended or anticipated. Beldan is deeply troubled. The Coordinator is deeply troubled. We are all deeply troubled. If we have misjudged some property of your planet, we need to correct the error in time to prevent future mishaps."

"Don't you think I know that?" Clark snapped. "Don't you think I'm troubled too? You don't understand what I'm up against." *They don't, either*, he reflected. *Literally. If what Sandy says she learned about their Coördinator is right, they could never understand what it's like to have all our information scattered around in books and individual minds, and every mind wanting to go its own way on the basis of its own little smattering of data.* The thought overwhelmed him. An hour ago he had felt relieved that a decision had finally been made, despite the albatross he must wear to the end of his days for having made it himself. Briefly, then, he had felt that he had done his part and the rest was up to others. Now he began to faintly see how much more he would have to do even before the others began to do their part.

That would take discipline. With deliberate effort, he forced calmness back into his voice. "I appreciate the problem," he said. "As soon as I know precisely what has to be done, I'll make every effort I can. You need information and local experts. We can start with that committee the U.N. saddled me with. What else?"

"The rest is what your people must do for themselves. The seismic problems you already know about; we're keeping them as small as we can. Do what you can for them. But even more urgent are the field distortion effects we have touched on briefly. Those will require prompt, massive, coordinated action on a global scale. The first thing that must be done—"

The phone interrupted harshly. Very briefly, Clark considered ignoring it. But Zhalāū broke off, Beldan quit piping, and Clark left a barely perceptible break before he finished Zhalāū's sentence: "—is to answer the phone." He walked over, picked it

5

up, and sat down on the bed. "Hello!"

"Henry Clark," a familiarly stentorian voice spat into his ear. "Gerber here. What's going on?" Clark noticed at once that there was something new in the U.N. head's voice. He was still projecting the stern authority figure—but he was a badly shaken stern authority figure.

"Be specific," Clark suggested.

"The news," Gerber grated impatiently. "I assume you've heard some news today. Disasters all over the world. Earthquakes, mostly. I don't know how many major cities in shambles; hundreds of smaller ones likewise. I was already swamped with requests for relief before I came into my office this morning, and they keep pouring in. I'm numb; haven't had a moment's peace all day. There's nothing I can do for most of them; too many. I'm doing all I can to muster up aid from outfits like the Red Cross, but they're up to their ears too. I've never seen anything like it."

"I doubt that any of us have, Franz."

"I could only take so much of this," Gerber said tightly, "before I started putting two and two together. All those things don't happen at once for no reason. They all have something to do with the aliens, *nicht wahr*?"

"Yes." Clark didn't even hesitate before answering, as he would have back when this all began, back in October. Those three months had wrought profound changes in him—mostly in the last few days. "Yes, Franz," he said, to leave no possible doubt, "we're on our way."

"What?" The phone was silent for a long time. Then Gerber forced out through obviously clenched teeth, "What did you just say, Clark?"

"You heard me. I hope it didn't really take you this long to figure it out. I mean, if you looked at what cities were involved, and at what times—it's pretty obvious, isn't it?"

Another lengthy silence. Without the picture switched on, Clark could see Gerber boiling only in his imagination. But that was vivid enough. Finally Gerber said, "I find it hard to believe even you'd do this. You say they've started moving the Earth. On whose authority?"

"Mine," said Clark.

"You had none!" the phone snarled. "Not to do that. Well,

you'll pay for it, Clark. As for the aliens . . . well, they'll just have to stop, that's—"

"They can't stop," Clark interrupted, losing patience. Gerber was wasting time. "We can talk about it later. We're going to have to talk about it, and soon. But there's no point in it until I've finished talking to Zhalāū."

"Who's Zha . . . who's that? And what do you mean, can't stop?"

"Kyyra engineer," Clark answered curtly. "And I mean we can't stop. I've got to find out exactly what we have to do."

"*You* have to come to New York. Right now!"

"Right after I finish with Zhalāū," Clark corrected. "If you want to talk sooner, you can come here. But if you do, be sure you get a message to me first. The world can't afford for us to waste time passing each other halfway. See you, Franz." He hung up without waiting for a reply and turned back to Zhalāū. "You were saying?"

Zhalāū had taken out a music-pipe like Beldan's and played a couple of short phrases to calm herself before answering. Then she said, "I was starting to explain the field distortion effects. The acceleration of the Earth along its axis feels like an added gravitational field, with the effect that the ground everywhere will seem to tilt toward the south. The acceleration is so low, so far, that you can't actually feel it. But it's not too low to make things happen. For instance . . ."

She proceeded to tell Clark what must be done. It took two hours, and he felt pale through and through when it was over.

But he had listened carefully and taken good notes. For the Kyyra, with their long experience in planet-moving, were mankind's only hope of getting safely to M31—the spiral galaxy in Andromeda.

By 2:20 in the afternoon, Clark was striding briskly onto the spaceport's auxiliary airfield. Tony, his uniformed chauffeur, had his plane ready, checked out, and waiting—a compact lemon-yellow jet with twin engines tucked neatly under backswept wings. As he hurried out to the ramp, attaché case in his good hand, Clark automatically sized up the weather. He hadn't done any of his own flying lately, but he still had his license and the habits he'd acquired with it. A fairly stiff breeze blew straight out of the north, just as he'd expect from Zhalãú's briefing.

(Although, he realized suddenly, neither of them seemed to have taken coriolis force into full account. It would be more complicated than he'd thought....)

There was still some clear sky to the north, stuck in among big gray and white cottony clouds. To the south the clouds had all coalesced into a formless gray mass that filled a third of the sky and gave a vague impression of pushing northward. It had no well-defined northern edge, and Clark realized that it was growing—as more and more water molecules diffused into the air—rather than moving north as a unit. Only to be expected, with the biggest reaction "engine" in human history roaring away at the South Pole.

Resigned to the fact that it wasn't going to be an especially pleasant ride, he climbed into the back seat. Tony glanced dutifully back to make sure his seat belt was fastened, asked, "All set, sir?", caught Clark's nod, and turned to the controls to get things going.

The take-off was bumpy and so was everything else. They climbed to a normal cruising altitude—Clark kept glancing over Tony's shoulder at the instruments, and especially the altimeter—but the turbulence seemed to be everywhere, and so, increasingly, were the clouds. After they had leveled off, Clark said conversationally, "Tony, what were the weather reports like?"

"IFR all the way, sir," said Tony, without looking back. He was concentrating unusually hard on his flying. "Patterns look a little odd. A lot of SIGMET's and such out, but nothing we can't get through. Winds are against us, but I'll do the best I can."

"That's all I can ask," said Clark. He hesitated pensively for a few seconds, then added, "Wouldn't hurt to check the reports a little oftener than usual—and the altimeter, too. Especially the altimeter."

He almost wished he hadn't said that, but Tony gave neither reply nor comment. Clark wondered how much Tony suspected about the weather patterns that he called "a little odd." Did he suspect a connection between those and the "acts of God" that the papers and casts had been full of all day? Clark surmised that he must, even if it hadn't yet reached the conscious level. *He* certainly wasn't going to ask—much less tell the young pilot how much more he knew about how all this fit together.

There was little to see outside, now, but there was plenty to think about. Clark lowered his seat back a notch and settled back against it, eyes closed and hands resting on the attaché case on his lap. He was used to the constant bounces and bumps from his own more active flying days, so they didn't interfere with his using the trip to turn the whole situation over and over in his mind. What had led up to this...what he would do when he was in New York and face to face with Franz Gerber...

Why (a piece of his mind wondered abruptly) was he going to New York at all? Why hadn't he insisted that Gerber come down to Florida instead, to save time?

Because (another piece of his mind answered) this way would save time in the long run. Because Gerber and those who worked with him were very, very human, and under the best of conditions Clark faced an uphill battle to make them see what they had to do and get them doing it in time to help. The fact that he had already forced everybody's hand was not going to make it easy. For him (whose official title was still nothing more than Lieutenant Commissioner of Grants of the World Science Foundation) to compound the offense by telling the head of the U.N. that he must come to see Clark rather than expecting Clark to come to him—

It would be too much. Far better to do it this way—to appear cooperative now so the U.N. people wouldn't waste still more valuable time trying to make him change his mind.

It would be worth it. Both for the big reason of improving mankind's chances, and for the very personal one of getting this whole enormous burden out of Clark's hands and into the ones where it belonged. How he looked forward to that!

Only—

Only it wouldn't be like that, he realized with shocking abruptness, and his throat went suddenly dry. For an instant he caught a clear glimpse of this whole situation as it must look to Gerber, and the glimpse blossomed into a terrifying picture of what was *really* going to happen. He felt his pulse quicken as he examined that future and gradually realized what he would have to do.

He didn't like it, and he was painfully aware that he couldn't see enough moves ahead. But what he had just envisioned seemed *so* likely that he had no choice but to cover it as well as he could.

Grimly, he squeezed the qualms out of his mind, reshaped them into resolution to do what he must, and squeezed that back in. That felt better. . . .

He looked at his watch. Still a bit more than an hour to New York. He allowed himself one more minute to ponder wording, then opened his attaché case, took out paper, and started writing. Oddly, his hand didn't shake, even with the soreness still in his shoulder. If anything, it seemed to have acquired a kind of firmness that it had never had before. There was shakiness in the writing, but only what came from the turbulence in the air.

He wrote—sometimes hurriedly, sometimes crossing out and pondering, then rushing on to make up lost time—all the way to New York. He took a short time out as the plane fought its way down a very bumpy final, bounced hard with one wing dipped, and roared down the runway, braking hard. By then Clark was writing again; his signature gained an added flourish from Tony's necessarily sharp turn onto the taxiway. As they taxied to the terminal, Clark sealed what he had written into an envelope, snapped the attaché case shut, and addressed the envelope:

JONEL AND SANDY TURABIAN

PERSONAL AND CONFIDENTIAL

As he climbed out into the bitter cold of an overcast intersection of January and New York, wishing he'd brought a heavier coat than he had, he handed the envelope to Tony. "I don't know how long I'll be," he told the pilot, "but guard this with your life. If I'm not back and you haven't heard from me by quarter of seven, you hightail it back to Kennedy Spaceport and deliver this to the Turabians. Personally and immediately, regardless of the hour, and make sure they read it right away. Got that?"

Tony's puzzled frown was thinly veiled, but he asked no questions. "Yes, sir."

Business was pretty much as usual in New York, with the

possible exception of the weather. Clark took a cab—an undoubted extravagance, these days, but still worthwhile in cases of real hurry. It gave him little chance to see conditions in Manhattan, since they used the Queens Midtown Tunnel and surfaced almost at the doorstep of his destination. But they were above ground, careening through the streets of residential and shopping neighborhoods, for a goodly distance before entering the tunnel, and nothing looked terribly unusual. Traffic was normal; pedestrians went about their business in quite ordinary ways. The dirty remains of last week's snow lay on the ground and fluffy new flakes swirled aimlessly but rather violently in the air. The winds whipping tree skeletons and pedestrians' hats about weren't really spectacular, but they boded far more than routine annoyance.

The taxi entered the frantic dream world of the tunnel and Clark stared blankly as the neatly tiled walls whizzed hypnotically past. Then up again into the steel and concrete and glass canyons of Manhattan, with the bustling and honking of early rush-hour traffic on the sidewalks and streets. Quieter and less crowded now than in his boyhood, Clark reflected, since even more of it was underground now than then and engines had become quieter and cleaner. But still crowded and noisy, by any standards.

For half a minute, after he paid his fare and got out, he was right in it, fighting the wind from the curb to the door. For that time he merged into the human stream, heard them talking, watched them pass the headlines on the ubiquitous newsfax dispensers—and saw no evidence that any of them cared.

But he cared. And he had reached his destination.

He stepped through the door into the warm lobby, but he felt no warmth.

Franz Gerber's office occupied a corner of the twenty-sixth floor, with huge plate glass windows, beginning less than a foot above the blue plush carpet, commanding a splendid view of the East River and lower Manhattan. But Gerber was by no means preoccupied with the view. Hardly a second passed after Clark rang his doorbell before the door flew open and the boyish-faced U.N. chief glared out at him, his dusky-blond hair thrown carelessly back and his smooth, round cheeks flaming even redder than usual. Boyish, perhaps, in ways, but his eyes were hard and fiery and his lips drawn sternly tight across his white teeth. "About time," his voice crackled. "Get in here, Clark. Have a seat."

He pivoted sharply, strode back to his big molded desk and sat down. He pressed a button, presumably to alert the front-office receptionist not to let anybody else in, and waited impatiently while Clark took his coat off and hung it on a hook beside the door. Gerber, ever impeccably dressed and usually impeccably groomed because he set great stock in such things, kept a half-length mirror on the inside of the door, and Clark couldn't help noticing himself in it before he turned away. His clothes wrinkled, his face more lined and his black hair and mustache more streaked with gray than they had been three months earlier—he looked harried. He looked like a man who had managed to get gracefully past his first sixty years, aging less than others—and then, abruptly, under the press of events, began to catch up to them.

But there was something else there, too—something he hadn't quite decided how to evaluate yet. Almost as if, shortly after this aging spurt began, it had taken another sharp turn, off in some other direction. To...where?

He thrust the silly thoughts impatiently from his mind and sat down in a leather-covered armchair facing Gerber. Gerber was leaning slightly forward, staring impatiently at Clark. The desktop between them, usually an extension of its owner's meticulous concern for appearances, was strewn with telegrams and memos and sheets of newsfax, all about the earthquakes and calls for help and sincerest regrets that no help was available. Gerber waved a despairing hand over them. "The fruits of your arrogance," he hissed. There were bags beginning to form under his eyes. "O.K.—you got us into this. Now get us out. After that we'll worry about what to do with you."

"I'm sorry," Clark said softly. "But that's impossible."

Gerber's eyes narrowed. "What, precisely, do you mean ...impossible?"

"We can't stop the Earth. It's on its way; it's using reactions that the Kyyra know how to control and we don't. But it's using the Earth's substance for fuel, and it's using it on a large scale. Did you ever try to stop a forest fire instantly because somebody said you must? You can't do it. You can control it, on a large scale. But once it's going, you can't just casually stop it or ask it to bypass your favorite flower. This is something like that."

"You're lying!" Gerber snapped. But his eyes had a haunted look of terrible uncertainty.

"Besides," Clark went on, "even if they could stop it, there'd be nothing to gain by it. Absolutely nothing."

"Nothing?" Gerber echoed incredulously. "We could pick up the pieces of all this and get back to a normal life—"

"For seventeen years," Clark broke in. "That's all. And even that wouldn't be normal. You'd spend a lot of it picking up those pieces. And toward the end of it even normal, short-sighted human beings would begin to realize what was going to happen to them, and they'd shatter into hysteria. By then it would be too late to do anything else. That's why I told the Kyyra to go ahead."

"*What's* why? Make sense, Clark!"

"You, for instance. You still haven't really grasped what's happening, have you? I'll say it very slowly, though you've heard it all for three months. The core of our galaxy has exploded, Franz. Radiation from it has sterilized planets all over the galaxy, and we'd get ours in seventeen years. Not a thing we could do about it, on our own. But the Kyyra have already been through it. They're fleeing to the nearest homelike galaxy, using their planets as ships, and they've offered to help us do the same. But they can't wait those seventeen years for our answer. They had to know now."

"But who gave *you* the right to decide? Since when can you play God with the whole human—"

"I finally realized," Clark lashed back, "that I was doing that either way. You politicos have had this thing long enough, and you haven't done a thing with it. It's become quite obvious that you never will, and the Kyyra were about to leave. So what would have happened if I hadn't gone ahead and made a deal with them? We'd have lost that chance. What choices would we have then? Sit here and talk and finally panic and die. Or we could burrow underground and sit here like rats in a hole—we and all our descendants for the next million years. Only we wouldn't have even done that. Seventeen years sounds too far off to get excited about, even if the problem'll take that long to solve. I finally realized that the only way to make people worry about a big, long-range, far-off danger is to convert it to a big, immediate, very personal one. So I did." He sat very straight and gazed defiantly into Gerber's eyes. "And no, Franz, I don't regret it. I'm sorry people are dying, but if I hadn't done it, everybody would. This is better."

Gerber was silent for a long time, staring, wheels turning behind his eyes. He hadn't seen much of Clark these last few months, since he'd been tied up with this affair at the spaceport. But he knew that before that Clark could never have done anything like this, or even talked this way to Gerber. Yet circumstances change men....

"You've gone mad," Gerber announced finally. "Completely out of your skull. I can't understand why *they* would try to make a deal with *you*. Surely they know—"

"They know I'm the only person in a position of any authority who even seemed to take them seriously. And they really wanted us to go—"

Gerber's eyebrows shot up. "You finally found out about that?" he demanded. The aliens' motives, which they had studiously avoided discussing, had been a very hot question up through yesterday.

"Yes," said Clark. "Just this morning. Beldan took a liking to Sandy Turabian—the girl who married Jonel after they followed him back here—and took her to visit their ship." *No need to go into all* that *story*, he thought privately. "She figured it out, and Beldan verified it. They—" He started to tell the first part of their reason, but caught himself and decided that was best kept under his hat. He skipped to the other part. "They're going to need help resettling when we all get to M31. They think we can give it."

"Over my dead body!" Gerber snarled.

"Very probably," said Clark.

Gerber's face went white. He fumed silently for a while. Finally he said ominously, "That's not funny, Clark. Does that damned space creature have a phone where he's staying?"

"He does," said Clark. "It takes a clearance to call it, but you can do it. I suggest you address him a little more respectfully than that. And think of him that way, too."

Gerber gave no answer except an indignant snort. At his touch on a button, a picture-phone screen popped up out of the desktop, facing him. He put a call through to Florida, taking more time and pushing more buttons than were usually necessary. Finally he leaned back, looking hard at the screen.

Clark couldn't see the screen, but he heard Beldan's mellow voice from the speaker.

"Yes? What is it?"

"I'm Franz Gerber," Gerber said distastefully. "Secretary General of the United Nations of Earth. You probably don't remember me, but—"

"I remember you."

"Then maybe you can explain what's going on here. We're scrambled. Mr. Clark tells me he's made an agreement with you and you've started the Earth on that intergalactic trip."

"That is correct."

"Mr. Clark had no authority to make that agreement."

Silence for a few seconds. "I'm sorry."

"*I*—on behalf of the U.N.—have that authority. So..." Gerber hesitated, as if what he had to say next tasted bad. "So would you please stop the reaction? Right now. Then the proper authorities can consider this thing, and maybe we'll do it and maybe we won't. But for now, the deal's off. Do you understand me?"

"I understand you." Pause. "But I'm afraid you don't understand the situation. The deal may be off, in your view, but the reaction is on. It can't be stopped—not soon enough to do what you want. The physical and technological requirements leave no alternative which is in any way preferable to continuing what has been begun. Hasn't Mr. Clark explained this to you?"

Gerber didn't answer. He glowered at the screen for a long time, breathing heavily. Then he said, "We'll discuss this later." He disconnected. The screen disappeared back into the desktop.

Gerber looked at Clark and forced a thin, sardonic smile. "So," he said, "we seem to be at an impasse. So what now? This morning you said we'd have to talk."

"Yes." Clark jumped eagerly at the possibility of finally getting to the meat of the matter. "Things must be done so people can survive. Time is of the essence, and I'm talking about minutes, not days. The U.N. will have to direct things for maximum speed."

"I'll humor you. What kind of things?"

"They're starting out very gently—"

"*Gently?* You call the worst rash of earthquakes in history gentle?"

15

"Relatively," Clark nodded. "It could have been much worse. They made the initial shock as light as they could, to minimize damage. It's been worse than they expected, but there was no way to avoid it altogether. But they do want to minimize it. That's why one of the first things we have to do is give Zhalāŭ all the information we can about the Earth, and a panel of experts to help them interpret it. Right away."

Gerber frowned. "Sounds dangerous. Maybe suicidal. How gullible do they think we are?" Pause. "What else?"

"They're building the thrust up to something like a thousandth of a gee. That'll take a few days; I don't have all the numerical details. They'll hold it there to give us time to prepare for the next phase, then run it up higher. That'll be a big job, but we'll have to put everything into it and get it done fast. It's hard and inefficient for them to keep the acceleration too low—and we'll hit some time limitations of our own from things like food reserves. Agriculture as we know it is finished. But that's not what matters now. Our immediate problem is just to get through the initial phase with enough people still alive to do what comes later. The earthquakes last night and this morning are part of it, but a small part. The main thing's going to be the flooding."

"Flooding?"

"We're accelerating, and acceleration feels like gravity. It means the ground everywhere on Earth is effectively tilting downward toward the South Pole."

"This room isn't tilting."

"Yes, it is. You just can't see it because the tilt isn't very much—yet. Everything outside's tilting too. That means the oceans are going to flow south. They'll flood land temporarily on the way, and they'll flood it permanently when the water piles up in southern latitudes. It'll be deep down there and gone up here. So the first thing we have to do is hold all the water we can in the north, and evacuate the areas that are going to be flooded. That's going to include a lot of the southern hemisphere. Whole cities, even whole countries, in some places up to thousands of feet above present sea level—"

"Hold it!" Gerber broke in. "Hold it. Evacuation of areas like that. Do you have any idea what you're asking? Do you know what it would *cost*?"

"Meaningless question. The economy is dead, Franz, all over the world. The sooner you realize that, the better off we'll all be.

Money doesn't mean a thing any more—but there are billions of lives at stake. I don't think you understand yet that we're in a situation where survival is the only problem we have time for."

Gerber leaned back and stared narrowly at him. "No, I don't," he said quietly. His manner had changed, as if he had finally made a decision that had eluded him for too long. "You admitted yourself that the earthquakes have stopped."

"Most of them," Clark nodded, frowning. "But the floods—"

"You're bluffing," Gerber said flatly.

Clark was stunned in spite of himself. "What?"

"You're bluffing," Gerber repeated, standing up and beginning to pace in an arc on the far side of the desk, looking down at Clark. "Beldan is bluffing. I don't entirely understand why, yet, but it's the only way I can make sense of it. You've developed delusions of grandeur and you've somehow got the aliens to put on a show for you, to make it look like there's a situation so desperate that we have to hand you virtually unlimited power. I still don't see what's in it for them . . . I'll have to talk to Beldan about it."

"There isn't time for that," Clark protested. "The evacuation—"

"I can't start anything that big until I'm absolutely sure it's necessary. Meanwhile . . . the earthquakes have stopped. Your show is over."

"The floods," Clark croaked. "Check ocean currents, if you don't believe me—"

"No time. That's a big job, and the chances of its being necessary look too slim. Meanwhile, I have real problems that need a lot of attention. All those earthquake victims. And you." He frowned, pressing his lips together, and added, "And those aliens. What *is* their angle in all this? It's obviously an act of aggression on their part—"

"Words," said Clark. "So what if it is? What kind of retaliatory action can you take against beings who mine stars and move planets?"

"None," Gerber admitted bitterly. "So we'll concentrate on you." He stopped pacing and riveted accusing eyes on Clark. "Insubordination at best—flagrant commission of acts for which you were in no way authorized. Mass murder and high treason at worst. You're a dangerous man, Clark. Too dangerous to risk letting you do any more."

Clark faced him with surprising calm. "What are you getting at?"

"Punishment can wait," said Gerber unhurriedly. "There's plenty of time to see what an international court can do with you. But it's immediately important to see that you don't get into any more trouble." He touched a button on his desk and smiled blandly. "Please remain seated, Mr. Clark. You're not going anywhere. I thought over our conversation this morning while I was waiting for you, and took the liberty of having a couple of security troops wait outside when you arrived. Just in case."

Clark heard the door open behind him. He turned sharply to see the two men in green and gold uniforms, armed and ready. Then he turned slowly back to face Gerber, forcing his body to relax and his face to appear calm. He drew some slight satisfaction from Gerber's visible disappointment that he did not seem very surprised.

But, of course, he wasn't.

Gerber wasn't as stupid as Clark seemed to believe. Sure, *if* it was true that the launching was real and irreversible and nothing could be done about it, he'd want to do everything in his power to prevent damage to life and property. Even something as mind-bogglingly expensive and formidably difficult as the evacuation program Clark was screaming for.

If.

But if it *wasn't* true . . . how could he possibly be expected to commit the kind of money and matériel and men and women Clark was talking about, and risk finding out when it was over that it was all a waste? It would be cataclysmic. The cost to the world, by any measure, would be shattering, particularly coming right on the heels of those earthquakes. The loss of confidence in the U.N. would destroy all the great forward strides that the world community had made in the last quarter century. He, Gerber, would be a global laughing stock, but it was far more than his own face and political skin he was concerned about. It was the welfare of all the people of the world.

He would have to find out, of course, and soon. If all Clark claimed *was* true, prompt action would be needed. But Gerber had no intention of plunging headlong into it until he was sure. A big crisis didn't warrant losing one's head—rather, it made it all the more necessary to keep it.

The possibility that Clark—and Beldan—were telling the truth haunted him long after the troops escorted Clark out. But still it seemed remote and therefore less urgent than the attempts to get aid to the earthquake victims. The launching irreversible? That above all Gerber found hard to swallow. The aliens manipulated stars and planets as men manipulated generators and automobiles. It seemed inconceivable that they could do all that and not even be able to shut off what they had started.

But... *Let me be right about that*, he found himself praying with unaccustomed fervor as he dialed a call to yet another relief organization. *Please let me be right.*

Actually, he wasn't even entirely convinced the launch was real. He still didn't see why the Kyyra should want to go to all that trouble for a strange and backward race. But he did know that Clark had been developing megalomaniacal tendencies out of this thing. Joe Sanchez had alerted him to that, before his involvement in that conspiracy. (*Too bad about that*, Gerber thought. *Sanchez's heart still seems in the right place. Pity he let bad judgment get him mixed up in a thing like that.*) That being true, and Clark being in closer contact than anyone else with the aliens, who knew what crazy deals he might have made with them? Gerber should have watched him more closely, he realized now. But it was too late to worry about that.

He concentrated hard on his relief efforts for forty-five minutes after they took Clark away. Telegrams, calls to agencies who might be able to help, calls to friends all over the world who might be able to pull strings at agencies who might be able to help, people who might take some of the load off his shoulders....

It left him drained. The day had been too much, without a moment's relief since the first phone calls ripped him from sleep in the wee hours of the morning. The last hour had been frantic. It was dinnertime. He needed food, but was afraid to take time out for it. He needed a drink even more, and was even more afraid to take that. There was so much still undone....

All he allowed himself was two minutes leaning back with his eyes closed, running through a relaxation exercise with such grim determination that it defeated the purpose. Then he dialed another call.

The face that formed on the screen was one that he had never been able to consider calmly. Before it he felt somehow intimidated—and there wasn't a man or woman on Earth who could intimidate Franz Gerber.

"Mr. Gerber," said Beldan, neutrally. "I hadn't expected to hear from you again so soon."

"You should have," Gerber said tightly. "I said I'd get back to you. We have a lot to talk about." He waited, but Beldan made no reply. He simply stared back, his limpid red eyes projecting an aura of stoical patience such as might grow out of a long and trying life. Finally, annoyed, Gerber broke the silence. "I didn't want to continue the discussion we started in front of Mr. Clark. But I have to pursue it with you."

"Where *is* Mr. Clark?" Beldan asked.

"Never mind that. Let's talk about stopping this thing you've started."

Impatience rippled faintly across Beldan's calm, then passed. "We told you that's impossible."

"I know. I don't believe you."

Beldan shrugged, but his face betrayed nothing. "I'm sorry. But that doesn't alter the fact."

"You actually expect me to believe you can start a thing like this and yet you can't stop it?"

"Not the way you want. As for believing it, do you have any alternative? I hope you will not waste so much time deluding yourself that irreparable damage is done."

"Irreparable damage has already been done," Gerber shot back, "But not by me. By you. Do you people have no consciences?" *That looks chillingly believable*, he thought. But he said aloud, "I can't believe you have so little that you'd go ahead and let the things Clark described happen."

"You refer to the flooding, I suppose?" Beldan looked deeply troubled. "Certainly we would not willfully cause such harm to your people. The possibility that you would act as you are doing—that *you* would allow them to suffer when you should be acting to prevent it—was inconceivable to us. I find your actions quite incomprehensible. But I am powerless. It's in your hands now."

Frustration pounded harder and harder at the inside of Gerber's head. "I still can't believe that," he muttered. He leaned forward, affecting confidentiality. "Look, Beldan, maybe we can make a deal. Obviously you hoped to get something out of all this. What?"

"Surely Mr. Clark has told you our reason." There was

something odd in his expression then, Gerber thought. But he couldn't figure out what.

"He told me what you claimed was a reason," Gerber said. "What's the *real* reason?"

Beldan looked utterly perplexed. "I don't understand you at all."

Gerber felt more and more exasperated. "What do you want from us? Admit it—you made some kind of a secret deal with Clark, didn't you? Well, he had no power to make a deal. You won't get whatever it was." He realized even as he said all this that it seemed absurdly futile in the face of events. But he knew nothing else to try. . . . "But if you deal with me, maybe you can. We'll see."

Beldan stared out of the phone screen at him, silent, seemingly uncomprehending. At length he said uncertainly, "I don't know what deal you think you're talking about, Mr. Gerber. I'm sorry you don't consider Mr. Clark an appropriate individual for us to have made arrangements with. That was my mistake, I suppose. We have never really understood your power structure. We have nothing like it ourselves, you know." He paused, then suddenly looked out at Gerber with the uncertainty gone. His voice remained placid, yet there was a strong note of urgency in it as he said, "But you really should listen to Mr. Clark. He knows more about this situation than anyone else."

Gerber made one last desperate try to find a point of contact with the alien. "Why can't you just start dealing with us instead? With me and the others here at the U.N.? *We* are the duly constituted authorities on Earth."

"But Clark," said Beldan, "is the one who knows what's happening. We won't waste time trying to teach you."

"Why?"

"Because it would be futile. If we waste that time, very simply, none of you will survive. Neither your race nor ours will gain anything."

And with those words, without waiting for a reply, *he* broke the connection.

For a moment Gerber fumed at the alien's audacity. Staring at the blank screen, he almost called back, then decided he would not give Beldan that satisfaction. Instead, he leaned back, exhausted, exasperated, hopelessly frustrated. He was still hungry and thirsty and—he finally admitted—scared. He badly needed sleep, but hated to take time for it.

However, he conceded, it had reached the point of necessity. Therefore, he would do it, for just a short while. There was just one more call he would make first.

After supper that evening, Jonel and Sandy Turabian sat on their couch continuing the day's long process of sorting out their thoughts and feelings. They talked little, for what they both needed would come more from within than without. Still, Sandy, leaning on Jonel's shoulder, drew great comfort from his nearness. But it was by no means a thing of passive dependence—she knew very well that Jonel was leaning on her quite as much as she on him.

But she felt sure that in some respects his adjustment was farther along than hers. That was his way. If a thing needed doing and there was no longer any chance of changing it, he could quite calmly thrust all regrets about might-have-beens behind him and concentrate his whole being on doing what he must. To some extent, so could she, but she was more sensitive to some things and sometimes that got in the way.

And she had been much closer to Beldan.

Her gaze fixed on the wall, her mind relived for the hundredth time the dizzying events of the last two days. The entertainment console provided a background of Vaughan Williams' *Sinfonia Antarctica*, not too loud—a thing she had chosen more to match her mood than for any literal appropriateness its title might have coincidentally had. Ozymandias the Mutt lay curled between her feet and Jonel's, unusually quiet, occasionally gazing up at him or her with big brown eyes full of worry about whatever was worrying them.

Twenty-four hours ago she had been aboard the Kyyra starship in orbit around Earth, a lone guest among Beldan's kind. In the few intervening hours had come the stunning series of revelations. She had been less a guest and more a hostage than she could ever have dreamed; Beldan had made his first known attempt at deception. She had confronted his dying "God" face to face—or mind to mind—and had learned of his ancestors' guilt in connection with the core explosion. And Henry Clark had played along with his amateurish deceit to the extent of committing the Earth single-handedly to the odyssey on which people had utterly failed to agree for three months.

And now there was no turning back.

That was what took the most getting used to. All this time, ever since the Kyyra had followed Jonel home from space, she had been in the very forefront of trying to learn what made them tick and whether men would do well to accept their offer. But, she had realized with stark clarity this morning, she had remained so objective through all that that she had never decided whether she personally favored going. Which would be better for two people in their prime: to live normal, vigorous lives into their forties and then die, or to trade all semblance of normality for more time and a chance for the grandchildren they might someday have?

She still wasn't sure. She had long since disposed intellectually of any outrage she had felt toward either Beldan or Henry. Both had had understandable reasons, probably even good reasons, for what they did. Shock had passed quickly; emotional turmoil was fading gradually. But she had not yet fully accepted the trip as something that had begun and would continue for the rest of her life, rather than something to be debated for decision at some vague time in the future. She had not fully realized that the cost would be so great—not even the first time she had sat in on one of the deliberations and become afraid as she had never been afraid before.

She had run through it all once more and was stuck on that again when the doorbell rang. The narrator on the record had just read the last superscription, the one that begins, "I do not regret this journey...." Sandy remained on the sofa, consciously hoping that wouldn't become too prophetic, while Jonel went to answer the door.

She frowned, perplexed, when she recognized Tony, who usually flew Henry's official plane. She couldn't hear all he said; he was speaking too quietly. But she heard, "He didn't come back.... No, I don't know what happened.... He said to be sure you both read it right away."

"Will do," said Jonel. He took an envelope from Tony and tore it open with his thumb. "Thanks, Tony."

The door closed and Tony was gone. Jonel sat back down next to Sandy and took a single sheet of paper out of the envelope. It was covered with Henry's handwriting, marred by an occasional crossed-out phrase or a place where something seemed to have bumped his hand. Jonel held it where Sandy could see it and they both read silently.

Dear Jonel and Sandy,

I hope you've managed to forgive me enough by now to read this and do what I ask. I'm writing this on the plane en route to New York. When we took off, I was looking forward to getting out of the driver's seat, but I've had enough time to think it over to decide I'm not going to get off that easy. What I'm afraid of is this: Gerber's going to be so teed off about my taking things into my own hands that he'll go overboard coming down on me for that instead of doing what needs doing. I had a long talk with Zhalāū (ask Beldan to introduce you) and I know there's not time for that. I know what needs to be done, and I'm going to try to do it through channels. (I'm not sure I'd bother if I could see a workable alternative.) But Gerber's likely to try to block me—I wouldn't be terribly surprised if he locked me up and put a muzzle on me.

That's why I'm writing this. If that happens, a lot of people are going to die unnecessarily in the southern hemisphere. I don't think you and I can prevent that, but if it happens, maybe we can use the shock of it to prevent too much more of it. I'm asking Tony to bring you this if I don't come back; if he does, it means I'm out of commission for some reason like that and it's up to you.

What I'm asking you to do is this: go to the media. Jonel, at least, should have no trouble getting air time or newsfax coverage. Use it, tonight. Give them at least some of the information I wanted to. Zhalāū can give you a list of the places that'll be flooded, and when, and where people can go to be safe. Some of the flooding will start within a day, so we've already lost the chance for an organized evacuation of the first victims, but maybe some of them can still get out on their own. What's even more important is that you make it very clear to everybody that these things are going to happen and we knew it. Make sure they know we can get through it if and only if southerners get out of low places and northerners start saving all the water they can. Above all make sure they know I told the world government and the world government didn't do anything. It won't save those people in the south but if they die and the survivors know somebody knew how to prevent it—maybe it will create some pressure to listen in the future. Pressure like that can cause explosions, but it can also be channeled to get things done. I don't see any other way....

I don't know what you should say about my role in this. Probably the less said the better. I find it hard to think about that....

No time anyway. We're landing now.

> *Please hurry,*
> *Henry.*

Sandy read it twice and then stared at it for a long time with growing dismay. She could see something of the same in Jonel's face. Mobs could be vicious, terrifying things; neither she nor Jonel felt comfortable dealing with people in large masses. "Poor Henry," she whispered. "But . . . why us?"

It was almost purely a rhetorical question, but Jonel answered it. "All kinds of reasons. As he says, I can get the exposure. Like it or not, anybody who brought the *Archaeopteryx* home with the news of the core explosion and the Kyyra not far behind is going to remain grist for the newsmen's mills. Especially when he wants to talk about what Henry wants us to talk about." He took another long look at the letter and remarked, "Henry's changed. Can you imagine him doing anything like this before the Kyyra came? Or even before he was shot giving that speech?"

"We've all changed," said Sandy. "And we'll keep on changing. Anybody would, under that kind of pressure. And Henry's been under the most of all."

"True. And you've been in closest contact with the Kyyra. If anybody on Earth knows what makes them tick, you do."

"That's a frightening thought, when I think how bewildered Beldan still makes me feel sometimes. Well, what are we going to do, Jonel?"

"Two choices, as I see it. We do what Henry asks, or we don't. Do we agree with him?"

Sandy chewed thoughtfully on her lower lip. "I . . . I'm not sure what I think. Again. I hate being that way. I'm not used to it. I hate the thought of doing what he wants and taking what the public and the U.N. are going to give us for our trouble. But I'm also afraid of what will happen to everybody if we don't."

"I think," Jonel mused, "Henry is in the same position, only more so. He's resigned himself to doing what he thinks he must, knowing full well it may mean he'll never have any personal peace again." He looked at Sandy and added softly, "And I think we're literally the only other people he even hopes support him now."

Sandy finished thinking it out. "I don't see that we have any choice," she said, and with that all hesitation was banished from her mind. She began planning moves, thinking out loud. "We can get in touch with a few people to announce that we have an announcement. Then while we're waiting we'll get the details from Zhalāū. I know her already, Jonel—I met her on the ship. And . . ." she frowned ". . . we're going to have to do some hard thinking about that last question Henry raised."

Jonel nodded, but he was already at the phone. "We should be able to make some eleven o'clock news," he said, pushing buttons. Then, to the phone, "Hello, this is Jonel Turabian. Yes, *that* Jonel Turabian. . . ."

Cecil Gordon sat on the hilltop overlooking the bay at dawn, leaning against a gumbo limbo tree and trying dazedly to comprehend what had been happening to him. He had first become aware of it in the middle of the night, when shouts and excited jabber in the old patois had yanked him from a sound sleep in his shack on the edge of Port Maria. The road and its margins swarmed with villagers, brandishing flaming torches and electric flashlights as they milled about, seemingly streaming toward the steep hill on the landward side of the road. Yapping dogs and bleating goats mingled with cries of children and shouts of adults trying to keep their own together. A lot of them were saying something about water, and Cecil was conscious of a steady undertone of rushing, lapping, wet sounds. He paid them no great heed at first. It had been a stormy night when he went to bed, with winds howling and shaking the coconut trees and plantain and banana plants this way and that, and waves battering the shore, sending towers of foam and spray crashing skyward when they hit the retaining wall. But there was nothing in that that should hold terror for any but a small child. So his first reaction when he got up was annoyance.

That changed to something much more, with literally chilling suddenness, when he stepped out of his front door to see what was happening. Still fumbling to get a torch lit, he didn't see the rushing water before his bare foot landed in it. He drew it back with a startled oath, frantically finished lighting the torch, and looked down incredulously at his brown feet. The water was lapping at his very doorstep, and there was never water on this side of the road—not since the hurricane that had struck the coast when Cecil was just a little boy begging rides in the fishermen's boats.

He held up the torch to look at the road. It wouldn't reach that far, but there was enough moonlight and flashes from his neighbors' lanterns to see that the road was covered and the Caribbean had spilled over it. Many of his neighbors were up to their knees in churning froth.

That realization sent Cecil's eyes frantically to the side of his house, where he kept the cotton-tree boat on which his living depended. It was gone. As well as he could by the blotchy mixture of moonlight and torchlight, he looked wildly around for it. He found no trace—unless it was one of those dark shapes bobbing on the water, too far out to go and investigate. He thought of the time and work he would have to put into making a new one if he didn't find it, and felt sick.

But he had little time for that now. He felt the water around his feet again, and he had been standing up out of it. It was rising. How high it would go, he had no idea; it shouldn't have even been this high. The only sensible course was to head for high ground.

The hill started up right behind his house, and so did he, without delay. He didn't bother trying to take the torch. It would be a nuisance, and he knew the hillside well enough to pick his way up it by moonlight, even allowing for its steepness and thick vegetation. But he did take his machete. It was one of the few times he was glad he lived alone now, with no family to keep track of and watch out for. Occasionally he saw other people, their dark faces and arms barely visible among the shadows, but he made no attempt to join forces with them. He could move faster alone.

He was tired, from climbing too far too fast with a body too little rested, when he collapsed against the gumbo limbo tree. He sat there the rest of the night, trying to sleep but with little *success. He did a lot of looking at the sky and water, and at some point it dawned on him that there was something wrong with the moon. Like any good fisherman who sometimes went out before dawn, he knew the sky well, and so he knew the moon was not where it belonged. It wasn't far off—not even enough that most people would notice. But for Cecil it was unmistakable and very, very disturbing. What did it have to do with the water in the streets below? He wished he could hear a newscast from Kingston or Mobay. But he didn't own a radio, and he doubted that any of his neighbors who did had had the foresight to bring it with them.*

So all he could do was wait. Now, as somber-tinted sunrise colors squeezed through cracks in gray clouds and ricocheted off the water—in the right place, thank God—Cecil still strove to put it all together. He could go back down now, he realized. He could see that the water had already receded and left the town behind. But he wasn't even sure that was an unmixed blessing—for it had receded too far. Looking out around Cabarita Island and along the arc off to its left, he saw the jagged top of the reef sticking out—more of it than he had ever seen exposed before.

Gerber woke at 5 A.M., wrenched out of a nightmare-laden sleep by the insistent buzzing of the telephone. He reached out for it groggily, struggling to clear his mind, first enough to distinguish the telephone from the alarm clock, then enough to distinguish bad dreams from reality. It wasn't easy. When he had the instrument in the general vicinity of his face, he muttered irritably, "What do you want at this hour? I've—"

"I'm sorry, Mr. Gerber," interrupted a female voice which might have been pleasant had its owner's nerves been less obviously frayed. "I don't like it either. This is Ms. Oliveira, the night operator at the office. You have an awful backlog of calls here that I thought I'd better let you know about."

"Calls, in the middle of the night? What kind of calls? Can't they wait?"

"This is the U.N., Mr. Gerber," Oliveira reminded him, with a plainly audible effort to avoid sarcasm. "It isn't the middle of the night everywhere. Some of these sound pretty urgent. I thought you might want to get an early start. You're going to have a busy day."

He winced and thought, but didn't utter, a particularly expressive oath in his native German. "Don't I know it," he muttered. "Well, give me a hint. What's urgent enough to call me now?"

"You haven't been listening to any news in the last few hours? Well, I guess the most urgent one is Melbourne."

"Melbourne?"

"Australia."

Gerber's spine began to tingle. He rolled closer to the phone stand. "Well, get on with it. What about Melbourne?"

"It's underwater." Her voice was suddenly shaky and her words spilled out in an uncontrolled torrent. "It's a drowned city, Mr. Gerber. A few people got out in airplanes, and some managed to drive to the highlands in spite of the traffic jams. Luckily there were highlands to drive to. But they had only a couple of hours' warning. Their mayor would very much like to know, and I quote, why the hell they didn't have a lot more."

By then Gerber was sitting up, wide-eyed, on the edge of the bed. He groped for words, but the operator found them first. "Frankly, sir, so would I. And there are a lot of people in Sydney and Buenos Aires and Cape Town and forty other places who want to know what you're going to do when the water gets to them. Which won't be long."

Gerber's throat was painfully dry and he felt his heart hammering in it. So he had misjudged—Clark and Beldan had actually made good on their threats. Now he would have to try to make up for lost time—and he was agonizingly aware that far too much had already been lost.

There was something else in Ms. Oliveira's words that brought him even more immediate chagrin. But he wasn't sure how to ask about it. "But I don't understand," he tried lamely. "Why do they assume we could have given them more warning?"

The scathing, incredulous contempt in her voice made him glad he was neither receiving nor transmitting a picture. "Come on, Mr. Gerber. Everybody heard the news last night. Didn't you?"

"What news?" he asked warily, afraid to admit he'd slept through it.

"Jonel Turabian was on. Claimed Commissioner Clark had all the information and wanted to broadcast it earlier, but you tied his hands—or worse. What do you have to say to that, Mr. Gerber?"

Gerber wanted to scream.

Clark's place of captivity was a spacious, comfortable, tastefully furnished apartment with only one overwhelming shortcoming: it was utterly isolated from the outside world. There was no telephone, no newsfax, no radio or television. He had thought it had those things, at first, but they turned out to be dummies. The entertainment console did have tapes and a working player, but those were at best static relics of an age that had died this morning—and Clark was in no humor to be entertained. There weren't even windows—only big holograms, neatly framed and draperied, which at first glance appeared to look out on the city and the world. But a closer look revealed that nothing ever happened in their world. Again, static reminders of the past.

Meanwhile, things were happening out there—tremendous things that urgently needed his attention and help. Frustration churned in his mind all evening and night. His guards brought him a good meal shortly after they deposited him here—a better meal than he could have dialed from the dispenser. He needed it and he ate it, but he was a long way from enjoying or appreciating it. He was too painfully aware of all that was going on out there, out of his grasp.

But he resigned himself to learning no more until Gerber chose to visit him, and he made a valiant effort to sleep. Without outside references, he lost his feel for time. But breakfast and an antique mahogany clock told him a night and a half a morning had passed when Gerber finally appeared.

The doorbell rang and Clark walked with deliberate slowness to answer it. He wasn't surprised that it was Gerber. The U.N. chief looked as if he had slept as poorly as Clark; the bags under his eyes were worse. He stepped in with a slight nod and no words. He seemed to be trying simultaneously to give Clark an infinitely dirty look and to avoid meeting his eyes directly.

Only when he had closed the door behind him did he speak. "You weren't bluffing," he said in a dead voice. He sat down in an armchair and leaned his head back and closed his eyes. "Melbourne's drowned. The water's piling up farther and farther north, just as you said it would. O.K., Clark, so you were telling the truth about that much. I blew it; I didn't believe you and didn't give them even what little warning I could have."

Clark sat down on the couch, shaking his head numbly. He had fully expected this, which dulled the shock a little—but not enough. In a sense he was still responsible, and nothing could relieve him of that knowledge.

"I didn't warn them," Gerber repeated dully, and then suddenly his eyes snapped open and flashed at Clark. "But Jonel and Sandy Turabian did," he said accusingly. "Made you look more blameless than you are, I'd say. But how did they know? About you being here, I mean."

"I suppose they could have figured it out," Clark said matter-of-factly. "But they didn't have to. I told them."

"You told them," Gerber echoed numbly. "I kept telling myself you must have. But . . . *how?* There's no way out of this room. There's simply no way."

"I'm not as naive as you think I am, Franz. Not any more. When I was flying up here I figured out that I was probably walking into a trap. So I wrote them a letter just in case. I still figured I should try to do it your way first, but I didn't expect it to work." He changed the subject. "Did they get their word out in time to help anybody in Melbourne?"

Gerber nodded. "Some. Not enough. But you undermined world confidence in the U.N. tremendously. Why did you do it, Henry?"

"To save lives," said Clark. "And," he added savagely, "to undermine confidence in the U.N. as thoroughly as you deserved. If you hadn't, it never would have happened. If you hadn't wasted time stalling and holding me incommunicado, my message would never have been delivered and you could have issued the warnings and made the arrangements yourself. As you said, you blew it. If you can't be trusted, people need to be shown that in time to quit relying on you. You've proved my point, Franz. Resoundingly."

"So you've set us up as the goat—and yourself as the could-have-been hero."

"Did I?" *Sandy and Jonel must have helped*, Clark thought approvingly. *I don't know what they said, but if they just came out and said I O.K.'d it, I wouldn't have a chance. They must have made Beldan look the villain—or at least made the whole thing look like a misunderstanding all around.*

"You know very well you did," said Gerber. "With all the repercussions that can have. It still looks suspiciously like a power play, you know. You make a deal with the aliens to create a situation where the world thinks it has to do what you say, instantly. Then when they've knuckled under and given you absolute power, *then* you discover something you overlooked. You can stop the world after all, and keep it here at home. But by then it's too late, and you and the aliens live it up milking the world you took over for its last seventeen years. You probably can't expect much more than seventeen yourself, and you know it."

Clark shook his head, amazed, pitying, appalled. "Do I really seem that infantile, Franz? Think about it. What kind of a man would it take to think that way? No kind that I can respect, much less be. All I want is a future for man. *My* last years could have been vastly more comfortable if I hadn't bothered." He paused. "You've seen what's happened in the last thirty hours. Are you *still* going to persist in wasting time with absurd accusations when you should be doing things? Have you no conscience?" (*Not quite fair*, he admitted to himself. *I know he does, despite all his failings. But a misguided conscience is more dangerous than none at all.*)

"I'm doing things," Gerber said tightly, obviously pained, and pointedly ignoring the reference to absurd accusations. "I have some water-holding and evacuation efforts underway. Too little, too late, but we're trying. Cape Town has Table Mountain right behind it, and Sydney has some high country not too far away. Not high enough for a permanent refuge, if your predictions hold up, but we can supervise getting people there with their own resources. Buenos Aires is in the worst position and has the most people, so we're putting our most direct efforts into that."

"Have you talked to Zhalāū?"

"I talked to Beldan." Gerber started to say something else, then snapped his mouth shut abruptly as if to bite it off.

"And?"

"I have the evaluation committee at Kennedy checking on your claim that they can't stop—and I know where I'd put *my* money." He stood up. "Meanwhile, you stay right where you are. I still don't trust you—and if you thought this little maneuver was going to get you right where you wanted to be, you're dead wrong." He started for the door.

"Franz," Clark said softly just before he got there.

Gerber, his hand on the knob, turned and glowered at him. "What is it?"

"Yesterday you told me, 'You got us into this, now get us out.' I'm willing. Not the way you want, because that's still impossible. But I can spell out a coordinated plan for maximum survival whenever you want. For everybody's sake, I hope that's soon."

Gerber turned and left without comment.

Sydney.
Cape Town.
Buenos Aires....

Carlos Esquivel brought the huge liner out under the clouds an uncomfortably short distance above the ground. He noted with relief that the microwave altimeter was still giving a believable reading, though the pressure-operated backup unit had strayed again. Smaller planes that depended entirely on that kind would be in a bad way by now, and getting worse.

The air was rough near the ground. Esquivel brought his ship in fast, to improve controllability, but he still had his hands full. Weather was especially bad this far south, this close to the violence being done to the atmosphere by the "rocket" at the South Pole. Esquivel was not at all sure he agreed with the sudden decision that had led to that state of affairs, but that was not his concern. The rocket reaction was running, whether it should be or not, and his job was just to get his plane in, load it up with as many refugees as he could, and get them back out to a safer place. Because of them, the turbulence near the runway was even worse than "natural" causes could explain. In their haste to get as many people out as possible, the controllers were hustling planes in and out in such close succession that there was even less time than usual for the wake turbulence from one to subside before the next roared into it. That's going to get them in trouble one of these times, *Esquivel thought grimly.*

He looked down at the seething sea of people crowding against the barricades and realized abruptly that the tower had not yet given him clearance to land. Hastily, he requested one; the tower shot it back testily.

The landing was rough despite his best efforts, braking was poor on the sheet of water that already covered the runway, and the air was full of swirling spray kicked up by earlier planes. Pretty soon, he thought as the reverse-thrusting jets screamed *their loudest,* they're going to have to shut the whole thing down until it gets deep enough to land on pontoons. Meanwhile they'll have to mount an awful lot of pontoons and find pilots who can handle them.

As he turned onto a taxiway and headed in for the terminal, he saw the hordes of hopeful passengers, now much closer. A drop in the bucket, *he thought with a sudden sense of futility.* Even packing them in like sardines and moving as fast as we can, how much of a dent can we make in the millions who live here?

He tried not to think about it.

On the ground, Rubén Marquina pressed forward among the sardines, tightly clutching the hands of Gabriela and little Javier to keep them together. Another plane was coming in now, a big one. Perhaps this one would have room. Surely the chances were better than two hours ago. Already they had quit trying to restrict passengers to seats with belts; they were letting some sit in the aisles now. And his little family had made progress toward the gate, though they were forever having to fight back those who would shove them aside.

The plane, awkward on the ground and bleak under the drizzly sky, rolled into its berth and stopped. Gangways lowered themselves with a soft whirring of machinery. Nobody got off; nobody was coming to Buenos Aires today.

The crowd surged forward. Somewhere up there, where Rubén couldn't quite see, that petite, clarion-voiced stewardess had opened the gate and people were streaming through it and up into the big silver cylinder that meant escape. Rubén and Gabriela and Javier almost made it....

And then the stewardess drew the chain back across the gate and tried to fasten it. "I'm sorry," *she called out.* "That's all this one will hold. The rest of you will have to wait a little longer."

"Not me!" *a big man not far in front of Rubén yelled.* "It'll take me!" *There was a scuffle and a shriek; Rubén couldn't quite see what happened. He saw two male attendants in uniforms trying to hold the man back, and then the man breaking free and running out to the plane. Nobody ran after him, but the last gangway was already retracting, and nobody paid any attention to his coarse demands that it be put back down.*

Craning his neck, Rubén saw the stewardess lying on the ground where the big man had knocked her down. She was struggling to get up, her clothes soaked and dirty and her expression hurt almost beyond endurance. Rubén looked away, embarrassed.

The plane was gone and he didn't know when the next would come to this gate. "Maybe we'd be better off at the harbor," he muttered.

A mild-faced stranger with horn-rimmed glasses overheard and shook his head. "No use, friend. I've called there. The docks are flooding. They're still putting people on ships, somehow, but there's no guarantee they'll go anywhere. They have to be fast enough to buck the current and prudent enough not to get too far from land or they'll just be swept south. And they're as crowded as this."

Rubén said nothing, but he had never felt such frustration. He didn't understand what was going on. There was something about moving the Earth, for some reason he still didn't follow, and some yanqui *named Clark who had something to do with all this and yet knew how to make it easier. Maybe he'd even caused it; some said so. But if he knew how to rescue people better than this, why wouldn't the authorities listen to him?*

None of it made any sense to Rubén. All he knew was the personal threat. ¡Madre de Dios! *he thought.* ¿Qué pasa? ¿Qué pasará?

New York....

Jez Johnson detested violence; she always had. But she believed in Causes worth fighting for, and this was surely one. She had not instigated the demonstration; rather, at first, she had been swept up in it and then along with it. By now enough adrenaline had been pumped through her system to make her feel a fierce pride in being part of the parade that had crowded all vehicular traffic off First Avenue. She pranced along proudly, tall body erect, flame-colored hair streaming behind her in the strong north wind as a beacon for all behind her. Once in a while a timid something in the back of her mind expressed a fear that she would get into trouble....

But every time she squelched that unceremoniously. This was important, and it was now or never. A placard waving near her expressed her feelings perfectly: LIVES NOW, RETRIBUTIONS LATER. What was Henry Clark's role in all this? Jez didn't know, but that could wait. What she did know was that she had seen Jonel Turabian on that talk show, and he had made it quite clear that Clark could have been saving those lives being lost down south. First Australia, now South America and South Africa.... The floods were happening, no matter whose fault

*they were. Turabian had told how Clark had known about them
yesterday morning and hadn't been allowed to tell. He was up
there, in one of the buildings Jez and the rest were marching on,
with who knew what happening to him. If he knew what was
happening and how to save people, why wouldn't they listen to
him? Turabian had explained how those hours could have saved
lives—a surprising number of lives—had they been used instead
of squandered. But that took coordination. Sure, the U.N.
bigwigs were making some motions now that would save a
handful of people—now, when it was too late to do more than
that. Apparently they hoped to soothe the public conscience, to
appease the masses. But people like Jez Johnson would not be
appeased by such empty gestures.*

*She could see the door up ahead now—the new, ornate,
multicolored glass entrance chamber to the Hall of Councils.
The mob surged forward; Jez's heart shifted up a gear or two.
She held her placard high, bracing it with an effort against the
chilling wind: CLARK KNOWS—LET HIM ACT. Another
nearby differed in only one small detail: CLARK KNOWS—
MAKE HIM ACT. Others all around carried aspects of the
general drift: THROW GERBER OUT! GERBER DOESN'T
WANT TO GET INVOLVED! LISTEN TO CLARK!
MERCY FOR THE SOUTH! CLARK HAS A PLAN—
WHAT DOES GERBER HAVE?*

*Jez thought she could feel her heart crescendo as the glass
antechamber grew closer, but she couldn't even imagine she
heard it. The shrill and hoarse yells of the crowd were already
much too loud, and growing fast. The quiet part of her that
worried looked around and managed to wonder for five
seconds. How many of these people understood why they were
here? For Jez, this was something she believed in; for Drew
Cabat, over there, it was so obviously a game that his attitude
infuriated her. How could he joke about cities and countries
being drowned?*

*Drew was not a very responsible person even away from a
mob. How many Drews were here today?*

*The front of the crowd had arrived; the others pressed in
around the entrance. The people in front began to chant: "No
more Gerber! We want Clark!" The chant took form, spread,
swelled. Jez was dimly surprised to notice that she had joined in,
screaming at the top of her lungs. Just as dimly and gradually,*

she became aware of sirens approaching from both up and down the avenue.

But she didn't think about them. Shouting rhythmically while that small part of her mind watched from the sidelines, she watched Drew Cabat's arm swing in a long, leisurely arc. Something dark and shiny sailed away from it; then there was a shattering of glass and everything inside the antechamber was flame, shooting out through the broken parts and making the rest glow and flicker even in daylight. Inside, new sirens wailed and heavy iron grilles clanked into place.

That snapped something in Jez. Suddenly the ardent demonstrator was hollow, cowering huddled into a corner of her head while the part that had been on the sidelines stepped forward and said calmly, "We've got to get out of here. Fast." And then she was trying to run, but all she could do was flail helplessly against packed, shoving bodies.

From somewhere—some inconspicuous door off to the side—men were streaming out, wearing the green and gold uniforms of U.N. security troops and waving long objects ominously at the crowd. Those are real guns, Jez thought. Beginning to panic, she turned away, dropped her sign, and tried again to run. This time she made a little headway—possibly because others had also opted for retreat—but to no avail. Other uniforms, blue ones of city police, were closing in from all other sides.

The Security Council met in a relatively new chamber on the fifth floor. In keeping with the recent popularity of windows, real or ersatz, it had a big one running the length of the outside wall. It was fairly soundproof, and at the moment it was covered with opaque, deep blue drapes. But it was a window rather than a wall, and some of the sirens and shouts and scuffles found their way in, distant and muted, but undeniable. Gerber sat behind the lectern, shuffling through his scanty notes, cringing with every sound from outside and earnestly wishing he were far, far away.

He stalled as long as he could. Finally the hushed whispers and fidgetings and clearings of throats became too pointed to delay any longer, and he looked miserably up into the seventeen hostile faces that surrounded him on the two-tiered semicircular dais.

Surrounded, he thought wryly. *Are they really as hostile as I think they are? Or have they reached the same conclusion I have? No matter—even if they have, they'll blame me. They'll need a scapegoat.* He rustled his papers slightly and the seventeen grew silent and somber. They waited. When Gerber spoke, his voice cracked—something it had never done before in all his years of politics and public speaking.

"Never before," he began, "have I addressed this assemblage with such cause for regret." *And that*, he thought emphatically, *is the understatement of my career.* "What I have to say this afternoon will be extraordinarily difficult, for me to say and quite possibly for you to accept." He paused, sipped water, resumed. "You are all aware of the unprecedented wave of 'natural' disasters the world has experienced in the last two days. Due to my written briefing before this meeting, if to nothing else, you are equally aware of the unnatural cause of those disasters."

"And the purpose of this meeting," said a smooth, Bantu-accented voice from the left end of the second tier, "is to take suitable action against Commissioner Henry Clark?"

Gerber reluctantly ignored the fact that the representative from Tanzania had not formally sought recognition before speaking. "Not exactly," he said, and the words were bitter in his mouth. "I will come to the purpose soon enough. You are also aware, I think, of what has happened to several southern cities today"—*(For which I myself must bear blame)*—"and of what is now happening in the streets outside this building." Several council members glowered. Gerber concentrated doggedly on his notes to avoid looking at the faces. "I am informed that similar rioting is going on in cities all over the world. We are going to have to take immediate and drastic action."

"Yes," said a voice from the front. "Rioters must be treated firmly—"

This time Gerber did not ignore it. "The representative from Indonesia is out of order," he interrupted sharply. "Do not speak without recognition." He shifted his tone back to his main point. "Punishing rioters is not the solution—though it may be necessary—because that is not the problem. Not the real problem.

"Let me summarize briefly what the real problem is. Item: Henry Clark, the Kyyra ambassador Beldan, and the Kyyra engineer Zhalāū"—he fumbled with the alien names—

"unanimously claim that the reaction with which they are dislodging the Earth from its orbit and incidentally causing the earthquakes and floods cannot be stopped. Naturally, I have been suspicious of this claim from the start, but I have been unable to sway any of them from it. If it is a conspiracy, it is well rehearsed."

He drew a deep breath. "Item: While Henry Clark has been following the discussions of the aliens' proposal more closely than any other human individual, he has not been alone. Almost since the beginning, last October, I have seen to it that a hand-picked committee of experts has been following the talks at Kennedy Spaceport, scrutinizing the technical details of the Kyyra proposals. I have been in consultation with them—and had their findings cross-checked by independent specialists—during the last day." He paused, sighed again, waited and finished. "They were not very helpful. Each of them has looked closely at some specific area. None of them claims to have the comprehensive overview that Clark does. And none of them has been able to absorb enough of Kyyra science to evaluate all of the details. They cannot confirm the claim of Beldan and Clark—but neither can they prove it false."

He looked down hard at his paper, then forced himself to look up and out at them. "Item!" he snapped, talking louder and faster. "The flooding Clark predicted has begun, catching us unprepared, and all indications are that it will become worse before it becomes better.

"Item: Clark claims to have a relief plan—and Beldan refuses to spend time explaining it to anyone else. So . . ." Gerber looked back down at his notes. His voice drooped with his head. "They have us over a barrel. A nasty, nasty barrel, but I see no way to escape it. Yes, the aliens and Clark conspired to start this thing without this organization's approval and consent. Yes, they *should* be stopped and they *should* be punished to the fullest extent possible. But I see no way. Stop the Kyyra? With what, gentlemen? Their capabilities are so depressingly far beyond our own that I see no conceivable leverage we can use against them—now or ever. Punish Clark? A consummation devoutly to be wished—but at this moment millions of people are dying or being driven from their homes, and Clark seems to be in the sole position to get any significant number of them through it alive."

"So," said a voice with a touch of French accent and more

than a touch of suspicion, "exactly what are you proposing?"

Gerber shut his eyes. He didn't need his notes for this and he didn't want to look at them. "I see no choice," he said quietly but firmly. "I'm asking you to authorize Henry Clark to do what he's offered to do."

He heard pandemonium. Snapping his eyes open, he pounded hard and yelled louder than they for order. A semblance of it came, but most of the men and women in the two raised semicircles looked ready to pounce on him and claw his eyes out. "If you have discussion," he said peremptorily, "you will request proper recognition."

A half dozen buttons before him instantly glowed. He selected one at random. "The representative from Federated Panarabia."

"It seems to me," Hajji ibn Mada'ini snarled, "that the Secretary has been listening too much to the rioters in the streets. I and my constituents will not be dictated to by gangs of hoodlums."

"The fact that we do what the hoodlums demand in one instance," said Gerber, admitting privately that it sounded pretty lame, "does not mean we're letting them dictate to us. It's coincidence. They are demanding what we must do anyway, for entirely independent reasons. Although it's true that, with their numbers and the mood they're in, we could never command enough respect to govern if we ignored those reasons." He glanced down at the lighted buttons. "The representative from India!"

"But you are," said Masudan Gujarati, rising respectfully, "suggesting that we let Henry Clark dictate to us. For if I understand correctly, you are in effect asking us to grant him essentially dictatorial powers over the world community. Is that correct?" He remained standing.

"It amounts to that," Gerber admitted bluntly. "But there are situations in which such things must be done and have been done. What I'm asking, to be very explicit, is that we designate Henry Clark special administrator of emergency operations, effective immediately. Until such time—if any—as we find a way to force the Kyyra to stop this, we're going to need such operations, and they're going to have to be run so efficiently that they'll have to be controlled through one man. Clark, unfortunately, is the only man who has the right background—

and contacts—to do the job. I don't like it any more than you, but I see no workable alternative. So I'm asking this council to grant him emergency powers, with all the operating resources of the U.N. and its affiliates at his disposal."

"Including the military?"

"Including the military." Gerber realized that he was almost pleading, for something he believed in only out of desperation. "That sort of thing has been done before. Often."

"But not," said Gujarati, "on a global scale or to a man who has already betrayed the people he is supposed to protect—and is also known to have dangerously powerful outside connections."

"The Kyyra will deal with no one else," Gerber pointed out impatiently.

"Precisely. I'm sorry, Mr. Secretary, but I cannot approve such a thing lightly or hastily." Gujarati sat down.

"May I point out," Gerber said tensely, "that the decision is going to *have* to be made rather hastily? The representative from Brazil!"

"I merely wish to underline that," said João de Castilho. "I hope my colleagues from more fortunate latitudes will make some effort to realize how this situation looks, for example, to someone in Rio de Janeiro who faces the prospect of destruction in hours or days. We need action *now*."

"Then may we vote?" suggested Gerber. "Let me emphasize once more that the emergency powers I'm requesting will be only for the duration, and Clark will still be responsible to us. When the need for him is past, he will be removed from power and will have to answer to us for what he did this week. If he fails to produce better results, he will be removed much sooner." Gerber thought sourly of what an utterly futile gesture those stipulations were, if Clark chose to treat them as such. But of course he said nothing. He seriously doubted that anybody present was actually fooled. "Are we ready to vote?"

Miraculously, they were—for what it was worth. The first vote disappointed but didn't really surprise Gerber. Straight along latitude lines, almost—severely threatened southern and extreme northern countries were for emergency powers, those in relatively well-off middle latitudes were against.

"Ten to seven," Gerber announced, trying not to let his desperation show. "Emergency powers are granted."

"Objection!" sang out Marcel Guyot of France. "The issue is substantive and the permanent members have not all concurred. Emergency powers are denied."

Gerber sighed. He hadn't really expected to get away with it. "My mistake," he said. "May I remind the Council that no issue is automatically substantive or procedural? You could vote to classify this as procedural."

Guyot flashed an oily smile. "Such a ploy will only waste time. Such a vote is doomed to fail because it still needs the concurrence of the permanent members and you will not have that of France. Surely I don't need to remind the Council that the question of whether a question is procedural or substantive is substantive."

Wearily, simultaneously thinking of all the parliamentary tricks he might try and wondering how many people had died during Guyot's last sentence, Gerber said grimly, "Well, gentlemen, then I must ask you to reconsider. May I point out that the very difficulty we are having is a good illustration of why we shall *have* to go to one-man decision-making...."

They came around, of course. There was really nothing else for them to do, and eventually even they realized that. But it took hours, and during those hours Clark was still a captive and people were still losing homes and lives with only the most makeshift efforts at rescue or aid. There was a bitter aftertaste in Gerber's mind when it was all over—and in that of all the other council members as they filed out (though by no means all for the same reasons).

Clark, too, felt bitterness when they came to tell him—and deep, haunting sorrow that it had taken even this long. Gerber had relented to the point of giving him newsfax, and he felt things he had never felt before as he read them.

But he was beyond letting them cripple his thinking. He had resigned himself to finishing what he had started two nights ago. This evening, waiting for Gerber to finish his announcement and introduction, he fiddled absently with the two index cards that held his opening notes, while his mind roamed soberly over what had happened to him in the last three months. *Well, Joe*, he thought as he remembered two incidents out of a past that included Joe Sanchez (one of them just two days ago), *it's come to this. Maybe you were right. But I was right too. It doesn't bother me the way it used to.*

Gerber, his face weary and drained of its usual color, was speaking into the other microphone, the two live cameras on him. "...an announcement of gravest importance to all the peoples of Earth," he was saying. "It has become clear that a global emergency exists and must be reckoned with. Emergency situations sometimes require emergency measures which would be intolerable in normal times. . . ."

Clark, preoccupied, only half listened. He remembered the last time he had given a public speech—only days ago, incredible as that seemed. He had already lost track of how many, though he was sure it was very few. It had been a nightmare, with a big live audience and swarms of microphones and cameras and interpreters in glass booths.

And the assassination attempts that had ended it, by two independent gunmen with ironically opposite motives. One of them was responsible for the present condition of his shoulder.

Clark would have no more of that. This room, at his firm insistence, was a very ordinary television studio, with three cameras and two mikes and a skeleton crew. The rest of the world could get what he said electronically. And what he said, this time, would be no idealistic plea for world unity. That, now, seemed far away and naive.

"...so the Security Council has this afternoon empowered Henry Clark to administer all affairs associated with the emergency." The pain and distaste in Gerber's face were evident to Clark, but he hid them rather well from unfamiliar eyes. "Let me emphasize that all areas of life, everywhere, are directly touched by these, so Mr. Clark's authority will be essentially absolute and general, for the duration. All facilities and instrumentalities of the United Nations are subject to his direct command—and that includes the forces which can be used to compel cooperation. Think of it, if you like, as martial law. And cooperate, for therein..." he seemed to choke "...lies our only hope of survival." Pause; then, very low, "Mr. Clark."

The little red light on the one camera already facing him, and his face on the monitor, told Clark he was on. He began immediately and directly, his voice carefully firm and calm. "Let me assure you that I hate and fear autocratic rule as much as any of you," he said, looking straight into the camera. "But a ship under battle conditions must have one commander. The job has fallen to me simply because I am more familiar with the problem than anyone else.

"Battle conditions, you may ask? Where's the enemy? The enemy is our own galaxy turned traitor, and the only strategy we have is retreat." (*The things people say in speeches!* he thought.) "We are on our way, to a new galaxy which will offer sanctuary, if not to us, at least to our descendants. But the trip will be hard—harder than anything in our history. Whether we will go is no longer a question. The only question is whether we will survive. Those who fail to cooperate will not. Those who listen and cooperate . . . may.

"I am not speaking of coercion by man against man. I have the power to coerce; I will use it whenever and only when I see it as necessary. But the numbers of people in the world mean that you cannot rely on the world government or your own government to keep you alive. Ultimately, that is up to you. *You* will have to make your way to a place of safety, though we will help where we can. *You* will have to make your dwelling safe for the trip. *You* will have to collect and preserve water. *You* will have to stretch your food reserves until *you* have established new sources. We will provide guidance in how to do all these things, but it will be up to you to do them. Self-reliance and cooperation with the central authority will be the keys to survival. We will tell you what things you can do. Those who do them will have a fighting chance; those who fail to, will die. It's that simple.

"Enormous problems lie ahead. But for now we can afford to think only about those of immediate concern. If we survive those, we can tackle the next phase. The principal immediate problems are food, water, and evacuation of flood zones. Listen closely. Here are detailed instructions, prepared in cooperation with the Kyyra earth-moving team. . . ."

Zhalãū had given him the particulars in two hours, but he had had an extensive background to draw on. The people of the world did not. He took three hours to give them the first batch.

When the little red light and the monitor finally went out, he let himself realize that he was tired and his throat was dry and his brow was moist. But it was done; a beginning had been made. Gradually, now, the destruction might slow, and out of it some hope might begin to emerge.

Would I have done it if I'd really known what it was going to cost? he wondered. And he answered himself: *Maybe not. So maybe it's just as well I didn't.*

Well, it doesn't matter now. There's work to do.

• • •

As it turned out, it cost even more than Clark anticipated, even then. If ever he had expected the mere assurance of survival to lead to instant acceptance of his rule, he was sorely disappointed. In the early days resistance and inefficiency were rampant, both of them fed by the galloping hysteria that followed the initial shock. He himself had to gain practical experience in wielding the power that was theoretically at his disposal, and that experience was in itself a baptism of fire. He learned quickly—but external, human obstacles were huge. People in cities which had plenty of time for orderly evacuation in private cars panicked, ignored instructions designed to keep the flow smooth, and drowned in gigantic traffic jams. Work forces balked at having their services commandeered without pay, not yet realizing that money was a thing of the past. Some of them did not live to regret it. Scattered individuals everywhere simply ignored everything until it was too late.

Perhaps the saddest cases were those in backward countries where education was neglected and communications were primitive: people who simply got caught in things, not understanding what or why, not knowing what to do, and so doing nothing and being overwhelmed. Or perhaps sadder still were those scattered cases where populations suffered because their local governments, objecting in principle to accepting decrees from Clark, blocked his every effort at help that might have saved them. In a few of those cases, he finally forced himself to send in U.N. troops to topple the obstructive government. It served the purpose, apparently—but he was glad he didn't have to be there to watch, even though he couldn't hide his responsibility from himself. The first time it happened, he admitted to himself that he could never have done it had his sensibilities not grown protective calluses. *But*, he kept telling himself, *it's necessary....*

Somehow they muddled through—some did, anyway. The early mishaps and fatal stupidities hammered home Clark's point far more effectively than any number of words: those who cooperated had a chance, those who didn't, didn't. After watching more and more of their neighbors succumb, more and more of those who remained determined not to. Then they listened, out of desperation.

Five days out, Zhalãũ's worldwrights changed the driving reaction at the Pole from the rocketlike one that they compared to a detonation cap to the far more efficient exhaustless one that

45

only they understood. Then, with vast quantities of water no longer boiling into the atmosphere, the skies largely cleared, and by then changes were becoming large enough to be noticeable to the casual observer. Many reacted with superstitious fear, of course, but many, at least nominally enlightened, simply realized down to their bones that Clark was in no way bluffing. The Earth was *moving*. The sun itself didn't look very different from before—to the naked and uncalibrated eye, it was neither significantly smaller nor significantly dimmer than it had ever been. But the Arctic and Antarctic circles were visibly creeping toward the equator. The oceans that had swallowed Melbourne and Sydney and Buenos Aires and Cape Town saw less and less of night. But in the north, and gradually farther and farther south, the sun set for the last time; a cloak of final darkness spread slowly but inexorably over the northern hemisphere.

With all that happening, people's attention had to focus on the reality of the survival problem. Too often the response was still blind panic—but increasingly often it was constructive action. Within two weeks, things were progressing at a level of effectiveness for which Clark had wished but in the early days had not dared hope. Now, to some extent, he felt vindicated. *Sometimes*, he thought one day after reading a pile of reports that contained a small nugget of hope among all the despair, *people do better with a problem that's really too big for them than with one just the right size. Must be that the reasonable one doesn't challenge them enough to bring out even what they need....*

Within a month, the darkness covered most of Canada, Germany, Poland, Russia; all of Scandinavia and England. Those places had perpetual night sky, full of stars that still showed no sign of change. The moon, after an initial effort to follow, had been left far behind. Nobody in the north saw it any more; those in the south who still got a few hours of darkness sometimes saw it as a bright speck, almost a southern pole star, barely discernible as a half-lit disk reeling uncertainly in a violently perturbed orbit.

The howling, destroying winds and rushing waters subsided. The first plateau had been reached: Zhalău's crews had stabilized the acceleration at its low preliminary value, and the oceans and air had largely stablized with it. It was temporary, of course—but it was a much-needed moment of respite.

• • •

It was a somewhat older and considerably wiser Clark who walked slowly out onto the airfield, savoring the ruddy sunshine and the restful, almost forgotten stillness of the air. Tony had come to meet him; his little yellow jet waited under a deep blue sky—a rather deeper blue than he had been used to. It glistened in the light of a sun which hung low and red in the southern sky, though it was but little after noon, and would soon set, not far west of its present position.

"Hello, sir," Tony said softly, with a note of something that was almost awe in his always polite voice. "Good to see you again. You've been busy."

"Good to see you, too," said Clark. "We've all been busy."

They talked little during the flight south. Clark used much of it to rest, stretched comfortably in the back seat, often with his eyes closed. But often they were open, too—for the face of the land had changed utterly since last he saw it.

They took off from New York—a refreshingly smooth take-off—over an ocean that was no longer an ocean. Where once blue water had stretched sparkling off to the eastern horizon, now there was only parched mud spotted here and there with dead seaweed. And, far off to the left where he could just make it out, the naked edge of the continental shelf, where it dropped off toward the Hatteras Abyssal Plain.

Yes, he thought, awed by the sight, *something's been happening, all right. Hopefully something with as much of beginning as of ending about it. Hopefully.*

They flew lower than they once would have, in the somewhat thinned air, and it was chilly when Clark deplaned at Kennedy Spaceport. The sun now stayed as low here as it had in New York before, and the little heat the Kyyra let seep out to the surface from the driving reaction was distributed more uniformly than sunlight.

Jonel and Sandy were waiting for him just inside the terminal and came out to meet him with warm friendly smiles. He was surprised at how much that meant to him, and realized that he had doubted whether he had any friends left in the world now. It was good to know that he did.

"Welcome back, Henry," said Jonel, shaking his hand. "Nice work." Sandy hugged him; she had never done that before.

"I don't know," he mused, some of the old doubt and anguish returning. "A lot of people died. A lot more will."

"But not because of you," Sandy objected. "In spite of you.

47

More would have without you." (*Would they?* he thought. *I think so. But will I ever know? No.*) "Come on, let's go back to our place to talk."

He let them lead him back to their apartment, a pleasant little place that had taken on more of their personality since he had last seen it. Then the walls had been nearly undecorated; now they abounded in the photography and artwork that so often expressed both of the Turabians' multifaceted zest for living. Oz lay snoozing on the floor, a classic image of a dog on a hearth even in the absence of a hearth.

And there was another guest. Beldan was waiting on the couch and stood up—and up and up—when Jonel and Sandy led Clark in. "Welcome back," he said quietly. "The first phase is successfully past."

"Yes," said Clark, shaking his big hand. "I suppose you could call it successful. There are survivors, anyway." *Though how many, I'm afraid to guess.* He had had moments during the last month when he had wanted to lash out furiously at Beldan for not having made more explicit just how costly it all would be. But he had put those behind him now. He still—or again—felt well-disposed toward Beldan, if Beldan could still reciprocate. There was an awkwardness there, he suspected....

Sandy had wandered off into the kitchen. As she returned with a tray containing a bottle of rosé wine and four glasses, Clark said to her and Jonel, "I have to thank you two for doing what you did. But one thing puzzled me. How did you keep them from wanting to lynch me?"

"We didn't entirely," Sandy chuckled, setting the tray down. "We just sort of talked around the details of how it got started. We concentrated on the clear and present danger and the fact that you could do something about it. Never mind the fact that you also started it; we evaded that." She paused and her pixyish face became momentarily solemn. "It wasn't always easy."

"But if you didn't at least encourage them to think—"

"That it was all our fault?" Beldan broke in with a surprisingly puckish grin. "They did. Not explicitly, but by omission. You're wondering if I was offended? Rather more amused, I'd say. Sandy explained it all to me—and I'd never hoped for popularity among your kind." He took out his music-pipe and doodled a little. It sounded rather more melancholy than his words. "Actually," he remarked, breaking off, "this whole business of deceit among your species fascinates me."

"Not too much, I hope," said Clark, sitting down. "It's not very admirable. But when surrounded by it, sometimes it seems necessary to practice it." *It still bothers me, though.*

"And I have a question for you," Sandy said as she handed Clark the first glass. "When you wrote that letter, were you expecting things to work out the way they did?"

Clark sipped his wine thoughtfully before answering. "To some extent," he said finally. "I'm not sure how much. When I took off for New York, all I really hoped to do was get the U.N. to take over. I should have known better. I should have learned by then that when you want something done, the only way to be sure is to do it yourself. Well, I've learned now. I started something when I O.K.'d the launch. I wrote the letter when I realized I might have to finish it." He took a longer draught and gazed at—or beyond—one of the pictures on the wall. "Once," he said slowly, "Joe Sanchez really got my goat by saying he saw me starting to think of myself as a dictator. Caesar Clark, he called me. That hurt and scared me. Another time I got his goat by saying I didn't see how we were going to get through this without one. That scared me too, and I assure you I never thought of myself in the role. But now I've come to openly admit I was right. Somebody had to do it—and it seems to be me. I still don't like it. But I don't see any other way. Do you?"

"No," Jonel said soberly. "So wear it well."

"'Some are born great,'" Sandy quoted softly, "'some achieve greatness, and some have greatness thrust upon them.'"

"Hm-m-m," said Clark, pondering. "Thrust, yes . . . though I doubt Shakespeare meant it quite so literally. But greatness?" That could be judged only by results, and it was much too early. It was still a long, long way to M31. The problems that lay ahead—immediately, and far into the future—were even more formidable than those now past. Not long ago, even Clark would have thought them almost certainly insuperable.

But now he wasn't so sure—because now, at least, he felt ready to tackle them. "We shall see," he said solemnly. "We shall see."

First Interlude

REMEMBERING, ONCE STARTED, can be hard to stop. The memories were long ago and far away—both literally and figuratively—but Sandy found that each one she dredged up dragged others with it. *If I keep this up*, she thought, a little annoyed with herself, *I'll wind up sitting here rehashing the whole trip.*

But then she thought, *Well, why not? Somebody ought to once in a while, for perspective. And I have some time now. I can't do anything important until Jonel gets back.*

She stood up and moved to the couch, with one end mounted on jacks so it could be kept perpendicular to the current "up-down" direction. She or Jonel had to readjust the jacks at least every couple of days now. Before long they would go through the most awkward stage and then have to move the furniture back to the floor, as it again became a floor and the walls walls.

The room shook slightly as she lay down, but she paid that no attention. She stretched out, closed her eyes, and let her mind remain in the past. It would be brought back soon enough.

The lull at the end of the first phase was illusory. Violent as its application had been, the acceleration reached had been too low to be useful for long. Preparations for the next phase were no less frenzied, but they lasted longer. Plenty of people still got hurt—or worse.

At the very least, the effort demanded sacrifice of everyone. Sometimes the prices it exacted were rather unusual. . . .

Caesar Clark

"One year?"

Domingo Menéndez Consuelo, alone in his office, stood hunched over the ancient line printer in the corner, watching helplessly as the unexpected new dispatch from the north clattered out. He felt a growing, dry tightness in his throat as he read.

HIGHEST IMPORTANCE INSTRUCTIONS TO ALL REGIONAL AND NATIONAL HEADS OF STATE, it began, after the curt attention-grabber that had triggered his shock. READ CAREFULLY AND ACT PROMPTLY.

We're busy, he protested silently. *We're terribly busy.*

But the machine clacked heedlessly on, spewing neatly folded paper into the output bin as fast as he could catch its drift.

A NEW AND MUCH LONGER PHASE OF ACCELER-ATION WILL BE INITIATED AT THE END OF ONE YEAR. THOUGH THE INCREASE OF THRUST WILL BE SPREAD OVER SEVERAL MONTHS, THE ONSET WILL

52

BE ATTENDED BY PROBLEMS SIMILAR TO THOSE OF
THE LAUNCH.

It'll take longer than that just to dig out from those,
Menéndez Consuelo thought. *It's only been . . . What? A month?
How can we even think about new ones now?*

. . . EARTHQUAKES, the printer continued, ignoring his
thoughts, FLOODS, AND IN SOME REGIONS VOLCANIC
ACTIVITY. PREPARATIONS TO MEET THESE CON-
TINGENCIES MUST BEGIN IMMEDIATELY. EVEN
MORE URGENTLY, IF POSSIBLE, WATER HOARDING
MUST CONTINUE AND RECYCLING BE BROUGHT
INTO FULL OPERATION AS QUICKLY AS POSSIBLE.
THE WORLD GOVERNMENT WILL STRIVE TO DIS-
SEMINATE RECYCLING PLANTS AND INFORMATION
AS RAPIDLY AND EQUITABLY AS POSSIBLE. MEAN-
WHILE, FOOD MUST BE RATIONED STRINGENTLY,
BEGINNING NOW. REPEAT: NOW. AGRICULTURE IS
ALREADY DEAD IN MANY AREAS AND WILL NOT
LONG SURVIVE FARTHER SOUTH. RESERVES MUST
BE STRETCHED TO THE UTMOST IF EVEN THIS
MODEST DELAY IS TO BE POSSIBLE.

LOOKING BEYOND, OTHER AREAS MUST BE
ATTACKED SOON, BUT WITHOUT QUITE THE EX-
TREME URGENCY OF THESE. AIRTIGHTNESS OF
DWELLINGS IS NOT QUITE AN INSTANTANEOUS
NEED. A COMMUNICATIONS NETWORK OF UN-
PRECEDENTED QUALITY . . . NEW SYSTEMS OF
TRANSPORTATION FOR THE LIMITED TRAVEL
THAT WILL BE REQUIRED AND PERMITTED WHEN
THINGS GET BAD. . . .

When things get bad, Menéndez thought numbly. *As if
everything's fine now.*

DETAILED INSTRUCTIONS FOLLOW, REQUIRING
IMMEDIATE ACTION. FIRST. . . .

Menéndez walked away from the printer, stunned. The
instructions could wait, at least until he had them all on paper.
He walked to the corner windows and looked out, trying to tune
out the clattering mechanical devil behind him.

He looked out, across the cluster of makeshift tents and
shacks in the Parque Central at the city and volcanoes beyond,
resting under a sun that was too low in the sky. (But at least it

was there. Up north, they said, the sun never even rose any more.) Over to the left, he could see another part of the Palacio Nacional, slightly damaged. Beyond that was the central market, forced into the streets by damage to its buildings for the second time in Menéndez's life.

He still vividly remembered the first time. He had been a boy of eight or nine then, and when his house fell down he and his family had taken to an improvised shack of cardboard and burlap and corrugated tin, on the hillside below the Ermita del Carmen. A shack much like those that now dotted the park in front of the palace.

He could identify with those people; he had been through it himself. He had been proud of his people then, for the way they pulled through and never lost their spirit, and he was proud of them now. The quakes last month had been just as bad—four decades had allowed severe strains to build up again—and the response had been just as admirable.

But there were limits to what they could do. They were only human, after all. Even if they were humanity at its best, it made no sense to expect them to go through all that less than one year after such a disaster.

Menéndez felt the anger welling up in him again—the anger he had often felt toward the increasingly meddlesome U.N. under Franz Gerber, and then more recently and more often and more strongly toward this character Clark who had somehow deposed Gerber. Menéndez still wasn't clear on how that had come about, or just what Clark had to do with the quakes and all that had come with them.

But it was pretty clear that he was somehow behind the atrocities now pouring out of the line printer. To Menéndez, they seemed crazily, cruelly unnecessary. But very soon, one way or another, he would have to act on them. . . .

A day earlier and a thousand miles away, Henry Clark had stared across an oval table at two tall aliens with much the same dismay. *"Half a gee?"* he echoed incredulously.

"Would you prefer three thousand years?" Beldan asked. His olive-bronze face loomed over the humans, its solemnity contrasting oddly with the flamboyant iridescence of his robe. "Three thousand years," he repeated emphatically. "That's how long it would take at our present acceleration. We—the Kyyra—can't accept that. I wouldn't think you could either."

"We don't want to," Clark said stiffly. "But half a gee. . . ." He shook his head, feeling trapped. He'd been so busy getting things under control during the first month of Earth's flight that he hadn't had time to think beyond that. But beyond had become now. The first phase was over; the acceleration had been stabilized at a low value that could be held while preparations were made for another boost. How big a boost was proving a far less simple question that he had hoped. "Of course I don't want it to take three thousand years. That's no different from forever, to a human. It wouldn't work."

"Exactly," said Beldan. "But to get a shorter trip, you have to go to a higher acceleration. There's no way around that."

"That much higher?" Clark frowned and looked to his right, at Jonel Turabian. "Jonel, what do you think? Is it reasonable to think about that high an acceleration?"

"I'm skeptical," Turabian said slowly. "It's scary, and I don't see how it can be done. But then, I don't even see how they got it this high. I would have thought the Earth was much too fragile."

"Only for the most obvious ways of producing the acceleration," said Zhalāũ. She spoke slowly and carefully and her face was more alien than Beldan's; talking to humans was still relatively new to her. But she understood the technical details as Beldan didn't, so it was she who answered such comments as Jonel's. "Of course you can't just push hard on the surface. You'd break it. But the danger comes not from acceleration itself, but from accelerating different parts of a body at different rates. If you could apply a gravitational field-type force equally to all parts of your planet at once, you wouldn't feel a thing, no matter how great the force. We can't quite do that, but we can come close, with our reactionless drive operating under remote control at a vast network of points throughout the Earth's interior."

"But," Jonel objected, "the way a force is transmitted through a fluid—"

"Not this force," Zhalāũ interrupted, shaking her head. "The fact that it's unidirectional and fieldlike makes all the difference. We've been through this before."

"Yes," said Jonel, "we've been through it, but you never say much more than that. If you expect us to buy a high acceleration, can't you explain enough of the method to convince us it's safe?"

Clark looked at him with some surprise. Jonel had been

pretty quiet since he brought the bad news home, leaving the decision about the Kyyra's disquieting offer largely to other people. Now, with the trip underway, he was taking a much more active interest in charting its course.

"No," Zhalãũ answered flatly. "You have no conception of how much intermediate knowledge lies between your technology and an understanding of ours. There's not time to try to fill in the gap. And there's no need to fill it. We can handle these matters for you. Your efforts are needed elsewhere."

Jonel's eyes narrowed as if to say, *And it couldn't have anything to do with your having something to hide—again?* Beyond him, Sandy, who had done more for communication with the Kyyra than anyone else, listened and watched intently, but her face was carefully noncommittal. Jonel looked back and forth between Beldan and Zhalãũ several times before he said, "O.K. I'll grant that you've got us this far without completely ruining the planet, and you've brought your own planets out from the core and for all I know you've used higher accelerations. But you certainly haven't done it without incident. We have millions of people dead and more hurt and homeless from earthquakes and floods and drought. Even if you can control things inside the Earth, isn't it true that there's going to be more of that sort of thing on the surface when you raise the acceleration? And that the more you raise it, the worse it'll be?"

Beldan nodded. "To some extent, yes."

"But not," said Zhalãũ, "as much as you think. Much of the recent trouble was due to the nature of the priming reaction and the fact that we had to start it at the south polar surface. We're through with that now. The exhaustless drive is working, it's well distributed through the interior, and we'll have time to distribute it even better. We can add quite a bit of acceleration with relatively little disturbance of the crust. And you'll have time to brace for what disturbance there is."

"But enough?" Clark protested. "I don't think so. The earthquakes weren't the worst of it, you know. The worst were the field distortion effects, the flooding and atmosphere changes. Nothing you've said is going to keep those from being worse with a larger acceleration. At a half gee, even the crust and mantle must suffer a lot."

Neither Kyyra replied—and that was a reply. Especially when they both took out music-pipes and began improvising unearthly melodies.

For the first time, Sandy spoke. "Beldan," she said softly, "you don't understand how it looks to humans. You're used to doing things on a scale which we'd only dreamed about until you came. I doubt that you can really grasp what it's like to have to throw your whole body and mind into making one house livable—though you'll learn, when we get where we're going and you have to build something new. But believe me when I tell you it's asking too much. Jonel and Henry have shown me the calculations on what a really high acceleration would mean. Go right to that, and the demands and terror will drive most people to give up in despair, even if you can hold the Earth together. Give them something less—something challenging, but within their grasp if they stretch just a little more than they thought they could—and they'll meet it. We're funny that way."

Zhalãũ stopped playing and looked at Beldan. Beldan played on for a few seconds, ending on an oddly questioning note, and looked at Sandy. "Then," he said with a slight frown, "you're suggesting a compromise?"

"Of course she's suggesting a compromise," Clark said impatiently. "She's right. We can go to a higher acceleration—we *must* go to a higher acceleration—but not that much higher. It can't be."

"But..." For a moment Beldan's expression became inscrutable. "We can do it, I tell you. You don't believe it, but we can. If we do, we can be there in a decade. Isn't that worth the effort?"

"It would be," said Clark, his voice becoming increasingly firm, "if it had any chance of succeeding. But it doesn't. I'm responsible for billions of people's lives, and I know those people as you don't. In the time we have, they could never get ready for that much tilting, technologically or emotionally. A hundredth of a gee, maybe. A half a gee, no. So we compromise, or it's all been a disastrous waste. For the Kyyra and for us. Well, Beldan, do we compromise?"

Beldan played a nervous tune, then broke off and said, "But a hundredth only gets the trip down to three centuries."

"And you've only been on the way for one," Sandy nodded. "Well, we've been on the way a month. Three months before that we couldn't have even imagined this. Who do you think sees those centuries as worse?"

A moot question, Clark thought, studying the layers of expression in Sandy's face. At times, in ways, she reminded him of the wife he had once had. *How would I feel if I'd been fleeing something for a hundred years and saw a chance to finish in ten and somebody told me no, you'll have to wait another three hundred? Lord! What we're asking of them is every bit as hard as what they're asking of us. Maybe harder. I hope Sandy can make them understand that I understand. For whatever it's worth....*

But compassion had its limits too. Just because he understood that it was hard for them, he couldn't give in and make it *that* hard on his own billions. "True," he agreed. "Three centuries. Many lifetimes, for us. A goodly while for you. I'm sorry. But I just don't see how we can go any faster."

"Suppose," Beldan said suddenly, stiffly, "we ignore your request. Zhalãũ controls the drive; humans can't. Suppose I simply tell Zhalãũ to run it up to half a gee, regardless of what you want. What will you do then?"

Clark made himself answer with a straight face, neither chuckling nor shuddering. "The question won't come up," he said. "You still don't bluff very well, Beldan. You know we haven't lied to you. If you do that, we won't make it. And if we don't make it, you've no reason to bother with us at all. Right?"

Beldan stared glumly at the tabletop before answering. Clark wondered how much of his dismay was at the consistent failure of his few attempts to deceive. "Right," the alien ambassador said finally, resigned. He played a few more phrases on his faintly flutelike pacifier, then added with faint hope, "But if it works out better than you expect, maybe we can raise the acceleration again later."

"Maybe," said Clark. "But I doubt it."

There was much to do even before that meeting could break up. Sandy sat through it with some of the same discomfort she had felt the first time she and Jonel sat in on a meeting with the Kyyra. But this time she was braced for it, and did not get unnerved to the frighteningly unfamiliar extent she had then. She said less than she often had in the past, and Jonel more, for more of today's discussion was in areas where he was more at home than she. But she listened and watched—and she grew increasingly convinced that there were important things not being said.

She said nothing—hopefully not even her face revealed what she suspected—until that evening, when she was alone with Jonel in their apartment after supper. "Jonel," she said, staring through a haze of memories and emotions at the swirled-metal sculpture Beldan had given them on his first visit here, "what was Beldan hiding today?"

Sitting next to her, looking as pensive as she, he showed little reaction. "Hiding?"

"Yes." They both knew the Kyyra apparently didn't lie—but they certainly could avoid mentioning parts of the truth. "Over and over he looked like he wanted to say something but thought better of it. A couple of times I could tell he wanted to reach for his music-pipe, but resisted. As if he thought it would make us suspicious. He's learning—but so am I." She looked carefully at Jonel's face. He wasn't looking quite at her; he, too, seemed to be trying to say no more than he must. After a while Sandy said quietly, "They're going to have to raise the acceleration again, aren't they?"

He nodded calmly. "Probably. I didn't see any point in mentioning it now unless you did. Besides, I'm not *sure* they will."

Sandy frowned. "How can they avoid it? The radiation from the core will get here in seventeen years—"

"Uh-huh. We'll start getting it a little later, and keep getting it as long as we're below light-speed. But that seventeen years is to the beginning. A core explosion lasts a long time and has to spread from its starting point. I don't know what the buildup curve looks like. The Kyyra should be able to tell us. Maybe it isn't too bad at first."

"Beldan said the levels would rise sharply and dangerously," Sandy reminded. "Henry told us that when he was filling us in on the first meetings."

"But he also said they'd keep rising for years. How dangerous did he mean? Bad enough to kill somebody out in the open for a few minutes? Even my measurements make that doubtful. Bad enough to cause dangerous mutations in people who grew up in it? We'd call them both dangerous, but there's a lot of difference. If it's not too bad, maybe we can shield well enough to hold out for a few years, or even decades. There'll have to be shielding anyway, if only against interstellar hydrogen when we pick up speed. Our little ships used field generators for that, but they only worked on bow radiation. We don't know what the Kyyra have. But the fact that they're willing to even consider a lower acceleration suggests they can handle it."

"Or think they can."

"M-m-m . . . yes." Jonel shrugged. "All I know is that in not much more than seventeen years, we'd better either be going fast enough to jump to super-c, or be prepared to weather the storm until we can."

Sandy didn't say anything right away. He hadn't told her much that she hadn't figured out for herself, but his opinion lent conviction to it. Eventually she said, "Do you think Henry knows? Or should we point it out to him?"

"He must know," said Jonel. "But I wouldn't mention it anyway. He's got too much else on his mind now."

"But this is important."

"Sure. And in a year or two we'll have time to think about it. But until then, we're all going to have our hands full. And what we have to do now is the same no matter which course we take later."

They said no more about it then. Later that night, as they were going to bed, Sandy bent to scratch Ozymandias the Mutt behind the ears, and found her thoughts concentrated with painful sharpness on the year at hand. *It's February*, she thought, picturing Oz romping through the woods and fields near her abandoned cottage in the mountains to the north. *Almost spring. Only . . . there isn't going to be any spring this year. Maybe Henry should change the calendar so it doesn't remind us.*

For Clark, the day did not end as gently as for the Turabians. Beldan's grudging acceptance of a compromise acceleration—a compromise equally unsatisfying to Kyyra and humans—was only a beginning. It led immediately to the question of how soon the increase would be made, and Beldan immediately pressed for an answer. Clark, aware (though only dimly, he feared) of the hardships it would impose and the preparations that would be required, wanted as much time as possible. Beldan insisted that that wasn't much, and that an absolutely rigid deadline was required. Clark suspected, reluctantly, that he was right. But he couldn't buy a deadline only seventeen months off.

"Why?" he demanded, feeling beads of sweat on his forehead.

Beldan couldn't explain. Part of it, he claimed, was the need to establish a timetable for matching velocities and linking up with Beldan's planet, already bound for M31 but presently traveling at a speed far below that at which it and Earth would complete the trip together. Part of it concerned technical difficulties and inefficiencies involved in holding the acceleration too low—details concerning their propulsion systems which neither he nor Zhalǎǔ would try to explain to humans.

But neither would they budge from their year-and-a-half deadline.

Clark finally left the meeting for a hurried and haunted supper alone. *Half a gee*, he thought. *Then a year and a half.* The compromise was an improvement, perhaps, but it was still far from satisfactory. Clark shuddered every time he thought of what the mortality rate would be if that was all the time humanity had to prepare. And the psychological consequences, the loss of morale....

Maybe there was still some small hope that Beldan could be persuaded to extend it, once Clark could show him some figures of his own. And with Sandy to help him explain....

The population of Earth would face its own limitations, of course. Clark had known that only too well, from the beginning. What he didn't know was exactly what they were. There hadn't been time to think about it before. But now he would have to. Tonight.

As he ate, he organized the questions in his mind. Exactly what had to be done? The closed organic life-support systems developed for distant-planet missions before the turn of the century—and before the Rao-Chang faster-than-light breakthrough—were the key. But how fast could they be produced and distributed? How could they be produced and distributed in the numbers required? What kinds of industrial facilities could be quickly converted to present needs? How could shipping facilities best be used? How about power and communications?

And what would people eat in the meantime? What were the world's food reserves, and how fast could people be taken off them as home recycling spread?

That was the most pressing of all.

As soon as he finished eating, Clark plunged into an evening—which stretched far into the night—of harried consultations with United Nations and World Science Foundation agencies and the central computer here at Kennedy Spaceport. Finally, utterly unencouraged, he linked the spaceport computer with the U.N./W.S.F. units in New York.

He left the resulting team with instructions to ponder all the answers he had been able to gather and all the others it could gather from the combined data banks at its disposal.

And call him in the morning—or whenever it had reached an answer to his question: what was the optimum preparation time before increasing the acceleration, the time which would allow the highest possible survival rate if they did everything right?

That was at three in the morning. It called him at six-twenty.

Though tired, he had remained so tense that he was not far below the surface of sleep when the buzzer summoned him. He literally jumped out of bed and ran to the terminal he had brought here.

The answers were a neat tabular array of softly luminous green letters and numbers on the big CRT screen. His throat went dry and tight as he read them. *The* number was there, and a multitude of others—answers to subsidiary questions to support the big one and provide the details for the message he would begin sending all over the world within the hour.

He looked at them all, hoping they would change as he came more completely awake. But they didn't. And all of them pointed at *the* number.

Less than eleven months from now. Almost exactly one year after the trip's beginning. Even worse than Beldan's deadline. *One year.*

That was the figure that stuck and throbbed and burned in his mind.

. . . And in Domingo Menéndez Consuelo's.

Finally the line printer ceased its clatter behind him. He remained at the window a few moments more in the silence that followed, then walked silently over to read the long message. He tore the stack of paper off along the perforations and took it over to his big desk of carved *conacaste* wood.

His thoughts traveled on two parallel tracks as he put on his rimless reading glasses and scanned the big sheets of paper. One track simply absorbed the staggering burden this Clark—worldwide "special administrator of emergency operations"—wanted his people to shoulder. The other reflected on how much this burden was like others they had handled in the past.

And how different.

In ways, it was like the big quake of '76, the one that had driven Menéndez's family into the shack below the old church. The view out the window now was very reminiscent of conditions then; the causes of that view, to one who couldn't read the papers, seemed little different. But Menéndez knew they were very different. He could see where the sun was in the sky, and that the days were getting shorter. He understood— though not clearly—that utterly unprecedented threats were on their way.

And there was another difference. Then, his country, in its time of trouble, had been unique, attracting sympathy and help (though too often the wrong kind of sympathy and help) from all over the world. Today it was just one of many. Everyone else was also in so much trouble that there would be little outside help. If his people were to muddle through this time, they would have to do it on their own.

Could they? Well, they had done it then, his parents and others like them. They would just have to do it again.

The only thing that threatened to crush all hope was that deadline.

Menéndez was a realistic man. He had no delusions that Clark was bluffing. After the first month of the trip, it was hard to believe that anybody in the world could believe that. If he said these things would be done at the end of the first year, ready or not, they would. But perhaps...*perhaps*...he could be persuaded to reconsider.

Menéndez thought a moment, then got up and stepped to the keyboard next to the printer. His fingers flying deftly over the keys, he tapped out the necessary address codes and then his message:

URGENT AND PERSONAL, TO SPECIAL AD-MINISTRATOR HENRY CLARK: WE ARE IMME-DIATELY INITIATING EMERGENCY PREPARA-TIONS AS PER YOUR COMMUNICATION OF THIS MORNING. HOWEVER, ON BEHALF OF MY NATION'S CITIZENS, I MUST REMIND YOU THAT OUR LAND WAS BADLY HIT BY THE EARTHQUAKES AND COASTAL FLOODS AT-TENDING THE LAUNCH. WE ARE STILL SO BUSY WORKING TO RECOUP THOSE LOSSES THAT

*THE PROPOSED TIMEFRAME FOR THE NEW
MEASURES SEEMS NOT ONLY DISCOURAGING
BUT UNREALISTIC. OTHERS MUST SURELY SEE
IT IN THE SAME LIGHT. WE SHALL DO ALL WE
CAN, BUT I URGE YOU AS STRONGLY AS
POSSIBLE—I IMPLORE YOU—TO IMMEDIATE-
LY AND VIGOROUSLY SEEK WAYS TO POST-
PONE THE DEADLINE.*

*DOMINGO MENENDEZ CONSUELO
PRESIDENTE DE LA REPÚBLICA*

He glanced quickly at the copy the printer had made for his
records—there was much more he would have liked to say, but
this was better politics—and then went back to the windows as
his mind, gathering speed, turned over what he must do first.

Right out there was some of it—the market, the streets full of
vendors, many of them still Indians in traditional garb come in
from the countryside to sell produce and crafts. Or rather,
"distribute"—"sell" was no longer the word. Money no longer
meant much, here or elsewhere. Menéndez had found ways to let
it still circulate, which was vaguely comforting to some who
didn't understand what was happening, while at the same time
assuring reasonably equitable distribution of goods. Now even
that would change. The market would still serve as a distribution
center, but money would no longer serve as even a nominal
medium of exchange. Now there would be strict, tight, meager
rationing—for all, including him—and more soldiers roaming
the market to make sure it was done.

Already he saw what must be done about that; it was merely a
matter of starting orders down chains of command. He spun
about and strode quickly back to the desk and lifted the phone.
He paused just a second or two before punching out a number,
to gaze at the yellowed placard that still hung on the wall behind
the desk. He had saved it from his family's shack, that year in his
boyhood, one of thousands all over the city and the country
proclaiming the defiant motto of reconstruction: "¡*Guatemala
está en pie!*" "Guatemala is on its feet!"

"*Otra vez,*" he murmured grimly to himself. "*Espero.*"

But he felt little hope as he crossed himself, punched buttons
on the phone, and began snapping out instructions. Even as he
did that, the other track of his mind was planning the next step.

• • •

There were a million things for Clark to do.

In essence, there were only two basic problems that had to be solved within the year, and the work would be shared by all the people of Earth. But the two basic problems resolved themselves in practice into a vast, interlocking complex of smaller but by no means small ones. And the whole effort, to have any chance of success, had to be coordinated by a single individual. So Clark would remain, in essence, the first truly global dictator. A couple of months ago, he could hardly have imagined a less likely candidate than himself for such a role. But circumstances—in which he had played one small but crucial part which had so far luckily escaped public notice—had forced him into it.

Now, stuck with it, he determined to give the two problems all he could so as few additional people as possible might die. Basic problem number one was simply the surface activity that would come with the change in acceleration. The oceans and atmosphere, already significantly redistributed by the distortion of the apparent gravitational field, would shift still farther south. That meant storms everywhere, temporary or permanent flooding in central and southern latitudes, and permanent drought in the north. And, even though the Kyyra used their reactionless drive with a delicacy which shortsighted human engineers insisted was impossible even while it was happening, they could not avoid *all* stress on the crust. The biosphere—what was left of it—was so thin, compared to the whole planet, that a globally tiny perturbation would seem catastrophic to people caught in it. There would be earthquakes, and here and there volcanoes would grumble in their sleep and bury cities under molten rock.

The addition of new thrust, in short, would bring problems very much like those brought by the original, now stable, thrust. The crucial difference was that this time people would know it was coming. They would have a few months to prepare—to strengthen houses, to move out of especially vulnerable places.

Basic problem number two was less familiar and more complex: food and water supply for people suddenly deprived of all their traditional sources. The southward flow of water not only flooded the south (such cities as Melbourne and Cape Town were drowned and abandoned), but left the north without natural reservoirs. Water had been collected and held from the beginning, but better ways would soon have to be applied to recycle it. The food problem could be stated quite simply:

agriculture was dead in the north and dying to the south. Indeed, practically the whole ecosystem was dead. Between the drought and eternal darkness spreading over the northern hemisphere, and the flooding and perpetual but waning daylight over the southern, most plants and animals would already be extinct except in protected collections and in and near the tropics. That left people entirely dependent on existing reserves of food—canned, dried, frozen—until they got substitute sources into operation.

The substitute source was the working element of those life-support systems: the edible aquatic plant complex which would also recycle organic matter, water—and air. It was clearly urgent to get them into widespread operation as fast as possible. It was even more urgent than food and water considerations alone would dictate. Even airtightness of dwellings was more desirable, sooner, than might have been thought from the present rate of atmosphere escape alone. It was best to consider the whole life-support system as a package, and at least as urgent as earthquake protection.

On the face of it, it sounded impossible, even described in these grossly oversimplified terms. Such hope as there was rested on the fact that the life-support and sealing systems had already been refined to a simplicity and ease of installation undreamed of before people began seriously concentrating on making long manned spaceflights possible. The Kyyra suggested further refinements. The things that were needed could be added to existing dwellings by the occupants themselves, with little need for special tools or skills.

But it could only be done if the materials and know-how were available. That meant they had to exist and they had to be where they were needed. Big indoor farms were established to grow cultures of the organic soup for the recycling tanks. Small quantities could then be distributed as starters for home cultures, which would then thrive when fed practically any organic matter—and there was no shortage of that. The algae grew and multiplied quickly, but at the beginning there was difficulty finding enough to start the process toward large-scale production. The tanks themselves had to be manufactured, in kit form, in unprecedented quantities. Likewise artificial light sources, both for the tanks and for people to see to work where the sun had already set. Factories already equipped to do such things ran around the clock at expanded capacity. Others, formerly devoted to products now useless, were massively and hastily converted. Zhalāū and her cohorts showed how to tap the driving reaction for electrical power at the surface—a process as seemingly magical as the drive itself, but fortunately rather easy to do.

As fast as tanks and lights and starter cultures and sealing compounds could be made, they had to be distributed. At this stage, that was still a matter of making the best use of existing transportation, some forms of which could still be used. With the materials had to go instructions for using them. That meant instructions had to be written and translated and printed in hundreds of languages, and teachers trained to take them orally to speakers of those and still more who had not learned to read. All that made it possible, even to the extent that it worked, was that the emergency was so clear that a rapidly growing number of people accepted—though often grudgingly—the need to deal with a hierarchy of dictators.

But the political and human problems were by no means small. The subordinate hierarchy took some of them off Clark, but he still put in thirteen and fourteen hour days of virtually nonstop work, and he still felt frustration at not being able to give details the personal attention they deserved. Solidarity and morale were still lacking. He early found it necessary to establish what he privately called a propaganda mill and publicly called the Central Information Service. Some of its first important products were the instruction manuals; another was the New Age calendar Sandy had suggested, dating from the launch and eliminating references to irretrievables like spring and summer. Attempts to explain why things were being done the way they were were still another, and very important. There were dangerously divisive controversies, and time for only shotgun methods to try to smooth them out. In some cases there were easy answers. It was easy to explain why the Kyyra's alternate power source went first to places that had depended on hydroelectricity. But there were other questions of priorities, far less simple, that left festering feelings on both sides of the splits they produced.

And there were complaints about the deadline itself, mostly from places badly hit by the original launch. Clark had a huge pile of messages, some earnest, some irate, some both, from officials in places like Australia, Japan, Guatemala, Peru, Mozambique, . . . all wanting to know why they couldn't have a little more time. There was a pamphlet, but Clark kept all those messages and from time to time got them out and looked at them, longing—intending—one of these days to answer them, to *really* answer them.

But he never found time to do more than look.

During the first part of the year, Menéndez was too busy and too hopeful to think very often or very long about failure—or about the fact that Clark hadn't answered his note.

A typical noon in early April—"Month Four, Year One," they were calling it by then—found him strolling north on Séptima Avenida, out of the downtown shopping district (now hardly recognizable) and into the modest residential area beyond. His boyhood home had been more or less up that way— he could see the Ermita from some of the open intersections now—and he still liked to keep the common touch. Unlike some of his predecessors (and like others), he often strolled unaccompanied among the populace, mingling and chatting. For him, it worked.

Noon, now, was the only time he could take his walks in anything like daylight. Soon even that would be gone, but for now the midday sun rose almost high enough to see. Not quite— it couldn't quite clear the mountains south of the city—but close enough to paint the sky deep blood red behind the silhouettes of the government buildings and the big hotels along La Reforma. During that hour the city got something a shade better than twilight, and Menéndez liked to look at it then. He thought of it almost as paying his last respects.

The streets were full of workers, much as they had been on that other occasion. But now they had lanterns, for the street lights needed work and during most of the day there was no other light but the stars. Menéndez walked slowly, nodding and trading pleasantries with men and women wielding picks and shovels by the curb and hammers and other tools both inside and outside pastel-painted houses. The damage hadn't been as bad here as in '76—people had learned a lot about adobe construction after that one—but it had been appreciable. Looking at the work these folks had done already, he was sure it would be much less in the next one, even though he was just as sure that was less than a year off.

He paused in front of a pale pink house where the front door stood open while a wiry man of fifty and a chunky woman a little younger hammered something around the frame. A scrawny black and white dog, the white tinted pink by the sunsetlike light, snoozed underfoot, oblivious of their labors. *He'll be food one of these days, like as not,* Menéndez thought. But he forced that away and smiled and said, *"Buenos días, Pablo, Carlita."*

They flashed cheerful white rows of teeth back at him and returned his greeting. *"Buenos días, Señor Menéndez." "Buenos días, Señor Presidente. ¿Cómo está?"*

But they didn't stop working.

"Well enough," he assured them. "Looks like everything's coming along nicely here."

"Not badly," said Pablo. "It'll hold, I think. We've got the sealing kits; that's what we're working on now. We missed out on the first shipment of tanks and soup, but there's another due soon. We'll get that one."

"Sure," said Carlita, holding a strip of something against the wall while Pablo did something to it as smoothly as if they had rehearsed the whole thing many times. She grinned. "We're in no hurry to start eating algae soup anyway. Can't say we're eating well, these days, but at least what little there is is still real food."

They exchanged a few more pleasantries before Menéndez excused himself, saying he had to hurry back to the office and dig into a pile of work. Pablo and Carlita nodded and waved as he turned away. "Until next time," they both called after him, and Pablo added, *"¡Guatemala está en pie!"*

Menéndez smiled to himself as he walked back toward the palace, toward a southern sky where the reds were already giving way to deepening grays. He had revived the old battle cry at the beginning of this thing, and it had caught on as quickly now as when he had originally heard it. At times like this, seeing and talking to people like Pablo and Carlita, he could almost believe it.

Especially with most of the time still to go. But, he knew, there were disturbing notes too. . . .

The village, somewhere among the neat terraces that had been farms in the rugged hills near Lake Atitlán, was so little it didn't have a name. It had never even occurred to Mario that it was a village until the Teacher said so, although he had lived there all his life.

He was a strange bird, this Teacher—not like any of the few others Mario had known. He had come up from the capital, he said, bouncing along the dirt road to the village in a noisy old panel truck with feeble yellow headlights. The truck was full of strange boxes and gadgets which the Teacher insisted on passing out to the villagers. It was very important, he said earnestly, that they learn to use them. Naturally Mario was suspicious— though not as suspicious as some of the older folks, like Grandmother Laura—but he was inclined to listen. If the Teacher was a threat, he had to be understood before he could be counteracted.

And maybe he wasn't a threat. Maybe he actually brought the help he claimed. No one could deny that these were strange times.

So Mario listened. He and two dozen others sat in a semicircle on the ground, under the black and starry sky—it was always like that now, though it still paled ever so slightly near the southern horizon around noon—and they listened to the Teacher. He was tall and thin and young, with an aquiline nose jutting protectively over a bushy black mustache. The nose cast a long shadow across his cheek on the side opposite the single dim electric lantern standing on a rock. Mario had tried to tell him there was no need for that—there was lots of wood and dead cane that could be burned for a stronger light—but the Teacher wouldn't hear of it. "No fires," he had said quickly, shaking his head vigorously, becoming strangely upset. "Mustn't burn anything, ever again. Not unless it's absolutely necessary."

Mario had shrugged and let him have his way. Now he stood at the hub of the assembled group, gesticulating and telling them, "When the air outside goes bad, you'll have to stay inside. And you'll have to keep good air in with you, so—"

"Excuse me, señor," interrupted a polite voice from the other side of the circle. "Why will the air get bad, again?"

The Teacher sighed. He had tried to explain it many times already, and Mario knew he would have no more success this time, because he always said the same thing. "Because the galaxy's exploded," he said, and Mario mouthed the words with him, "and the Earth is being moved to a safe place. The motion's pushing the air to the south, and things have died so they can't keep the oxygen and other gases in balance any more. . . ."

Gibberish, *Mario thought again, impatiently, as the Teacher droned on. What's a galaxy? What's oxygen? How can anybody move the Earth? Where could they take it? It was all so silly. Grandmother Laura, sleeping fitfully in the hut, had her own explanations for what was happening, curiously compounded of Catholic preachings and ancient Mayan traditions. Mario was beyond accepting them at face value (though he would never tell her so), but they made at least as much sense as the Teacher's version.*

When the Teacher finished his answer, he paused, leaving an awkward stillness in the warm, stuffy air. "Now," he began anew, "as I was saying—"

"Excuse me again," said the voice from the darkness. "You say we will have to stay inside. But for food, and water—"

"The tanks will take care of all that," the Teacher interrupted, growing impatient. "And you'll get radiophones to talk to your neighbors and get instructions from the government. But, please, all that comes later. Listen to me now. I already told you about the tanks. They'll keep your air fresh. But to keep your fresh air in, you have to seal your houses. You take the paste in these containers and smear it along all the cracks—"

He broke off, taken aback by the ripple of laughter that swept the circle. "What's wrong?" he demanded. "What's funny?"

A hush. When he saw that nobody else was going to answer, Mario stood up. "Señor," he said with a kindly, patronizing smile, "you speak of smearing all the cracks with this stuff you bring. Have you looked closely at our houses?"

The Teacher didn't answer right away. "No, I'm afraid I haven't."

"Come over here with me," said Mario, starting toward his hut. The Teacher picked up his lantern and followed. "Speak softly, please. My grandmother is sleeping inside, and she hasn't been feeling well." Mario gestured at the wall, made of vertical cane poles with big open spaces between them, and at the thatched roof. "Things here are not as they are in your big city," he said. "Patch the cracks, you say? How much paste did you bring, señor?"

The Teacher, staring wide-eyed at the wall and roof, looked as if he needed to sit down. Inside, Grandmother Laura, disturbed by the shafts of yellow light streaming in from his lantern, stirred and made little noises in her sleep. "I'm going to have to think about this," the Teacher whispered.

Emilia, seated under one of the decorative wall lights at the side of the colonnaded patio, finished reading the instructions and let them fall in her lap with a feeling of quiet dismay. She stared ahead into the blackness, broken by the tiny oasis of the one remaining box of red and yellow flowers, basking under a floodlight. The others here, and all outside the house, were dead and shriveled now. These still gave color and fragrance—but, as Emilia read the instructions, even that might not be for long.

Her eyes wandered to the left, to the crates piled in the harshly shadowed corner, and then to her husband. "That's all they sent?"

Rodrigo, his broad yellow hat resting on his knee as he sat in the wicker chair recuperating from the drive back, nodded. "That's all."

"For all of Finca Ramirez? For our house and the workers' quarters? It's not enough!"

Rodrigo shrugged. "But it's all they gave me. I tried to make sure it was right, but they just hurried me through. They were very brusque." He forced a weak, humorless laugh. "Maybe they thought the Indians had all gone home, now that there's no more coffee to pick."

"But they have nowhere else to go. This is their home, now." Emilia sat silent, breathing slowly, thinking of the rows of neat little thatched cottages along the plantation's winding drive— tiny and humble, but clean. And she thought, one by one, of the faces and voices she knew in them. She opened the instructions to look at the figures, to make sure she'd read them rightly. She had. "Rodrigo," she said slowly, "we can't just let them do without. They'll die."

His face was blank. "What else can we do?"

She drew a deep breath. "We could share it with them." He started to say something and she went on quickly, "No, listen. We can't do all of our house plus the cottages with this. But we can do just part of the house and have some left over. It's a big house, Rodrigo. We don't need all of it."

"No!" he said with surprising vehemence. "I can't live cooped up like that."

"They do," she said quietly. The quiet became silence, too long. Emilia grew acutely conscious of the absence of all the sounds that should have been there when it was dark outside, all

the non-human but somehow friendly things that were no more. When Rodrigo had been silent for far too long, she said, "If you don't want to do that, maybe we could fix the whole house and let them use part of it."

"How is that better?" he said scornfully.

She was stunned. He had always been good to his workers— at least as good as any other finca *owner she knew. She would never have imagined him so unfeeling toward them in a crisis. "This is an* emergency, *Rodrigo," she said—still quietly, but with a coldness in her voice that had not been there before.*

"But it's forever," he said. "As far as we're concerned. That's what they say, anyway. I don't think you realize what it would be like, Emilia. All of us and them under one roof, getting on each other's nerves. . . ."

"In an emergency," she said harshly, "everybody has to sacrifice. And maybe it will be temporary. Maybe there'll be more supplies later—"

"And maybe there won't. I'm sorry for them, too, Emilia. But we can't let our emotions drive us to do something we'd regret the rest of our lives. We'll just have to fix what we can now, and then hope we get enough more in time to help them too."

"But—"

"I'm sorry. It's out of the question."

She rose from her chair and looked down at his harshly lighted face, her lip quivering and her eyes feeling hot and wet. "You think so?" she said ominously. "I thought I knew you, Rodrigo Ramírez Colón. Well, I can tell you this. You're not going to leave them out there to die. Not if you want me to ever so much as speak to you again. Now think about it!"

She stomped off into the house.

By Month Nine, it was apparent that it wasn't going to work. One of those thought-tracks in Menéndez's mind had been trying to tell him that for some time—that there were still too many people not taken care of and too little time left to take care of them. The other track kept trying to pretend it wasn't so— that things would still work out all right. It took an incident to drive the two tracks back together.

Menéndez went to the airport that day, at what the clocks called late morning. It was dark, of course. The city was eerie: the street lamps were all working now, but dimly, to conserve power. There was little traffic, with headlights dimmed, so he made good time. The plane was already on the ground when he arrived, but hadn't started to unload yet. And the airport was crowded—much more crowded than it should have been.

Menéndez saw that as soon as he got inside the terminal and had to weave and dodge and elbow his way through the throngs. A time or two he even thought of the advice he was too often receiving (and ignoring) from his cabinet, that he should not go out in crowds without bodyguards. "No," he always told them, "trusting my people is too important a part of my image. . . ."

But these crowds disturbed him. The airport had not been closed, but passenger traffic had virtually vanished, and with it the usual airport crowds. Those here today could only have been attracted by the plane Menéndez had come to meet—and they could only get in the way.

They thickened as he turned down the concourse where it waited. The gate area was cordoned off, but people pressed in on it, milling around the rope and guards. Menéndez struggled through to the chief guard and got himself let through. He found an almost-quiet corner and took out his pocket radiophone to call General García back at central headquarters. "Menéndez here," he said curtly. "At the airport. Just want to make sure you know—there's quite a crowd here. I don't like it. Maybe you'd better get some more troops out here."

"Yes, *Señor Presidente*. Raigosa has already called. They're on their way. Thank you for calling."

He contemplated the little gray box for a moment before putting it away. Not very different from those in the cargo of the big plane waiting outside. Many thousands of them—but, rumor had it, not enough thousands. He had hoped the rumor could be contained, but, looking around, he doubted that it had been. He felt a gnawing fear that these people had heard, and were here to look out for themselves. For the radiophones would be crucial in the months—the *years*—to come. One of them would become each sealed household's only everyday link with the outside world.

He stepped closer to the glass, to cut down glare, and looked out at the plane. He could see it clearly—aviation was demanding enough, these days, without the risk of bringing vital cargoes into poorly lit airports. So here the lights burned bright. The plane gleamed in dazzling patterns of pinks and yellows—

Aviateca had used colorful planes for as long as he could remember. A long caravan of military and civilian trucks waited, the first near the plane's main cargo hatch, the others lined up behind. And the hatch was opening.

It swung down and out, slowly and silently, spilling out a shaft of warm light and a conveyor that snaked down to the first truck. The truck adjusted its position, just in time to catch the first crate from the belly of the plane. A worker crouched in the hatch, loading crates onto the top of the belt; another swept them deftly off at the bottom and stacked them in the truck. Three soldiers with submachine guns paced around the truck and conveyor.

Abruptly, a sharp cry burst simultaneously from many throats behind Menéndez, and there was no quiet after that. He whirled to face a solid wall of civilians vaulting the rope and running toward the outside door and windows. The guards moved quickly to stop them, but there were too many. The first wave knocked the rope down, and then the whole mob surged forward. The guards yelled; the crowd yelled louder. Somebody threw something and the big window near Menéndez shattered. Flying glass narrowly missed him; he saw blood appear here and there among the crowd. But nobody stopped or even slowed. The tidal wave of people poured through the door and window, straight for the conveyor. Both out there and in here, echoing loudly, warning pistol shots rang out. But they had no effect. Seconds later, the submachine guns chattered out by the trucks. People screamed. For the first time, the crowd faltered; some started back toward the building. Through the channel that opened up, Menéndez glimpsed bodies lying motionless on the ground.

Then someone was tugging at his arm and saying, "This way, *Señor Presidente*." He jumped, then saw with relief that it was a soldier brandishing a submachine gun.

Or am I relieved? he thought as the soldier led him swiftly along the wall toward an exit. Remembering some of the more turbulent days of his country's politics, he thought, *Maybe they've had enough of me....*

But it wasn't that. The relief had been justified. The soldier merely escorted him back to his car and asked him if he'd like an armed escort back to the palace. Menéndez hesitated a second, then said grudgingly, "That might be a good idea."

He got in and let the soldier in the other side. He drove too fast all the way back to the palace, but of course no one questioned him. Neither he nor the soldier spoke. Menéndez shook all the way; his thoughts and emotions churned violently. *I had no idea!* he thought. *I should have closed the airport. But there was simply no hint of anything like this before....*

Back at the palace, he hurried immediately to his office and locked himself in. His analysis of what was happening had crystallized by then, and his anger had congealed into determination. He punched out a long-distance call, waited, and finally got a bland answer.

"This is Domingo Menéndez Consuelo," he announced tightly, in English. "President of Guatemala. I must talk to Administrator Clark at once."

"I'm sorry, sir," said the voice at the other end. "Mr. Clark cannot take calls at this time. Would you like to leave a message?"

"No, I would *not* like to leave a message! It's vitally important that I speak to Mr. Clark personally, right away."

"I'm sorry, sir. Mr. Clark is extremely busy."

"So am I. My business is his."

"Lots of people believe that, sir. My job is to screen them. If your business is as urgent as you say, I'm sure Mr. Clark would recognize that and call you back. If you'll leave a message—"

"Somehow," Menéndez said, as acidly as possible, "I doubt that. Look, I *have* to get through to Clark. When do you go off duty?"

"I'm sorry, sir, but I don't see—"

"You wouldn't." Menéndez slammed the phone down and sat glaring at it. He had expected a runaround, of course. But he wasn't going to be stopped by it. He wasn't going to be stopped until he got through to Clark and got what he wanted.

He wasn't going to be stopped.

Clark readjusted his glasses on his nose and stared through them again at the report on top of the pile. In itself, in another time, it would have been consuming cause for grave alarm. Now it was just one item among many. Still, it warranted a second look. Atmospheric changes and medical problems, the heading said. The body summarized an observation by somebody in the technical hierarchy about a possible link between an increase in various health problems and changes in atmospheric composition resulting from the collapse of the ecology.

Well, who can say? Clark thought wryly. *With all the malnutrition and everything else to confuse the issue.* . . . Atmosphere changes were inevitable, of course, but not instantaneous. Ecology was a complicated science, immature among humans and forgotten among the Kyyra, and data on what had happened were sketchy. So the estimates of how fast the changes should occur were far from unanimous. But there was pretty general agreement that oxygen would not fall to a dangerously low level, nor carbon dioxide rise dangerously high, for a goodly while. There was even a surprising amount of photosynthesis still going on in the enlarged ocean of the southern hemisphere, where perpetual daylight partly compensated for the fading sun, and the demise of some species fed a final burst of glory for others.

Even that was temporary, of course. And individuals vary in their adaptability. But the real danger now, the report suggested, might lie in much smaller amounts of other materials—poisons released by vast quantities of unburied dead things all over Earth.

Here in his office, with efficient recycling already in full swing, Clark might have found the report comfortably remote. He didn't, but he did recognize that while the matter deserved investigation, there was little that could be done even if the writer's suspicion was true. Little, at any rate, that was not already being done. So he stamped it CONFIDENTIAL, shoved it into a folder addressed to a suitable section head, and attached a scrawled note that said, "Look into this."

Then he shoved it into the OUT basket and out of his thoughts.

He paused, eyes closed, to grab a needed minute of rest before looking at the next item. Thirteen hours, he estimated, since he had started. A typical day, now. He wondered how he took it. A year ago, he knew, he couldn't have; but now he held up surprisingly well under the constant stress. *Something like Dianne*, he thought with faint amusement, remembering his late wife back when they had had their one son. *With a child to take care of, she could be run so ragged she should have dropped, and yet she didn't. Well, there's a resemblance . . .*

The door opened softly and Rose FitzHugh came in. "Coffee, Mr. Clark?"

He opened his eyes and laughed wryly. "You use the term loosely," he said, reaching out to take the steaming cup. "But thanks anyway." He sipped it; Rose didn't leave. Already Clark was tired of the taste of the stuff, but so far he had resisted grumbling about it. He should have been overjoyed that the systems actually worked well enough to produce it—and that he was still alive and not still waiting to get one. Still, he hadn't had any *real* food or drink since they got his going.

Better get used to it, he told himself. *It's only been a few months now. And it's going to be forever, as far as I'm concerned.*

He looked up at Rose, still waiting. "Something I can do for you?"

She hesitated. "I guess not. I was just going to mention that President Menéndez called again. He's awfully determined."

"President who?" The name sounded vaguely familiar. . . .

"Menéndez. Of Guatemala. He's been trying to reach you since noon yesterday. Insists it's very urgent."

"They all do." Clark hated to sound callous, but there was only one of him and only so many hours in a day. "Did he leave a message?"

"Yes. The second or third time."

Clark picked up the thick sheaf of "ultra-urgent" message slips and riffled through it. Answering them all would have been a full-time job in itself. . . .

He found Menéndez's. It wasn't very specific. "Must discuss time bind and possibility of extension. Remind you of previous appeal, lost or disregarded, early Month Two. . . ."

He remembered now. Guatemala. One of the first of the messages he had kept meaning to answer back around the beginning of the one-year plan. He glanced at the message, watched a quick succession of thoughts tumble through his mind, and announced his decision. "I'll return this one now, Rose. Put the call through, will you?"

The call came as Menéndez was getting into bed, but he didn't complain. Somehow he even managed to sound reasonably civil as he sat in the leather chair beside the bed and explained what was on his mind. "The people are getting desperate," he said. "Immediately before I tried to call you yesterday, I witnessed a riot at the airport here. Our first big one; we haven't even had any real food riots. Now they've looked at the calendar and seen how little time is left, and when that planeload of communicators came in, they were afraid to depend on the distribution centers. They'd heard there weren't enough, so they tried to help themselves right from the plane. There *weren't* enough, you know. And now there are even fewer." He paused, then said very carefully, "We need an extension, Mr. Clark. I told you that months ago, and I'm surer than ever that it's true. We simply aren't going to be ready by the end of Month Twelve. We can't."

"I'm sorry," said Clark. His voice was quiet, sympathetic— but his sympathy was empty. "I understand what you're up against. But I can't help you. An extension simply isn't possible."

Menéndez's civility faltered. "*Do* you understand, Mr. Clark? I find that hard to believe. We are here and you are there. I have a newsfax copy of yesterday's *Prensa Libre* here with an article reprinted from one of your own papers, boasting of how nicely the preparations are coming along in the highly developed countries of North America and Europe. Mightn't your view be colored by the fact that you are in one of those countries, and no doubt quite comfortably settled in?" He resisted the temptation to press the issue of *why* those countries were so much better prepared than places like Guatemala. With a carefully amiable chuckle, he smoothed his voice again. "Forgive me if I sound bitter, Mr. Clark. If you understand, you will understand that too. *No* extension is possible, you say?"

Clark seemed to hesitate, almost but not quite imperceptibly. "No significant extension can even be considered. The computers and the Kyyra agree—"

"Ah," Menéndez interrupted, "but an 'insignificant' extension might be considered?" He didn't wait for an answer. "At this point, Mr. Clark, no extension is insignificant. A couple of months, even one month, even a *week* would save some lives and therefore be worth it. Please understand, sir. Guatemalans do not sit around begging for mercy or favors rather than working to help themselves. I wish you could see how they've been working. In spirit and background, we are better suited to recovering from disaster than most of your people. We've had practice—and many of us have fewer artificial attachments to feel the loss of. But by the same token, we lack the technological head start of some countries. This time that matters. This is not just another earthquake. For the technical changes we must make, we need a little more time. That's all I'm asking."

"I appreciate that," Clark assured him gently, in fairly decent Spanish. "But," he continued in English, "there's little I can do. The situation's too complicated to explain easily. But what it boils down to is this: we have to stick to the deadline. Look, Señor Menéndez... it's not as bad as you think. The increase won't be instantaneous. There'll still be time to work after it starts—"

"Easy for you to say," Menéndez grated, his temper beginning to rise, to struggle free of its harness. "Where you are, far from fault lines. Here we will have quakes again. Have you ever tried to work during a quake, Mr. Clark?"

"No. But—" Clark started to say something else, broke off, and remained silent for several seconds. "I'll think about it," he said. "Will that satisfy you for now? I'll think about it, and double-check, and call you back. I can't promise you anything beyond that, but I will think."

Menéndez, far from satisfied, pondered his reply for many seconds before he spoke it. "I will wait."

The call, and the promise he had made, rankled in Clark's mind. His sleep, though sometimes very deep, was fitful. When he woke in the morning, he found himself relieved that he hadn't dreamed about Dianne.

It was a clear sign that he needed to talk it out with somebody. Dianne had filled that need as nobody else ever could, and no doubt it was a subconscious effort to regain that that had led him to dream about her so often during the last months of the Old Age—those agonizing weeks of indecision about whether to accept the Kyyra offer. But those dreams had twisted Dianne into such tormenting travesties of the woman he had loved that they were far from welcome. He had been tremendously relieved when they stopped after the decision was made—and he had no desire to see them return.

As he dressed, he decided without effort what to do first today. He had been fortunate, in a way. Jonel and Sandy had, to some extent, come to replace that one part of Dianne: somebody to talk to, somebody who would listen sympathetically to the things he had to say but could not say in public. It had come about gradually and without plan (as such things must), and it was entirely unofficial—officially, the Turabians had no connection with the emergency government. But in a certain special sense, he reflected as he started out to visit them, they were one of its most important parts.

Their apartment was not far from his—a short walk across a courtyard under a black velvet sky studded with clear, bright stars. He passed through the building's outer airlock—an ingenious design which Clark hoped eventually to have added to most houses throughout the world—and down the hall to the Turabians' apartment.

He found them working on some reinforcements, but not frantically. For the most part, they were well settled in, and with weeks to spare. They had time to visit.

Now, as he faced them there on the couch and told them about the call from Menéndez, that bothered him. That, and the security of his own quarters....

"So I'm tempted," he said as he finished summarizing. "I do sympathize with their situation—and I know it's not unique. It's just the one where I happened to talk to somebody on the spot, and it drove the point home to me. Maybe I shouldn't have done it. Maybe it's cost me my objectivity, my perspective."

"Maybe," said Jonel.

"That's why I had to talk to you. Help me get it back. Should I even be considering an extension? Not a big one, you understand. That's out of the question. But how about a little one?"

"What does the computer say?" Jonel asked.

"The computer still gives the same answer. But it's not really out of the question. Those projections have so many variables and such hazy estimates of some of them that even the Kyyra Coordinator can't be sure. Maybe enough people are onto home life-support systems—and enough others have died—that we could stretch the food reserves a bit farther." He thought of what it would have been to try this with the reserves that had existed before the world government's advances of the last two decades, and shuddered. "But the longer we wait, the less head start we have on the radiation. And I'm concerned about the psychological effects. Mightn't people take false advantage of the reprieve and slack up on the preparations? I don't think Guatemalans would. I think Menéndez has sized them up fairly; they'd make good use of the extra time. I hate not to give them every chance. But how about the world as a whole? People aren't all alike. I'm afraid if I do this in the hope of saving a few more lives, the subtle side effects might wipe out the gains. Maybe even more than wipe them out. Maybe *more* people would die."

Sandy's normally cheerful face was solemn, her long brown hair falling very still over her shoulders. "I'm glad I didn't talk to him," she said. "I think I would have been convinced. But I'm not sure I would have been right. I'm afraid maybe you're right."

Clark smiled slightly at her. "But you're not sure?"

"Definitely. I'm not sure."

He turned to Jonel, calm and self-assured as usual, but seemingly taking special pains to be neutral. "Jonel?"

"I don't envy you the decision, Henry."

"But you're not going to help me make it?"

"I don't think I should. I don't think I *can*. If I could point out facts you'd overlooked, that would be one thing. But I don't know any more than you do. Probably less. I will admit I'm also afraid of the long-range consequences of changing the deadline. Move this one up, and it'll be harder for people to take the next one seriously, and that might be bad. The galaxy isn't going to give any reprieves, period." He shook his head as if annoyed with himself. "But here I sit spouting the personal opinion I said I shouldn't. Remember that speech you gave when you took over, Henry? 'A ship under battle conditions must have one commander,' you said. Right. And he has to command. He doesn't dare get bogged down trying to satisfy committees. So don't let us act like one. You're the commander, Henry. Decide what you ought to do, do it, and don't look back. We'll be behind you."

"Jonel's right," Sandy said. "You have to do it. I've never liked military-type decision-making, but I can recognize when it's necessary. It's in good hands this time. Just remember the basics."

"Which basics?"

"Don't do anything you'll regret, and don't regret anything you do."

Clark nodded slowly, mildly disappointed. He stood up.

"Noted," he said. "Thanks." They had helped—not the kind of help he had come hoping for, but they had helped.

He went to the door and stepped out. *And*, he thought, *the computer may be right.* . . .

Glumly, he walked slowly across the dark courtyard, almost decided.

A part of him knew what he must tell Menéndez. Another part kept wishing he could find a way not to.

Once more Menéndez found himself sitting at the *conacaste* desk glaring angrily at the phone he had just hung up. But this time he made no effort to bridle his fury; he let it boil.

And while he did that, one of those tracks in his mind coolly pondered and laid plans.

Snatches of the phone conversation echoed in his mind. This time he had not slammed it down in anger. This time he had lowered it to its cradle gently, slowly. . . .

Numbly. This time Clark had ended it, not in an emotional outburst, but certainly with appalling curtness. "No," he had interrupted when Menéndez tried to appeal his unfavorable ruling, "there's nothing to discuss, and we both have mountains of other work to do. I'm sorry."

And that was that.

Menéndez didn't waste time trying to call back. He just sat there, simmering, for half an hour. And then he made his decision.

The intercom was just a small box attached to the telephone, with a dozen extra buttons. Menéndez picked up the phone, pressed three of them, and waited. Within five seconds a crisp voice answered, "Intelligence."

"Menéndez here. Tell Perales I need to see him right away. My office." He hung up, knowing he would not have long to wait.

Guillermo Perales Alberti was there within three minutes. He came in after a single rap and no perceptible wait, a gray-haired man of moderate build and unprepossessing garb, but somehow radiating efficiency. "Yes?" he said, fixing his eyes on Menéndez's face and helping himself to the matching chair on the other side of the desk.

"I need some information, Guillermo," said Menéndez.

"You're come to the right man."

"I know. I've been trying to get this Clark to give us a little more time. He won't budge. I need leverage."

Perales nodded, waited, said nothing.

"You have men in New York and Florida and such places, right? Well, put them to work. Find something I can use. Fast. Anything you can about Clark's background. How this all got started. What he had to do with it. What happened to Franz Gerber. Kind of funny, isn't it? Head of the U.N. until right after the launch, then out of a clear blue sky he turns everything over to Clark and nobody hears a peep out of Gerber any more. Yes, that's funny." Menéndez shrugged. "I don't know what you'll find, but there's got to be something somewhere in all that. And *soon*, Guillermo, soon. That deadline's getting close."

"I understand, Domingo. Anything else?"

"Just details. You can handle them."

"Will do." Perales rose and went out. As soon as the door clicked shut behind him, Menéndez picked the phone up again and pressed a new sequence of intercom buttons.

"Public Information," a contralto answered.

"Menéndez," said the president. "I want to make a radio speech and announcement to the press, in an hour."

"Yes, sir. Domestic only, or international?"

"Everybody," Menéndez said darkly. "Everybody."

It took three days for Menéndez's statement to come to Clark's attention. There is a lot of news in the world; unless it is overtly sensational it tends to spread slowly from one area to another—particularly if it originates in an area not generally considered of great global importance. And sometimes it takes time for even an agency such as the Feedback Monitoring Division of the Central Information Service to recognize the importance of an item.

When this one finally reached Clark's desk, it came as a newsfax clip with a note attached from the division chief, scrawled in big red script and circled twice. "Read carefully," it advised. "This thing's already attracted far too much attention in underdeveloped countries."

Clark read carefully. "GUATEMALAN PRESIDENT CHARGES GENOCIDE," the headline proclaimed, and Clark's throat went dry as he read what followed. Key sections leaped from the page as if to bodily attack him. ". . . announced deadline and aid policies clearly discriminate against poor people and poor nations, wiping out large portions of their populations.... Cannot reasonably be expected to make such radical changes as rapidly or as easily as those beginning with advantages of material well-being and superior education. ... Policies should compensate by giving extra aid in the form of special attention to efficient distribution and education. Instead,... quite obvious that powerful nations have been preferentially served.... Refusal even to consider a small extension seems to show Clark is determined to keep the disadvantaged that way.... Perhaps the resulting extermination is not actually planned, but...."

It stung. It had all been through Clark's mind thousands of times, but seeing it here, spread all over the world, still stung. For many reasons, not the least of which was the fact that it contained a large and ugly core of truth. Certainly not the part about deliberate genocide—nothing could have been farther from the truth, no accusation more painful. But the *de facto* discrimination against the poor and uneducated—there could be no denying that, anyway privately. It had bothered Clark every day since this thing began—but no one had ever suggested a workable way around it.

So what could Menéndez possibly hope to accomplish with his inflammatory tirade? Maybe he honestly thought some good could come of it; maybe, due to limited perspective, he really misunderstood things to that extent. But Clark knew it could produce nothing better than divisiveness among people already strained almost to the breaking point. It was not the first public statement critical of his programs—not by a long shot. But it was the first that used quite that kind of language, that had that kind of punch and wide exposure....

It was the first that he saw as literally dangerous.

He stared at it for a long time, searching for a way around the decision he felt himself making. He found it odious, its implications far-reaching and distasteful.... *But it's necessary*, he told himself grimly.

Is it? he shot back at himself. *Or as you just getting panicky because the deadline's getting close?*

Maybe a little, he admitted. *Everybody is. That's why it's necessary.*

He hesitated a little longer, recognizing some of the old

indecisiveness in himself, recognizing that he must not let it come back. For an instant, he let himself consider again the idea of granting a short extension. Then he caught himself up sharply.

No, he told himself sternly. *You've rejected it, and you haven't found any new reason to change your mind. Right or wrong, you've decided it would probably cost more than it would buy. Live with it. Act on it.*

It's necessary!

Reluctantly, he picked up a notepad and pen and composed a brief, firm message. He read it over once, then took it to the keyboard and set the controls to scramble, so nobody but Menéndez could intercept it.

Then he sent it, typing fast as if anxious to get it done before he changed his mind.

YOUR STATEMENT ABOUT ALLEGED GENOCIDE IRRESPONSIBLE, DANGEROUS, AND INTOLERABLE. I REQUEST AND STRONGLY URGE IMMEDIATE AND UNMISTAKABLE RETRACTION AND APOLOGY TO COUNTERACT DAMAGE ALREADY DONE. IN ANY CASE, THERE MUST BE NO MORE STATEMENTS OF THIS NATURE. REPEAT, THERE MUST (REPEAT, MUST) BE NO MORE....

His head beginning to ache, he turned away from the keyboard. It was done. It was on its way.

Menéndez watched the printer in his office clatter briefly and read with growing disbelief as the message emerged. It did not clatter long—the message was so short that he barely made it from the desk to the printer before it stopped. It was so short that he read it through several times, fuming while a coldness grew in the pit of his stomach, before he really knew what his reaction was.

Censorship! So it had come to that. Never before now....
Or had it?

It was a new threat, or at least a threat newly come to light. It warranted its own strong response—and the world would see how Caesar Clark responded to *that*.

Meanwhile, Menéndez retained enough presence of mind to recognize that the old threat, the one that had prompted his statement, still remained. The genocide, planned or otherwise, was still going on. But now the public *was* aroused and Clark was on the run. The one thing Menéndez could not do now was let that drop. He had to pursue it, hard. The goal was still that delay. More—much more—was desirable, but that was the one thing he could actually hope to win for his people and all who shared their plight, all around the world. A little more time....

If he pressed his advantage. He stepped to his keyboard, thought briefly, and tapped out his reply, not bothering to scramble.

CONCERNING REQUEST FOR RETRACTION AND APOLOGY: CERTAINLY. I WILL ISSUE RETRACTION AND APOLOGY WITHIN TWELVE HOURS AFTER YOU ANNOUNCE DEADLINE EXTENSION OF AT LEAST TWO WEEKS. REPLY WITHIN TWENTY-FOUR HOURS. DO NOT (RE-PEAT, NOT) DISREGARD.

MENENDEZ

Twenty-four hours, he thought as he finished. *That's generous enough.*

And now there was this matter of the threat about no more critical statements. The world would be interested in hearing about that. Menéndez turned away from the keyboard and seated himself at the desk to begin composing his new statement on this latest turn of tyranny. He wouldn't release it until his deadline for Clark's reply, but he might as well begin getting it ready.

He felt strangely sure he would need it.

Less than an hour after he started that—during which he got little done, because of half a dozen urgent interruptions—Perales called him back. "I have information, Domingo," he said in a quiet, smug voice. "Do you have time to listen?"

Menéndez laid his pen down with grave satisfaction. "I certainly do."

"I'll be right there."

He was. Moments later, the Intelligence chief had slipped into the room, locked the door after himself, and settled into the carved chair facing Menéndez. "Information," he mused, flipping rapidly through a folder he had brought with him. "A good deal, as you can see, Domingo. Particularly good, I'd say, for a mere three days' notice. But," he said with a shrug and a fleeting plastic smile, "I didn't come to boast. I believe this item—" he pulled one double sheet out and laid it on top"—will be of most use to you. Your hunch, it seems, was a good one."

"My hunch?"

"Your hunch that Franz Gerber's rather precipitous descent into obscurity was a worthy object of curiosity. I had a couple of agents in New York concentrate on that, and their findings were quite interesting. It was not terribly difficult for them to talk to sources who were relatively close to Gerber but relatively uninformed, but such people were relatively little help. They gave only enough glimmerings of an underlying pattern to make us sure it was worth pursuing. Then it occurred to one of our agents that members of the Security Council who were present at the meeting at which Clark was made special emergency administrator had also been strangely quiet since then. The fact was only less obvious than in the case of Gerber because they had been less conspicuous to begin with. Our agents managed to interview a couple of them, and found that in certain areas they said very little, but looked to a trained observer as if they wanted to say a great deal more—"

Menéndez found himself growing impatient. "Come to the point, Guillermo. You have an excellent agency, but when I'm busy, I'm no more interested in hearing every detail of how they did their job than I'm interested in hearing every detail from my plumber. But I'm very interested in the results."

Perales broke off with a startled look and a barely perceptible sigh of disappointment. "Very well, Domingo. The results. My best New York agent finally managed—despite considerable difficulty—to spend half an hour talking to Gerber himself. He manipulated him, played on his emotions, and trapped into an admission that he had not only been instrumental in maneuvering Clark into power, but had quite actively worked to conceal Clark's original role in starting the trip."

Menéndez's interest perked up. There was something not quite right about what Perales was saying, he half recognized. There was something that didn't quite make sense about Gerber helping Clark into power that replaced and transcended what he himself had already held. . . .

But the disturbing wrongness of that was momentarily

overshadowed by Menéndez's curiosity about what Perales' man in New York had found. "Well," he prompted, leaning forward, "what *was* Clark's role in starting the trip?"

"Exactly that," said Perales. "He started it. By himself. He single-handedly made a deal with the aliens. We're not sure what his part of the deal was, but he told them to start the reaction. On his own, with no consent from any governing body, *he* told them to do it. And they did."

"Incredible!" Menéndez breathed. His mind raced, taking the shocking new fact and seeing how it drew together so many things no one had quite understood during the last several months. *Somehow* the Earth had been launched, with all the effects that had brought with it. People everywhere had been so busy working to survive those effects, and others yet to come, that they had had little time to think about exactly how it had started.

Now, suddenly, it was clear—all too clear. To Gerber, and Perales, and Menéndez, and a handful of others in the entire tortured world.

As his thoughts assembled the picture, Menéndez's emotions mixed themselves into a single cauldron of boiling acid. The frustration that had been simmering over the impossible task facing so many of his people now exploded into an enormous rage. To think that Clark was solely responsible for the entire complex of problems! Not only would he do nothing to improve their chances of solving the problems in time—he had *created* those problems in the first place.

He, and he alone.

There was little more for Perales to say. After he had gone, Menéndez sat staring at the summary sheet he had left. After a while he found the speech he had been working on, crumpled it, tossed it into disposal, and set savagely to work on a new one.

He finished that one in less than half an hour, and knew right away that it was a blockbuster. But, eager as he was to get it before the public, he forced himself to wait. Not out of any regard for honor in dealing with Clark—he no longer could muster that—but out of a purely pragmatic regard for the safety of his country. For only Clark could grant the extension it so desperately needed.

But the deadline Menéndez had given Clark came and went, with no sign from either printer or telephone. Fifteen minutes later he was giving his speech, and within hours it was all over the world.

Far too early the next morning, he woke to an insistent pounding on his door and went groggily to answer it. He found himself staring into the faces of five men. Four of them wore the green and gold uniforms and carried the sidearms of U.N. security troops.

The fifth was not uniformed, but it was he who stood in the center and addressed Menéndez. "Señor Domingo Menéndez Consuelo?" he said in resonant, flawless Spanish. He did not look the part: he was blond and fair-skinned, and his high-necked blue suit was tailored to emphasize his considerable height.

Menéndez frowned warily. "Yes."

"I," said the stranger, "am Robert Novelli. I've just been appointed Emergency Administrator of Guatemala. You are relieved of your duties until further notice." He nodded slightly to one side. "Take him away."

Two of the U.N. troops stepped forward and grabbed his arms—firmly, but not viciously. "Don't struggle," one of them whispered in English. "There's no need for anybody to get hurt."

They led him off, stunned, as Novelli and the other two troops went their separate way.

Once more Clark, who had kept out of sight whenever possible, found himself forced into the uncomfortable and unwelcome role of speechmaker. But this would be, quite possibly, the most crucial speech he had ever made.

It was all out in the open now. Menéndez's latest speech had spread so fast that within hours a hysterical populace had abandoned work for riots. They wanted Clark's hide. Too late, he realized that the attempt to silence Menéndez which had seemed too harsh had in fact been far too mild.

But too late it was—too late for prevention, too late for regrets. He had hoped to keep his role in the launch quiet, at least until time could better be spared for inevitable reactions. Hindsight said that hope, like so many he had held in the past, had been misplaced. No matter; he had had it, and it was gone. In the next few minutes, it was up to him to turn it to his advantage.

For them, he reminded himself stubbornly. *Because if I can't get them together again, they're dead.*

He waited nervously for the cue to begin. He was at his own desk; he had just enough occasion to make public announcements that he had had a pair of television cameras permanently mounted here. Now there was a cameraman behind each of them, and he felt fidgety and very exposed before them.

But when the red light came on on one of them, his posture was poised and erect, his gaze into the camera confident and forthright, his voice solid and steady. "Word has reached me," he began, "that many of you are disturbed by a recent and unfortunate statement by President Domingo Menéndez Consuelo of the Republic of Guatemala—and by reports that Señor Menéndez has been removed from office and replaced by a U.N. official. Let me say at the very outset that both the statement and the report are true. It would not be in your interest, which I try to serve, to conceal the truth from you, or to dress it in pretty disguises. But let me further beg your indulgence to listen carefully as I explain *why* these things have happened."

Is that too much to ask? he asked himself. *To listen? Maybe so. Sometimes it seems people* never *really listen. . . .*

He cut the thought off sharply. A performer can't afford to indulge in that sort of thing during a performance, and this was a performance that would take all the skill he could muster.

"Señor Menéndez," he continued after a pause that few listeners could have noticed, "has told you that I, on my own initiative, gave the Kyyra permission to begin moving the Earth. I confess: I did exactly that. But I make no apologies. I ask you to remember what things were like almost a year ago. The threat from which the Kyyra had offered to rescue us was still distant enough, and the rescue itself frightening enough, that we humans simply could not agree on a decision.

"Yet the threat was real and inevitable; there was no question about that. And the Kyyra were our only hope of even partially escaping it. If we did not go with them, we were all going to die. Period. In just a few years. I could not bear to see that happen. So when I had the chance to see that we would not condemn ourselves to that, I took it. It was the only way humanity was going to survive more than seventeen years—and only by being committed to the trip would we finally get together and do what we must to survive it.

"What did I get out of it? some of you have asked. Nothing. Nothing except the hope that my species—our species—will survive. Personally, it has cost me a great deal. I have sacrificed my conscience, my peace of mind, to buy us this chance. Because I knew that if we started the trip this way, we would start unprepared, and many would die, and I would never be free of the guilt for their death.

"But I don't ask for your sympathy. I did not make the decision lightly. I knew what I was doing. I even knew that the destruction and death would fall most heavily on the disadvantaged. But not, as Señor Menéndez has suggested, out of any desire for anything so horrible as genocide. It would be so only because, despite our best efforts, those so disadvantaged simply could not absorb aid as fast as those starting from more fortunate circumstances. This, I think, has haunted me most of all. But the only alternative was for all to die—and who could prefer that to offering a chance to as many as possible?"

He paused, wondering whether his forehead was as moist as it felt. He spoke his next words with special, gentle care. "Concerning Mr. Menéndez. I know the fear in your minds; my own is full of it. Censorship. Tyranny. Things we normally could not tolerate. But these are harsh times. There is much work to be done—so much that we cannot afford the luxury of the kind of discord fomented by statements like Mr. Menéndez's. If you doubt the danger of such statements, only look at yourselves and your neighbors in the last day or so. I think you will see why, during this emergency, I was not able to tolerate Menéndez's rash remarks—and why we will not tolerate similar actions in the foreseeable future."

He paused again, to let that sink in and to set off his conclusion. When he launched into that, his pace was faster and his voice again subtly changed—for he must end on a positive, hopefully stirring note. "So we must get back to work. More people will die, unfortunately, but the more diligent and heroic our efforts—all of us—the fewer they will be. I ask you this: think not of how many are dying, but of how many are not. For without these measures, we all would. Not today, but far too soon, and man and all his dreams would die with us. This way, there is a tomorrow—a tomorrow a long way off, but a tomorrow nonetheless. Hate me if you must; I'll understand. But cooperate with me—because there's no turning back, and it would be truly terrible to have gone through this to no end at all. I did what I did because I was sure, even though we could not get together last year, that we are a race well worth saving. Help me: together we will show ourselves, and the Kyyra, and the universe, that I was right."

He said no more. The light on the camera glowed uncertainly a few seconds longer, then went out. After that, Clark could only wait, filled with doubt. His audience was too remote and too scattered for their applause or catcalls to reach his ears.

The first returns came in some three hours later, in a phone call from Bill Flamsteed, head of Feedback Monitoring. Bill had one of those voices that are too loud and jovial for a telephone, even when bearing good tidings. He bore them now, Clark supposed, though his feelings were mixed.

"Tremendous, boss, tremendous!" Bill boomed. "I heard it myself—inspired and inspiring."

"Knock it off, Bill," Clark said gently. He felt tired and vaguely embarrassed. "What did anybody else think?"

"Same thing. Not everybody; I won't claim that. But I've got reports from field men in two dozen spots around the world. General consensus is that it worked wonders. Most places, most people are back to work and in better spirits than they've been in weeks. And more solidly behind you than ever before. When you came on, they would have boiled you in oil if they'd had the chance. When you finished, they were cheering."

"Hmph." *Well,* he thought, oddly discontented, *that's what I was after, isn't it? So what's the problem?* "Have you heard anything from Guatemala?"

"Just a minute." A brief silence, during which Flamsteed presumably checked his notes. "No. Not yet."

"O.K. I'll be interested in that one." *(And a little afraid to look at it.)* "Look, Bill, I've got to get some rest. Keep me posted—but with notes instead of calls unless something really urgent comes up. O.K.?"

"Sure, boss."

Clark hung up and walked slowly over to the cot he had had brought in for days when he was too busy to go back to his apartment to sleep. He lay down, eyes closed, and tried to relax, despite a weird mixture of exultation and disgust.

So he had pulled it off. Gradually, he had learned what it

took—how much of the truth, what visual image, what intonations, what gestures, what figures of speech.... He had seen evidence that he was learning before, and if Flamsteed's preliminary reports held water, he had come a long way: He had even become coolly, professionally methodical about it. He pretty much knew what he was doing when he spoke now, and what effect he could expect.

Don't be so cynical, he scolded himself. *It's part of what you have to do. For them.*

For them. Do I still believe that? he wondered. *I hope so. I really hope so.*

Involuntarily, he found himself thinking of a man called Hitler, about whom his parents and uncles and grandparents had had stories from their own memories. Frightening stories, for this Hitler was a man who had orated and schemed his way to both power and popularity....

And today Clark had won the cheers of millions with words about saving humanity—just hours after he had had a noble and well-meaning man dragged from his office and thrown in prison for speaking his mind.

He shuddered.

The rest of the day was not very productive. Flamsteed sent him several more reports of reactions to the speech, generally supporting the first batch. There were still pockets of resistance—Guatemala, not surprisingly, was one of the worst. But, in general, popular support for Clark and his programs was at an unprecedented high, and soaring.

He went to bed early, but he didn't sleep well. But at least the dreams didn't come.

Not quite.

In the morning, as Clark breakfasted on a feeble imitation of scrambled eggs in the dining nook of his apartment, the phone rang insistently. Mouth full, Clark went to answer it, but he consciously resisted running for it. The last couple of days had reminded him forcefully that a man with too much to do will reap only short-term gains by too much haste to do it all.

He picked up the phone. "Henry Clark."

"Bob Novelli," the faceless voice identified itself. Clark's imagination supplied the face, while wondering irritably why

Novelli should be calling him personally this soon. "Hope I didn't get you up."

"No. No matter, anyway. What's up?"

"Well . . . to put it bluntly, things are out of hand, and I'm not getting them back. I heard your speech, and I heard it made a big hit in most places. But not in Guatemala."

Clark frowned. "Exactly what seems to be the problem?" He refrained from adding, *That you can't handle yourself.* He had never felt really confident of Novelli's abilities; he had never really liked him personally. Privately, he had thought when he sent him that Guatemala deserved better. But Novelli was who was available. He was there, and Clark would back him.

"They're not listening," said Novelli, a bit defensively. "I don't think we had any idea just how popular this Menéndez guy was. The people love him. They heard your words about saving the race, but all they really see is that Menéndez is in the clink and I'm in his chair and they want nothing to do with me. The only thing keeping me alive is a heavy bodyguard from the U.N. But I'm not getting anything done. The cabinet and palace staff pretend they don't even hear me. Nobody outside's doing any work. When they get Menéndez back, they say, but until then nothing else matters. It's crazy, but that's the way it is. I can't apply any force with local resources; I'm practically a prisoner in his office. I think I need some U.N. troops, Mr. Clark."

"To gun them down?" Clark snarled. "Look, Novelli, have you forgotten what you're down there for? We're trying to help them stay alive. Massacres don't fit in with that. Listen . . . this problem's a lot more delicate than you realize. I'd better think about it and call you back."

"All right. But don't think too long. Oh . . . I guess I ought to mention one other thing."

Impatiently: "Yes?"

"*One* of them *has* been talking to me. Menéndez. Keeps raving about wanting to talk to you. Demanding, he says." Novelli's voice sneered, but Clark made himself ignore that.

"I thought Menéndez was in prison."

"He is. But he still says he has to talk to you. That's all he'll say. He's frantic."

Clark mulled it over without saying anything. Finally he reached his decision. "Put him on," he said quietly.

"Er . . . I can't right now, sir. He isn't handy. And he wants a picture-phone connection."

"O.K. Do it. My office. Within the hour." He hung up.

The call came back in half an hour—a half hour which Clark spent alternately wondering what they were going to talk about and what he could do to get Guatemala working again.

He had never met Menéndez, but he had seen newsfax pictures. The face that formed on the picture-phone screen was familiar—swarthy, strong, proud.

But, in addition, it was now surprisingly, obviously contrite.

"Everything has come out wrong," Menéndez said in English with only the faintest trace of accent—and even that, Clark suspected, due only to stress. "Horribly, horribly wrong. I still am not convinced you were right, but, as you say, that doesn't matter now. What matters is that I was trying desperately to win my people a better chance, and I ruined it beyond my wildest nightmares. I didn't understand why they couldn't have it, and I thought I could make you change. But it's backfired. I see now the pressure isn't going to work. But because of my efforts, the very people I was trying to save are up in arms over me and not getting anything done to help themselves. I tried to make it better for them, and I made it worse."

"So it seems," Clark agreed, sourly and sympathetically at the same time. "I suppose you called to suggest something?"

"Yes. Let me talk to them."

Clark stiffened warily. "How do I know you won't make things still worse?"

Menéndez looked pained. "Please, Mr. Clark, can't you see that's the last thing in the world I'd want to do? I've done enough damage; all I want now is to fix it. That's what you want too, isn't it?" He leaned earnestly closer to the pickup. "Still, I understand your desire for assurance. Very simple. Let me tape my speech, under supervision of whoever you appoint. Let me tell them I was wrong, and you, under the circumstances, are right. Let me tell them that no matter what has happened to me, they must cooperate with all their might with this puppet of yours. Because only so will Guatemala survive. I understand them, Mr. Clark, and they understand me. I can tell them that so they will believe it; I doubt that anyone else can. And you can check the tape privately and broadcast it yourself."

"H-m-m." Clark thought it over. It might well be what was needed—but Menéndez didn't carry it far enough. "Sounds fair enough," Clark said slowly. "But let me make you a counterproposition, Señor Menéndez. Let me ask you a favor."

It was Menéndez's turn to be wary. "What's that?"

"Would you consider taking your job back?"

Menéndez stared incredulously. Finally he said, "You can't mean that."

"Yes, I can. If one speech from you would do as much as you think—and I tend to agree—how much better would your actual return to the presidency be? I think you can lead Guatemala through this as nobody else could."

"True. But you couldn't trust me. There has to be some catch."

"Nothing very subtle," said Clark. "Oh, you're quite right . . . after what's happened, I couldn't turn you completely loose. I'd have to keep very close tabs on you. I have to have somebody who's going to cooperate in that job."

"You're asking me to be a *puppet!*" Menéndez exploded. "Like . . . like Novelli!"

"I don't like to think of it that way," Clark said quietly. "But yes, it would amount to that. But your people don't have to know."

Menéndez's glare was infinitely contemptuous. "You dare ask me to lower myself to that level?" he hissed. "And to hide the truth from the people whose respect I've earned by trust? One speech is one thing; a lifetime of humiliation is another. You don't know what you're asking!"

"Yes, I do," said Clark, as quietly as before. "Far better than you realize. What I'm asking is something I'd never ask anybody unless I were desperate. I am. I'm pleading, Señor Menéndez. We both want the same thing: we want your people to pull through. I think this is what you can do that will help them the most. You'll get no medals for it; you may feel like a heel. But you'll know what you did. Think about it. Can you help them more another way?"

He waited, feeling tense, projecting calm. Menéndez was silent a very long time, his face an agonized mask of confusion, suspicion, and profound distaste. But at last he said, very quietly, "You win, Mr. Clark. I'll do it."

"Hopefully," said Clark, "we *both* win."

He hung up, when it was over, with a feeling of deep respect for this man he had never met. He could appreciate, as perhaps very few others could, the sacrifice Menéndez was making.

We're more alike than you realize, he thought in silent salute. *If I may say so.*

Clark watched Menéndez's tape twice before he sent it on to the CIS for translation and broadcast. His Spanish was not as good as he sometimes wished, but it was good enough that two screenings made him sure the speech was one of the most moving things he had ever witnessed. It would not affect anybody else in the same way, of course, but he felt confident that it would have the effect that both he and Menéndez desired.

The frantic few weeks that followed between then and the deadline proved him right. With Menéndez back in "power," and playing the part so well that few ever suspected his humiliating deal with Clark, Guatemala rallied to a last-ditch effort that inspired all who watched it. And with Guatemala's example, and the Menéndez affair apparently cleared up, and the C.I.S. driving hard for solidarity, the pockets of resistance in the rest of the world dwindled and they, too, approached the deadline with heroic determination.

It wasn't enough, of course. The most deserving do not always get the best treatment from the universe; heroic determination and nobility of spirit can go only so far as substitutes for proper tools and knowledge of how to use them. When the deadline came, there were such New Year's Eve parties as people could manage, and on Day One, Month One, Year Two, the Kyyra began raising the thrust inside the Earth. And the new quakes came to places like Guatemala, and some weathered them but again a discouraging number didn't.

And this time, it was worse for those who didn't. For when their houses fell down, there was not food for them to eat while they rebuilt, and the sky was cold and black and starry all day. Many died under that sky and had no one come out to bury them.

Such things happened in many parts of the world, but for Clark the images of Guatemala were especially vivid and painful. But he was far too busy arranging help where help could be arranged to think too long at a time about it. And there was, on the positive side, the fact that this time many more people and homes emerged virtually unscathed. For that, there was a growing consensus that the high survival rate was owed very largely to Clark's leadership.

For eight months the acceleration crept upward, multiplying tenfold, and people struggled to cope with the changes it brought. Sometimes—often—coping was far from easy. Many times during those eight months Clark felt sure the dreams of Dianne would return.

But, ironically, it wasn't until the end that they actually did.

That day the acceleration stabilized at the value that would be held until further notice, and possibly all the way to the jump to super-c. That would require more preparations, too, but for now the urgency was gone. Now, for the second time since the trip began, there was the prospect of relative peace and stability—for a while. In the old days, there would have been dancing in the streets; now, people didn't go out in the streets unless they had to. But there were celebrations. Wild celebrations, even big celebrations, where people gathered by radiophone and laughed and drank with people they couldn't see or touch, and hopped from one celebration to another with the turn of a dial. Clark did some hopping—listening more than participating—and found that, now that that phase was over, he was the object of a kind of worship he could not have imagined when he made that crucial decision of twenty months back.

Worship? Yes. For the survivors, that decision, once viewed by many as an act of betrayal, had become an act of salvation.

And Clark found the role of savior even more uncomfortable than that of ruler.

He grew more and more uneasy as he visited the celebrations, hearing the boisterous laughter and the unpolished songs portraying him as a jolly good fellow, until finally he was sure he wanted no more. At that point he switched off the radio and went to bed, telling himself that by reaching this milestone he had earned a rest.

Many shapes, shadowy and disquieting, moved in his sleep. One of them, for the first time since the trip began, was Dianne.

He watched, half afraid, as she slowly approached him. She was fairly young again, honey-blonde, wearing a yellow dress that faded out into vague mists around the edges. She came quite close without speaking, without even showing any expression, and he feared that when she tried to speak, no words would come—or, worse, laughter.

But, for the first time since the Kyyra had come, it was not that way. "Problems?" Dianne said, simply and softly.

He was overjoyed. There was still an aloofness, a coolness, but it was a beginning. Finally he had Dianne to talk to again, at least in his dreams.

He nodded. "A few."

She studied his face, then let her eyes wander slowly down his body and back up. "You have blood on your hands," she said matter-of-factly.

He looked down at them and saw them red and wet. He looked back at Dianne. "Yes," he agreed. He added defensively, "So does a surgeon."

She looked at his hands again. Her face showed a hint of a dubious frown, her shoulders a hint of a shrug. "Perhaps," she said.

"There's another thing," he said, feeling frustrated. "I gave a speech. I said, 'Think not of how many are dying, but of how many are not.' They're taking me too literally. Now that they've made it, they're forgetting too fast. All the ones who didn't make it, who starved, or got sick, or—"

"Maybe they have to," she said. He noticed that she was farther away now; her voice sounded farther still. She wasn't walking (though he couldn't see her feet), but she was receding.

"But they like me too much," he complained. "Nobody should like a dictator that much. That's what worries me most."

"As long as you worry about that," said Dianne, "I won't. When you stop worrying, then there'll be something to worry about." She had turned away and was receding faster, becoming less distinct, fading back in among the other dream-forms.

"But don't you see the problem?" he called after her, frantically, afraid he was losing her again. "How do they get rid of me? I read a story once where men kept deposing tyrants and then becoming tyrants themselves 'for the duration of the emergency.' But they never quit until somebody deposed them, and it just kept repeating. How are they going to get rid of me, or somebody like me, when all this is over?"

Dianne's voice drifted back to him, a pensive murmur from very far away. "Hm-m-m," she said. "That is a hard one. I'll see what I can think of. . . ."

And then he saw her no more.

Somewhere along there he realized that he was no longer quite asleep, but lying in his bed and his own sweat, staring into darkness and an uncertain future.

So will I, *he thought with determination.* Between us, we'll think of something.

After that, he slept.

Second Interlude

The lull that time was no illusion. For the first time, some time could be spared to think. Henry Clark, appalled at the destruction and loss of life in building the acceleration up this far—resulting largely from the fact that it had to be done hastily—was very determined to give plenty of thought to what was done next. He declared a one-year moratorium on most preparations for the rest of the trip, so the options could be weighed before they became commitments.

But time to do that meant too much time for other things. The loss of morale Henry had worried about had not yet become the problem he had feared, because during the build-up preparations people were far too busy to dwell long on their plight. But the letdown that followed the end of that frenzied activity sent morale crashing to abysmal depths. Suddenly there was time to be bored, to realize how much had been lost, to see that the tunnel was too long to ever reach the light at the end.

Sandy, these decades later, still remembered those days too

well. Even with a better-than-average understanding of what was happening, and a great desire to keep life going, she had not been immune to the depression. Sometimes, during the long artificial "nights," she would lie awake realizing too fully how much life other than human had perished through the actions of humans and Kyyra, with no chance to defend itself. Sometimes she wondered bitterly whether humanity was worth saving, even at a price less than had already been paid.

But those were her blackest moments. Basically, her problems were not uncommon ones.

It was still odd to think what had pulled her out of those doldrums and made her see what was needed. But it hadn't been cheap.

She got up slowly from the couch and went to open a drawer of a battered wooden cabinet, also leveled with jacks. She dug through a pile of papers until she found one of her oldest journals since Before. The open drawer quivered weakly with another faint tremor. She closed it and took the journal back to the couch.

After a slight hesitation, she opened it, flipped through the pages to a certain entry, and began to read.

Pinocchio

I'M AFRAID I've been neglecting these notes lately, and especially since we reached the second acceleration plateau. I could rationalize it by saying that the paper and ink we stockpiled isn't going to last forever, which is true. (I've been consciously writing very small when I do write.) But the real reason is that so little has been happening these last months that it's driving us up the walls, and writing about it only makes it worse. Well, this trip up north is something happening, and I'm going to keep full, careful notes, if only for the duration.

It's funny what makes an impression on people. I think what thrilled me the most about the invitation was the fact that Dr. Orlik said I should bring a bathing suit. I still have one—a nice orange bikini I'd only worn twice—but I never expected to get to use it again. At home we never get any closer than sponge baths now, and even that too seldom. I really need to get away, and the prospect of enough water to get all the way into is Elysian.

104

I'm only sorry Jonel can't come too. But, much as I hate to say it, I even need to get away from him for a while. And he needs to get away from me. There's so much we both have to sort out.

And I'm not at all sure how I'm going to react to meeting Pinocchio.

Flipping back through these pages, I notice this has all happened so fast I haven't given a very coherent account of just how it came about. I'll have to try to fill it in as I go, in case anybody (including me) tries to read this sometime years from now. But time's still going to be a problem, I suspect. After all these months of so little to do (imagine *me* complaining about *that*!), I'm going to be busy.

But I do have a little time now. We're here, and I'm alone in my room and more than ready for sleep. But I really should try to finish what I started on the plane before I turn out the lights.

Beldan came with me; he said it was his duty as the Kyyra ambassador when he heard there was another intelligent race involved. (Of course, I know it goes deeper than that....) Anyway, we came up in Henry Clark's official plane, the same little yellow twin jet Tony's been flying for him for as long as I've known him. Henry doesn't use it much any more—even he doesn't travel unless absolutely necessary now—but he tries to keep it in shape and Tony in practice. As emergency administrator of Earth, he has to be able to go anywhere fast if the need should arise. He's had to have it modified, of course—altimeter revamped to compensate for latitude, jets souped up to let it fly in thinner air, fusion rocket boosters to help it when it has to go so high that even the modified jets aren't enough.

We did that once today. I wanted to see my old cottage in the Tennessee mountains, near the Carolina line. It was out of the way, but Tony said it wasn't too far, so we swung inland. And as we started up over the Appalachians, he cut in the rockets, even though we would only clear the highest peaks by a thousand feet. There isn't really that much less air, yet, but most of what there is is in the southern hemisphere.

We passed my place around noon. There wasn't anything to see out the windows, of course, except blackness and stars (and we could see those, because we were flying with no cabin lights except the soft glow of the instruments). But the plane now has an infrared ground scanner with an image intensifier, and Tony let me come up front so I could see the screen. I watched it intently, but I'm not sure it was a good idea. I recognized the hills, and I even caught a glimpse of the cottage where, less than three years ago, Jonel and I had looked forward to living. But it was a different place now—the mountains which should have been alive with sunshine on soft greens and pinks now held nothing but darkness and black skeletons and death.

There was a lump in my throat and something in my eye as Tony turned the scanner off. I went back to my seat next to Beldan and we turned northeast. I guess I could have written some more then, but I didn't feel like it, and none of us talked much the rest of the way.

We had a smooth landing at Hyannis, uneventful except for the striking effect of flying over a landscape of almost complete darkness and having an entire airport outlined in bright lights spring suddenly into being at Tony's request. It was beautiful. (Flights are so infrequent now that few airports keep their lights on except when they know somebody's coming in or leaving.)

We put on respirators before we got out of the plane. There's still enough air to breathe, for short times, but the quality isn't what it used to be. No point in taking chances, Tony says, and I suppose he's right. So we put them on, and I felt like a caricature of a nurse going into an operation as we got our feet back on the ground. Tony said good-bye and went to the pilots' lounge to rest up before taking the plane back to Kennedy.

Henry doesn't worry about keeping Beldan out of sight when he leaves the spaceport any more. Everybody knows who he is now, and presumably everybody knows we can't get along without him, now that we're committed to the trip. In ways, I prefer the new openness, but sometimes I wonder about it. There are still enough nuts in the world that someday one of them might take a potshot at an alien just because he's an alien. Rational arguments have little effect on such people.

Luckily, most of them—like virtually all of us—are confined under what might as well be called house arrest. So I guess the danger isn't really very high.

Anyway, the car that had been sent to meet us was an ordinary car, and we walked like ordinary travelers through the airport corridors and out to the parking lot. But our car was the only one there, and our driver was the only other person in the halls. He'd been wandering around looking for us, not sure where we'd come in. When he saw us come in the gate he ran to catch us. He gave Beldan's flamboyantly robed seven-foot form a wide-eyed glance, tried to cover it, and looked straight at me. "Excuse me," he said. "Are you Sandy Turabian?"

"Yes," I said. "And this"—I gestured—"is Beldan."

"Awfully glad to meet you, ma'am," he gulped. "And you, too," he added hastily to Beldan. It took a slight effort to keep from laughing at his flustered state. He kept casting furtive, curious glances at Beldan, as if he'd never seen a Kyyra in the flesh before. (Which was undoubtedly the case—very few people have.) "I'm Bill Maracek," he told us. "I've a car outside to take you to the Institute."

It was an electric car, of course. You never see anything else now, even if you happen to be out; internal combustion engines don't run well enough to be worth the trouble. Unfortunately, it wasn't a very big car, so Beldan had to scrunch up in a way that couldn't have been very comfortable. Luckily it wasn't a very long ride. It's not very far, the road's pretty good (though the surface could use quite a bit of work), and there was no traffic and no traffic cops. We didn't see a single moving car on the whole trip, even in downtown Falmouth.

There wasn't even a parking problem in Woods Hole—we could have any place we wanted! A far cry from the one other time I was here, when I came down as a girl to catch the ferry for the Vineyard with my uncle and we spent so much time looking for a parking place that we almost missed the boat. But then everything's a far cry from what it was then. The ferries have long since been cannibalized, and there's no water between here and the islands—or a long way beyond.

Seeing that at close range, I think, made arriving here even spookier than flying over the cottage, even though I had lived many very happy months there and only visited here once. It wasn't cold, but I shivered as we parked in front of the main building of Oceanographic, with lights on in a few thick windows, and got out onto the deserted street.

Water Street, I thought, reading the sign up at the corner. *None of the names fit any more. Water Street, with no water in sight. Oceanographic, with its ocean miles and miles away, and in the late stages of dying.*

I looked up. *And a stunning, chilling Milky Way in the middle of the afternoon.* I tried not to think about it but the thoughts tumbled through well-worn grooves before I could stop them. *The sun's still back there; they still see it in the southern hemisphere, as the pole star they never had before. A bright pole star—as bright as the full moon used to be—but just a pinpoint to the naked eye.*

And only faith tells us northerners it's still there at all. But it is—six or seven hundred astronomical units back. We've come that far—which only leaves a couple of million light-years to go.

Or a couple of hundred million times as far as we've come. No wonder I feel like we're not getting anywhere.

I shook the thought out of my head and followed Bill Maracek. It was about time I concentrated on what I'd come for—I should be excited about it, yet I hadn't actually thought about it since we landed at Hyannis.

The dolphin facility was right across the drawbridge, the rusty old drawbridge that has nothing to do now. The channel under it, formerly connecting Eel Pond to open water, was now just a deep, ugly gash in the Earth. One orange brick wall of the building formed a side of the gash, extending well below the former low-water line. Near the bottom was an elaborate gate arrangement, now tightly sealed, which I knew was where the participating dolphins had come and gone in the heyday of Mason Orlik's work. I hadn't seen the gate before—the building was still under construction when I was here fifteen or twenty years ago—but in the last couple of days I'd been reading about what Orlik had done here. Just how much he'd accomplished had come as quite a surprise to me—but then, the most important parts had happened in the last couple of years before everything changed, and he hadn't had time to publish it.

We reached the door, pressed a call button, and waited. I noticed the entrance had been fitted with both kinds of airlocks—the self-sufficient kind with its own cycling pump, and the cheaper kind with no pump but just a nipple for rescue crews and such to attach a portable when they need to get in or get somebody out. Here, presumably, it's an emergency backup, but for most people it's all they have. Just one of the umbilical cords—along with power lines, recycling systems, radiophones, delivery chutes, and on and on—connecting them to this precarious makeshift civilization we've built to stay alive. If any one of the cords fails, the person or family attached to it dies, unless it can be fixed very fast. And they do fail sometimes, because it's all been built so hastily there wasn't time to get all the bugs out.

No wonder we feel vulnerable.

A voice from a rattly speaker asked who we were. Bill told it, and a moment later there was a hiss that ended in what sounded like a sigh of relief. The words *PLEASE COME IN* glowed at eye level, and we opened the outer door to go in and meet our host.

Mason Orlik is thin, wiry, intense-looking but soft-spoken, and so instantly likable I can't help wondering whether he had more reasons for asking me to come than he's told me so far. He must be close to twice my age, but looks quite youthful, with smooth skin and close-cropped black hair cradling his face in a thin fringe beard with a sharp point at the chin. There's a little gray among the black, but not much, and it doesn't call attention to itself.

He rose from his gray steel desk as we walked into his fluorescent-lighted, book-and-tape-lined office. Beldan had to duck to go through the door, and Dr. Orlik gave him an odd glance that I didn't understand. But then his eyes came back to me and he smiled and extended his hand. "Terribly glad you could come, Mrs. Turabian. Mason Orlik, at your service."

I shook his hand. "I'm flattered that you asked me. I only hope I can help."

"If you can't, I'm afraid we'll have to give up." Close up, I saw that worry lines were starting to creep into his face. "I've heard so much about how you were the only human who could really talk to the Kyyra. And how helpful Caesar Clark has found yours and your husband's advice since all this started."

Caesar Clark, I mused. Lots of people call him that now, but the fear and hate with which they used to say it is so far gone from their voices now that it scares Henry. But Orlik didn't say it with quite the reverence some people do....

I shrugged. "He asks us what we think, we tell him. That's all. Dr. Orlik, I'd like you to meet Beldan, the Kyyra ambassador."

"An unexpected pleasure," Orlik said, extending his hand to Beldan. But his eyes said he wasn't quite sure. "I ... er ... didn't realize you were coming with Mrs. Turabian."

"Sandy," I corrected, trying to put him at ease. "I told your secretary—"

"I'm afraid she garbled the message a little," Orlik

apologized. "She just told me there'd be two people and we'd need two rooms. Does...er...His Exellency need any special arrangements?"

I laughed in spite of myself. "No. Nor titles. 'Beldan' is fine. A fairly long bed would be nice, but he's quite adaptable. Right, Beldan?"

"I try," he said. Orlik's consternation made him a little uncomfortable, but I doubt that Orlik knew. Nobody else can read them the way I can.

"Good." Orlik looked relieved. He turned back to me. "Sandy, I know you're anxious to meet Pinocchio, but you must be tired after the trip. I think it would be better for you to wait until tomorrow, when you've had a night's sleep and a chance to go over some background material. You'll want to know some things about our facilities and what we've learned and how you should act before you go in."

I nodded vigorously. "I certainly will. I must admit I've been a little nervous about the whole prospect. I have lots of questions—"

He cut me off with a wave of his hand and an understanding smile. "Later. I'm going to give you some reading material—preprints and some notes we've written up for you—and some tapes to study in your room tonight." He looked at Beldan. "Beldan, are you going in to meet him too?"

Beldan nodded. "I'd very much like to."

"Then I'll have copies made up for you, too." Orlik turned back to me. "Go through this material tonight; it'll probably answer most of your questions. Any that it doesn't, ask me in the morning and I'll try to clear them up. Fair enough?"

"Couldn't ask for more."

He picked up a briefcase with my name tape-labeled on it and ushered us down the hall to a little room labeled OFFICE SERVICES. He handed the briefcase to a spectacled young man (who tried not to stare at Beldan) and told him, "We'll need copies of this right away, for Mrs. Turabian's companion." He turned back to us. "They'll be delivered to your rooms shortly. Supper when you call for it." I noticed he didn't ask if Beldan needed anything special—but then I'd told him Beldan was adaptable, and besides, there's really only one kind of food to choose from now.

He took us to our rooms, a pair of cubicles with bed, dresser, and desk, sharing a small lounge area between them and a bath (such as it was) opening off that. The whole thing, he explained, had been created by partitioning up a former lab. It was a pity, he said, that work had shriveled so that labs had to be abandoned—but maybe it was just as well, since transportation outside had become so difficult that people had to live where they worked whenever possible.

Just before he left us, he looked at me and said earnestly, "I will give you one extra bit of advice right away. When you meet him, be casual and take your time. He'll have to get to know you before he wants to talk about anything as personal as what I want you to talk to him about. If you try to rush it, you might blow the whole thing. I'm sure you can understand that."

"I think I can," I said, a bit stiffly.

Do I ever!

He left. Beldan and I retired to our separate rooms, and that's where I am now. It's been a long day. I've been through most of the papers and tapes Dr. Orlik gave me, and I guess I ought to go through the rest. But I'm too tired, so I'll try to finish them first thing in the morning.

I want to be well-rested then; I'm eager to get into this thing (though a little afraid, too). But I'm not too optimistic about how well I'm going to sleep. Unfamiliar quarters, and too much on my mind—Henry's problem about future plans and acceleration; my personal problems (which I must try very hard to keep separate); and my job here. I'm very serious about that.

It's not every day I get asked to try to save a species from extinction.

15/5, 3

My dreams were haunted by dolphin distress calls—eerie pairs of shrill, sirenlike whistles, ascending sharply and then descending in a second or so—which I've never heard except on the tapes last night. I have to be careful not to let such things color my thinking.

I finished the tapes and books this morning; now on to reality. I put on my bathing suit before leaving my room, and threw a long shirt on over it. Then I went out to knock on Beldan's door. As expected, he came out in his usual long robe. I was hardly surprised, but a little disappointed. We humans still don't know what the Kyyra look like, except for their faces and hands, and we can't help being curious.

Dr. Orlik glanced at my bare legs and smiled when we walked

into his office. "Well, I see you're all ready." He looked at Beldan. "How about you, Beldan? Are you going in the water?"

"I think," Beldan said carefully, "I'd rather just watch from the side, if you don't mind."

"Oh. Well, I suppose that'll be all right. You should understand, though, that they love physical contact and you'll win his trust faster if you get in and touch him and let him touch you."

"I'm aware of that, Dr. Orlik. But I'm afraid I would feel uncomfortable. I'm sorry."

"No matter. Pinocchio will understand, I think." He changed the subject. "Do you have any questions before we go in?" Beldan and I both shook our heads. "Good. Let's go." He stood up.

"No need to be afraid of him," Orlik said as he led us down the hall to an elevator. "He's big and powerful—and very gentle. Just treat him with ordinary respect and he'll return it."

We got into the elevator and started down. "I think you'll be surprised at how fast it goes. It used to take a long time to get a dolphin's trust, but that was because we couldn't get past all the barriers and actually talk to each other. Human and dolphin languages are mutually unpronounceable, for all practical purposes; most of what they say, we can't even hear."

The elevator stopped and Orlik motioned us out ahead of him. "And the content and idea patterns are literally worlds apart. The everyday things that they and we talk about have little in common, and we organize the ideas very differently—for very good reasons. For all practical purposes, Pinocchio's language doesn't use words. And they find the fact that ours does amusingly strange and unnecessarily obscure."

We had already stopped in front of an unlabeled door and been standing there as he talked. He stared at the doorknob as he finished, "But with modern electronics that can render one mode of expression into a fair approximation of the other, the whole thing becomes much easier. You can talk to Pinocchio, he can talk to you, and suddenly the whole thing is on a much more civilized level." He looked up with a smile, as if he had just finished a well-rehearsed sales talk for an inspector from a grant foundation. (Quite likely, he had.) "Well," he said, as if he had just become aware of the fact, "we're here."

He opened the door (double, with an emergency airlock) and we followed him in—into a different world. At first glance the white walls and bright, even lighting reminded me of a handball court, but almost the whole floor was taken up by a square pool of clear, sparkling, dancing water. A dry ledge ran around three sides of it; the fourth lapped right up against a wall. The fourth wall, I noticed, looked different, as if it had been built at a different time from the others. And if I looked carefully along it, I could actually see the slight "tilt" of the water surface produced by the Earth's acceleration.

The air was damp and warm and full of a heavy fragrance reminiscent of both seashores and swimming pools. And at the far end of the tank, with the tip of its dorsal fin projecting above the surface, lay a magnificent animal, a sleek, steely-gray torpedo nine or ten feet long, with broad flukes at one end and a bulging forehead and slender beak at the other. The pool was only some twenty feet square and must have seemed pretty cramped to the dolphin, I thought. But I couldn't remember when I'd last seen so much water in one place. I could hardly wait to get in.

Before I could ask what I should do, Dr. Orlik gave a little whistle and cheerfully (but in an ordinary conversational tone), said, "Good morning, Pinocchio." Then he quickly grabbed my arm and pointed at a large screen hung at one end of the pool.

I tried to watch the screen, but my attention was divided. At that same instant, the dormant torpedo came suddenly alive, stirring, bending into a smooth curve and darting toward us. In the split-second it took him to get here, the air filled with a rapid succession of what I might crudely describe as clicks and whistles.

And the screen lit up with words, in clear red letters, big enough to read from anywhere in the room:

GOOD MORNING, MASON. •	• FRIENDLINESS,
•	•
•	• MODERATE
•	• CHEERFUL-NESS.
•	
• IS THIS SANDY?	• CURIOSITY,
•	•
•	• EAGERNESS.
•	•
•	• SONAR.

"Yes, it is, Pinocchio," said Orlik. "And she's very eager to meet you."

Pinocchio had stopped directly in front of me and raised his head out of the water, looking me over with big, surprisingly human eyes—and, presumably, ultrasonic pulses. Close up, I noticed that his otherwise smooth skin bore a goodly number of small scars and the hundred or so little teeth in his open beak were worn flat on the tips. He seemed to be grinning at me.

And suddenly I no longer needed to be told what to do. As usual, anticipation was more frightening than reality. I grinned back. It seemed the most natural thing in the world as I shucked off my shirt and stepped off the ledge into 80° water that lapped playfully at my legs somewhat above my knees. "Hi, Pinocchio," I said quietly. "I've heard a lot about you." I bent slightly to pat his bulging forehead, carefully avoiding his eyes and blowhole.

I heard a succession of strange underwater sounds, dolphinlike but coming from somewhere else, and then Pinocchio's blowhole wiggled and more sounds came from him. "And I've heard a lot about you," the screen told me he'd said.

He was nuzzling my legs, exploring them with his beak. It tickled, and I felt so gloriously good that I was only half listening to Mason's explanation. I knew most of it anyway. I did notice that he seemed a little surprised that I was already in the water. "There are microphones," he was saying, "to pick up dolphin sounds either underwater or in the air. The phonation apparatus in his blowhole is divided and he can use the two halves singly, jointly, or independently. Our computer's in the next room, beyond the screen. The first two columns of the display give a very free verbal translation of what he's saying, or both messages if he says two things at once. Some of the sounds carry connotations to compensate for the lack of an expressive face, and the third column has comments about those. When you say something, it generates an approximate translation into his terms and plays it through underwater speakers for him. Only approximate, of course, and it can't handle everything. . . ."

More words from Mason; more clicks and whistles from Pinocchio. He slapped the water with his tail, splashing me, and started swimming around me in tight circles, rubbing his smooth sides against my legs and nudging me toward the center of the pool. Beldan watched us with obvious fascination. The screen said Pinocchio was excited and pleased and had told me, "It's been too long since I had anybody new to play with."

I laughed. "Me, too." Faint dolphin noises from the underwater speakers, then more from Pinocchio, and new words on the screen.

"Come on!" Pinocchio told me (with "playfulness"). "Get wet!" And before I finished reading it, he startled me by whirling about and slapping my calves with the side of his tail, almost but not quite hard enough to throw me off balance. For a split second I struggled to stay standing, briefly afraid, then realized his intent and let myself fall laughing into the water. He could have killed me with that tail, if he'd wanted to—so he obviously hadn't. I relaxed and let myself go completely under and come up with my hair dripping. It felt as heavenly as I'd anticipated.

Pinocchio was nuzzling the parts of me he hadn't been able to get at before. I ran my hands over all of him I could reach. The thought crossed my mind that Mason must have given me quite a build-up—and Pinocchio must trust him very deeply—for Pinocchio to take so quickly to me.

I had finished struggling into a sitting position before I realized that Pinocchio had helped. Now he was slithering across my lap and coming to rest there. He twittered. "Rub me between the flippers." I did, and the screen showed, "Ah-h-h!" with no further comment. I laughed, both at Pinocchio's reaction and at the way Mason had programmed the translator.

With another of his mercurial changes, Pinocchio darted away from me and over to the side of the pool. He stopped directly in front of Beldan, looking up at him as he had looked up at me. "And who is this?" he asked.

Mason smiled down at him. "I've brought you a surprise, Pinocchio. This is Beldan, one of the non-humans from off Earth that I told you about Sandy talking to. She brought him with her."

"Fascinating," said Pinocchio. "I'm glad to meet you, Beldan."

"And I'm glad to meet you," Beldan said slowly. "I'm not sure what to say to you...."

Pinocchio laughed, according to the screen. "Then don't say anything," he suggested, "until you have something you want to say." (*An admirably simple and sensible idea*, I thought. *Wonder why it so seldom occurs to people....*) "You're coming in, aren't you?"

Mason, apparently satisfied that all necessary ice was broken, quietly opened the door and slipped out. Beldan's big red eyes jerked slightly back in their sockets, then forward. "I'm afraid not," he told Pinocchio. "I'd love to join you, but I'm not a water animal."

For a very brief moment, Pinocchio was almost silent. There was one brief burst of noise, soft and cut off abruptly, as if it wasn't meant for us and he decided after he started that he didn't really want to say it at all. The translator screen indicated DISTRUST(?) SUSPICION(?). His face, as Mason said, gave no more clue to what he was thinking or feeling than a mask. But after a tiny pause he said lightly, "Sandy's not a water animal either. But she came in with me." He swam once around me, rubbing his side against my back, and went back to Beldan. "Are you afraid of me?"

"No," said Beldan. "Please don't think that. But I can't come in the water. I'm sorry."

Pinocchio swam slowly back to me and cradled his head in my lap. "Why is he afraid of me?" he asked, perplexed and a little hurt. "Or is it that he—"

He broke off abruptly, listening. Beldan had taken out his music-pipe and was playing one of his haunting improvisations. For a moment Pinocchio listened and scanned Beldan with eyes and echoes. Beldan kept playing. After an uncertain few seconds, Pinocchio came back to me. "What's he doing?"

"Why don't you ask him?" I suggested, stroking him. "I think you've upset him by making him think he's hurt your feelings. But he didn't want to do that. He's just even less of a water animal than I am. You wouldn't want somebody to make you get out of the water, would you?" He lay silent and motionless— thinking, I suppose. "But why don't you ask Beldan?"

"O.K." And he was off, back to Beldan. "Beldan, what are you doing?"

Beldan stopped playing but didn't put the pipe away. "What Sandy told you," he said. "She's a very perceptive young lady, Pinocchio. We Kyyra often play tunes on these pipes when we're agitated." He paused, with obvious hesitation, then knelt down at the pool's edge and held the pipe out to Pinocchio. "Would you like to look at it?"

I was impressed by the gesture—I knew what his pipe meant to Beldan or any other Kyyra. But Pinocchio just looked

quickly, touched it once lightly with his beak, and drew away.
"No, but thanks," he said. "I'm not good with tools. I might
break it. I'm sorry if I made you agitated. I've got in the habit of
mistrusting humans who say they want to meet me but refuse to
come in the water. You look so much more like a human than a
dolphin that I guess I thought of you that way. But you're not
human, are you?"

"No," said Beldan.

"Then I must learn to think of you as what you are, instead.
Please be patient with me." He paused, but he talked so fast that
the pause was barely noticeable to human ears. "'Tunes,' you
say. What are these tunes, and how do they help when you're
agitated?"

Touché, I thought. *One of those questions that sounds
simple—and is really so profound you can talk about it for hours
and never really answer it.*

"That's hard to explain," said Beldan, warming to Pinocchio
and the subject with a human smile. "The tunes are patterns of
sound that express our feelings and can alter them—"

"Are they elements of your language?"

Beldan thought it over, and I remembered the time he had
told me about their "musical puns" when I visited their convoy
ship right before they started moving the Earth. "No," he said
slowly, "though there can be very close relationships. We make
the tunes up—"

"Ah," said Pinocchio, with the excitement of dawning light,
"then they are something like our [UNTRANSLATABLE]."

"Your what?"

"Our [UNTRANSLATABLE]. It's hard to explain. Dolphins have a large body of traditions, of sequences of sound that
we tell each other from one generation to another. Some are
simply patterns of sound that we find enjoyable but tell no tales.
Others tell stories of things that happened long ago, or things we
need to remember. Still others tell stories of things that never
really happened. The distinction is not clear-cut; a good bard
always improves on the compositions he repeats—except the
unchangeables." He paused, again briefly. I marveled at how
rapidly he said things which, in translation, were long and
complex. I had to read like lightning to keep up with him.

He was speaking again, to Beldan. "From what you say, I
suspect the connection between your tunes and language is not

as intimate as ours. Does your language consist of words, like human speech?"

"Yes—" said Beldan.

And I saw a chance to get back into the conversation. "Mason said yours doesn't," I said, splashing over to sit on the bottom next to Pinocchio. "What did he mean, exactly?"

"I'm not sure I understand the 'word' concept well enough to give you a good answer," Pinocchio said with mild amusement. "But I gather a word is a little sound-symbol which is always the same and represents a primitive idea-element, and you string them together like beads or building blocks. We do rather little of that. Our language, we suspect, grew out of descriptions, and our descriptions are much more graphic than yours must be. You might say we talk in pictures."

"Example?"

"Not easy. Suppose I say—" The screen showed, "'A fish just swam by above and to my right.' Mason tried to tell me how that came across on your translator, and it wasn't easy—and not much got across. Our world is primarily a world of sound, and we do a lot more with it than humans do—and our perceptions and communications are much closer. If there were really a fish here—don't I wish!—to see it I'd make certain noises and listen to the echoes. What I really said was, 'I made such-and-such kind of feeling noises, and this is what I heard.' Another dolphin, when I repeated my echoes, would literally see that fish—what kind it was, how big it was, where it was, how fast it was going, what was around it. . . . Does that help?"

I nodded, trying to visualize something of his world, wishing I could see it too. "I think so." *To think that we've been sharing the planet with something like this for all this time and never realized it until now—when it's almost too late.*

Maybe more than almost. . . .

"Do humans have tunes?" Pinocchio asked me.

"Yes," I said, thinking of how simple, how primitive human ideas of tunes must seem to a dolphin. Again I remembered myself back on the Kyyra starship, eating and drinking with Beldan in a room filled with his kind, talking of our languages and musics. And the other experiences we'd shared with sound communication. . . . "With us," I told Pinocchio, "the line between music and speech is even sharper than with Beldan's people. But we do have some things you might be interested in hearing." Abruptly, belatedly, I was surprised. "Hasn't anybody played any human music for you?"

"Not that I recall."

"Well, I'll have to see if I can't fix that. Meanwhile. . . ."

And so it went, for several hours. Three of us, of three species, chatting with animation, eagerly comparing notes on differences and similarities among our three very—but not hopelessly—alien cultures. Gradually I began to know Pinocchio, to like him, to admire him as a remarkable individual who was equally a playful child and a philosopher of wide-ranging interests and wisdom. For one exhilarating day, the three of us got so wrapped up in learning about each other that we could forget the more painful aspects of the circumstances that had brought us together.

But when the afternoon was over, I had to remember again—and it was that much more painful then.

Beldan and I had dinner with Mason in his apartment (which, like ours, is a hastily converted corner of a former lab). The quarters were cramped and the food the same wretched fare we have at home—a handful of slightly different forms of thinly disguised essence of algae from mass-produced recycling plants. Hardly surprising, of course, but a little disappointing anyway. I think a part of me had subconsciously dared hope that in a special, exotic place like this the food would be special and exotic too.

Well, I'll get used to it. I'm going to have plenty of time to practice. Still, once in a while I can't help wistfully imagining a real lobster or hamburger or a steaming ear of corn dripping with butter. . . .

And this is clambake country.

Mason made a valiant effort to play the gracious host, making sure his guests were comfortable and well-fed and lubricated with small talk before getting down to business.

(Small talk is a lost art these days. What do you talk about? The weather? Nobody sees it; nobody cares about it. Sports? There aren't any. With the struggle we've had just keeping this many of us alive this long, there's no time or energy to spend on football stadiums or hockey arenas. How bored and miserable you are? Everybody else is too, and for the same reasons, and they were the same last week and they'll be the same next week.)

Anyway, Mason tried. I guess the liveliest topic we came up with was his curiosity about Beldan's food converter, the gourd-like gadget he carries to produce an antidote to poisonous ingredients in alien food. If that was the peak, you can imagine the valleys. After a while the effort to force innocuous conversation grew so obviously strained that I jumped into a lull with what we all really wanted to talk about. "Pinocchio," I blurted out, "is quite a guy, isn't he?"

I think Mason was relieved. "Yes," he sighed. "You enjoyed your visit with him?"

"Immensely. But one thing puzzled me. He isn't . . . the last, is he? The reason you asked me to come—"

Mason looked a little surprised. "He didn't tell you about Topsy and Turvy?"

"No."

"Two females who came back with Pinocchio the last time." He looked thoughtful, as if trying to remember how much he'd told me. "You remember that when I wheedled the administration here into building this lab, the central idea was that dolphins should be free to come and go. They did, and it's a good thing because Pinocchio wasn't one of the originals and we could never have made the real breakthroughs without him. He heard enough stories about us from other dolphins to convince him we were intelligent, and he was interested enough to make a big personal effort to communicate. So he learned all he could from the others about the crude communication they'd achieved, and then he came here, on his own initiative, and showed us how to build on it. That was only about three years before the launch. When the Earth started moving, he was off somewhere, but he quickly saw that the oceans were being destroyed and everything that lived in them was in mortal danger. None of them understood why, but Pinocchio guessed that we might know something about what was happening and we might be able to provide a refuge. A lot of the dolphins were as afraid of coming here as they were of what was happening in the oceans. But he convinced a few of them that staying was sure death while coming to us was a long-shot chance for survival. Those few came with him. It was a harrowing trip—get him to tell you the story sometime. But Pinocchio and Topsy and Turvy made it, and we got them into an indoor tank—had to seal off the outside connection, of course. And then we got to start trying to tell them what had happened, and why." He emitted a dry chuckle. "Don't think that was easy. Their picture of the world doesn't include much detail about things outside the water. To them, the stars were just lights in the sky, and the sky was something very peripheral and unimportant that they glimpsed when they jumped at night. So you can imagine— faintly—how much background, and what utterly alien background, we had to give them before we could tell them the galaxy had exploded and we were trying to ride the Earth to a new one to save our skins."

"But not theirs." I pondered silently. Beldan didn't say anything, but he did start playing something very slow on his pipe. Finally I said, "And now they—"

Mason nodded. "As far as anybody knows, they're the last three bottlenose dolphins alive."

I didn't feel like eating any more. I said, "But I only saw Pinocchio. Where are the others? Can I meet them?"

Mason shook his head. "Sorry. They're here, in this building, but I doubt that you'll be able to meet them. They were never here before Pinocchio brought them, and they've had a rough adjustment. Dolphins have always been hard to keep in captivity, and Topsy and Turvy's circumstances are especially unfortunate. Contact with humans upsets them, so we try to minimize it. They don't take well to the synthetic food we have to give them, since the fish are all gone. And ... Topsy hasn't been feeling well. She's always tended to be a bit sickly. I worry about her a lot ... especially now."

Beldan was still playing his pipe, and I knew he was unlikely to join the conversation—though I also knew he would listen intently to every word. I said, "Is that why they're separated from Pinocchio?"

"No ... though if she comes down with anything, it might be a good idea. The separation was Pinocchio's idea. That's what I want you to talk him out of."

Finally. Mason had told me, in very general terms, why he wanted me to come to Woods Hole. But he'd been vague about details. Maybe now I would finally find out exactly why he thought he needed me—and what he thought I could do.

I waited. Finally he said slowly, "Dolphins play a lot; it's a very pervasive, integral part of their whole way of life. And a lot of the play is very uninhibitedly sexual. With no technology, abstinence is the only form of birth control they have available. So Pinocchio decided they'd better not play—and that meant they'd better live apart."

I still didn't understand. At all. I frowned, momentarily sidestepping the main issue, hoping it would clarify itself. "You mean there are three of them here, and Pinocchio deliberately cut himself off from all contact with the others?"

"Not all contact. Just physical. They talk, but they don't touch. Because if they do, sooner or later one or both of them will get pregnant. And Pinocchio doesn't want that to happen."

Nothing had clarified itself. "But that's what they need! Birth control is the last thing in the world you need when there are only three members of a species left. It doesn't make sense."

"I agree. Pinocchio doesn't." Mason frowned, picked his words carefully. "When he heard our story, he got depressed—not even angry, mind you, but depressed—and he gave it a lot of thought. He decided that living conditions here were just too alien, too restrictive for dolphins. *He* could stand it—he doesn't want to die, and once he made his decision he even became reasonably cheerful again. But he decided it would be unkind to produce new calves who would have to spend their entire lives cooped up in tanks, with no prospect of an end in sight. And I haven't been able to budge him."

I thought about it for quite a while before I answered. Pinocchio—through Mason—had struck a nerve, a currently very active and responsive storm center in my own thoughts and feelings. "I'm not sure he's wrong," I said finally, with careful restraint. "But he's too nice to become extinct. If he's typical—"

Mason laughed. "I wouldn't say typical, exactly. He's plenty special—but only in having typical traits highly developed. Like an Einstein or a Schweitzer among us. He's unusually capable, and he's the oldest one we've ever worked with."

I nodded, but wondered about one thing. "Old, you say. Does that matter, as far as—"

Mason shook his head with a slight grin. "Nope. Old dolphins never quit."

Now, sitting here finishing off today's entry, I find myself thinking about Jonel. I ought to call him. But not yet, not tonight. I still haven't sorted myself out.

I do find myself thinking about the similarities in our

situation and the dolphins'. But it isn't really the same.
Is it?

16/5, 3

I dreamed about a recognizable incident from my past—
something I don't often remember doing. But this was one I'd
dreamed about before. It was the day I first realized the dolphins
were going to be in trouble if we decided to accept the Kyyra
offer, a gray, windy day, too cold for Florida even in December.
Beldan was with me—this was in the days when the politicians
were still arguing and I was becoming his only human friend. We
stood together by an inlet near the spaceport, watching dolphins
or porpoises playing in the water. I told Beldan they were
intelligent, and he admitted he didn't know what could be done
about them. I think it bothered him as much as me.

I don't even know what species they were; I didn't know
much about them then. But in my dream one of them was
Pinocchio, and two were Topsy and Turvy.

I moved slowly when I got up, trying to think about the few
things I could do. I'd promised Pinocchio I'd show him some
human music; it seemed hard to believe nobody had. Music—
sound patterns shaped by intelligence and culture—would seem
one of the most likely areas of shared interest for humans and
dolphins.

And Kyyra.

Not that I believe in trite nonsense about music being a
universal language, of course. The first time Beldan and I
managed to improvise a duet on his pipe and my oboe, I was
flabbergasted at how much we'd achieved in a very subtle kind of
communication. But, difficulties notwithstanding, such things
are an important part of both our lives and we've learned a lot
about each other by comparing notes on them.

I couldn't resist the temptation to make it a three-way
comparison. I took Pinocchio a recording of the same
symphony I'd tried on Beldan the first time Jonel and I had him
over.

Pinocchio was intrigued. He lay quietly in one spot for most
of it, but once in a while he would stir slightly or even dart
around the pool and slap his tail on the surface or make
untranslatable pronouncements as if reacting to the music. *How*
he was reacting, what he felt, I could only guess.

I had explained to him beforehand that the sounds were made by many humans using artificial instruments in a consciously coordinated way. Like Beldan, he found the ensemble idea novel; unlike Beldan, he was equally unfamiliar with the use of instruments.

When it was over, he lay beside me and began vocalizing loudly. The translator showed that he was pleased and excited, but also curious and puzzled. "I enjoyed it," he said. "Of course, there was a lot I didn't understand. . . ."

"Not surprising," I assured him. "After all, it's as new to you as your speech is to me. But you did find enough in it to like?"

"Oh, yes. Though of course it seemed rather empty in the ranges that we can hear and you can't."

And vice versa, I thought with faint amusement, but I didn't say it. I saw another chance. I asked quietly, "Do you think Topsy and Turvy would like it?"

I was unprepared for the sharp annoyance the screen showed with his "words". "What do you know about them?" he demanded. "How do you know about them?"

But I stayed cool—reasonably, anyway. *May have been a mistake*, I noted. *But I had to start somewhere. . . .*

"Mason mentioned them," I said, trying not to say more than I had to. I knew I mustn't lead Pinocchio to think Mason had put me up to pressuring him. "He said they'd come here with you and were in another tank. I'd like to meet them too, but Mason said I probably won't be able to. So I have to ask you about them." I paused uncertainly. "I'm a little surprised you're not with them. I would have thought you'd want to be together."

He hesitated too—a long, long time, for him. "Do you know what would happen then?"

"I think so," I said. "What's so bad about that?"

Another lengthy silence. "Is this any life for a young dolphin? It's too bad you can't talk to Topsy and Turvy. They're relatively young, and they're not holding up even as well as I am. The three of us are already here; we have to hold up. But we don't have to inflict this on lives which haven't yet begun."

"But it's not going to always be like this," I told him (a little hollowly, I admitted to myself). "This is just to get somewhere else. We'll move onto a new world, with open skies and seas—"

"Where is this new world?" Pinocchio asked suddenly.

The question caught me off guard. "I don't know, exactly," I said. "In M31—"

"Have you seen it?"

"No. But—"

"Do you really believe you will ever see it?"

The question hurt far more than it should have. I'd known the answer for a long time. But sometimes you can stare at something for a long time before you suddenly really see it, and then it's blinding. "No," I said very quietly. I looked down at the dancing wavelets and then closed my eyes. "*I* won't. The trip will take much longer than I live, at the rate we're going now. But the kind of world we need is common enough. There'll be one out there, for our descendants."

"Maybe." CYNICAL LAUGHTER, the screen said. It ill became him.

"It will," I insisted, reaching out to stroke his back. "And if you and Topsy and Turvy don't get together, there'll be no dolphins to enjoy it."

"Maybe that's just as well," he said, with surprising calm. "Maybe it's best."

"But how can you think that? It's hard for a while, but don't you want something better for your descendants? Not your children, of course, but later. . . ."

"If we don't have any descendants," said Pinocchio, "it doesn't matter, does it? I can see you don't understand. Dolphins and humans see future and past differently. We have traditions from our past, and we provide for our immediate offspring's well-being. *Their* offspring are their concern. And where there is conflict. . . . Let me explain it this way. You say I should father children so that maybe their children's children can have a good life. All I see is that my own will not, and the farther future is uncertain. I have no right to produce lives which will only be used as an instrument for the benefit of others who may never even exist."

I struggled to get hold of it. A view that reflected an alien outlook, but I could see and respect it. "But," I said, making one final weak effort, "don't dolphins have an instinct for preservation of the species?"

"The value of intelligence," said Pinocchio, "is that it can overrule instinct when instinct is wrong."

I could think of no reply to that. We all sat silent for a minute or so, with no sound except the water lapping around us and the air and water circulation systems humming softly in the walls. Wordlessly, I rubbed Pinocchio between the flippers; he rolled on his side and drifted slightly closer to me. Finally I said, very softly, "Pinocchio, do you hate us for what we've done? Humans, or Kyyra, or both?" *I would*, I thought.

But the screen showed no hatred in his answer. Instead, almost embarrassingly, it showed gentle reassurance, and he nuzzled my side. "I can't hate you for what others have done, Sandy. And I can't blame them for doing what they did to save their own kind. In their position, I suppose I would have done the same. But I had no opportunity, and things have come out against us. Unfortunate, but there's nothing to be done."

I think I felt a tear on my cheek.

After that, we led each other away from such highly charged topics and back into tamer conversation. Beldan got back into it, and we talked all day, missing lunch.

Mason was tied up with some urgent business at suppertime, so he didn't eat with Beldan and me. He had our dinner sent to us, and we ate it together at the table in the little lounge between our bedrooms. We didn't talk much as we ate; I was busy composing myself and I think Beldan was too. But by the time we finished, I found that I was ready to talk—or at least I didn't want Beldan to go off to his room and leave me alone.

I looked at him and said, "You know, Beldan, in ways they're more like you than us."

He looked at me uncertainly as he tucked his food converter back inside his robe. "You mean in the relationship between various uses of sound that we were discussing yesterday? Yes, I suppose so."

"No," I said, "I mean a lot more than that. Things about their whole outlook. Social relationships, for instance. Except when we're talking about certain things—like what's happening to them—I have the feeling you find Pinocchio more congenial than most humans."

"That's true. Of course, I also find you more congenial than most humans."

I shrugged. "Well, from what I've read and seen and heard, I think dolphins have some characteristics in common with Kyyra. When you first came to Earth, you said you were bothered by the prevalence of suspicion and distrust and deceit among humans. Remember?"

"I remember." I could see that the question disturbed him

because it made him remember a lot more than that. It reminded him that the Coordinator—the huge telepathic computer that continually molds everything on his planet and its convoy ships, including individual minds, into a harmoniously functioning whole—is dying. He almost reached for his pipe, for solace, but successfully resisted—as if preparing himself for the day when he must get along without even the memory of the Coordinator.

"Well," I said, "it seems to me they're like you that way. But they don't have a Coordinator. Do you suppose their openness comes from the fact that their bodies are largely transparent to the sound waves they use for sensing?"

"It sounds possible," Beldan said thoughtfully. "I suppose if your visceral reactions are obvious to everybody, you don't waste much time trying to lie."

I must ask Pinocchio.

17/5, 3

I asked Pinocchio about that matter of the transparency of their bodies and the openness of their dealings with each other and with us. He suspects I'm right, but he never thought about it before; the whole thing is so much a part of them that they've always just taken it for granted. We talked quite a while about that, and how things look to him, and how the Coordinator has had a somewhat similar effect on the Kyyra, and how humans— neither telepathic nor controlled nor transparent—have made various sorts of deviousness a pervasive part of our cultures.

Pinocchio found that amusing ("It must make life awfully complicated," he mused), and we all found the whole subject quite interesting. But otherwise it was a relatively unproductive morning. Pinocchio just wasn't as talkative as usual. I have a hunch (though the translator gave me nothing concrete to support it) that some of the things I said to him yesterday have him a bit rattled.

Well, that's fair enough. Some of the things he said to me have me a bit rattled.

We quit early and Beldan and I met Mason for lunch. I told him about my hunch, that Pinocchio was giving my remarks more thought than he yet chose to admit. He nodded but didn't quite smile. "Could be a hopeful sign," he said. "Maybe." He put down his fork and dabbed at his mouth with the corner of a napkin. "On the off chance that it is," he said slowly, stretching,

"I guess now would be a good time to tell you the other reason I asked you to come."

I waited without comment. I'd half expected this since I first met him. (Human deviousness, again—he tells Pinocchio one reason for my coming, me another, and now that I'm here he tells me still another. Well, I'm human too. I'm not surprised.)

"Suppose you succeed," Mason began, "and they do start a family. Where will we put them? Obviously we can't turn them loose in the sea; they'll have to stay in tanks like we have here. The ones we have could take the added load of a calf or two while they're young, but only while they're young. If they survive, we're going to need more tank space."

He paused. His eyes took on a distant expression, his voice a hint of deliberately suppressed anger. "This place has never really accepted me, you know. When I came here as a young man, the administration was so conservative I couldn't even tell them what I really wanted to do. To get even this facility, I had to justify my proposal in terms of things like EEG studies of wild dolphins and possibilities of training them to help us in field research. Flunkeys—like grad students. Then, gradually, I could let my important findings emerge as 'accidental' by-products."

I was embarrassed. He might have some legitimate complaints, but his attitude seemed to smack unnecessarily of sour grapes. "'Even this facility,' you say," I said. "Isn't this a good facility?"

"It was acceptable," he conceded, "when the tanks were open to the sea and the dolphins just came in for visits. But they're much too small for permanent confinement." He shrugged. "Well, none of us are living in luxury these days, and they're intelligent enough to understand that. But there are limits. We're at rock bottom now, for the dolphins we have. If we get more, we're absolutely going to need more space. And my fearless leaders keep making threatening noises about closing down even what we have."

"You can't be serious," I said, genuinely shocked. "How can they even consider—"

"Expense," he said with a sardonic smile. "We don't measure it in money any more, but it's still very much a factor. In terms of materials and effort, even rock-bottom dolphin facilities aren't cheap to build or maintain. They have to be big. We have to constantly circulate and treat the water and air;

temperature and chemistry are critical. We have to feed them. I'd like to give them fifteen or twenty pounds of butterfish a day, but we have to make do with equivalent amounts of synthetics. And the form of the synthetics is more critical than for humans."

"But surely," I said, "we owe them at least that."

"I think so," Mason nodded. "And I hoped that if you called the matter to Henry Clark's attention, he would agree strongly enough to see that we do get what we need."

So that was it. As if Henry doesn't have enough on his mind. A lot of people think the moratorium means he has a lot of free time, but it doesn't—not by a long shot. So far the effects of either going to a very high acceleration or changing the acceleration very often look so terrifying that we're all very doubtful that we'll do it that way—but we (and especially Henry) are very busy checking all the angles we can on all possibilities. We want to be sure. "He's terribly overworked," I said.

"But surely, if he knows it's literally a matter of life or death for another species of intelligent and civilized natives of Earth—"

I nodded. "Oh, yes. He's already interested. When he really understands the situation, he may even be able to do something. If Pinocchio decides to have a family."

Mason appeared to relax a little, as if satisfied that he had done all he could for now. "Good enough," he said. "So I guess we have to solve that one first." With a smile, he tried to shift back to small talk. "Tell me, do you and Jonel have a family?"

"No," I said—rather curtly, I'm afraid. I almost added, "Not yet," but it didn't feel quite necessary, so I left it at that.

I don't think I wanted to talk about it.

And now Orlik had really complicated things. I'd been looking forward to spending the afternoon relaxing, thinking, coming to terms with myself, getting back in tune with Jonel. And maybe coming up with some new angle on Henry's acceleration problem, or even how to get through to Pinocchio.

And now Mason's given me something else to think about.

18/5, 3

Pinocchio caught me completely off guard today. Thinking back, I wonder if Mason was reading me better than I realized yesterday, and talked to Pinocchio alone sometime after lunch. Or maybe it was just coincidence.

Anyway....

One thing kept disturbing me about Pinocchio's attitude toward all this. I didn't know how to broach it, but I kept it in the back of my mind, waiting.

It seemed to me that he was in a bit of a mischievous humor when Beldan and I went in. There was nothing about it on the screen, but I think I'm learning to tell a lot more about his mood than the translator tells me.

He was more interested in playing than talking when I first got in—going limp and having me push him around, then expecting me to do the same so he could push me around. I cooperated, enjoyed it, and got tired before he did. But he sensed when that happened and suggested, "Let's rest."

I sat down on the bottom, slouched down so the water could lap at my chin, and he hovered in the water beside me. Our play had been so completely non-intellectual that I found myself sitting there trying to think of something to start a conversation with. There was one thing I was sure I didn't want to use....

And then I remembered something Mason had said. "Pinocchio," I said, rubbing his back lightly, "Mason said I should ask you to tell me about your trip here."

"I prefer not to talk about it," he said. "But I think I should...because I care what you think, and I sense that you think we've quit too easily, that we've given up without a real struggle." It was as if he'd read my mind. That was exactly what had been bothering me. Despite what both he and Mason had told me, there was the nagging feeling that the dolphins had not done all they could.

For a moment the first two columns on the screen were blank while the third showed little flickers of agitation. "I was south," he said finally. "Down the coast. I don't know how to tell you exactly where, but it doesn't matter. It was a goodly distance. The first indications we had of something wrong were the quivers, the little shock waves in the water that told us the bottom was shaking. And then the currents, the tug of something trying to pull us and everything else south. We couldn't see the sunlight fading yet; that was too slow. But we felt the currents and the tremors and saw our food being swept away from us. We followed it for a while, and when the while became too long and it showed no signs of slowing, we began to realize something was very wrong. Then we noticed that the bottom was warming in a way it had never done before. Gradually we began to feel fear—not the fear we feel when we meet a shark, which is deadly but we know how it is deadly, but the far worse fear of something unseen and unknown. Worse yet, it was a fear that grew slowly, because it took time to be sure something was happening. At first we argued about it; by the time most of us realized the extent of the danger, we had drifted quite far to the south. And we knew nothing to do.

"I thought of Mason. I'd been here before; I liked and trusted him; I knew humans understood some things we didn't. And I knew there were shelters here. I persuaded a dozen of my fellows to come back with me. Many more would not; the prospect of placing their lives in human hands was too unfamiliar, too terrifying. We hated to leave them—there were many dear friends/relatives—but we decided it was best that some of us go and some stay. That way at least some of us might survive. In those days, Sandy, we were very concerned about saving our kind.

"Thirteen of us started—upstream. It was very far; it was hard swimming against the current; it was hard to navigate because so much was changed. Food was scarce; by the time we started, too much had been swept away or destroyed. We swam without stopping for several days, pushing ourselves hard. Eight of us—including four of my sons and daughters—died of exhaustion or hunger. Two more were battered to death in storms. Only Topsy and Turvy and I remained. Each of us was too tired and hungry to feel like continuing, but we prodded each other on. We passed landmarks I knew; I knew we still had hours to go. But only hours, now; somehow, we could make it. But the water was getting shallower....

"And then it stopped. Miles before it should have ended, miles before this place, we were at the foot of a beach, struggling not to run aground, and there was nowhere else to go. I think that was when we lost hope, and we never got it all back. We lay there in the shallows, in the dark, huddled together, feebly crying our distress to a sea that no longer had anyone to hear us.

"To our astonishment, someone did, but it wasn't a dolphin. It was a ship full of humans from here, roaming the sea, hoping to find survivors like us. They followed our calls, picked us up, carried us back here. We vaguely remember what you would call a nightmare—though we don't dream as you do—a nightmare series of slings and hands and tiny tanks and long rides. Mason said the longest ride was in something that flew through the sky and made a continuous nerve-wracking noise. And then we were here, and they fed us things that weren't fish and tasted terrible but were better than nothing. And Mason told us what happened. We could only partly grasp it, but we grasped enough to know that there was nowhere else for us to go, nothing else for us to do.

"You think we didn't struggle, Sandy? How many of you have ever struggled as we did? But there comes a time when all the struggle is used up, and there's barely enough energy left to live out your own days with a minimum of pain. That's where we are, Sandy. If there were more of us, or conditions were much better, or there was any hope of their getting that way...."

"Suppose we could get bigger tanks," I said. "Much bigger—"

"Still just tanks," he said curtly. "You can't give our ocean back. No, we've fought all we can. Or choose to."

I understood that. I still wasn't satisfied, but I understood. I'd felt the same way myself on more than one occasion—and never with a tenth as much cause. I sat there trying futilely to think of something to say.

And that was when he caught me. Abruptly, the mood column on the screen changed to lighter things and Pinocchio said, "But this is depressing; let's talk about something else. I'll have no more children, but I'd love to hear about yours. How many do you have?"

The question hit me like a bombshell. It was so simple, so obviously related to things we had talked about, that I should have anticipated it. But I hadn't. And now I was afraid he would see me as a hypocrite when he heard the answer.

But I couldn't lie to him. "None," I said softly.

He didn't answer right away. From a human, I would have considered any further pursuit of the question plain, nosy rudeness, and wouldn't have hesitated to tell him so. From Pinocchio, I couldn't consider it that. It was I who had first raised the subject. He had fully as much right to ask me such questions as I did to ask them of him. But he waited as if uncertain whether he should continue. Finally, with the third column showing gentleness and reluctance to pry, he said, "I don't understand. You have no mate?"

"Oh, yes," I said. "A very nice one. His name is Jonel."

"And you live with him?"

"Yes."

"And you play together?"

"Yes. And work...." I toyed briefly with trying to explain some of the differences between human and dolphin work and play, but quickly decided they were much too complex and subtle.

And, of course, that wasn't what he was driving at, anyway.

"Then I don't understand," Pinocchio was saying. "How can you not—"

"For humans," I said, "playing together doesn't necessarily lead to babies. We have ways of preventing it. We have babies only when we want to. But if we don't want to, we don't have to hide from each other."

"Interesting," said Pinocchio, the third column blank. "'Ways?'"

"Technological ways. Mason can tell you about them."

"Hm-m-m." He pondered. "It sounds unnatural to me. I don't think I'd like it." I felt a tiny flare of anger, thought, *As unnatural as locking yourself away from Topsy and Turvy seems to me?* But he didn't give me time to waste much energy on that. He said, with a sonic equivalent of a shrug, "But that doesn't matter. Our backgrounds are different. What does puzzle me is why you've chosen to do it this way."

I think I blushed; I know I felt very uncomfortable, very aware that the conversation had gotten completely out of my control—and onto ground where I was more sensitive than I liked to admit, even to myself. And especially to Pinocchio.

"Jonel and I," I said lamely, "think it would be better for us to wait a while and see how things develop." (*No,* I corrected myself sternly, *let's be honest. I think that. Jonel has been anxious to start a family for quite a while now. I'm the one who's been stalling. And hating myself for it, just like the day we got married....*

We hadn't planned to do it that day; we hadn't even thought much about setting a date yet. But I'd just sat in on my first meeting with the Kyyra, shortly after they came to Earth. Jonel had already told me about the core explosion; now, when I heard Beldan and Henry and Chandragupta Rao talking about what it would mean if we accepted their offer to move the Earth, I was scared. I was scared as I had never been before, and confused and helpless. And since I wasn't used to feeling that way, the fact that I did was scary in itself. Jonel and I went out to the beach and decided to get married right away, and I kept saying things that didn't sound like me about how maybe it would be better not to have the children we had always planned.

That passed quickly, but lately, with things settled down to what Rao called "spaceship-style living," I find myself feeling some of the same doubts again. With the isolation, the monotony, the dependence on all those umbilical cords, the epidemic depression—and no end in sight—I just don't feel like becoming a mother. Eventually, I keep telling myself, but not now. Not just yet.

Jonel's been telling me it's more important than ever that people like us have children now, and throw everything into raising them well. Intellectually, I still agree with him. But I want it to *feel* right. . . .

All those thoughts raced around in my brain as I sat there in the pool trying to think how to explain my feelings to Pinocchio. They were interrupted, to my surprise and annoyance, by a series of loud noises that sounded remarkably like human laughter.

And the translator said they *were* laughter.

What's funny?" I snapped.

"The irony," said Pinocchio. "Your situation is just like mine, and yet you've come all this distance to try to get me to change my mind. Perhaps I should turn the tables and try to change yours."

"But it's not the same," I protested. "Similar, but there's a very important difference. There are lots of humans, but only three of you."

"Hm-m-m," said Pinocchio, again with mild amusement. "Makes your problems sound pretty trivial compared to ours, doesn't it?"

"You twist everything I say," I complained, annoyed because of that (and even more annoyed because he was right). "Yes, in a sense, that's true. But what I meant is that what you decide determines the whole future of dolphins. But there are so many humans that what Jonel and I decide doesn't matter."

"Ah, but how many of those humans feel the same way you do? If it's too many, the effect may be the same."

I was beginning to feel cold. I hadn't really thought about that, but it's true. And there's plenty of evidence that too many humans do feel that way. Vital statistics are pretty sparse these days, but it's quite clear that births are way down and disease deaths and emotional disturbances and suicides are all up. Cannibalism has started to crop up here and there; some clergymen vehemently denounce it, others find ways to make it sound positively noble as the ecologically best way to dispose of undiseased dead. But some people have a simply morbid fascination with it. . . .

No wonder I'm not as cheerful as I used to be. No wonder I'm reluctant.

But how can I tell Pinocchio all that? He has enough problems of his own.

"Maybe," I said tightly (and I think this is as low as I ever got), "after what humans have done to you, we deserve to die too."

"And what good would that do?" he asked gently, undulating over to rub his side very slowly against mine. "It's too late for us. But suppose you let yourselves die out too. Suppose you've done this much and then not even you carry on. Then everything is lost, instead of just almost everything. All the destruction—for nothing. Do you want that? I don't."

I reached out to rub his forehead. It was impossible to stay even mildly annoyed with somebody who could hold that attitude in his situation. "I don't either," I told him. "Especially if you feel that way. But for myself . . . my heart's still not in it."

"Then we should all talk about it," he said suddenly, and he was darting away, his dorsal fin brushing my hand aside as it passed. Before I could try to guess what he was talking about, he pressed a big red button at one end of the pool with his beak. Then he swam back to me and kept making nervous little motions.

"What was all that about?" I asked.

"You'll see."

Moments later, the door swung open and Mason Orlik appeared at the side of the pool, having obviously hurried. "What's up?" he asked anxiously.

So Pinocchio had called him. "Can you arrange a long-distance conference call with my translator hooked into it?"

Mason looked as surprised and puzzled as I felt. "I suppose so. It'll take a little while to set up, but I don't see any reason why it can't be done. . . ."

"Good," said Pinocchio. "Sandy and I would like to talk to her mate."

It's crazy, I thought over and over as I waited. I had no idea, either that the possibility existed or that Pinocchio would take so active a role in trying to change my mind. I can't say I'm enthusiastic about the idea, but I didn't try to stop him. I'm not sure why. Maybe I want to cooperate with anything he suggests because I'm still clinging to a desperate hope that somehow I can get him to change his mind. I don't want them to be the last. Or maybe I feel guilty because I haven't called Jonel yet and I'm using Pinocchio's crazy idea as an excuse to make me do it.

Or maybe part of me is secretly hoping that he'll succeed.

Mason says we'll do it this evening. I'd rather just go ahead, but he says he has to rearrange some of the electronics to get the picture-phone circuits and the pool mikes and translator working together.

Waiting, as usual, isn't much fun. I keep thinking too much. I think about what Pinocchio said about human problems being small compared to dolphins'. It's embarrassingly true, of course. For that matter, Jonel and I are more fortunate than many humans. We still have an entertainment console that works (though we don't often find it very entertaining); more importantly, we have some of our personal things like pictures and books and my oboe and guitar. Our recycling plant is in a central location in the building so it doesn't clutter up half our apartment. We still have Ozymandias the Mutt, though he's beginning to get old. We even get to see a few other people in the flesh once in a while.

But very seldom. It's too much trouble, and too many of the people we'd like to see died in the acceleration buildup (and had their homes cannibalized for material to fix those of the survivors). The food is monotonous and meagerly rationed, and the air is always stuffy and stale. So is the routine. I'm an outdoors person, and the outdoors isn't there anymore.

I like to think I'm an adaptable person, too, but it's taking a while. It's just *so* different from everything my life was full of.

I'll come around. But . . . today?

Beldan has been pretty quiet through all this. He likes Pinocchio and enjoys talking to him—usually. But when we get to talking about what's happening to the dolphins and what can—or can't—be done about it, he's so completely at a loss that he doesn't say anything.

But he plays his pipe a lot.

19/5, 3

I'm still a little dazed, but I must try to reconstruct what happened last night and today and get it on paper while I'm still close to it.

Mason had it arranged within an hour after dinner. He took us into Pinocchio's room and explained the setup, then left. Beldan stayed. I didn't feel quite right about having him there for this, but I couldn't bring myself to ask him to leave.

And I'm glad I didn't.

I dialed the phone—located on the small cart of extra equipment Mason had wheeled in and hooked to some cables brought through the wall next to the screen—and sat down on the edge of the pool to wait. I heard the irritating buzz of our phone ringing at the spaceport, and then Jonel's voice. "Hello?"

I was very glad to hear him. "Hello—" I said. But I was drowned out by Pinocchio. The screen showed him saying, "Hello, Jonel. I've enjoyed talking to Sandy so much I wanted to meet you too—"

"What?" said Jonel, obviously puzzled.

"Turn your picture on, Jonel," I said. "It's Sandy."

"Sandy!" he exclaimed. "I've been wishing . . . O.K. It's on." We still didn't see him, unfortunately; Mason hadn't hooked up a picture receiver. "Now, what was that? Is your voice changing?"

I laughed. "No, that was Pinocchio. Pinocchio, say it again. He couldn't see the translation."

Pinocchio said it again. I watched the screen; a direct electronic pickup sent Jonel the signal without the need for a camera to block my view. "Did you get it that time?"

"Yes. I'm glad to get the chance to talk to you, Pinocchio. I didn't expect—"

"Don't let him fool you," I warned. "He has ulterior motives."

"Ulterior motives?"

"Yes. He wants to play marriage counselor."

"What?"

"He thinks you and I should start a family, and he's taken it upon himself to try to sell us the idea."

"Sounds fair enough," said Jonel. "That's about what you went to do to him, isn't it?"

"Yes—" I began, reflecting that Jonel knew very little of the details.

"—but I'm afraid," Pinocchio interrupted, "she's failed." I broke off and listened intently, watching the screen, seized by a sinking intuition that this time it was final and I really had failed.

"I've thought about it all day," Pinocchio said, "and while what Sandy suggests is tempting, in a way, it would not be wise— for us. We are different enough—humans and dolphins—that I don't know whether I can make her understand why it would not be wise. But I know it wouldn't—and Topsy and Turvy know it wouldn't—and we are so certain that we've decided not to think about it or talk about it any more. There's no point in tormenting ourselves."

"Topsy and Turvy are two females who came here with Pinocchio," I explained to Jonel. It seemed to me that Pinocchio looked surprisingly calm, and the little that appeared in the third column of the screen bore that out.

"Yes," said Pinocchio. "Sandy tells me we should keep going because there'll be a better future. This is probably true; for your sake, I hope so. As I understand humans, the belief can sustain you through a lot. Futures mean much to you, and you can adapt to confinement and discomfort. We can't—or at least we can't without pain that seems too great to inflict on children. We're too used to open space; play is too big a part of our lives. We can't give it up for several generations."

A trace of amusement appeared in the third column. "I suppose," Pinocchio mused, "it must seem to humans that we're frivolous, that we have too much playfulness in us. It looks like they're right—under the present highly unusual circumstances. But it seems to us that humans often have too little. We hope you make it through this—if you do, we'll be satisfied that it wasn't a total loss—but in doing so, be careful not to lose what you have of that.

"It's going to take special people to be sure that doesn't happen. Sandy is a special person, Jonel—and I can tell you must be too. If all this is going to make any sense at all—"

And suddenly everything stopped except his clicks and whistles. In one tiny fraction of a second, the translator screen went dark, the hums of the machinery in the walls cut off, the lights vanished and we were plunged into utter darkness.

And my insides twisted themselves into a knot.

The umbilical cords—

I'm sure I didn't scream, or anything like that; I'm not a hysterical person. I do remember croaking, "Jonel!" and choking it off as I realized he couldn't hear me any more. Whatever Pinocchio was saying faded abruptly. For a time that felt terribly long, though it was probably only seconds, the silence became almost as complete and oppressive as the darkness. Almost, but not quite—there was still the soft *lap-lap-lap* of the water, and the muted thunder of the blood pounding in my ears. But otherwise there was nothing. The hum of the machinery was hardly noticed when it was on, but its sudden absence was overpowering.

Soon new sounds started up in the blackness. Pinocchio swam around, making creaking door noises, stirring the water up. Beldan's pipe began to weave something simultaneously plaintive, frenzied, and (to my ears) eerie. Pinocchio came to rest against my leg and for a second or so was silent. And then he began the distress calls, those shrill, haunting whistle-pairs I'd previously heard only on the briefing tapes and in troubled dreams.

But now they were real.

A shivery feeling chased itself up and down my spine. Simultaneously, I reached carefully to touch Pinocchio, and started trying to collect my thoughts.

What happened?

Power failure; that much was clear. Completely unexpected—as they always are. Whether it was confined to this room, or the building, or covered a much larger area I had no way to know. But it was complete, at least here. It had knocked out too many things to be a malfunction in only one of the operating systems.

It got them all.

I wasn't ready to think about what that could mean. It wasn't necessary yet; with luck, it never would be. But already it was nibbling at the back of my mind.

I realized I didn't really know what all had happened even in this room. I knew all three of us were alive—my ears told me that—and since I wasn't hurt, I suspected the others weren't either. "Beldan," I asked softly, "are you all right?" My voice sounded hollow, with most of the background noise gone. And it seemed terribly wrong not to hear dolphin sounds from the underwater speakers right after I spoke.

Beldan's piping stopped. "I'm all right," he said. I wished futilely that I could ask Pinocchio. "Do you know what happened, Sandy?"

"Not exactly. We've lost our power; that's all I can tell."

"What can we do?"

My answer was as hollow as my voice. "Wait."

"That's all? We can't call for help, or go out in the hall and see what's happening there?"

"We don't dare, yet. Mason or somebody might know what's happening and be able to help. But the electrical communications are dead, and the room's practically soundproof. And they may have lost pressure out there. If that's happened, we wouldn't want to open the door until somebody comes to cycle us through the emergency lock. So we sit and wait. They'll get it fixed, or get somebody down here, before too long." *I hope*, I added to myself, biting my lower lip. I thought a moment and added, "I can try pounding on the door."

I climbed out of the pool, groped my way to the wall and along it to the door, hit it with my fists and yelled a couple of times before I remembered that it *was* an emergency lock and I was wasting my time. Nobody'd hear that either, and I should have known it. *Slow down*, I warned myself. *Take it easy. Panic's not your style. Just wait.*

I felt my way back to the edge of the pool and sat down, trying hard to take my own advice. It wasn't too bad for the first hour or so. Pinocchio kept up his distress calls, over and over, with unchanging urgency, for most of that time. I kept wishing I could tell him what I'd told Beldan, tell him that he might as well be quiet until the trouble was fixed or help came. The endless whistles could easily get on anybody's nerves—especially in the dark with Beldan piping too. But finally Pinocchio did quit, of his own accord.

Then I worried about whether something new was wrong with him.

And all the while I kept thinking of what must be running through Jonel's mind, wishing I could tell him I was all right.

And hoping he was. After all, I didn't really know the extent of this thing. . . .

I lost track of time. I have no idea how long that "first hour or so" really was; I do know subjective time sense can be wildly distorted by stress or sleeplessness or any number of other things. Even allowing for that, I eventually felt quite sure that the time we'd been trapped there in the dark was measured in hours rather than fractions.

And that made it harder to keep the other thoughts down—though I did manage to resist talking about them for quite a while.

What's keeping them? I thought. *Have they forgotten we're here? Surely somebody should have come by now, if only to reassure us and take us somewhere else.*

Unless something's happened to them. . . .

I didn't want to think about that. But I did, more and more often.

And I thought of people I'd known whose umbilical cords had failed. Some got them fixed in time to regale their friends with tales of the experience.

Others. . . .

Well, they did provide much-needed subjects for small talk.

Beldan and I talked occasionally, but not often or long. I think we started when one or the other of us felt an especially acute need for comfort, and stopped when we realized that neither of us felt up to talking very long. Sometimes he piped; once he asked me to sing, and when I did Pinocchio rubbed against my feet and made noises of his own.

Discomforts accumulated and grew more insistent. First there was just the darkness and the silence and the fear and uncertainty. Later, in addition, I found the air feeling stiflingly damp and stuffy; it stank, and seemed to be getting colder. Sometimes I would start shivering, and it seemed to me that my pulse was too fast and I was having trouble breathing. I tried to estimate how soon we would be in any danger from carbon dioxide narcosis, with the recycling plant not working, but I couldn't. I was too tired. I couldn't remember clearly, and I couldn't do calculations in my head.

And I was hungry, and thirsty. . . .

"Beldan," I said, and I was appalled at the weakness of my voice, "do you remember the fresh water tap on the wall near you?"

He had to stop piping to answer. "Yes."

"Does it work?"

"I'll see." I heard him moving cautiously, heard him find the faucet and try to turn it on. "Nothing comes out."

Not surprising, I thought. *Pump's out, and who knows how much else.*

I drew my feet out of the water and sat huddled up, hugging my knees against me for warmth. "Beldan," I asked slowly, hating even to mention it, "what would happen to everything . . . out there . . . if anything should happen to you?"

He didn't answer right away. "It will carry on. It will complicate matters, of course. But the Coordinator will prepare a replacement for me." He hesitated, then added almost inaudibly, "If there's enough left of the Coordinator."

Then he went back to his piping.

Not long after that, I stretched out on my back and tried to sleep. I must have dozed now and then, but it was always shallow and full of dreams I could easily have done without. Sometime during one of the half-awake, half-asleep episodes, I remember thinking, *If I ever get out of here, I'll. . . .*

And the thought stopped, idling against an immovable obstacle. What could I do?

A long time later I thought of an answer. A bitter, hard-to-swallow answer. *If I ever get out of here*, I thought, *I'll go back to doing the same old things, with just as little control over them. And I'll pass every day in fear of this happening again.*

For as long as I live.

That made me angry. I was too groggy to try to do anything about it, but I lay there letting it simmer in a dreamy stew.

And suddenly I saw, with such simple clarity that I marveled at how it had eluded me for so long, what was wrong with everything.

And for the first time, I actually saw something I *would* do. If I ever got out.

I was sleeping a little more soundly when they finally came. Gradually, dimly, I became aware that the noises of someone trying to get in existed outside me and not just in my dreams. I turned my head slightly toward where I thought the door was, but otherwise I didn't move. *It's over!* I thought, and in the same breath warned myself against premature poultry-counting.

The door swung open and the glaring tips of two flashlights appeared, enough of their light bouncing back from the walls to show Mason Orlik and Bill Maracek, looking a bit sinister in the darkness. "Everybody all right in here?" Mason asked softly.

"Yes," Beldan said dully.

"Still living," I said, managing a weak smile. "What took you so long?"

"Sorry," said Mason. "We didn't know where the trouble was—in the building or out. Had to check everything we could right away in case it was here. This room's pretty far down the line."

"And you found . . . ?"

"Nothing. Trouble's outside somewhere. We kept checking with a radiophone on emergency batteries, but for a long time it had nothing. I think some idiot thought he'd reduce panic by not admitting the trouble was widespread. But they finally announced that it covers at least the whole Cape."

I shut my eyes. So it wasn't over yet. The danger was still real, and still unresolved. "So what now?"

"We wait some more. But at least we can wait together, and a little more comfortably. I'd suggest that all of us land-dwellers go up to my apartment. Meanwhile . . . I brought you some things." He knelt beside me and I laboriously sat up. Bill went over to Beldan. Mason wrapped a blanket around my shoulders. "Thought you might be a little chilly," he said. "And thirsty. . . ." He handed me a quart bottle of water, and I downed half of it in one greedy guzzle. "And hungry." An algae patty. It had been a long time since I had any idea they could taste so good.

"Infinite thanks," I told him, feeling a shade better. "Have you been in touch with Jonel since we were cut off?"

He shook his head. "Afraid not. The 'phone doesn't have much range on E batteries. We tried, but no luck."

He must be worried sick, I thought. *Well . . . not quite. Not Jonel. But plenty concerned.* For a wistful moment, I envied him. I can stay fairly cool in a crisis, but he does it better than anybody I know. I guess an astronaut has to.

But we're all astronauts now. . . .

Mason put a flashlight in my hand and helped me up. He and

Bill and Beldan and I went out through the dark corridors and up the stairs to his apartment. I told Pinocchio we'd be back, though I knew he couldn't understand me.

We sat around by the light of a single flashlight pointed at the ceiling and waited some more. According to Mason's wind-up watch, it was almost three in the afternoon when we went up. Time passed a little more easily now, with human furniture to sit in and more of us to talk. But still it dragged, and though we said little about it, I'm sure we all thought more and more about the things that would happen if power wasn't restored soon.

It came back all at once, with no warning from the radio, a little after seven. One second we were sitting there in darkness and uncertainty; the next, the lights were on and cozy hums came softly from the walls and everything looked very ordinary. (Except that I was sitting there in a wet bikini with a layer of drying salt on my skin and a blanket wrapped around me.)

"Thanks," I murmured, too drained to do more, "to whomever it may concern...."

And then I jumped up with a startled cry of remembrance. "Pinocchio!" I ran out the door and down the hall, the others close behind me. We used the stairs again, afraid to trust the elevator until we were sure everything was really back to normal.

The lights were on and the walls humming in Pinocchio's room, but there was an unpleasant smell of air and water that had sat too long without recycling. Pinocchio lay motionless right where I had left him.

"Pinocchio," I asked anxiously as I threw the door open, "are you all right?"

He flipped his flukes and swam closer, but he looked tired. He made a complicated series of vaguely excited-sounding noises.

But the translator screen remained blank. And I realized beleatedly that nothing had come from the underwater speakers when I called to him.

Mason swore. "Of all things to get knocked out and stay out! Well, I'll get somebody working on it right away. Meanwhile, I know what some of those noises mean. He's starved."

I smiled. "I can sympathize with that. So am I. But I've got a phone call to make before I do anything about it."

I called right away, from my room. There was a little trouble putting the call through, and I was momentarily afraid something was still wrong. But it was nothing serious, and within a couple of minutes I had Jonel's voice in my ear.

And it sounded *awfully* good.

". . . power failure," I explained. "Still don't know the details, but it was all over this area. For a lot of hours there, Jonel, I really wondered whether I was ever going to get to talk to you again. And I didn't even get to say good-bye."

"I didn't know what to think," he said. "But it certainly is good to know you're all right." He chuckled. "Have you ever noticed, Sandy, that when you go off on excursions with Beldan you have a habit of getting into situations that scare me more than anything that's ever happened to me?"

"Yes," I laughed. "Sorry about that." I leaned eagerly closer to the phone. "But I learned something from this one, Jonel. Something important. I'm ready to start that family now—"

"Great!"

"—on one condition."

His voice took on a slight tinge of caution. "Well?"

I was talking fast, excitedly. "In the middle of all this, I realized that our problems—my attitude—are a microcosm of what everybody's up against. And if we don't solve them, we're going to. . . ." I trailed off. I was going to say, "go the way of the dolphins," but I still couldn't bring myself to admit out loud that Pinocchio was the end of their line. I didn't finish that sentence. "The basic problem," I went on, recomposing myself, "is that we're so completely, helplessly, pathetically dependent on this artificial environment we've thrown together. And that there's no end to it."

I paused, waiting to see if he would say anything. He didn't. I went on, "Do you remember, back at the end of the first month, when Henry and the Kyyra were conferring on how high an acceleration to use?"

"Yes."

"Henry rejected the high value Beldan wanted us to use because its side effects would be too drastic. And he rejected keeping the low one we'd already reached because it would take too long. Three thousand years, he told Beldan, is no different from forever, to a human. So we compromised. Well . . . three hundred years is no different from forever, either. And that's what's been bothering me, and a lot of other people who feel the same way."

"But what can we do about it?" He already knew what I was

driving at; I knew that. But he had to hear me say it—to be sure.

"The high acceleration Beldan was pushing for," I said. "The half gee or so they claim they can do. Jonel . . . do you think they really can?"

"I think so," he said slowly. "I've talked to Zhalāū some more, and I think they can use a pretty high acceleration and get a significant part of the planet and some of its inhabitants to their destination. *But* . . ." he paused for emphasis ". . . the acceleration effects *would* be much more drastic. Conditions would be a lot worse than they are now."

"I realize that. But they could have an end, within the lifetimes of people now living. That would make all the difference in the world to me—and I think to a lot of other people, too. And we could take more time to get ready for it. I think it's worth it, Jonel. I didn't before, but I do now. Very strongly."

He was silent for a while; I wished I could see his face. Finally he said, "Do you realize how *much* worse it would be?"

"You showed me the calculations," I reminded him. "But I'd rather have a tooth pulled once than a permanent toothache for the rest of my life."

"Even without anesthesia?"

"Even without anesthesia." I tried to picture a dentist finding a way to get forceps into my mouth while I was biting a bullet. . . .

Jonel was silent even longer that time. Then he said, "I'll talk to Henry. I love you, Sandy."

"I love you, too."

And now it's late and I'm exhausted and I'm going to my bed and collapse.

And hope.

20/5, 3

Morning: Jonel called me back—woke me up, but I didn't mind. Henry's rechecking the high-acceleration options, with the computer and Zhalāū and his own judgment. And this time he's paying special attention to my hunch about the psychological factors.

Some other news isn't so good. They still don't have the dolphin translator fixed; it seems to be a worse problem than Mason thought at first. He's concentrating everybody he can on that right now, and he's working on it himself.

And Topsy, whose health has always been a concern, is definitely sick. Mason isn't sure what it is, but he thinks it's some sort of a virus. It must have already been there, but her resistance was lowered by a combination of factors like psychological strain (which was already pretty bad) and loss of proper environmental control during the blackout.

He's afraid Turvy's coming down with it too. He's given them both shots which he thinks should help.

Pinocchio shows no signs of it. But I certainly hope we can talk to him soon.

Jonel called again this evening. I'm delighted, and Beldan is as pleased as I've seen him in a long time. Henry's finished his reanalysis of the acceleration problem, and he's reached a decision, well before the end of the moratorium he'd set aside for it. He's convinced that the psychological problems of the way we're doing it now more than outweigh the physical dangers of the other way. He and Zhalāū have worked out details, checked with Beldan, and Henry's decreeing a twenty-year plan to prepare Earth for high acceleration.

It'll be hard, all right, and the whole thing will still take over thirty years—maybe even forty, depending on how tricky things get toward the end. But it gives me a fighting chance to see the end. That's all I ask.

Like I told Jonel yesterday, it makes all the difference in the world. I feel more like myself now than I have in months. I'm actually eager to start a family again.

I don't know why I didn't think of it sooner, but this may make a difference to Pinocchio, too. I have to talk to him as soon as possible, but the translator's still out.

21/5, 3

I'm numb. The translator still isn't fixed, and it doesn't look like it's going to be. They found the trouble this morning; Mason says a power surge when things came back on apparently blew a couple of special IC's that'll be well nigh impossible to replace these days. He doesn't understand why the usual surge protection failed, but that's no consolation; it did.

Worst of all, both Topsy and Turvy died during the night. Pinocchio still shows no signs of catching what killed them, and Mason doesn't think he will. But he's definitely the last now.

Mason says he doesn't have to be; he's saved cells which he thinks the lab may be able to keep till the end of the trip and then use to grow new dolphins. But he doesn't understand. They weren't just an organism. They were a culture, a civilization.

And that will die with Pinocchio.

Tony's flying up this afternoon to take Beldan and me home. I can hardly wait to get back to Jonel. But before Tony comes, I've got to go down and tell Pinocchio good-bye. He won't understand my words, and I won't understand his—"words." But we can communicate, a little. I'll get in the water with him, and I think I can make him understand my sympathy (for what little that's worth) and at least a little of the more complicated things I feel for him.

And then I'll go home to Jonel and we'll start getting ready. Somehow, we're going to have children who can stay hopeful— and playful, Pinocchio—right through all this. We have to. I'm not in that kind of a mood now, but I'll get there as this passes. With the possibility of an end in sight, I think we can do it.

And after what we did to Pinocchio....

We owe it to him.

Third Interlude

Well, Pinocchio, Sandy thought as she closed the book, *I kept my promise as well as I could.*

Just a little while longer, Scott....

Scott was born a little over a year after Sandy's trip north, and Greg sixteen months after that. The creation of an attainable goal had given Sandy the will to have them, but they taught her that goals aren't enough. A sunny day thirty years in the future is meaningless to a two-year-old. To raise them as she had promised herself, Sandy and Jonel had to make life meaningful and interesting and fun for them *now*. Finding ways to do so taxed their imaginations, but they rose to the challenge and in the process rejuvenated their own ability to get the most out of an uninspiring present. They both made up games and stories, both true and fanciful. Sandy added songs, both to entertain and to keep alive at least vicarious memories of the old Earth and anticipation of the new. Despite the conditions, so limiting for one who remembered what had been, the years of helping Greg and Scott grow contained many bright moments. The two boys did not respond identically; they were individuals from the start, and diverged as they developed. But they both responded.

The needs of children were not entirely dissimilar to those of people in general. The target date and the work needed to meet it made a good start toward restoring morale, but they were not enough. Entertainment, education, and indoctrination were necessary as well. The huge communication network, already started and now consciously expanded and improved, was the key to all of them, and often they merged. Entertainers who could function in the available media were at a premium. Like past depressions and wars, the twenty-year plan spawned its own generation of comedians and songsters. Sandy contributed occasionally, at Henry's urging; some of her "Songs of Old and New Earth," composed for her boys, gained wide popularity.

A great deal of energy went into building morale, and it was built. Despite the increasingly drastic measures taken to keep the race alive and get the work done, people adapted to their new way of life.

And that brought problems of its own.

Dark Age

IT WAS DARK all over by then. Even the south pole star (which once had been the sun) had faded into the same league as its myriad fellows; Sirius and Canopus actually outshone it. No point on Earth had any sky but a black and starry one.

But the real dark age—the time that would make this one seem ablaze with light—was yet to come. Soon.

If it was allowed to.

There were those, as the twenty-year plan neared its culmination, who feared that it wouldn't.

And there were those who feared that it would.

"Please, no names." The other man in the small, nearly bare room interrupted with a peculiar smile. "Ideally," he said, "we shouldn't even know each other's names. I do know yours, of course, but the circumstances are unusual. We mustn't use it here, or anywhere that we meet in the Cause. The walls, alas, have ears—and they're growing new ones all the time.

So . . . here, you are Brad, and only Brad. And she, if you must mention her, is Rosanne. Do you understand?"

"Brad" nodded slightly. "I understand," he said coolly. "Brad. Rosanne. And you . . . ?"

"I am Moses."

Brad glanced at him with double surprise, but he didn't let it show. The slightly built, early-thirtyish man on the other side of the table, with his hollow cheeks and thinning, dishwater-blond hair, was a far cry from the heroic image his radio voice evoked in his comnet listeners' minds. But people never look like their broadcast voices, and what he looked like was immaterial. The voice was right, and what mattered was the ideas he stood for. Brad accepted the fact that this was Moses.

The other source of his surprise was harder to dismiss. "I didn't expect to meet you personally," he remarked. "I thought you didn't let yourself be seen." When Moses said nothing, he added awkwardly, "Do you live in Titusville?"

Amusement flickered across Moses' otherwise placid face. "Where I live," he said, "is one thing I never discuss. Let's just say I'm a good deal more mobile than most people these days. If I weren't, I couldn't have lasted this long. You'll never see me in this room again." He looked hard at Brad. "And you're quite right that I normally don't let myself be seen. But, as we already agreed, circumstances are unusual. Normally we'd be reluctant to use somebody as young as you, or as new to the Movement, for such a delicate and critical assignment. But time's running out. We may not have much choice."

"Should I feel honored?" Brad asked wryly.

"I don't particularly care how you feel. All I care about is how you perform. We've been checking up on you; you come well recommended. But in this one case I thought I'd better talk to you personally, in spite of the risk. Partly to look you over for myself, and partly to impress upon you the extreme importance of what we're asking you to do." He chuckled harshly. "Don't think I've done it without thorough precautions. Remember that if you get any ill-advised second thoughts."

Such talk in itself could at least suggest second thoughts. But Brad only asked, "Exactly what are you asking me to do?"

"Ah." Moses smiled a smile of uncertain meaning. "Very well, Brad, we come to the meat of the matter." He lifted his gaze, focusing somewhere above and behind Brad's left shoulder. "As you well know, in just a few days the Kyyra will begin raising the Earth's acceleration again, this time farther and faster than ever before. The *sine qua non* of our program is to make sure that doesn't happen. Because if the build-up is allowed to begin, there's no way we can prevent the miseries that come with it and establish the alternative order."

Brad nodded but said nothing.

"We've been working on many fronts, but what we'd prefer to do is persuade Henry Clark to call the whole thing off. Unfortunately, Clark is a very stubborn man."

Brad smiled thinly. "I know." Everybody did.

Moses did not smile. "We've already applied a good deal of pressure to him, but it hasn't been enough. With the deadline so close, we're going to have to push harder. Much harder."

"Meaning?"

Moses told him what he had in mind. And for the first time, Brad's reaction was too strong and too automatic to hide. "Is that necessary?"

Moses' eyes narrowed. "Yes," he said sharply, "and you can't afford that kind of doubt while you're doing it. Get rid of it." His voice softened a little, but only a little. "You question the necessity. Think about it. Under Clark we've had the work draft, the contraceptive restrictions, Matchmaker. You haven't been affected much by those—"

"Not personally. But I have a brother."

"Indeed. So you've seen something of what tyranny can be. If things go on as they have, you'll see more. You were lucky enough to find a wife for yourself before Matchmaker got you—"

Brad frowned. "How do you know that?"

"Come, Brad. I told you we checked up on you. Such matters are among the first and most basic that we check. But that's beside the point. The point is that you were lucky. You found her. You have each other, and you both want to keep what you have. Right?"

Brad hesitated slightly, not because it wasn't true, but because it seemed nobody's business but his and..."Rosanne's." But he didn't hesitate long. "Right."

"Well, I might point out that while you escaped Matchmaker, you still have the other things to look forward to. How big a family do you want? Caesar Clark will see that you have as little choice as possible. Will you be there to enjoy it? It depends. The work draft can still get you. I don't think I need to be too graphic about that."

"No," Brad agreed, thinking of his brother and several friends.

Moses' voice grew intense, picking up the fervent intonations, even some of the words, of his radio speeches. "It doesn't have to be that way. Clark has justified his totalitarianism by a state of emergency. Despots always do. But the emergency doesn't have to go on. The promised land, for us, is not in some alien jungle in M31, years in the future. It's here, now. Life isn't so bad any more, except politically. If we abandon the high acceleration plan, Clark has no justification for continuing his dictatorial measures. Get rid of them, concentrate on improving living conditions, and we can build something truly worth keeping. Here, now. Maybe we can get rid of Clark. Maybe, in time, we can even reinvent democracy."

Brad carefully suppressed emotional reaction. "You want me to be completely convinced? Then let me play devil's advocate for a minute. Your program sounds fine—except that if we adopt it, we'll never see the new world. We won't get there in our lifetimes. The whole point of the twenty-year plan was that by enduring hardships for a while, we could."

"But is it worth it? The new world has been overadvertised, Brad. Life isn't going to be easy for the settlers who have to tame it. Who wants it so badly, anyway? People who are nostalgic for the Earth they lost. People like you and I don't have that handicap. We never saw Old Earth, or at most we saw too little of it to matter. Why should we miss it?"

Brad sat silent for several seconds. Finally he said slowly, "Maybe we shouldn't. But I'm not sure. Maybe it hasn't been as oversold as you say. If we never saw Old Earth, how can we know?"

Moses' nostrils flared slightly and he forced a thin, distantly ominous smile. "Well, Brad, maybe we don't *know*. But I suggest that you think very carefully about how much of what you *have* you're willing to gamble away betting that a fairy tale is true. Meanwhile...where do you stand? We need your help now. We've already taken the first step. Are you with us?"

Brad stood up. "Maybe," he said. "I need to think it over."

"We need your answer now."

"Even if it's no? You also need me, or so you say. Well, then, you can wait till I'm ready to commit myself." He turned toward the door, but not too fast to see Moses' thinly veiled anger.

"There's not much time," Moses said tightly. "Here ... take this with you, so we can keep in touch, at least. It may be crucial."

Brad turned back around. Moses was holding a small metal cylinder out to him. It looked like an ordinary pocket communicator, but Brad stared at it for quite a while before he took it. And he turned it over in his hands, looking some more, before he put it in his pocket.

"We'll call you if we need you," said Moses. "Meanwhile, remember what I said about precautions. Now that you've seen me, you can't just fade away. But I hope it won't come to that. I hope you'll see that the Cause really needs you—and deserves your help."

Sandy and Jonel went to Clark's office-apartment as soon as he called them. What he had to discuss *might* not be urgent, he had said—but on the other hand it might. He didn't want to take chances, and neither did they. There was too much at stake.

Clark looked up as they came in, but he remained seated behind the desk. He didn't move around any more than he had to, now; his age was finally catching up with him. "Ah, you're here." He motioned vaguely at two chairs on the nearer side of the desk. "Sit down. How are things?"

Something's wrong, Sandy thought as she took the chair on the left. Clark was little inclined toward small talk, and he never had much time for it. Least of all now, she would think. "Not bad, with us," she said. "With things generally ... you know."

"Yes." He seemed to ponder something. Sandy studied his face, more conscious than ever before of how old he looked. Slowly, his hair had become long and thin and gray, his cheeks sunken, his skin loose and wrinkled. He wore his glasses all the time now. But the firm set of his jaw had grown steadily since the beginning, and the eyes behind the glasses were as steady and intent as ever.

And haunted—by ghosts he had kept at bay by constant effort for over twenty years.

He snapped abruptly out of his reverie, but he still skirted whatever was bothering him. "How's Alycia?"

"Not bad." *It's still hard to believe*, Sandy thought, *that I'm*

about to become a grandmother. But it's true. With luck, Scott
will even be home with Alycia when it happens.

"And the newlyweds?"

"Greg and Roberta? They're fine." She frowned. "What's up,
Henry? This can't be what you called us in here for."

He sighed. "No, it isn't. But it's not pleasant to talk about."
He stared at the desktop in front of him. "Fifteen minutes before
I called you, I received a threat on my life. An anonymous caller
told me that if I don't very promptly and convincingly call off the
acceleration build-up, I'll be killed and the build-up stopped in
spite of me."

"Moses' gang?" Jonel asked.

Clark nodded. "He didn't say so straight out. But he didn't
leave much doubt, either."

"And you believe it?"

"I have to believe it—or at least act as if I do. That call was on
my private phone line, and I'm sure it wasn't anybody who was
supposed to have access. Therefore it was somebody who
shouldn't—but does." He stood up carefully, pushing up with
his arms on the edge of the desk, and walked silently to where
there had once been a window—before buildings had been so
thoroughly sealed and barricaded that people spoke of
themselves as living "underground." He walked slowly and a
little uncertainly now, and when he stopped he stared
thoughtfully at the former window as if Kennedy Spaceport
were still there to see. "You know about this Moses character,"
he said. "We've been hearing his rabble-rousing on the comnet
for some time—and whenever we try to trace one of his
broadcasts and catch him, he's not there. Sometimes we find a
tape—but that's all. And never in the same place twice. So far
we've been able to live with it. He's built up a sizable following,
but it's still a minority, and there's a fairly definite age
polarization effect. His followers are young—people too young
to remember Before, who can't really visualize what we left
behind or what we're going toward. People who remember
could never settle for what we have, so most people are still with
us. But we're just now realizing—too late—how little our goal
means to people who've never known anything but the trip."

He turned around and looked intently at Jonel and then at
Sandy. "But there's more to Moses than that. There's more than
I've told you until now. Moses talks—but he also acts. He has a

much more effective subversive network than you might have thought possible, with travel and communication as restricted as they are now. People find ways. A threat on my private line is just one symptom. We've been hearing scrambled transmissions that we can't unscramble on the public talk channels. How many people can build the equipment that takes—or even get the parts? Yes, Jonel, they've got their tentacles well into the comnet. And if they can infiltrate that, why not the life-support systems? We're all vulnerable there. There's already been some sabotage, trying to pressure me into changing plans. I've held out and now they're getting desperate. They threaten assassination."

Jonel nodded. "What can we do?"

"Too little that we're not already doing. You, Jonel, might try to anticipate technical angles on things they might try and countermeasures we can take. In particular, there's a danger that they'll find out where the drive control stations are. Any ideas you have for tightening security there, we need." He shrugged and laughed wryly. "As for assassination—the fact that my life is threatened is, in itself, unimportant. I'm on borrowed time anyway. I'm almost eighty-four. Have to be replaced one of these days in any case, and history won't care just how it happens. But I do want to be sure the machinery for getting my job into other hands is well lubricated. That's why I called you."

Jonel frowned. "I thought that was all taken care of. You've already told us—"

"I've shown you the file with the transition instructions in it, and told you how to get at it. It's all still there—my successor's name, with alternates; instructions to get him started; safeguards to make sure it doesn't fall into the wrong hands. But it's not enough any more. I've added some new safeguards and precautions. As my closest advisors, you need to know about them. Under the circumstances, I don't want to talk about them, even here. So I've prepared this." He walked over, took a sealed envelope from his pocket, and handed it to Jonel. "Both of you read it as soon as you go back to your apartment. Don't talk about it, but memorize it and destroy it. Right away. Got it?"

"Got it," Jonel said. Sandy nodded, a little shaken.

"There's not much more to say...." Clark proved his point by saying it all in less than five more minutes. Then Jonel and Sandy descended into the network of dimly lit, massively reinforced tunnels which now linked the buildings of the complex. They did not talk. People who are as close as they sometimes need no words to know their thoughts are exploring the same territory.

Aside from personal concern for Henry's safety, two themes haunted Sandy's thoughts above all others. One was the newly vivid realization that Henry *would* have to be replaced, one way or another—and that she knew very few possible successors, and none that she really liked.

The other was the realization that whatever was going to happen—with its outcome deciding nothing less than whether the whole twenty-year plan had been wasted—would have to happen soon. It would have to happen before the scheduled beginning of build-up.

And that was less than three days off.

Clark watched them go with a feeling he might have called amusement, had it not been for the other things mixed with it. *They're rattled*, he observed. *As well they might be. But I only scratched the surface. They have no idea just how deep the rottenness runs, or how wide.*

Or how long.

An absolute dictator of Earth—even a crippled, mortally wounded, shell-shocked Earth, literally running scared—cannot have an easy job. Time and again, Clark had wondered how so many men in past history could have actually thought they wanted it enough to aggressively seek it.

He knew better. Earth was big. There was so terribly much to do, even with a worldwide hierarchy of subordinates to handle details, that he constantly had to drive himself as no human should be driven.

And the supporting hierarchy itself was a liability. From the very beginning, individuals and groups, neither understanding nor supporting Clark's programs, had tried to use their positions to undermine his. He couldn't watch them all; had that been possible, he wouldn't have needed them. But he had long since accepted, as an unpleasant but necessary part of his workload, the need to spot-check some of the programs carried out by subordinates. That way he found and stopped some of the plots that developed—often by the silent midnight justice he had always deplored—and hopefully discouraged a few others.

That was one matter in which he had never sought the

Turabians' advice or help. That one he bore alone, doing what he thought he must and letting the casualties add fuel to the already roaring fires of his conscience. No need to inflict that on Jonel and Sandy, he had always told himself.

But now the need was at hand. This one was serious.

Tired of standing, he returned to the desk. *I get tired too easily*, he thought as he eased himself into the chair. *I should exercise more*. He thought it often, and he saw that the C.I.S. reminded everyone else constantly. Having become used to a slowly weakening gravity as the driving reaction ate into the Earth's mass, people who didn't exercise would find their hearts and muscles ill-prepared when the effective gravity rose to, and beyond, what had once been considered normal.

But Clark himself seldom felt like it. And there were too many excuses—too much else that he had to do.

Now he took a few minutes to rest, elbows braced on the desktop and face cradled in his hands. But his mind could not rest.

It had all seemed so simple, once. Back in the first years of the Earth's flight, morale had sunk to a level that threatened the very survival of man. There were many reasons, from boredom to resentment of human dependence on the Kyyra, but foremost among them was the bleak prospect of centuries of desperate flight.

And if that was the problem, the solution had seemed obvious: shorten the trip. Get it over with within a human lifetime.

But that meant a much higher acceleration, with all the agony that would entail. Not as much agony as it might first seem; that would be intolerable. The Kyyra could ease the shock by a variety of means, from redirecting a small part of the drive to counteract disruptive forces, to modifying the structure of crucial parts of the shell. But the effects on human life would still be severe. The twenty-year plan was needed to prepare for them.

Now it was almost complete. And the new problem, as Clark saw it, was ironic: the plan had succeeded too well.

Back then, it had seemed critically, urgently essential to get people out of the doldrums, by work, propaganda, some semblance of entertainment—above all, a goal. It was only recently, with hindsight, that Clark had identified the most insidious ingredient of those doldrums.

Withdrawal symptoms.

Consider the obvious ingredients: Tedious routine; totalitarian rule. Meager and monotonous diet; medical care poor and scarce. Constant exposure to a high risk of death from uncontrollable perils. All of that leading to a low life expectancy, insecurity and boredom, and no hope for improvement.

But those things have been the normal lot of man through most of the world and most of history. Yet he endured. Modern man had simply become addicted to a host of luxuries that his ancestors had never dreamed possible.

And when they were taken away, he—like any addict— reacted unfavorably. He rebelled, he complained, he sank deep into depression.

But in time the withdrawal symptoms passed. When the survivors found themselves still alive, with the memory of their drug faded and no hope of getting it back, they learned to live with the things their forebears had always lived with. They grumbled, but they endured. Some learned to endure comfortably enough, with what little they had left and what little was added under the plan, that they would rather keep that than give it up for the new tortures of high acceleration—even for the chance of seeing sunshine again.

And those who had never seen sunshine in the first place were even less sure that it was worth the risk—or the emergency measures the effort made necessary.

But it's not all the young, Clark reminded himself. *Or only the young. I might be one of them myself, if I had nobody else to think about. High acceleration's not going to be easy on me, and I can't kid myself that I'll live to see the promised land.*

He sat up straight. *But I can't just think of myself. Or them. I know things they can't know—and most people don't agree with them anyway. We have to go through with it, at all costs.*

Don't we?

He reached out resolutely and picked up the phone. As he dialed Security, he wondered how secure even this call was.

McDugal answered—a good man, one Clark trusted as much as any. Of course, Joe Sanchez had long ago taught him—the hard way—not to trust anybody too completely.

Clark told McDugal about the threatening call on his private phone. "Check it out," he said. "Thoroughly, and fast. It should be recorded—though Moses has enough contacts in the comnet that he may have been able to block that. Anyway, start there, and go wherever it leads you. If you find a way to stop it and there's no time to consult me, don't worry about it. Just do whatever's necessary. We can talk about it later."

"Yes, sir." McDugal's image in the small screen at the base of the phone reached out of view, moving as if he were already pushing buttons. "Anything else?"

"Yes. Arnie, if somebody wanted to attack me, how would he go about it?"

"Well, I assume it would have to be through the support systems where you are. Somehow—"

"Of course," Clark interrupted, a little impatiently. "We've assumed that for a long time. We've even taken some precautions—but not enough. I've thought of half a dozen ways the security on those systems needs to be improved—immediately. I'm sending you a memo. Get somebody on them, and cover anything else you can think of at the same time. And, Arnie—"

"Yes?"

"Be sure you do your part. The guys who do the actual work will be from Systems, but you make sure they're screened before they come here. And I mean screened." He thought for two seconds and added, "It might not be a bad idea if you sent a security agent with them. A *good* security agent."

"Yes, sir. Anything else?"

Clark smiled thinly. "You can take it from there."

He made one more call, this one on the hot line to Beldan. "Bad news," Clark said. "We have reason to believe that this Moses' conspirators may have some leads on the control stations. We're not sure, yet, but if they do find out where they are they're sure to try something there. You'd better alert all your engineer crews to strengthen their security. If they find any human they're not sure of near any station, make it clear that they're to take any measures they must to keep him from getting at it."

"Any measures," Beldan repeated carefully. "Up to what?"

"Whatever it takes," said Clark, and Beldan's eyes twitched in their sockets.

"I can imagine cases," Beldan said after a pause, "in which a would-be saboteur might be stopped by nothing short of death."

"So can I," Clark agreed grimly. "Very easily."

"But if one of our engineers kills a human—"

"I'll take full responsibility. You take no chances. And don't delay. I'll keep you posted on any new developments."

"If it must be done," said Beldan, "it must be done. How about the jump induction stations?"

"They should be careful, too. But the main threat is to the drive stations. They're the ones that do what Moses wants to block right now. If he succeeds there, he doesn't have to worry about jump stations."

"True. I'll do what I can."

When Clark hung up, he left Beldan trying to compose himself with a distraught improvisation on his music-pipe. But Clark knew he was also already composing his message to the Kyyra engineers, and would deliver it in minutes.

As he left the meeting with Moses, Brad's thoughts were troubled by the drasticness of what Moses had asked him to do. He couldn't shake off the feeling of being followed as he hurried along the chilly, dimly lit branch tunnel, his footsteps echoing too loudly off the walls. There were no tunnel bugs waiting at the platform, so he summoned one from the call box and then paced nervously as he waited for it.

It came within five minutes, a small, ungainly electric car with a single cyclopean headlight. It pulled up alongside the platform with a quiet hum and a faint scent of ozone, and stopped. Brad looked inside to make sure it was empty before he opened the door. Once inside, he felt a little more secure. He stuck his license-key briefly into its slot on the dash, then slightly tilted the joystick between his knees, taking partial control away from the autodriver. The bug slid away from the platform and turned into the main tunnel.

He drove almost automatically; he knew the route well. The tunnels were a fairly recent development, having existed within towns for several years, between neighboring towns for only a few. This one, opened when Brad was twelve, had opened a new world to him—a world of personal contact with more than a handful of other human beings—and he had used it as much as possible from the start.

Sometimes he dreamed of expanding his world still more, of traveling tunnels that linked not only nearby communities, but distant cities. But such tunnels did not exist. If the acceleration was raised as planned, they never would, and any travel beyond the most provincial would remain virtually impossible for ordinary people.

Yet another reason, he thought, *for supporting the Movement. So what's bugging me?*

It was not, he told himself, that he had doubts about what he was doing, or whether he would in fact do it. He had his father's ability to size up a situation, make a decision about it, and act on that decision without looking back. Unfortunately, like so many people these days (or had it always been thus?), he had reached a decision that was different from his father's. Never again, he knew, would their views come back together—or be compatible.

That was sad, but could be accepted. But did it have to mean getting mixed up with such sordid things as this plot? Did it have to mean dragging Rosanne into it? For he was. Not directly, but the very fact of calling her Rosanne—of calling her anything but her real name—was an involvement, and he resented it.

Another bug whizzed by in the other direction, its headlight beam splattering into little rays of brightness in the scratches in Brad's windshield, and then was gone. *I'm at a crossroads*, he thought with grim amusement, alone again in the blackness. *With what I know now, I can get the Movement over the hump. Or I could blow the whole thing wide open and put an end to it.*

Or could I? Moses uses drastic means to his ends, too. What was that he said about precautions? Maybe that communicator he gave me is more than just a communicator. It could be rigged to monitor everything I say—and explode if I say the wrong thing.

That, he decided, was what bothered him most. Not the possibility of a personal threat, *per se*, but the shock of finding that Moses, so idealistic in his broadcasts, would use such cold-blooded expedients because of "emergency."

Just like Henry Clark.

So how was Moses better?

He was better, Brad told himself sternly, because he offered a chance for continuance of the good things they already had going, and the end of at least some of the bad.

And there *were* good things going. Looking back, Brad could remember a multitude of happy sights and sounds and feelings, centering about days and nights of conviviality with Rosanne and their friends in Titusville. And he could imagine still better things to come, with them and the children he and Rosanne would have.

If they didn't have their world turned up on end and shaken to pieces, figuratively if not literally, by high acceleration. And if they could cast off the yoke of Clark's "emergency" regime.

Are those things, a voice within him asked, *as good as what we could get on a new planet?*

He wasn't sure. But certainly, from where he sat, they were more real.

And so were things like the ever-looming specter of the work draft.

The buzzer sounded in his earphone and the alarm beacon on the barracks winked red and green, red and green....

Sagittarius was rising.

Wearily, Scott Turabian put down his tools and looked across the rolling but otherwise featureless plain at the southeastern sky. He recognized some of the pinpoints of light against the blackness there, but he couldn't see the one that mattered. The galactic center had not yet grown bright enough for its visible light to show through the thick clouds of dust. But less obvious, less friendly radiation had been getting through for quite some time.

Normally, for that reason, the buzzer and beacon would mark the end of the work day and time to retreat to the barracks. But not any more. Now it was just the shift change. There was too much left to do, and too little time, for the work to ever cease.

For a moment Scott turned back to survey the unfinished induction station with quiet dismay. From his perch high on the framework, he could see the whole thing, black and shadowy under starlight, but its outlines clearly traced by lamps strung along its beams—like dewdrops on a spiderweb, Scott's mother might have said. Scott had never seen a spiderweb, but he could see the resemblance to things she had shown him in pictures. The resemblance went only so far. This thing had none of the delicacy of a spiderweb, and it was much more three-dimensional. It sprawled over thirty acres, partially sunk in a deep pit so its towers and ramparts could not topple when it tried to lean.

Human figures, tiny by contrast, scurried along the beams

and down ramps and ladders, merging into a single stream bound for the barracks. Ironic, Scott thought, that they had built this thing, yet none of them understood how it worked.

It was enough that the Kyyra did. When the time came, it and others around the world would induce the transition to super-c. Even the stars would vanish from the sky, and the Earth would hurtle onward in solitude, chasing the unseen galaxy M31 at speeds up to a million times that of light. It would be almost six years before the stars came back. . . .

And then man and Kyyra would find a new home.

Scott had hoped the jump stations would all be finished and he would be home by now, or at least before the acceleration toward jump speed began to build up. But it didn't look likely. Not with barely two days left.

He started down the ramps, his skin-tight protective suit bending reluctantly with his body. He passed men streaming out for the new shift, their suits doubly reinforced against radiation, and went directly to the barracks and the low-ceilinged room he shared with eighty other men, packed in like sardines. (Another obsolete simile, but still in wide use for lack of a better one.) Once through the lock, he peeled off his breather mask. At his cot, he traded his suit for the tattered but reasonably comfortable outfit he'd brought from home. As he finished changing, amid locker-room chatter and smell, and stashed his work gear in his footlocker, he saw Luis Mamani standing by the inner door, watching his work crew come in. Like a mother hen, Scott thought, knowing how that infuriated Mamani. "Hawk," the foreman insisted his Inca surname meant, and that was how he wanted to be regarded.

It was not, at least in its more favorable connotations, how Scott regarded him. Especially now. He walked over to the crew boss and asked, "Do you think we'll make it in time?"

Mamani looked down his long, hooked nose at Scott. "We will make it."

"In time?"

Annoyance flashed in Mamani's black eyes. "We will make it when we make it. We can do no more."

The anger which had been lying in wait began to stir. Scott gestured at the room around them, at the shoddily built and poorly reinforced walls. "What about this? If we're out before the build-up starts, fine. But if we might not, shouldn't we be spending these last days reinforcing our quarters? This place isn't ready—"

"It is strong enough."

"Marginally, even on paper. We need to be sure."

"That is my concern. Not yours."

"I have a small stake in it," Scott snapped. "I have a wife back home expecting a baby in a few weeks. Even if I never see her again, I want to be sure they finish the trip."

"They will finish."

"But if the crew gets wiped out—"

With a surprisingly slight shift of his body, Mamani loomed threateningly. "Look, Turabian, I am in charge here. I do not have to listen to your insolence because you are Jonel Turabian's son. Now, are you going to bed like a good boy? Or are you going to continue this and make me do something neither of us likes?"

Scott stared at Mamani's leathery face for many seconds, seething. But in the end, he said quietly, "I'll go." He turned.

"You'll go, what? Turn around, Turabian."

Scott stopped and turned slowly. He had to force the words out, without meeting Mamani's eyes. "I'll go, sir."

He returned slowly to his cot, thinking. Mamani and his kind, their judgment warped by petty power, could cause whole companies to be wiped out, leaving their projects undone.

And if that happened often enough, the biggest project of all could come to nothing.

Briefly, as he crawled into his cot, Scott considered taking his frustration to Sklynel', the Kyyra overseer of the Salina Station project. But it would do no good. Sklynel' was too shy among humans, too reluctant to interfere in their affairs in any but a purely technical capacity. He made Beldan look like a social climber. And Scott's willingness even to talk to Kyyra had already brought him too much trouble with his human co-workers.

So the idea faded quickly. And the lights faded as soon as he was under the sheets.

Staring into the darkness between himself and the ceiling, he found himself thinking of Alycia. He imagined her slim, almost frail form; the pale, smooth skin and hair that bespoke her Scandinavian ancestry; her voice and smile, which could be *tremendously soothing—when she wanted them to be.*

He wished she were lying next to him.

Strange, he thought, that he should miss her so now. Thrown together by Matchmaker at eighteen, they had both found the first months stormy and uncertain. Scott had gone into it handicapped by a childhood allowing little direct contact with other people—especially those near his own age—before his teens. The tunnel to Titusville had come too late. Alycia Svensson was the first girl he had got to know well—and he met her the day they were married. She was somewhat better off, having long had access to the older tunnels within Titusville. Nevertheless, she came into marriage unwilling, resentful, sullen, with an overdeveloped talent for sarcasm. There was ample fuel for needling and quarrels. Their family backgrounds differed greatly. Scott was close to Clark and Beldan; Alycia had a distrust of them acquired in her association with a wide range of other humans. Assigned to the tiny spaceport community instead of her home town, she felt stranded, cut off from civilization, even though that was no longer really true, with the tunnel developed as it now was.

From such beginnings their marriage had had to grow, and, almost miraculously, it had—at least, it had made a good start. Scott, imbued since babyhood with the worth of the trip and its goal, had endured stoically at first—not happy, but quietly determined to make it work. Gradually—very gradually—he had begun to get through to Alycia. Cautiously, she began to change, to let him closer. As their first year progressed, he began to see some faint glimmering of what life together could be.

And he wanted more and more to make it that.

Just when they were becoming hopeful—just five months after their marriage and a couple of weeks after Alycia knew she was expecting—Scott had been work-drafted. Ripped away to serve in places like this, working for people like Mamani on jobs like building induction stations or cannibalizing houses full of death.

They kept in touch. Not often enough, but whenever possible. They talked about the baby, and they both had a lot of time to think.

And now he missed her.

Restlessly, he rolled onto his side. Seeking sleep, he tried to imagine walking on the surface of a planet, with no special suit

*or mask, under a clear blue sky made light all over by a single
star so huge it looked like a disk and so bright no others could be
seen. The ground covered with soft green leafy things that waved
in the breeze and smelled good, with animals of all shapes and
sizes wandering about....*

*(The only animal he'd ever seen was Ozymandias the Mutt,
and Oz had died of old age before Scott was eight.)*

*Maddeningly, the chain of thought led back to an early
conversation with Alycia. She'd been chiding him about being
so determined to get to a new planet, and he'd been thrown on
the defensive. "You don't know what it's like," he told her. "You
should hear my mother tell about Earth before the trip. Or sing
about it...."*

*"I have," said Alycia. "She recorded some of those songs for
the comnet, remember?"*

"Well, she wrote them for me. And Greg."

*"Touching." Alycia could be exasperating at times. "Old
people always exaggerate about the good old days."*

"She's not old," Scott snapped. "She's not even fifty."

*Now, trying to get to sleep in a barracks somewhere on the
Great Plains, he added to himself, "And she's not exaggerating.
She's telling the truth.*

"She has to be."

Alycia called Sandy quite late at night. Sandy didn't mind;
she wasn't getting to sleep anyway, and she welcomed any sign
that Alycia was feeling more like one of the family.

But Jonel was already asleep, so she left the lights out—
except the little phone-screen—and spoke softly. "What is it,
Alycia?"

Alycia smiled apologetically. "Sorry to bother you, Sandy. I
couldn't sleep."

"That's O.K. I couldn't either. What's wrong?"

"Scott. I haven't heard a thing from him lately."

"Well, there are a lot of people on work crews, and only so
much radiogram equipment in the field. You've never heard
from him often, have you?"

"No, but now's special. He's supposed to be home before the
build-up, and there's only a couple of days left. Do you suppose
something's happened?"

Sandy studied the image for several seconds before

answering. Alycia wore an elaborate, frilly nightgown that did not hide her ripely bulging shape. It was beautiful, and she had made it herself—from the same roughly recycled materials which in most people's hands became the severely functional, multiply patched garments now in almost universal use. "I doubt it," Sandy said after a while. "But we can't be sure."

"You can't get Mr. Clark to find out?"

"I'm afraid not. All we can do is hope for the best and brace for the worst."

"I'll try. But I can't help worrying. About him—and myself. I'm a little afraid, you know."

"Afraid?"

"Of the build-up."

"No need," Sandy said, showing a little more confidence than she felt. "Remember, we've spent twenty years getting ready. Even if it seems a little scary, the place you're in can take it."

"And Scott? What if he's still up there when—"

"Any place with people will have to be prepared too." Sandy tried to change the subject. "How's the baby?"

Alycia grinned. "Alive and kicking—usually when I'm trying to sleep." The grin ended abruptly. "I'm a little afraid about that, too. Does having a baby hurt much?"

"It can," Sandy admitted. "But quite a few worthwhile things do, for a while. Just remember what your doctor and I've told you, and you'll be O.K. How are you feeling?"

"Pretty good, mostly. I have spells once in a while. I wish Dr. Hartzel could see me oftener."

"It would be nice. But doctors can only do so much, and there aren't nearly enough."

"I guess. Well, thanks, Sandy. You've been a help. I won't bother you any more. Good night."

"Good night, Alycia." Sandy didn't look away from the screen until some time after the image had faded. Alycia, she reflected, was still burdened by more than her fair share of fears and anxieties. But she'd come a long way since her marriage to a stranger whose main point in common with her was that he wasn't ready for it either. They'd both come a long way.

As she crawled back into bed, Sandy was very conscious of how fortunate she and Jonel had been to be able to choose each other. Their younger son, Greg, had had the same good fortune in finding Roberta, but that was regrettably uncommon these days. But then, Greg's path had always seemed smoother than Scott's. He'd adapted much more readily to the social life in Titusville—he'd been visiting friends there just today—and in so many ways seemed to draw more pleasure and less pain from life.

Eventually, Sandy hoped as she fell asleep, some of his luck might yet rub off on his brother....

"Yes, Beldan." Clark, increasingly harried, began to grow impatient. "I'll call McDugal right away. We'll do what we can. Meanwhile...if you should be directly threatened, don't hesitate to act on your own."

He hung up.

For a moment he sat staring absently at the phone, too conscious that he no longer bore the pressure as well as he used to. The "Movement," he thought, was getting desperate. Only desperation, brought on by the closeness of the deadline, could explain the rebels' appealing directly to the Kyyra. Surely they must know how determined the Kyyra were to complete the trip as quickly as possible. Clark very vividly remembered how stubbornly Beldan had resisted his early, misguided efforts to keep the acceleration low.

Admittedly the call Beldan had just received was not an actual threat. It was a fairly calm, reasonably worded plea for reconsideration, offering arguments and containing only one pointed reminder that the Kyyra would be dependent on human help when the time came to colonize a new world.

That was how their campaign against Clark had started, too. Reasonably, lawfully presented petitions with considerable backing—which Moses could never have expected him to accept. Their real function had been to undermine support for Clark by making him look unresponsive to the desires of the people.

Thus paving the way for the more sinister measures of the real revolution to follow.

Beldan had learned enough to guess that threats would soon follow in his case too. Especially since his call, like the earlier one to Clark, had been on what was supposedly a very private line.

Still more evidence of how deeply the comnet had been infiltrated.

And the incidence of sabotage and terrorism had increased within the last day.

Clark shook off his torpor and picked up the phone again. McDugal looked surprised when he answered. "Ah, Mr. Clark. I was just about to call you."

"That's good. I'd been wondering why you hadn't. Look, Arnie, I was just talking to Beldan. He got a call, too."

"Assassination threat?"

"Not yet. But he's afraid that'll come next, and he's probably right. He wants more protection."

McDugal looked harried, too. "I'll try," he said—a little doubtfully, Clark thought. "We're terribly busy just now."

"Aren't we all? But we do what we must. Do this. You know we can't let anything happen to him."

McDugal closed his eyes momentarily. "Yes, sir. Anything else?"

"Plenty." *I'm getting nasty*, Clark thought. *I don't want to, but lately it always happens at times like this.* "It's been over a day since I talked to you about tightening my security, and I haven't heard a thing. Have you traced that call?"

"I'm afraid not. We tried. But they blocked it, just as you said. So I've had men rounding up and grilling all the known or suspected revolutionaries they can find."

"And?"

"Nothing. Not much, anyway. But we're still working on it."

"Hmph." Clark scowled. "Well, when are you going to fix my systems? Over a day, Arnie. That's a lot of delay on something like this. What's up?"

"Sorry. As I understand it, Systems got into some internal hassle about which of two ways to do something. But—"

"I could be killed while they do that. Doesn't anybody over there know the meaning of emergency?"

"As I was saying, sir, they should be coming soon. I'll check on it."

"Do that." Clark pressed his lips tightly together. "You said you were about to call me."

"Yes. Bad news, I'm afraid. You knew the conspirators were trying to locate the Kyyra control stations and get saboteurs to them—"

"Yes?" Clark straightened up abruptly. "They've succeeded?"

"Not yet. But we've intercepted communications that indicate they know where at least some of them are."

"That they really do, or they want us to think they do?"

"They really do. Unfortunately, we don't know exactly which individuals do, or where they are. We're afraid some of them are on their way. That would mean they're somewhere on or above the surface, in commandeered vehicles. There's a lot of space out there, all in the dark, and not many men or vehicles available to search it. And some of those could be rebel saboteurs who've infiltrated legitimate surface parties to gain safe passage to their targets."

Clark began to feel trapped. *I don't know why*, he thought. *I've been handling this kind of pressure for almost a quarter of a century. I hate to admit it, but I guess I am getting old.* "Do what you can," he said.

"It's not going to be enough," McDugal said bluntly. "Not the way it is. I've told you we're already busy. You've just thrown me another job. There aren't many vehicles outside, but there are too many to find and search them all. I was hoping you'd help."

"What can I do? I'm busy, too."

"We need a way to filter out suspicious vehicles. If you could—"

A flash of his old insight stirred in Clark's mind. "Suppose," he broke in, "I issue a general ban on intercity travel until further notice. It would be nice just to stop it in the vicinity of the control stations, but I don't see any way to do that without giving their locations away to more people than already know. If we order all motion to stop—any saboteur who complies isn't getting any closer to his target. Any who keeps going, your agents can pounce on, and they'll have a lot fewer to worry about."

McDugal brightened with relief. "Very good, sir. That should help a lot. The only thing that bothers me is that some of the jump stations aren't finished yet. We may block the flow of needed supplies—"

Clark nodded. "True, and I don't know how much we can do about it. But if the drive stations can't raise the acceleration, the jump stations aren't going to be worth much, are they? I'll try to include some provision for legitimate supply crews to be identified and sent on their way as quickly as possible."

"Good idea. But that takes manpower, too. What if they're still delayed too much?"

"We'll just have to try to see that that doesn't happen. But if it does . . . well, jump stations can be worked on after the build-up starts. We'd hoped they wouldn't have to, because it'll be harder and more dangerous. But it's not impossible. If it has to be done, it'll have to be done."

"Yes, sir. I guess that's the best we can do. If I think of a way to improve on it, I'll let you know."

"Only if I need to know, Arnie. Otherwise, just do it."

Clark hung up and closed his eyes, breathing heavily. Arnie was right. There was too much. But it all had to be done, somehow. Measures like the one he'd just suggested were full of unpleasant possibilities, but at this point might well be the least of the available evils.

Even so, they might not be enough. As Arnie said, blocking the saboteurs, even this way, bore a marked resemblance to needle-hunting in haystacks.

Would it work?

For a painful moment, Clark thought of the plot succeeding, destroying all the work of the last twenty years, hurling the dream of a normal, sunlit life back into the inaccessible future from which it had been so laboriously wrested. . . .

That was so painful his mind drew back from it like a burned hand. But there were other specters closer to home. He thought of what he had told Arnie about jump station work continuing into the build-up, and that reminded him that some might have to do that anyway. The one at Salina, for instance, was cutting its schedule dangerously close. . . .

And Scott Turabian was there.

He tried not to think about that, either. But the thought lingered—and, quite abruptly, it suggested one more idea. He opened his eyes and thought hard about it, staring at the wall where the window had been.

He was pretty sure it could be done, though he would have to check with Beldan. But it was so drastic he couldn't bring himself to actually do it. Not yet, anyway.

When the pocket communicator woke him with its quiet but insistent beeping, he almost forgot he was Brad and said his real name. But he remembered in time. Groggily, afraid the thing would wake Rosanne, he shut off the beeper, held the pickup end near his mouth, and whispered, "Hello?" He glanced nervously at Rosanne. He couldn't see well in the dark, but she seemed to be sleeping soundly.

"Brad?" said the communicator.

"Wait a minute." He got out of bed with as little disturbance as possible and tiptoed barefoot across the slightly warm floor to the bathroom. He closed the door, turned on the overly bright light, and sat down. "O.K. I can talk now."

"This is Moses, Brad," the voice said unhurriedly. "Time's getting very short and our other measures haven't been completely successful. We'd like you to help us in the morning. Are you ready?"

Brad didn't answer right away. Images passed through his mind, faces of people he would hurt if he agreed, and of still more he would hurt if he didn't. The personal danger, oddly, didn't even enter his mind. Finally he sighed, "Yes."

"Good. You understand the priorities?"

"I think so."

"Tell me."

"I'm to persuade if I can, kill if I must." He thought about that. What were his chances of persuading? Not at all good, he feared. "And if both of those fail...what?"

"Don't fail," said Moses. "There's only one alternative beyond those, and we're not sure it'll work. We've located most of the control stations and we have agents on their way. But we're still not sure of a couple of the locations, and Clark's learned enough to make it hard for our people. There's a good chance they'll make it, but you shouldn't count on it. It's strictly a last resort, anyway. If we're forced to tamper with the stations, we may unknowingly disturb their operation at their present level instead of just blocking the build-up. Obviously, we'd rather not do that."

"I understand."

"Excellent. Let's go over some details. . . ." Moses spelled out the specifics, tersely but thoroughly. "Carry your communicator," he concluded, "and call us at once, win or lose. If you fail, the saboteurs will have to go ahead, if they're able. If you succeed, we'll have to be sure they don't. And if we don't hear from you—we'll have to assume you failed. Good luck, Brad."

"You'll hear from me," Brad said. The communicator made no reply.

He turned out the bathroom light and returned slowly to bed. He was relieved that Rosanne still showed no signs of waking. He tried to go back to sleep until morning, but with little success. His thoughts were too active—and this time, spurred by Moses' parting words, they included a few about the danger to himself.

He was awake when the room lights began to come on. As they crept almost imperceptibly toward their "daytime" levels, Brad looked at Rosanne, her face tranquil on her pillow and long black hair streaming behind, and decided he didn't want to talk to her before he left. He got up carefully and dressed slowly, half afraid she would wake up and ask him where he was going. When he finished, and made sure he had the two things he needed, the lights were halfway up and he could see her and the room fairly clearly. He let his eyes wander around, ignoring the poor furnishings and bare recycling gear, dwelling on the other things—personal items of Rosanne's, pictures on the walls, small gifts from friends in Titusville. He bent over to kiss Rosanne as she slept. *I'm doing this for you*, he thought. *And us, and all the others. I hope you'll understand that—if you ever know.*

And then he squeezed all sentimentality out of his mind and went out to wander the tunnels until it was time to do what must be done.

"Then you can do it?"

"Yes," Beldan said. "Everything's ready, as far as that goes. I'll alert all the station chiefs to be ready. And if the need should arise, you'll call me?"

"Yes," Clark nodded. "Or buzz you. I'll try to have that special alarm button added to my end of the hot line. But I don't know if I'll get the chance."

"Hopefully," said Beldan, "we won't have to use it, anyway."

"Hopefully." Clark hung up. *Last night*, he thought, *I hoped I wouldn't even have to mention it to you. But that was last night.*

He still felt a little groggy. He'd been to bed too late and up too early, even by the grueling standards he'd been used to for years. Such sleep as he'd had had been rudely punctuated by a series of new calls on his private line, warning him that he had better act soon on the Movement's ultimatum. The last two, with pointed references to his "last chance," claimed to be from Moses himself. But Security was unable to trace any of them.

Very early in the morning, McDugal had called with a new and unencouraging report on the conspirators' progress toward the control station. Two saboteurs had been intercepted, but the chances looked better than ever that they would reach at least two stations. That would be enough to force postponement, at least, and Clark could see no advantage in that. So, finally, reluctantly, he had called Beldan to set things up for the one new option he had thought of.

As he sat at his desk thinking over the call—and in particular his reference to a special alarm—he realized with a flare of anger that Systems had still not been here to tighten the security on his life support.

And that he had been too busy to even think of it since yesterday afternoon.

Scowling, he rang up McDugal and snapped, "This is ridiculous, Arnie! Almost two days. If you don't get somebody over here right away—"

"Sorry," McDugal interrupted curtly. "They're on their way. You don't want me to waste time explaining the reasons, do you? They'll be there. If they're not there in twenty minutes, call me back."

He hung up before Clark could. Clark seethed briefly, then deliberately calmed himself. He tried to work on the pile of papers on his desk—the pile that seemed never to have got any smaller in the last twenty years—and then thought of a way to speed things up.

If a Systems man ever got here.

He arrived nineteen minutes after Clark talked to McDugal. By that time Clark had finished the diagram he'd been working out on a magic slate. "I'm coming," he grumbled when he heard the knock, and he thought, *I sound like a grumpy old man.* The slow, awkward gait with which he went to the door did little to restore his self-image.

He checked through the peephole before he opened the door. He didn't relax completely even when he saw the young man in the blue-gray uniform of a Systems maintenance tech, but he did open the door.

"Systems," the man said. An assortment of tools dangled at his belt. "You requested some work, Administrator Clark. My credentials." He fished a worn imitation leather pouch from a pocket and passed it to Clark. Clark inspected it carefully. Identification card with a picture that matched the face and a name that matched the one on the uniform . . . job authorization, correct and detailed . . . security clearance . . . approval stamps and countersignatures from complex and building guards. . . .

Everything seemed in order. Clark handed the pouch back. The tech said, "I need to get at some connections in here. May I come in?"

"Certainly. It's about time." Clark stood aside to let the tech in and close the door after him. "I have a small last-minute addition to the work order." He returned to the desk and got the diagram he had drawn. "I know you're not a phone specialist, but you're here and this is urgent. Can you do it?"

The tech studied the drawing for a few seconds. "Sure."

Clark paced the room, never taking his eyes off the technician as he worked, both under the desk and on the things he had originally come to fix. *Do all dictators become paranoid?* Clark wondered. *I think we must.*

The tech worked for less than half an hour, but Clark felt definite and strong relief when he finished. Clark escorted him to the door, showed him out, and was about to lock the door after him when he heard rapid footsteps and a familiar voice from the hall.

"Henry, do you have a minute?"

"Greg!" Clark smiled as the bright-faced, curly-headed young man drew to a halt outside the door. "Not much time to spare, I'm afraid. But you know I'm always glad to see you. Come in." He turned and started back to his desk, leaving Greg to close the door. Clark's closeness to the Turabians had begun before the trip, grown steadily, and extended automatically to both their sons. He needed such people, at times, to keep him convinced the race was worth saving. "I haven't seen you for a while," he said as he eased himself into the desk chair and motioned Greg to one of the others. "Been busy?"

"Partly," said Greg, making himself comfortable. "And visiting friends. And getting used to having Roberta around the house." He grinned.

Clark grinned back. "How is Roberta?"

"Just fine." His expression grew serious. "Except she's worried."

"Worried? About what? I can't imagine what she'd worry about that you or Sandy couldn't help her with better than I could."

"The build-up," said Greg, and Clark felt a twinge of surprise. "She's afraid of it. So's Alycia. Especially Alycia, I think, with her condition." He hesitated. Clark thought he saw a peculiar unease in Greg's manner, so subtle and unfamiliar that it took him a while to recognize it and even longer to have any inkling of what it might mean. "I know I couldn't ask you to do anything about it just for them, but it's not just for them. I was in Titusville a couple of days ago, and there's a lot of the same kind of feeling. They asked me to talk to you."

Clark frowned. "Well?"

"They want me to ask if you could delay the build-up."

Clark looked at him for a long time, startled. Something in a remote corner of his mind squirmed uncomfortably, but since this was Greg, it did no more. "Well, Greg," he said finally, with a light laugh, "I've had the same kind of pleas before every major transition in the whole trip. I think you know why it's impossible."

"Is it, really? Completely impossible?"

"Yes." A memory stirred, of the one time Clark had allowed himself to hesitate on such a point. He found himself staring at the new row of switches the tech had installed under his desk, and jerked his eyes self-consciously away from them. "Yes," he repeated, "it's impossible. How long a delay are they talking about?"

"Long enough to convince everybody it's really the thing to do. That it's safe enough—and worthwhile."

"Everybody?" Clark said softly. "A long time ago, Greg, I was desperately hoping to get everybody to agree on something like that. I was very naive then."

"Were you? Or were you maybe wiser? Maybe you've lost something."

"Probably." Clark nodded slowly. "Probably both, in ways. But I can only do what looks right to me."

Greg's unease gathered itself into impatience. "But if it's so right," he demanded, "why can't you show us why? Look, Mr.

Clark"—(he had almost never called Clark that since he was very small)—"you forget that some of us never saw the kind of life you say you're taking us to. We don't feel sure it's real—or that we'll like it. But we know we have the makings of a decent life here—if we don't have to worry about high acceleration."

Clark looked at him sharply, suddenly very conscious of what had been bothering him. "You sound like one of them."

"Them?"

"Moses. The so-called Movement."

Greg smiled. A rather ordinary smile, superficially—but it was the most chilling thing Clark had ever seen. "That's right," Greg said quietly, producing a tiny pistol from a hidden pocket. The smile vanished. "Fold your hands on your desktop, Mr. Clark. Moses calls me Brad."

Clark obeyed, moving slowly. *It's time for those buttons, he thought. But . . . this is Greg. And he knows Moses. Maybe I can still talk to him. . . .* "Well," he said, carefully keeping his voice and manner calm, "this is a surprise, Greg. Not a pleasant one, I admit. I wouldn't have thought you'd be taken in by such demagoguery."

"It was his or yours," said Greg. He held the gun and his gaze unwavering on Clark. "It took a while, but I finally decided his makes more sense."

"To you. Not to your father and mother. Have you thought about how it will hurt them if you succeed?"

He had hit a nerve. The gun didn't budge, but for an instant Greg's eyes dropped and torment clouded his features. He nodded almost imperceptibly. "Yes. And that's the real tragedy of it—that they and we can't both have what we want." The confident, almost fanatical facade snapped back. "But we're going to have to live with it longer. And our way is better for the next few generations. Isn't that how you decided?"

"More or less. But have you really thought about it? Have you thought about why people have been less miserable under the twenty-year plan than before? Largely because they've been kept busy and the end was in sight. Do it your way, and we'll go back to what we had before. You don't realize how bad morale got in those days, Greg. We would never have gone to the plan if we didn't already know the alternative was worse."

"And the work draft?" Greg challenged. "The contraceptive laws? Matchmaker?"

"I've hated them as much as you. But we were dying off a lot faster than we were being replaced, and voluntary measures weren't working."

Greg made a contemptuous noise. "That's what you say. Moses had other ideas. Why should anybody have to go through what high acceleration means, when our descendants could get there in a few generations just the way we're going? And we could have easier lives in the meantime."

Clark shook his head, more with sadness than anything else. "I had those ideas over twenty years ago, Greg. I thought they'd work, then. I really wish I could make you see how wrong I was—but apparently I don't know how." He looked hard at Greg. "But you make me surer than ever that we have to go through with it. If one generation can forget as much as you have, what would happen if we let it stretch out to fifteen or twenty? Who would remember even enough to get things going after we reached a new planet?"

Greg looked uncomfortable, but made no direct answer. He just said, "I'm sorry that's your attitude. They thought maybe I could persuade you to see it our way. I really hoped I could, because I've always liked and respected you, Henry. I still do. So I hate to do what I must. But you leave me no choice. There's more to care about than you." The muzzle of his gun shifted slightly.

Clark felt his heart hammering and his throat drying out, but he somehow kept his voice steady. "You actually intend to use that thing?"

"Yes. If you won't change your mind."

"Why?"

The gun twitched with exasperation. "You're making this very hard. Because the Kyyra have had all their dealings with you, obviously. With you gone, they'll *have* to delay, at least long enough to make the transition to a successor. That gives us more time."

"Not as much as you think. We've always known I might have to be replaced suddenly. We've made arrangements." *What am I waiting for? I should have already done it....* "We've made other arrangements, too, Greg. You know, if the build-up had already started, you'd have to rethink your whole scheme, wouldn't you? Your number one goal would be gone forever. Would it still be worthwhile to kill me?"

Greg's uncertainty showed for less than a second, but it was unmistakable. "What are you getting at?"

"Very simple. We've anticipated most of your moves—including your last-ditch offense that you don't want to use. We have a last-ditch defense that we don't want to use, either. But, as you say, you leave us no choice."

"What—"

"We start early." And as he said it, shaking with regret that he dared delay no longer to make sure it was necessary, Clark slammed his leg sideways against the new switches under the desk. Simultaneously, Greg moved his hand as if to shoot, and then yelled a startled oath as the lights died. He didn't dare shoot in the dark; there were life support devices he couldn't risk hitting. But there was a clatter and scuffle as he sprang from his chair, kicking it over, and came around the end of the desk, knocking papers to the floor.

An electrical call had already gone out for Security guards, and another was sounding Beldan's hot-line buzzer continuously. Both would trigger immediate action, but immediate meant at least seconds. Meanwhile Clark felt Greg's strong hands grabbing his throat and squeezing, wrenching, lifting him out of the chair and throwing him to the floor. He hit hard. A twisting pain shot through his right ankle and echoed through his whole body. But the worst was in his throat. The hard fingers pressed into him until it seemed that their tips must meet. *I*, he thought with crystal clarity through a haze of pain and fading awareness, *am being strangled.*

The fact seemed neither particularly exciting nor even particularly real. Another flashed by—*Greg couldn't do this. Not Greg!*—and was gone. He couldn't breathe. He felt consciousness going and struggled to hang onto it.

Dimly, he heard steps outside. Then a hard blow, a wrenching sound, and the door flew open. The lights came on and a blur of green and gold flurried by the door. *Security guards*, Clark remembered with an effort, forcing them almost into focus. *I sent for them....*

One of them was lifting a black gun to point at the maniac (Clark couldn't remember his name) who was strangling him. The fingers let go of his throat, and he dimly remembered that there was some reason why he didn't want the assassin killed, though he couldn't remember what it was. He tried to call out to tell the guards.

But the only sound that came was the sharp *crack* of the

guard's gun. The assassin flew backward off him with a grunt, slid across the floor and lay quiet. There was blood....

A voice deep in Clark cried out to him that something was very wrong. Then a reddish-black gauze curtain slid gently across his world and the lights dimmed behind it.

"You'd better come right away," the guard on the phone told Sandy. Something in his voice made her sure he wasn't exaggerating. She fought to keep her apprehension under control as she relayed the message to Jonel. But they half ran the whole distance, and her head swam and Jonel's face went pale as they reached Clark's open door and looked in.

Henry lay on his back near the desk, apparently unconscious, his face and neck red. Near him sprawled Greg, equally motionless, his shirt drenched with blood that spilled onto the floor around him. A guard in a faded uniform stood uncertainly over Greg, still holding a pistol. Another pistol lay on the desk. Another guard stood near the door. A smell of burnt powder hung in the air.

The scene blurred through the film that filled Sandy's eyes and the fury that filled the rest of her. She could barely get words out. "What happened?"

The guard near the door stepped toward them, almost as pale as Jonel. "We're not sure, exactly," he said woodenly. "We got a call on Mr. Clark's emergency alarm and came in. The lights were off and we heard fighting. When we got the lights back on, we saw a man trying to strangle Mr. Clark. It was clear-cut: Frank shot him. We didn't know it was your son until afterward." He lowered his eyes. "I'm sorry, Mr. and Mrs. Turabian. I don't know what else to say."

Sandy didn't answer. She tried to keep her eyes off Greg, but they kept being drawn back. The other guard, having decided he was harmless now, knelt beside Henry, checking his pulse and breathing. Jonel asked, "Is either of them alive?" Some of the color had returned to his face, but not enough.

"Clark is," the kneeling guard said without looking up. "Your son isn't." Clark stirred and made incoherent little noises. "He's coming around, I think."

Jonel went to kneel beside Clark. Sandy followed. Clark's eyelids flickered, then opened. At first they were blank, but then he seemed to recognize Jonel and Sandy. "What...." The word came out so badly that he cleared his throat and tried again. "What happened?"

"Just what we were going to ask you," said Sandy, even more roughly than she intended.

Clark closed his eyes again. After a few seconds he reopened them, but didn't look directly at Sandy or Jonel. "Oh, yes," he murmured. "I don't know how to tell you this. Greg . . . is with the Movement. Moses sent him . . . to assassinate me."

Sandy closed her eyes, almost too numb for the shock to register. She would never have dreamed it before, but with hindsight, it made a bizarre sort of sense. Greg had always seemed less responsive than Scott to her tales of old Earth and the promised land, and more so to social pressures. That had made him seem unusually well adjusted—but it had also made him more susceptible to revolutionary influences, and given him more to value in the status quo. And few people on Earth were as well situated as he to attempt what Clark said he had attempted. It was shocking—but not incredible.

"How is Greg?" Clark asked, almost inaudibly.

"He's dead," said Jonel.

Clark winced. The guard was bandaging his ankle. "Oh, Lord. I tried to stop them; I really did. I didn't want them to kill him."

"Why?" Sandy demanded fiercely. "So he could lead you to Moses?"

"Partly," Clark admitted. "But you know there's more to it than that. You can't believe I wanted this to happen." He paused as if searching inside himself. "Maybe I tried to talk too long. Maybe I should have called the guards sooner."

And maybe, Sandy thought bitterly, *you just didn't care that much. I'll try to understand, Henry, but it's not easy. All I see is that you're responsible for our son's death.*

And he was mixed up in something that wanted to destroy everything we've been living for.

I don't know which bothers me more.

"Maybe," she said finally, coldly. "I don't know. All I know is . . . I don't see how I can work with you any more. Not after this."

Clark tried to sit up, failed, and fell back in pain. "Oh, but you must!" he said earnestly. "More than ever. I'm not going to be much good for a few days, and you two have to pull things together. Listen...they were very close to stopping us. I arranged with Beldan to start the acceleration build-up early if we ran out of other alternatives. When Greg attacked me, I knew the time had come. I didn't like it, but I gave Beldan the signal at the same time I called the guards. The build-up will be starting any minute now." He looked at Sandy, pleading. "You see what that means? There's going to be panic, and then anger, fanned by Moses. You have to calm them. You have to make them understand why I did it."

Sandy stared at him for a long time, astounded at his request. "Just how far do you think I can go with justifying your excesses? Maybe you were all right, and Greg was all wrong. But he was my son. I have to live with my feelings." *And I understand how he felt, to some extent. I'm only sorry I couldn't make the promise more real to him.*

Clark somehow grabbed her hand and squeezed it weakly. But there was nothing weak in the gaze he fixed on her. "Don't you remember what we started all this for? Do you want it to lead anywhere? Or are you willing to just let it collapse into chaos?"

She was silent for a long time. "No," she whispered at last. "I don't want that." She smoothed her feelings as well as she could, suppressing what she must—for now. "If that's the alternative," she said stiffly, straightening up, "we'll cover for you. But it's the last thing I can promise you."

She stood up.

Minutes later, the quakes started.

The new quakes were not the terrific convulsions that would have shattered the Earth beyond all hope of even temporary repair, had the Kyyra not taken their elaborate and esoteric precautions. Mostly, the new tremors were less severe than those near the beginning of the trip, before the Earth could be properly girded against acceleration. But the changes now beginning were by far the largest and fastest yet. Even with the Kyyra's seeming miracles of preparation, they would be felt throughout the months of build-up. Though properly prepared buildings and underground dwellings would suffer little damage, their occupants would hardly feel secure with their china rattling in their closets for all that time.

And improperly prepared buildings, or vehicles caught out in the open, would not fare so well. They would perish as so many had at the trip's beginning, and sometimes in ways still worse. As the acceleration rose to levels approaching half a gee, the ground everywhere would tilt more and more steeply to the south. Until now, the apparent tilt had been unobtrusive; in the weeks to come, it would become obvious and then awesome. To the perils of earthquakes would be added those of landslides on an unprecedented scale. Tall buildings (where such remained), even mountains, would topple southward with thunderous groans. In places like Manhattan, cannibal crews during the preceding years had dismantled many skyscrapers, sometimes carefully picking them apart for recyclables, sometimes just getting them down fast so they wouldn't destroy the shelters beneath by falling all at once. But there hadn't been time to get them all down, or even to fully reinforce all dwellings. There would be— there were—casualties. There were even more casualties than there should have been, because of the day-early start. And panic out of all proportion to the actual increase in casualties, simply because people hadn't been expecting it for almost a day.

And violence, from casual rioting in towns to deliberate, savage, but futile attacks on Kyyra control stations.

Sandy and Jonel did all they had promised. They led the publicity campaign, personally broadcasting around the clock, pausing only for brief naps, quelling panic, explaining that the early start was a desperate measure made necessary by a plot to subvert all that the last twenty years had worked toward. They used every trick they could to rally popular support once more behind the plan; so highly charged was the public mood that nothing less would work. They painted the assassin as black as they could, while hiding both his identity and the much more complex feelings they really had about him. "Who," Sandy challenged in a typical speech, "could possibly support an opposition that would stoop to brutal, craven physical assault on a defenseless octogenarian? And not just any octogenarian, but one who for a quarter of a century has given his body and soul to saving mankind from sure destruction?"

Unseen crowds cheered. And every word tore her apart.

But it worked. Initially, even with its essential goal snatched irretrievably away, the Movement lashed out with no-holds-barred counterpropaganda, including vehement but unproved allegations that the assassin had been Jonel and Sandy's son.

Without dignifying the claims with a direct answer, they turned them back against the Movement by citing them as further examples of how low Moses' followers would stoop. They outplayed the revolutionaries at their own game. Moses had nothing to match sympathy and indignation for a properly described old man attacked by a young. In short order, his Movement was driven farther underground than it had been for months.

When Clark emerged from obscurity into public view at the end of the second day, he emerged in glory. Support for what was happening, determination to make it work, was at an unprecedented fever pitch.

And Caesar Clark was closer to godhood than any man had been before. Someone, somewhere, might still have dared to doubt that.

But no one, at that point, would have dared to say so.

Alycia, too young to remember the original quakes, was one who panicked at the unannounced onset. She told Sandy, when she finally reached her fourteen hours later, that she had tried to call her as soon as she felt the first tremor, and kept trying, with steadily growing tension, every fifteen minutes thereafter. She was on the verge of hysteria when she finally got through. "It just keeps shaking!" she moaned. "Won't it ever stop?"

"Yes, it'll stop," Sandy assured her gently. "But not for several weeks. We've known that all along. It won't hurt you, Alycia. This is what we've been getting ready for. You'll get used to it. Try to relax."

But Alycia couldn't relax. The following morning Sandy went to see her for an hour, to try to comfort her. She didn't look good. Her eyes were red, her fingernails ragged. The news that her brother-in-law had died violently, under vague circumstances which Sandy obviously didn't want to discuss, did not help her spirits. Sandy didn't tell her that Roberta had disappeared right after Greg's death, and investigators had found evidence that her whole relationship with him had been a subtle scheme to lure him into the revolution.

Sandy, despite the strain she and Jonel were under, invited Alycia to move in with them until Scott got home. She refused. She would be a burden, she said. Besides, she had been trying repeatedly to get a 'gram through to Scott and find out if he was all right, and she had to wait right here until she got an acknowledgment.

I've been wondering about that myself, Sandy thought as she left Alycia crying softly to herself.

But she had long since learned not to let such wonderings drive her to Alycia's present condition. She had had to. It was the only way to survive.

If only Alycia could learn that. . . .

In the middle of the night after the second day, Sandy's phone shrieked at her until she answered it. Alycia's voice was full of terror and anguish. "Sandy," she gasped, "can you come here right away? I think the baby's coming!"

Sandy's mind snapped instantly to full alertness. *It's too early,* she thought. *It's much too early.*

She went right away, without bothering to dress, and she took Jonel with her.

The first tremors hit the station during Scott's shift, and kept going. Nothing of significance fell down right away, but during the hours Scott spent on the crazily swaying framework, he felt sure things were weakening. And still Mamani did nothing to the barracks—except make his workers try to sleep in them. He did make sure they heard a comnet explanation of the plot and counterplot, the assassination attempt, the reason for the early start. Scott knew enough about what was behind it to believe it, after allowance for poetic license. And he knew that, in most places, the one extra day wouldn't have made much difference. But here. . . .

It took almost a day to shake things loose enough to produce disaster. Scott was lucky: his building was undamaged. The first collapse occurred next door, near the end of his sleep shift. He wasn't sleeping well, and he heard the first rumble, transmitted through the ground, before the barracks siren drowned it out. Lights came on; the room full of nominally sleeping men exploded into a flurry of activity as they sprang from their beds, confused, and fumbled for suits and masks.

Outside, and in the building where Scott spent most of the day, it was quieter. The siren there was stuck on for over an hour, but the holes in the roof and walls left little air to carry sound. As he walked among the jumbled cots, or surveyed them from above, he sometimes imagined he smelled the smell of death. He didn't, of course—but the scene was so reminiscent of his nightmarish days of cannibal crew duty that his imagination supplied the detail automatically. In ways, this was worse. The bodies sprawled on and among these cots were acquaintances of his. Not friends—he'd had no friends here—but people he had known when they were alive, people who should still be alive. Some of them were, moaning through breather masks, waiting with forced patience for help.

Scott was too dazed to think much about what he was doing, but he did it fast and well, almost automatically. And meanwhile the conscious part of his mind went over and over what had happened, trying to understand. Perched on the ragged edge of a hole, looking out at the stars and the unscathed latticework of the station, he felt the building still quivering, but the worst seemed to be over. But now what? The barracks would have to be reinforced, just as Scott had so often tried to tell Mamani. But now they would first have to be rebuilt—and all of it would have to be done under the added handicap of tremors and growing acceleration. And the quite unnecessary loss of dozens of men.

How could Mamani be so stupid?

Could he, Scott wondered suddenly, have been in on the conspiracy? Had he wanted this to happen?

All through the day, as he worked, he pondered, and his anger grew. Several times he found himself thinking of Alycia, hoping she was all right. No reason why she shouldn't be, *he told himself stubbornly.* I'm sure they had everything ready there.

The thought of getting back to her, he began to realize, was almost the only thing keeping him going now. It occurred to him late in the day, as he applied the final outer seal to the second last patch in the roof, that with this setback, by the time he made it back he would have a son or daughter to welcome him too.

He paused and looked up at the Milky Way, momentarily feeling better. It'll be worth waiting for, *he thought, with a defiant smile in the direction of Sagittarius.*

Physically and emotionally exhausted at the end of an overlong day, he stopped on the way into quarters to see if there were any radiograms. There was one, but his throat went dry and his world wavered as he read it.

ARE YOU OK? GREG DIED IN BUILD-UP. ALYCIA DELIVERED EARLY. PROBABLY

COULD HAVE SAVED BABY WITH INCUBATOR,
BUT NONE AVAILABLE. ALYCIA OK BUT GLUM.
SENDS HER LOVE, PROMISES MESSAGE WHEN
FEELS BETTER. OUR LOVE AND DEEP SYMPA-
THY.

—MOM AND DAD

A worldwide tragedy is inherently too big for a single human mind to grasp or respond to. One frail girl losing her first child, one idealistic young man drawn into a conspiracy and shot down, one old and valued friendship turned to ice—any of those is another matter entirely.

A month afterward, they all still troubled Clark. He felt personally responsible. And now he kept wondering. At the most inopportune times—in the middle of a conversation, or halfway through a pile of paperwork—he would find himself staring vacantly into space, reliving the day the build-up began, asking himself, *Was it really necessary? Or could I have found another way?*

He would never know, of course. But that didn't stop him from asking, over and over.

And that wasn't good, because there was still a great deal to do. He and Dianne had long discussions about it. She kept telling him he mustn't let the incidents keep bothering him, that he must get them out of his mind and get on with today's business. He told her that he already knew that, and she would be a lot more help if she could tell him *how* to take the advice he already agreed with.

He was staring and questioning now, with a pile of urgent reports only half done on the desk in front of him. Dianne, standing just uphill from the desk, smiled down at him. "Don't you have work to do?" she asked gently.

But Dianne had been dead for a quarter of a century. "You," Clark said gruffly, crooking a finger at her, "are a hallucination."

"Oh," she said, crestfallen. "I'm sorry."

She vanished.

The reports didn't. *A hallucination*, Clark thought. *Not a good sign.* He had welcomed Dianne when she returned to his dreams at the end of the first year. In his dreams, she soothed him; she helped him sort out his most troublesome thoughts.

She gave him the reassurance he so desperately needed, that what he was doing was worthwhile and maybe on the right track.

In that capacity he had been grateful for her, and she had been with him, off and on, for much of the trip—sometimes old, sometimes young.

But lately she had overstepped her bounds. He sometimes imagined that he saw her when he was awake.

Always young. Always about Alycia's age.

So far he had always consciously recognized her as a hallucination—a symbolic embodiment of things he needed. That gave hope that his mind was not too far gone. But he did see her, during the day. That was a sure sign that he was slipping.

A symptom, he thought wryly, *of senility.*

He lowered his eyes to stare at the top report. They didn't want to focus. *Senility*, he repeated slowly, letting it sink in. *Maybe it's time I did something about it.*

Several times in the last few days he had thought about stepping down, putting his burden on younger shoulders. But always there was one more thing that he had to take care of personally, or a resurgence of the belief that he was feeling better. . . .

Or that awkward obstacle that had plagued him ever since Greg's death.

Well, he thought, *I did something about that, didn't I? Just a few days ago.*

Was it enough? Maybe I should check the new letter again, and decide. If I'm satisfied, I'll turn it over. If I'm not. . . .

I'll fix it. Maybe I'll even talk to them.

It's time.

The decision made, he stood up. That was no trivial undertaking. The acceleration build-up so far made him feel as if he had gained over ten pounds in the last month, and in the same time he suspected he had also lost more strength than in any comparable period before. He grasped the handles he had had installed on the desk, strained and groaned, and wound up "vertical." Then, carefully (for his ankle was healing slowly), he inched along the edge of the desk to the handrail at the left.

The handrails were necessary, as were the heavy east-west ridges—not quite steps—covering the floor to improve traction. Nine or ten degrees of tilt is a lot steeper than a spry young person who hasn't thought about it might imagine. *And*, Clark thought as he stepped off the cradled platform that held the desk and chair apparent-horizontal and started dragging himself up the rail toward the filing cabinets against the north wall, *it's going to get a lot worse. Both the tilt and the weight.*

It was slow going. He took his time, stopping to catch his breath when necessary. *Should have listened to myself,* he thought, *when I told myself to get more exercise.*

Well...too late now.

The recurrent thoughts about Alycia and Greg and Sandy returned, unbidden and unwelcome. *Was it necessary?* he asked himself for the hundredth time. But now he went farther. He thought of all he had done, all the way back to the time when he told the Kyyra to go ahead and start moving the Earth. *Was any of it necessary? Or right? Are circumstances ever special enough to justify the things I did?*

I don't know. I'm just not sure.

Too late to do anything about it, he became aware of messages coming in from several senses telling him he was losing both his balance and his grip on the handrail. There was a dull pain in his chest, but that, like everything, seemed oddly distant and lazy and dreamlike. He watched with little more than curiosity as the corner of the desk rose slowly toward his head.

I tried, he thought simply.

And then the corner of the desk arrived and consciousness left.

Sandy did not make her decision lightly. Jonel never came to agree with her, despite frequent long discussions, but in the month of soul-searching and nightmares that followed Greg's death and Alycia's miscarriage, she grew more and more convinced that it was necessary. It was not, she kept telling herself, that she no longer supported the trip's goal. It was, rather, that her emotions about things actually done so far would make her unable to contribute effectively.

Do I really believe that? she wondered occasionally. *Or am I rationalizing?*

I believe it, I think. A clean break would be best for everybody.

She finally nerved herself to tell Clark. But she got no answer when she tried to phone him. When there was still no response a half hour later, she began to feel edgy. This was going to be hard enough without the irritation of repeated incomplete calls.

Four more times she tried, in half that many hours. Gradually, the irritation changed to apprehension. Normally, Henry answered promptly, and he seldom left his office.

Reluctantly, she left her apartment and went through the tunnels to his. He didn't answer his door, either, and it was locked. But Sandy still had a key.

She found him where he had fallen, head down across the floor ridges by the desk, motionless. Something cold settled in her stomach. "Henry!" she gasped as she hurried to his side. As she examined the bump on his head and checked for pulse and other vital signs, she was vaguely embarrassed that her dominant emotion was frustration and annoyance at being too late to deliver her message. Enough memories came back from pre-Movement days to make her sure she should feel deep grief.

But the grief wouldn't come.

When she had convinced herself there was nothing to do for Clark, she used his phone to call Jonel. He was there a few minutes later. They covered Clark with a sheet until he could be buried (such as it was) in the recycling plant. Then Jonel said, "I guess we'd better check that file."

Sandy nodded numbly, teeth resting lightly on her lower lip. "This is what I was coming to avoid, Jonel," she told him as they climbed the floor to the north wall. "I'm sorry; I know you didn't agree. But I had to. I was going to tell him to leave me out of the succession arrangements." *Partly*, she thought, *because it was my last semi-official connection with the government.*

And partly because I was afraid of where it was leading.

Jonel said nothing. He knelt to open the combination-locked file Clark had told them about, hidden in a false-fronted compartment at the back of one of the regular files. The paper on top was conspicuously addressed to him and Sandy, in Clark's hand, with the words "personal and confidential" added under the names. *I've seen that before*, Sandy thought with a sudden tightness.

The sense of *déjà vu* persisted as Jonel sat down on the sloping floor to open the envelope and she leaned on his shoulder to read. The single handwritten sheet he unfolded was uncannily reminiscent of one Clark had had hand-delivered to them over twenty years ago, desperately asking for their help right after the trip's violent beginning. It was written in a hand that was little changed, except for a little more shakiness that came with age.

And it began the same way, though it was dated just three days ago.

Dear Jonel and Sandy,

I hope you've managed to forgive me enough by now to read this and do what I ask. I know it won't be easy after what's happened—especially for you, Sandy. But there's really no one else I'd trust with it.

So I'm asking you. Just one small favor: Finish what I started. Take them home.

Please.

You shouldn't be surprised; you must have expected this. I've never bothered you with titles or such official claptrap, but you know you've been my closest and best and most important advisors for years. You know more about the total situation and strategy than anybody else now alive. You're a good team, and the public already knows you both.

The official claptrap will be necessary now, of course. The world will need to know that you're in charge—and don't let them forget it. You'll find detailed instructions here to get you started and fill in gaps in your knowledge. I've made arrangements to get you legitimized and recognized; all you have to do is activate them.

One more thing: it's not going to be easy. You already know that, but it may be even harder than you now realize. Expect it. Don't let it crush you. You'll have to do things you don't like. Try to remember some of the good advice you've given me about those.

Moses' Movement isn't dead—only waiting. We kept them from stopping the build-up, and drove them into hiding, but that's only strengthened their resentment and determination to get rid of us. You'll hear from them again, if only at the end. Don't underestimate them.

I hope I haven't scared you off—but I doubt that. If you honestly think somebody else can do it better, let them—but you'll have to find them. It's your problem now.

Thanks and good luck,
Henry

Her throat felt dry and her pulse raced as she finished reading. "That's what I was afraid of," she whispered. "I can't do it, Jonel. Not after all that's happened."

"We've been all through this, Sandy," Jonel said quietly. "If you can't, who can?"

"I don't know. I told you you should go ahead, if he asked us and you wanted to—"

Jonel shook his head. "You know I can't do it alone. We're a team, Sandy. I know some of the problems, but mostly just the technical ones. I can't talk to the Kyyra like you can. Or our own people, for that matter."

"You can find somebody else—"

"There isn't anybody else. Not with our background."

"I know." She bit her lip, wishing he wouldn't make this so hard. "I don't know what to tell you, Jonel. It's not that I don't want to, exactly. I've tried to understand, but after the last month . . . I just can't function well in this state. The less I have to do with the government, the better. That's what I was going to tell Henry."

"A cop-out," Jonel grunted. He looked straight at her. "You know that's not you, Sandy. When something has to be done, you can do it. Your feelings might make it hard or painful, but you overcome that like any other obstacle. Henry did it for over twenty years. How do you think he felt about some of the things he had to do? How do you think he felt about Greg and Alycia? You can't understand—"

"Can't I? How do you think I felt telling those vicious lies about Greg? Later, when I had time to think, I saw that we didn't have to do it that way. We could have been honest. But we didn't have time to see the ways."

"Maybe," said Jonel, but he sounded unconvinced. His tone softened slightly. "O.K. So you have begun to understand. Are you sure that's not what you're afraid of? If Henry could talk, he'd tell you that's just the beginning. We'll have to do a lot of things in the next decade that'll torture our consciences. But we'll do them anyway, because the alternatives look worse. If we do them, we'll have a chance of finishing what we set out to do when we left the sun. If we don't—they might not get done, and everything it's already cost us will be wasted. And we'll have to live with the knowledge that we might have prevented that."

He waited. Sandy stared for a long time at the white-sheeted form by the desk, feeling a glimmer of renewed respect—and sorrow that it was too late to tell him. More than ever before she understood what he had been through, and the burden she would be assuming if she did what he asked. Very softly, she said, "He left a big pair of shoes to fill, didn't he?"

Jonel nodded. "But he grew into them."

Sandy was silent a little longer. It still wasn't easy, but gradually she beat down the resistance to the decision she must make—and as the new burden settled onto her, another seemed to lift. "So will we," she said at last. "But someday, Jonel, I'm going to tell them the truth about Greg."

Together, they started through the file. They had a lot to do.

Fourth Interlude

IT HAD ONLY been a decade—actually not quite that, even—but what a decade it was. In the beginning were all the effects of rising to high acceleration, with shaking and tilting that shocked even many who were intellectually prepared for it. When maximum was reached, things stabilized, at least enough to eliminate most of the quakes. Two weeks later Scott finally came home, riding through unending night in a radiation-armored troop transport designed to run steeply downhill for fifteen hundred miles.

He and Alycia were so relieved to be back together that their marriage seemed finally to have become something strong and valuable. Shortly before the end of that phase—still under maximum acceleration—Alycia was again expecting. Though they both approached the event with excruciating apprehension, the birth was surprisingly easy, and their daughter Karen was healthy and (in their thoroughly objective view) incredibly bright and cute. Her subsequent development bore out that initial impression and worked psychological wonders for her parents.

Which made the end, when it came, that much harder to take.

Altogether there were four periods, each approximately a year, of steady high acceleration. Separating them were eight periods of increase or decrease, with all the transition effects of tremors and varying tilt, sometimes to the south and sometimes to the north, but generally increasing and requiring more and more drastic compensations. Humans installed stairways and leveling jacks and gimbaled platforms and eventually converted "walls" to "floors." Kyyra used increasingly devious structure modifications and drive diversions to keep land masses from collapsing southward down slopes become effectively vertical, or even, in very late stages and extreme latitudes, from flying off into space. When and where the effective gravity was strong, mortality increased because of added strains on body systems. When it was weak, progressive deterioration threatened to make people unable to face the return of "normal" gravity. Always, one way or another, there were threats, and sometimes there were measures that could be taken to combat them.

During the years of super-c—including twenty blessed months with horizontal floors and no acceleration—the major threat could have been psychological. People long exposed to skies of utter nothingness often became disturbed. But few people were out then, so few disturbances actually occurred.

Much encouraged by Karen, Alycia and Scott tried again. This time Alycia's due date fell early in the steady super-c cruise phase. But her pregnancy did not go smoothly this time, and early in the final acceleration decrease, the combination of high acceleration and transition quakes precipitated another miscarriage. That one killed her, too, and though Scott seemed to bear it bravely at first, he grew slowly but steadily more bitter and withdrawn thereafter.

The older Turabians' main task—which left them regrettably little time for their own family—was education. Once high acceleration started, the preparations that had dominated the previous twenty years became a thing of the past. Those who had prepared well (and were lucky) survived (though not much more) with relatively little further effort. Those who had not, could do little now to improve their chances. There was again a need for something to occupy people, and it was none too early to begin getting them ready to colonize New Earth.

But nothing was yet known about New Earth—not even its identity or location. So the Turabians sought out people who remembered and could teach any skill that might possibly prove useful—woodcraft, farming, hunting, fishing, mining, metal-working, textile-making—as practiced in all parts of the world and at all levels of technology. Specific techniques, they knew, were not likely to be directly applicable. But knowing them might give people some basis for inventing the new skills they actually needed. That seemed so important that the major efforts of the decade went into recruiting teachers and making their knowledge available via the comnet.

And renewing people's belief that it was all worthwhile. No survival training program could minimize the hazards that would surely be found on a new world—and might well seem temporarily worse than the rigors of flight. It was vital that people realize—especially young people—that beyond the initial obstacles lay the potential for something better than they had ever known.

Only when the Earth and Kyere—Beldan's world—were inside M31, and starting to slow down, did the Kyyra scout ships dart ahead to go house-hunting.

Earth and Kyere braked slowly, relatively; a planet makes a cumbersome and fragile spacecraft. Even with a deceleration bordering on recklessness, they would take some four years and fifty thousand light-years to come to rest. At the beginning, no stars, no visible evidence of the galaxy around them, could be seen. At the end, they would have to halt in a well-chosen place, for there would be no second chance.

So the scout ships went ahead. There were ten of them, at first—small (compared to a planet), refuelable, agile and maneuverable. As the refugee planets began the long process of stopping, the ships plunged on at full speed. Mere weeks later, at the far higher accelerations they could use, all but one of them slowed and dropped back to sub-c and the first starlight they had seen in years.

Humans and Kyyra, back on their lumbering planets, welcomed the news, sent back by the timeless communication "beams" of the Kyyra. And then they waited—for the news they needed was far more specific than the mere fact that stars still existed.

For a year, more or less, the scouts mapped skies containing nothing familiar, identifying, analyzing, cataloging the stars they could see. The ship that had not slowed flew on alone toward the galactic core, to make sure it had not suffered the same fate as the one they had fled. All the others concentrated on the tiny region of spiral arm where they had emerged, learning which stars were nearby and might harbor habitable planets.

And then came the tedious task of checking them out. The ships, dividing the stars among themselves, went for closer looks, approaching each prospect as closely as they must to determine that it did or did not have a planet that might be called habitable. Most did not, though sometimes far too much time was wasted before that was known. And time (as usual) was short.

A handful of stars had planets which could serve. None was perfect. Humans and Kyyra greeted each report with eagerness at first, and ended by hoping the next few weeks would bring something better.

Eventually no more weeks could be spared for waiting and hoping. By then the planets also saw stars again, and it was time to set their final courses. The leaders of men and Kyyra conferred. Decisions were made. Not perfect decisions, but decisions which would have to do.

Now, nine or ten months later, the decisions were long made and irrevocable. There was the star on the screen, and—

Sandy's thoughts were interrupted by noise up at the door, heralding Jonel's return. She studied his face anxiously as he came down, and decided not to mention her talk with Scott until she had heard what he had to say. "Bad news?" she asked as he settled onto the couch.

He nodded. "Afraid so...."

She knew what he was going to say, and what it would mean for her. Dogs that had been sleeping too long were starting to snarl and snap, threatening everything, and she would have to try to calm them. They had first begun to stir at that meeting she had just been thinking about, when the crucial commitment had been made....

The Promised Land

"YOU'RE SURE WE have to decide now?" Jonel's dissatisfaction showed plainly—at least to Sandy—in a slight scowl. "We can't let them keep looking a little longer?"

"I'm afraid not," said Beldan. Seated across the small round conference table from Jonel and Sandy, he looked no more content, but resigned. "There's only a little more than a year left. We'll have to start course corrections very soon to get wherever we're going. You can't do these things suddenly, with a planet. The scouts have exhausted the stars in their original survey zone. They've done a little additional looking, but they haven't found anything really worth checking out, even if they had time. So we must choose one of the planets we know about, and be on our way."

"Hmph." Jonel looked down at the summary sheets before him. Sandy scanned hers too, though they had both been over them so often as to have them practically memorized.

One of the two farthest-reaching decisions in human history,

Sandy reminded herself—a choice among five planets, all described by such meager data that it was hard to decide which was the most desirable (or least objectionable). Time was part of the problem, of course. It was a real tribute to the Kyyra explorers that they had been able to find even this much in such a short time. With the pressure they were under, there could be no hope of more than scratching the surface, of delving into the myriad subtleties that make a planet a world.

But there was more than that. The Kyyra culture was technologically so far removed from raw nature that they had little feel for what was desirable or dangerous in a virgin planet. The basic physiological requirements of both species—gravity, atmosphere, biochemistry—they knew. But the far trickier factors which can shape a civilization were quite unfamiliar to them. Their civilization had been shaped too long ago.

"It's too bad," Jonel said wistfully, "we didn't have humans on the scout ships."

"Perhaps," said Beldañ. "But you know that wasn't practical, and little will be gained by dwelling on it now."

"I know. So we have to pick one of these." He peered somewhat distastefully at the sheets, holding them almost at arm's length to compensate for recent changes in his vision. "Let's see...this one has a pretty high gravity and metal content, leading to a lot of volcanism. A bit too exciting, and the day's a good deal longer than we'd like, but everything's at least marginally within acceptable limits. Except that the atmosphere's pre-polluted with enough sulfur compounds and such to make us doubt long-term safety. Scratch that one."

He flipped to the second sheet. "Everything very nicely within limits—but the local ecology uses all the wrong stereoisomers. We'd be completely dependent on food we brought with us—and we definitely don't want that."

His scowl deepened. He flipped to the third. "Another pretty nice place, in itself. But you didn't look very closely because a neighbor at three light-years is a bad risk for a supernova. We don't want any more of that."

The fourth. "Short day, crazy tilt, hyperactive F3 sun, violent weather, primitive ecosystem. Almost no life on land; no soil to try farming with any plants somebody might have kept alive. We could live there, maybe, but we'd rather not try.

"Which leaves this." He stared at the fifth and final report.

"Not bad. G4 sun, twelve-degree tilt, nice homey atmosphere and gravity, fairly familiar day and year lengths, some native life forms we can eat. Nothing blatantly repulsive about that."

"And yet," Beldan said, "you have reservations about it?"

"That's a fair way to put it. Two things. First, I get the impression—though it's hard to be sure—that it's geologically younger than Earth. Not a lot, but maybe enough to make fossil fuels scarce. Second, its density's a bit low for its size. Together with its sun's spectrum, that suggests metals are scarce too. I can see even more possible ramifications, but those are enough to make me hesitate."

"But are they really so important? Low abundance is inconvenient, but it's not the same as absence. The planet is somewhat larger than Earth. More area to mine may compensate for lower relative abundances."

"Possibly. But it also means more hay per needle."

Beldan frowned. "Perhaps. But we have insurance against such problems. We'll have to take the Earth fairly close for the transfer operation. We can park it more or less permanently as a reserve supply of resources. Zhalāŭ assures me it can be done. We won't be able to go close enough for a truly stable orbit because that would disrupt the tides too much. But we can get a compromise between distance and stability that'll let us tap the Earth for as long as we're likely to want to."

"Yes," Jonel muttered. "And since you have the only operational spaceships, dependence on the Earth means human dependence on the Kyyra."

"May I remind you," Beldan said quietly, "that we are at least equally dependent on you in other ways? We're all in this together, as Henry Clark used to say. It pains me to see you concerned about this. After all we've been through, I would think you'd be convinced of our good will."

Jonel smiled thinly. "Sorry. But after all we've been through, I'd think you'd realize we're a distrustful lot. Maybe we shouldn't be, but we are."

And you, Sandy thought in unspoken aside to Beldan, *will become more and more so, with the Coordinator no longer molding your minds.*

Or maybe you already have. Is it my imagination, or are we all a bit edgy today?

"Actually," said Beldan, "we Kyyra were most concerned

about the presence of large predatory animals. But I don't think that's really a serious objection. It should be no great problem to exterminate them."

Sandy nodded, but with reservations. "Probably. But only if we're driven to. We exterminate only what we must."

Beldan eyed her with a look of slight perplexity. "You sound as if there would be some question about it."

"There would. We're determined to treat this planet better than the last one, and that means working with the ecology more than against it. Now that we've been through the shock of destroying everything we lived with, we want to be very sure we never do anything like that again." She saw the look of growing chagrin on his face, and thought of what she knew of the worlds the Kyyra had lost—from which the last natural life-forms other than Kyyra had long since vanished. A frightening realization dawned. "You sound as if you want to make Clark's World into another Kyere."

He nodded. "As much," he said, "as you want to make it into another Earth."

He took out his music-pipe and began to play. And Sandy felt herself trembling on the brink of the rift that had opened between them. She had never really thought about just how incompatible their goals might be. . . .

"I don't think," Jonel said quietly (though his face mirrored Sandy's concern), "that this is what we have to settle now. Our only problem now is to get down."

With an effort, Sandy dragged her mind back from that imaginary edge. Jonel was right. "We seem agreed," he said, "that this planet is the one. How do we get onto it? What do our people have to do?"

"I'll outline the method," Beldan said with obvious relief, "and give you our most pessimistic estimates of the precautions you should take. Chances are that things won't be that bad. But better too much care than too little—"

Another shock. "Wait a minute," Sandy broke in. "'Estimates,' you say. Haven't you done this before?"

"Not exactly—"

"But you told us—"

"That we had moved planets? Indeed. But not with such haste as we had to move Earth or Kyere, or with the extra indignities we had to inflict on Kyere to search for people like you. And we've never had to quickly evacuate a whole population from a planet that we'd just moved. The methods involve rather delicate manipulation of the last remnants of the exhaustless drive reaction—qualitatively similar to some of the things we've done to hold the planet together during the high-acceleration phases, but even more delicate. We couldn't have done it even a few years ago. But the alternative was to do it with ships, and that's more impractical than strip-mining with teaspoons, especially now. So we had to learn, and we did. Zhalāū's engineers have been working intensively on developing the techniques ever since you joined us. We feel quite sure they're ready to use."

But you've never actually used them, Sandy thought. *So you don't really know.*

She listened patiently, if somewhat apprehensively, through the explanation that followed. It was not very detailed—Beldan promised full details in the near future—but it gave a good general idea of what lay ahead. Half an hour later Beldan rose, smoothed his iridescent (though slightly faded) robes, and took his leave. He moved with peculiarly sinuous grace in the weak gravity produced by what remained of Earth's mass. Actually it was even weaker than it now appeared, for part of the apparent gravity was due to the planet's deceleration. And that changed the effective up-down direction enough that the present sloped "floor" was normally the north wall, and Beldan had to climb a ladder up the usual floor to the door.

"Well," Sandy said when he was gone, "it looks like we have our work cut out for us."

Jonel nodded. "Yes. And in our spare time, we'll have to get out as much information as we can on the new planet."

"Which isn't likely to be much, from what Beldan says."

"Probably just as well. We're not going to have time for much except getting ready to land." He thought for a moment and added, "And that's going to involve a lot more than logistics and hardware."

"Like Moses?"

Jonel nodded solemnly. "He'll be getting ready, too."

He had called himself Moses for so long he had almost forgotten his given name. And he had been in so many unfamiliar little rooms like this that they all came to look alike. The constant moving about had always been wearying, and it had been even harder during the high-acceleration phases that had occupied most of the last several years. With much previously available transportation now unusable, he was more dependent than ever on wangling government jobs that gave mobility and opportunity. It had been necessary, to keep the Movement and himself in the public awareness—but woefully inefficient. To avoid suspicion, he had to actually work at the jobs he held, and that sapped both time and energy in ways not directly contributing to the Cause.

Now, maybe, it would all pay off.

He finished checking the room for bugs—something he never failed to do personally—and eased himself into an old wooden armchair with loose joints and peeling paint. He cast a perfunctory glance at the chunky, red-haired young man sitting among the bare recycling pipes, then clasped his hands in front of him and closed his eyes. "So. You have news?"

"Yes," said Griffith, whose legal name was no more Griffith than Moses' was Moses. "You know they've announced the choice of a target planet. I have some details they haven't made public yet. If they're ready to get specific, we'll want to, too. This is it, Moses. The home stretch."

"M-m-m." Moses opened his eyes and leaned forward to take the scrap of paper Griffith held out. He looked at the heading and smiled. "Clark's World, eh? So they're naming it after old Caesar Clark. Hardly surprising. Well, we can use that. But carefully, Griffith, carefully. Such people tend to get deified, once they're safely dead. The living have to tread cautiously when they try to trample a dead god." He skimmed over the rest of the sheet and passed it back to Griffith. "What else?"

"The main thing at this point is propaganda. We've been steady but low-key since we worked back up to the surface after high acceleration started. Now it's time to become high-powered and hard-hitting. The name angle is a good starting point. Beyond that . . . we can use details on the new planet to stress the most unpleasant features of going there. Dust off all that wonderful old imagery of yours about sunburn and water falling out of the sky when you have no roof over your head—"

"No." Moses shook his head wearily. *Was I like that at his age?* he wondered. *Maybe so. But I've learned. . . .* "You're not thinking," he told Griffith. "That was appropriate a decade ago, when we were trying to cure people of wanting to reach a new

205

world. It's not appropriate now; it's too late. We're going to reach it now, ready or not, and Earth is ruined as a permanent residence. There's no point in making people feel miserable about the inevitable. We gain nothing by whipping up emotion unless it serves our higher goals." He paused thoughtfully. "Besides, they know about those things. The Turabians' colonist education program has given a fair picture of what they can expect, even if it has had a positive bias."

"Sorry," said Griffith. "I was only thinking—"

"You weren't thinking," Moses repeated. "I'm sorry if that seems harsh, but that's the way I see it. Before you lay out a plan of action, Griffith, you have to have clearly in mind what you're trying to achieve. You do know what we're trying to achieve?"

"Of course."

"It's to help people," Moses said quietly, "to get through the transition as painlessly as possible. And to give them back their freedom and dignity. To make sure we get rid of the dictatorship we've been saddled with since this all began."

Griffith allowed himself a slightly teasing smile. "It couldn't be that you have any dictatorial ambitions yourself?"

"Don't ever say anything like that again. Ever." But as Moses glowered, he thought, *It would be distressingly easy, if things go right. I've become a folk hero, of sorts—just by managing to stay uncaught and keep giving speeches for this many years. They see me as a sort of Robin Hood, or something. A droll contrast to the way I see myself. Forty . . . bald . . . I'd be getting a paunch, if I got enough food to support one.*

But in politics, it's the popular image that counts. I could use it, if I wanted to.

Griffith, startled by his reaction, muttered, "Sorry. But you are planning to take over the government—"

"Temporarily. Only temporarily. Only long enough to make sure we get rid of the house that Clark built."

Griffith grew bolder. "But if that's all you want, why take over? Why not just smash the existing government and let grow what will?"

"Because I'm not just a nihilist. If I smash what exists, I have a responsibility to put something better in its place. Things are going to be rough down there, Griffith. We're going to need all the cooperation and leadership we can get."

"And you're it."

"Yes." Moses frowned, reappraising his sometimes shaky confidence in Griffith. "The alternatives are to leave things headless, or take a chance on somebody else taking over. I know I can trust myself. I don't know about anybody else." *And would any of it be for my own profit? Of course. I hope to enjoy it while it lasts. And I might draw a little more of what the new world has to offer than most people.*

But I'll earn my keep.

He tossed his head impatiently. "We're getting sidetracked. We're here to plan actions. O.K. We step up the publicity, first of all. Not to make people feel negative toward the planet, but positive toward us, the liberators. 'With the Turabians all the way down, and not a step farther.' That sort of thing."

Griffith nodded. "'They take us down, then we take them down.' 'The emergency stops at the surface.'"

"Not bad. Just don't underestimate the popularity the Turabians still have. O.K. Work out the details and check with me. Meanwhile, it's none too early to start thinking about the takeover itself. What do we know about their plans for moving down?"

"Very little, yet. But we'll be watching."

"Good. The sooner we know what they're doing, the sooner we can plan how to use it."

Beldan had another Kyyra with him when he came down the Turabians' ladder for the third briefing session. The new one, to judge by the smoothness and clear bronze hue of his skin, was much younger than Beldan—quite a young man, by Kyyra standards, though in actual years quite possibly at least as old as Jonel or Sandy. He waited awkwardly when he reached the bottom of the ladder; like most Kyyra, he made no attempt to affect human facial expressions. Beldan gestured at him. "May I introduce," he said with a faint frostiness painful to Sandy, "your pilot, Qabrim."

"I'm pleased to meet you and glad to be of service," Qabrim said in English almost as good as Beldan's. He looked at Sandy. "You and I have already met, Mrs. Turabian. Do you remember when you visited our convoy ship that brought Beldan to Earth, shortly before Henry Clark approved the move? I was one of the young rowdies at the next table in the gathering hall."

"Oh, yes." Sandy smiled with instant recognition, not of

Qabrim as an individual, but as part of a scene etched indelibly in her memory. "The musical pun."

To her surprise, he ventured an approximation of a human smile. "Yes. I hope Beldan did not try to translate for you."

Sandy laughed. "No."

"Qabrim came two days ago," Beldan said. "The pilot station in Titusville is complete, and the crews are making provision for moving your government headquarters there when the time comes."

"With all due attention to secrecy, I trust," said Jonel. "I can't overemphasize how important that is. Moses almost stopped us from going to high acceleration, and he's been a thorn in our side ever since—a very slippery thorn. We're sure he's going to try a coup no later than planetfall. Everything we do, we're going to have to do with as little publicity as possible."

"Of course."

Jonel turned back to Qabrim. "Two days. Have you started your schooling yet?"

"Barely."

"Let us know how it goes. We're not really satisfied with that program, but we'll do what we can to make it as helpful as possible." The Kyyra would be even more dependent than humans on training for survival on Clark's World—yet their location, on Kyere and distant convoy ships, had made it impractical to send them nearly as much as humans had received. Their main hope was that the pilots they sent to Earth now could absorb enough in the year before planetfall to return to Kyyra settlements as teachers, aided by human volunteers. Not satisfactory, but—like so many things—it would have to do.

"There's only one of you," Sandy observed. "Did you come alone?"

Qabrim nodded.

Jonel looked sharply at Beldan. "No copilot?"

"There were not enough. We sent all we could."

"But ..." Jonel frowned. "Flying a city must be a tricky business, and there are a lot of lives at stake."

"Very true," Beldan agreed. "But there are a lot of cities, too. We kept the number as low as we could; some are actually bulkier than we'd like. You're lucky we were able to give you even one pilot for each."

"I understand that. The safety element still bothers me." It bothered Sandy, too. The thought of a slab containing an entire city being severed from the Earth and flown down to Clark's World was unnerving enough without its being in a single irreplaceable pair of hands. Jonel pondered it for quite a while, then asked Beldan, "Could humans learn to do it?"

Beldan, with a glance, referred the question to Qabrim. The younger Kyyra said, "It's hard to say. Offhand, I see no reason why not, anyway for a human with prior experience with spacecraft or possibly large aircraft." His face changed expression—in an unreadable way, but Sandy suspected he would have frowned, had he known how. "Except that every city is different, and we all had practice on simulators which would not be available to you. I wouldn't want anyone without simulator experience to act as sole pilot, except as an extreme last resort. But enough is automatic that such a person might learn to do a good job with a limited group of controls."

Jonel looked dubious. "Would that actually be good for anything?"

"It could. If the pilot were partially disabled, or the job unexpectedly became too big for him. Separation, for instance."

"Separation?"

"If parts of the city should become separated in flight, additional actions would become necessary to land them separately." He seemed to recognize both humans' alarm and added, "We have provisions for doing it; they just put excessive demands on one pilot. It's most unlikely, anyway. It would take a large external force applied too suddenly for the structure stabilization to respond to. A large meteorite, for example, shortly before landing, when the drive reaction is almost dead and hard to control."

Very unlikely, Sandy agreed. *Still, the more I hear about this operation, the less confident I feel.*

"So an assistant would be helpful," Jonel said, "just in case. O.K.—it's better than nothing. Qabrim, I'll learn whatever you can teach me about handling Titusville."

Qabrim looked at Beldan. "Objections?"

Beldan shook his head. "No. I only wonder about your doing it personally, Jonel. You two already have a staggering workload."

"But nobody else in the Titusville zone has my experience. And if the pilot station is going to double as government headquarters, I don't want any unnecessary outsiders anywhere near it. I'll find the time."

"There aren't enough experienced pilots to assign to all the cities," Sandy pointed out. "Could non-pilots help?"

"Probably," said Qabrim. "But in a more limited way."

"Then I'll try to learn as a backup for Jonel. Titusville's going to be especially crucial. And we'll recruit copilot trainees for all the towns. Pilots when possible, others when necessary."

Beldan looked faintly disturbed. "I hope this isn't going to occupy too much of our pilots' time. We're depending on them for other things."

"You're also depending on getting them down in one piece. It'll add a load on all of us; we'll just have to see that it doesn't get too big. But we'd better do it."

Jonel nodded. "And we'd better choose the candidates carefully. Every one's a security risk—exactly where secrecy is most essential."

"Secrecy?" Moses smiled with mildly cynical amusement. "We'll have to see what we can do about that." Seated in a rickety wicker chaise in yet another room he had never seen before and would never see again, he scanned Griffith's latest report. "Flying cities, eh? Well, why not, after what they've already done with flying planets? With Kyyra pilots in secret locations. Naturally." He finished reading, then glanced quickly over the whole thing again. "Very good, Griffith. We'll need lots more details, of course, but this gives us a definite starting point. I already see the general outline of how we'll proceed."

"You should spend some time with the other sheets, too," Griffith suggested. "They've issued some pretty harsh warnings about opportunists trying to use the confusion of landing to seize power, even locally. And they're prepared to back them up."

"Well, of course. Our agitation's beginning to get to them. Naturally they'll issue warnings."

"But we'll have to be careful. These warnings have teeth, Moses. They've developed a pretty potent arsenal, and ways of getting it where it's needed. Even after we're down."

"Of course," Moses repeated imperturbably. "That's what we're going to use. Look, Griffith—it wouldn't be easy to build up the machinery to run that whole planet ourselves; I'm not sure it would even be possible. It's been hard enough just to build an underground network of the magnitude we have. But the government already has administrative machinery, and ways to keep it running after we're down. So what do we have to do?"

"Take over what they have."

"Exactly. We can expect to seize each individual city. And if I personally take the part that holds the reins for the whole works—that's all we need."

"It sounds good," Griffith admitted, but with a hint of doubt. "They say there'll be five thousand cities, Moses. That's a lot of targets, and a lot of risk."

"And we have a lot of contacts. Very good contacts. We'll manage."

"Hm-m-m." Griffith looked away. "I'm not questioning you, Moses. But have you ever wondered whether this is all really necessary? The Turabians claim that one of their first priorities after we're down is a smooth and fast transition back to self-rule. Suppose—just suppose—they actually mean it."

Moses eyed him narrowly. "Are you willing to take a chance on that?"

For a moment Griffith looked as if he would capitulate as usual. But then he thrust his jaw slightly forward and said quietly, "I'm not sure, Moses. I've been thinking about it, and I'm just not sure. The risk isn't just to us. It's to all the people we say we're doing this for. The kind of takeover we're talking about is going to mean bloodshed and extra danger. If there's another way, wouldn't that be preferable?"

Moses pressed his lips together impatiently. "You think there is another way?"

"I don't say there is. I say we should make very sure there isn't. The Turabians have spelled out a pretty specific plan for easing themselves out of power—"

"And you think we dare believe them?"

"We can negotiate safeguards to make sure—"

"Negotiate? Come on, Griffith. We can't even show our faces."

"Not us, directly. Citizens' groups under our influence."

Moses shook his head vigorously. "Dangerous thinking, Griffith. You've got to understand what we're up against. This is the first real worldwide dictatorship we've had; our goal is to make sure it's the last. No matter how benevolent it may seem, it's too dangerous to tolerate any longer than necessary. Trying to negotiate with it—even if it would admit to having time to talk—is out of the question. It's so firmly entrenched that its word is meaningless. It can promise anything—and then do whatever it wants. The only way to be sure we get rid of it is to get rid of it—by force. I don't like it either, but there's no alternative." He paused and looked darkly at Griffith. "So how do I count you? Help or hindrance? Friend or foe?"

Griffith didn't answer immediately. But after a few seconds he said, "I'm with you all the way, Moses."

"That's better." Moses, though still not quite satisfied, returned his attention to the report. "This thing's much too sketchy. The first thing we're going to need is details—like exact locations of pilot stations and government headquarters." He snorted. "Confounded government secrecy! Last time we were on the verge of a coup, we had to track down the control stations for the planet's drive. Now it's pilot stations for cities—and this doesn't even specify which cities they're using." He looked at Griffith with sudden fierce determination. "But we'll find out, won't we? We have ten months."

He laid the sheet down, leaned back, and looked up at the drab ceiling. "Meanwhile . . . we're going to need all the popular support we can get. We have a loyal following, but it's too small and the campaign we've been waging is too mild. The public at large is too enamored of Clark's memory and the Turabians themselves to help us throw them out. We need something really potent to turn public sentiment our way. Do you have any ideas, Griffith?"

"Nothing I haven't already mentioned."

"I do," said Moses. "You know, even before she came to power, Sandy Turabian was widely known as the closest of all humans to the Kyyra. Wouldn't it be interesting if something turned up to provoke a sudden wave of anti-Kyyra feeling?" He chuckled dryly. "Of course, there's a rumor that things aren't all peaches and cream between them right now, but that doesn't have to interfere. Maybe we can even use it, if there's anything to it."

Griffith's eyebrows rose and fell. "Do you think it's wise to antagonize the Kyyra before we're down? We are dependent on them—"

"And they on us." The shadow of a thought darted across

Moses' mind, but he couldn't quite catch it for a close look. "I didn't say we should antagonize them, Griffith—though I didn't say we shouldn't, either. We're looking for strong medicine." He dismissed Griffith's discomfiture with a light laugh. "Just investigate, Griffith; that's all I ask—for now. You know, there's always been some feeling against the Kyyra. I imagine there was quite a burst of it back near the beginning, when somebody found out that Henry Clark had singlehandedly made a deal with them.

"Who knows what else we may find?"

Education remained an important task of the Turabian administration into the final year, but it changed character—and, to a growing extent, it was crowded aside by other things. With New Earth—Clark's World—finally chosen and being explored, the half-blind general survival training could be supplemented by some specifics. One comnet channel carried a continuous picture, so people could watch their new sun brighten and grow with the passing weeks. But there were too few hard facts. The eight remaining scout ships, charged with finding several thousand usable landing sites within a year, had little time for close study of the places they visited. So the reports they sent back were infrequent and sketchy.

And the occupants of Earth and Kyere had little time for study—for this last year, as the planets veered slightly on their homing "beams," must be given largely to logistics. The human survivors, in particular, were too scattered. All, before the year was out, would have to be gathered into the major population centers designated for transport by the Kyyra. That was no small task. There were nowhere near enough transport facilities to move everybody at once. Priorities were too often too easy to decide: in many areas the extreme tilt and lack of suitably modified transports made it impossible to start relocating until the acceleration had decreased, and the decrease didn't begin until halfway through the year. People who had to wait worried that their turn would never come. Those whose turns came early suffered long exposure to crowding conditions even worse than they were used to—with all the tensions and frictions that implied.

The tensions and frictions were not alleviated by Moses' ever more insistent propaganda. Counteracting that—and trying to end it—consumed a growing amount of the Turabians' time and patience. They understood Moses' distrust of the existing government and its avowed intention to do away with itself; the problem had plagued Henry Clark from the very beginning. But they couldn't simply let Moses have his way, for he gave every indication of being that most dangerous animal, a Man with a Mission—who had not yet consciously realized how attracted he was to personal power. Yet the prospect of widespread violence and destruction to block him seemed cruelly unnecessary—especially when they knew he could not win as much as he hoped. Even as they publicly fought his propaganda with their own, privately they tried desperately to talk to him, to convince him there were other ways.

But every effort they made, he rejected out of hand.

It was conceivable that Moses might have nothing to do with the most ominous element of the growing unrest. But it wasn't likely. . . .

Three months to go.

Aldo Wisniewski, World Director of Education, looked as much like a football coach as anybody could under today's conditions. Big and burly, with black hair tipped with silver, he sat with muscular hands folded on a wooden desk that was long overdue for a paint job. The office looked crazily tilted with respect to him and the desk. Even had it had a north wall to serve as a floor, it would have appeared fairly steep now, with the acceleration well on its way toward zero. But this room had never faced squarely north, and so it seemed to lean sideways as well.

The faded pictures of sunsets and seascapes on the "wall" behind Wisniewski did not lean, Jonel noticed; the Director must adjust their suspensions at least every day. Normally Jonel would not have been here to notice such things; these days were even more hectic than usual, and he preferred to keep all unnecessary traffic out of the tunnels while the acceleration was changing. But this matter was touchy, so he had come anyway, leaving Sandy to handle anything that came up at headquarters.

"What I really want to know," he asked, tiring of bush-beating, "is whether you've seen any direct evidence of agitation about this within the educational system."

Wisniewski laughed loudly, but just a bit self-consciously.

"Well, now, that's sort of hard to say. Campus riots pretty much went out with campuses." He spoke with enough Texas drawl to remind Jonel of the existence of different regions and make him wonder how much life had diverged in them during the decades of isolation.

But he wasn't answering the question. "I was thinking," Jonel said, "more of incendiary material worked into your curricula."

"Oh." Wisniewski looked mildly startled. "None that I've recognized, Mr. Turabian. Certainly none that I've approved or encouraged. Of course, I haven't been able to screen every word of every instructor, but we have tried to be careful and reasonably thorough."

"I see." Jonel watched Wisniewski's face carefully as he considered where to go next.

The wait and the implicit almost-accusation made Wisniewski uneasy. "I can tell you this," he said to fill the void. "I don't think you have to look for deliberate agitators to explain this. Education makes people inquisitive, if it's any good, and most of the population has been primarily students for years. You get that many people doing that much thinking and talking about the trip, and some of them are sure to start wondering how it all started. We've always had questions and speculations about it— the same kind of youthful iconoclasm that's always led some students to think their teachers are old fogeys who don't know the score. They've just gotten a little noisier lately."

"It would be an understatement to call that an understatement. These rumors are so rampant that a lot of people are ready to act on them whether they know or not. Dangerously many people, and it's all happened surprisingly fast. Isn't that true, Mr. Wisniewski?"

"Oh, yes. The question is very hot, all right."

Jonel looked pointedly at him. "Rumors don't usually do that well unless they're encouraged."

"Well, I don't know about that." Wisniewski looked thoughtful. The pictures behind him rattled and flapped with a slight tremor, but neither man paid any attention. They were more than used to such things. "I suppose I agree, but does the encouragement have to be as deliberate and purposeful as you seem to think? Couldn't it just be the pressure that builds up when you herd people into tight quarters and let them think about how their whole lives are going to be changed in one swell foop a few weeks from now? It's going to be just like the birth trauma all over again, Mr. Turabian. Except they know it's coming."

"My wife," said Jonel, "compares it to waiting for Christmas morning when she was a little girl."

"But not everybody can see it that way. Especially people who've spent their whole lives on the trip."

"Yeah." Jonel understood that only too well. The reminder could open a whole hornets' nest of memories for either him or Sandy. But he refused to let it.

"Maybe," said Wisniewski, "we should be flattered that our teaching efforts have made so many people start thinking."

"Maybe. But they shouldn't be wasting it on that. Not now." Jonel stood up. "Thanks for your time, Mr. Wisniewski. We may want your help in trying to calm them down. I'll let you know." He started along one of the floor ridges to the door, which here opened "down."

"I must confess," Wisniewski remarked as Jonel steadied himself and opened the door, "I've often wondered myself just what did make our galaxy explode. We teach all the popular scientific theories, once over lightly, but they're all so . . . theoretical." He smiled. "You don't suppose there's any truth in these rumors, do you, Mr. Turabian?"

"Even if I knew," Jonel said flatly as he started down the steep stairs to the corridor, "I wouldn't comment just now."

That was the news Jonel brought back on the day Scott's gloomy mood started Sandy reminiscing. "Wisniewski wasn't very helpful," he said, "as far as fixing blame is concerned. But he agrees that the damage is done, and as bad as we thought—though of course he has no idea just how bad that is."

She nodded. "But you think I should tell everybody?"

"I think you'd better."

"I was afraid of that." *But not surprised*, she thought. She considered silently for a few seconds, adjusting her frame of mind to the task. Then she stood up. "I'd better talk to Beldan first."

Over thirty years ago, when it had become clear that his relationship with Earth was to be a permanent one, Beldan had arranged to have a few personal things sent down from the starship that had brought him. Not many—just enough small samples of their exquisite swirled metalwork to make him feel a little more at home. To a human visitor they made his quarters seem slightly alien. To Beldan, the pervasive reminders of man in such basic things as the shape of the room must have made it even more so.

He was visibly apprehensive when he saw Sandy at the door; he knew the Turabians' feelings about unnecessary personal visits. He welcomed her almost as graciously as ever—though with an underlying chill that had been there since the day they chose Clark's World, and still made Sandy ache. But as soon as he had shown her to a big gimbaled chair, he asked quietly, "Is something wrong?"

She nodded slowly. "I'm afraid so. Beldan . . . I'm going to have to tell them how the core explosion started."

His eyes jerked violently. "The truth? That our ancestors did it?"

"I'm afraid so."

He took out his music-pipe and for half a minute played something quietly frenzied. When he stopped, he said, "I don't understand. Why should that be necessary after all these years? Only four humans have ever known, and two of them are dead. Why can't it remain your secret?" He played a little more, then broke off as if startled by a sudden realization. "Are you doing this because of the difference in our goals for the new planet? I've heard of humans doing things for such reasons, but I never thought you—"

"No," she said quickly, "it's nothing like that. Please forget that, Beldan; I'm trying very hard. That's something we'll have to work out after we're down. Worrying about it now can't accomplish anything."

He nodded very slightly—and stiffly—but said nothing.

"I have to tell them," Sandy said, "because they're dangerously close to figuring it out for themselves. People have been asking questions about how it started, and some of them have guessed the right answer and started blabbing it around on the comnet. The questions are getting more and more pointed, and they're pointed at us."

"Lie," said Beldan.

Sandy winced—not so much at the suggestion itself, as at the realization that Beldan had become capable of making it. When they had all been guided by their Coordinator, no Kyyra could understand—much less practice—the deceit or violence long familiar to man. But the Coordinator was dead, and the need to deal constantly with humans was forcing its heirs to learn new ways. *We seem*, she thought, *to be learning each other's worst traits.*

"We've tried," she said. "I don't think we dare try any more. They're too close to knowing, and we're pretty sure the process is being helped by Moses' professional agitators. We suspect they started it, in fact—it may have just been a lucky guess at first, but it's gone far beyond that now. We've tried some censorship—actually caught a couple of speakers—but that just provokes demands for explanations and makes the original question still hotter. They're in an ugly mood. They're demanding to know whether Kyyra did cause the explosion, and we have the choice of trying to weave an ever more intricate web of lies, or finding the best way to tell them the truth before they're so sure we have to admit it. If that happens, it'll demolish our credibility, and in the first few years we're going to need all the cooperation we can muster."

"But they have not yet established the truth on their own," Beldan said. "They might not—"

Sandy shook her head vigorously. "Wishful thinking, Beldan. You've learned a lot about people, but still not enough. In the first place, the chances of getting away with it are almost nil. And it doesn't really matter whether they know it's true. If enough of them believe it, the effect will be the same. Bad. For you."

"You mean they'll want to refuse to help us with colonization, and you know how badly we need that help. It's been a *long* time since Kyyra have tried to live on an undeveloped planet." He piped through a brief pause. "But if you actually tell them, that will guarantee that that happens."

"No. My hope is that it will soften the blow. It's going to happen regardless, Beldan. That's so certain you can consider it assured. It's that bad. But if I talk to them before they have us backed into a corner and their fangs sharpened, I can appeal to their better nature. I can emphasize that the explosion was an accident and no living Kyyra had any part in it. I can make it very clear that we're fully committed to helping you in return for what you've done for us. If I do it now, some of them will listen and I can make them understand. It won't stop all the adverse reaction, but it'll help. If I don't do it—you'll get no sympathy. They'll lynch anybody who tries to help you, and they might not even wait till we're down."

For a long while Beldan just played or stared blankly into space. Then he said, without looking at Sandy, "I have no alternatives to suggest, so I will trust your judgment. Needless to say, though, I don't like it."

His face showed how inadequately that expressed his feeling, and that intensified Sandy's ache. *And so the rift widens*, she thought. *Just when we need each other most.*

Like Henry Clark before her, Sandy had developed a good feel for what to say to the public, how to say it, and what reactions to expect. Her "confession" and plea for understanding on behalf of the Kyyra brought few surprises. With the fact confirmed, there was a predictably savage outcry against giving them any help after they were down. But it was not as savage as it would have become had things been allowed to continue on their own. And it was balanced, to some degree, by more compassionate voices.

Beldan was less pleased. He saw only that there was now overt agitation against the Kyyra, and that scared him—both because he still couldn't quite understand it, and because it might lead to action. He withdrew even more into himself, talking less to the Turabians and spending more time with his pipe when he had to talk to them. Sandy often wondered uncomfortably what he was thinking but not saying.

In the remaining weeks, the star on the special comnet channel, already far brighter than its background, grew steadily more brilliant, became a visible disk, and grew into something that actually looked like a sun. Eventually it was too big and bright to look at, and the view shifted to Clark's World itself, first just a pinpoint of light, but growing brighter and brighter and then becoming a partial disk.

With it grew Sandy's feeling of Christmas Eve anticipation—but marred by the gathering doubts. The controversy over help for the Kyyra grew steadily hotter; Beldan grew steadily more distant. Sandy could imagine Moses—whatever he looked like—sitting back in some room somewhere, coolly sizing up the opinion trends and calculating how to use them.

And then flitting quickly to another such room, again evading capture and thus adding another notch to his popular glamor.

But neither she nor Jonel had much time to dwell on that, for there were too many practical problems still to be solved. As the time drew near, too many people still remained outside the flight cities, beset by growing panic that they wouldn't be moved in time. That in turn helped Moses undermine trust for the Turabians. Sandy did all she could to combat the panic and distrust and Moses' propaganda; Jonel worked with Zhalãü to make sure everybody was moved and the cities ready to go; Security and Intelligence tried with partial success to anticipate Moses' moves and plan countermoves.

And sometimes Sandy found a few seconds to remember just how frighteningly tricky that whole untried landing operation sounded.

With only days remaining, the battered remains of Earth slid into parking orbit around Clark's World. (There wasn't enough left of Kyere to bother; its remains were simply broken into small pieces, some of which its occupants would ride down while the others were abandoned in space.) Sandy somehow found five minutes to stare at the blue and white globe on the special comnet channel, while Jonel listened and talked on an extra set they'd brought in.

It looks a lot like Earth, she thought, *from way out here.*

And from right down on it? Who knows? We know so little about it, really. And we're going to live there from now on. All billion of us.

Almost a billion, anyway—but just "billion" sounds better. A far, sad cry from what we started with.

But it's a far cry from what we'd be down to if we hadn't done it, too.

For a moment she thought of the things already living there. She didn't know what any of them looked like, but she felt a certain sadness for them on the eve of their invasion. For some, she knew, it had already begun. Even at the compromise distance chosen for the parking orbit, Earth would already be increasing and complicating the tides below. It was all too easy to imagine millions of shore organisms drowning in salt water as the seas swept higher than ever before, while marine forms baked and shriveled in the sun below what a month ago had been low-water line.

Her thoughts were jolted away from that by the words that caught her ear from Jonel's transceiver. The voice was unmistakable, and the oratory of unprecedented bluntness. "Your rulers," Moses boomed, "have promised you that we will continue to pour human resources into helping the very aliens who destroyed our galaxy and made all this necessary. But I promise you that we will not. The hour is almost at hand when we, the people's liberators, will take our destinies back from the tyrants and into our own hands. And then, you may be sure, you will get all your due, and they will get theirs—which is nothing."

Though voices of reason could still be found on the comnet, the dominant impression during the next hour was one of bloodthirsty frenzy as caged humans rallied vocally around Moses. Before the hour was out, Beldan was at the Turabians' door, his face blazing with a kind of anger Sandy had never before seen there.

The floor was again the floor, and for all practical purposes horizontal. So Beldan walked in, with a gait that looked as if it wanted to be an enraged stomp, though the feeble gravity turned it into a dreamlike half-float once reserved for men on the moon. "You've heard this threat of Moses'?" he demanded, his voice reverting to the odd leaps of pitch he had laboriously trained away over the years.

"Yes," said Sandy.

"And the reactions to it?"

"Yes."

Beldan glared. "What do you intend to do about it?"

"The same things we've been doing," Sandy said tightly. "We've tried repeatedly to talk to Moses; he's pointedly ignored us. You know about the Security and Intelligence efforts against the conspirators, the defense plans to hold them off—"

"What assurance do I have that any of that will succeed?"

"None," Sandy said bitterly. "No more than we do. You have only the knowledge that we're as anxious as you to stop them, and we've done everything we can. But we're not without limitations. We may fail."

"And if that happens—how much chance will we have here?" Beldan started to say something else, but broke off and lifted his pipe to his mouth. For a minute or more he played a long, winding tune that seemed to wander here and there and find nowhere satisfying to go. When he finally stopped playing and spoke, his voice was low and his expression somber. "Many years ago, when you told Henry Clark why we had offered to move the Earth, I told you our offer was good whether you helped us or not. Now that the time has come, I begin to understand that things have changed. Of course, with the Coordinator gone, I suppose I see things differently." Abruptly, he thrust his pipe into its hidden pocket, straightened up, and stared down hard at Sandy. "Perhaps," he said in an altered voice, "your efforts to deal with Moses would be surer of success if you had a stronger incentive to succeed. Perhaps I should remind you that we have things you may need even after we're down. Only we have the ships which will provide easy transport between colony sites. Only we know how to make the converters which enable humans or Kyyra to eat food containing substances they normally find toxic."

"I know that," said Sandy. "I've tried to make people understand—"

"I might also point out that we outnumber you." His eyes narrowed to slits as he said it—a human gesture Sandy had never before seen him use. She shivered. *So now you're threatening us*, she thought, astonished. That, too, would have been unthinkable when he first came to Earth. The Kyyra had not yet lost enough of their old orientation to deal successfully with man on his own terms—they had lost the Coordinator too late and had too little chance to practice—but the time would come.

If they got through the present crisis.

"I understand all that," she said in a voice as cool and level as she could muster. "Jonel and I are as afraid of what can happen as you are. But we can't promise you anything. We're doing all we can."

Beldan looked away, but from the side she could see his eyes jerk back and quiver in their sockets. After a lengthy silence, he said, very low, "We also have the pilots." He turned back to stare at her, his gaze suddenly steady and harsh. "Suppose we don't take you down. Suppose we just keep orbiting."

Sandy made her answering gaze as steady as his. "What good would that do? We'd all just die here in space, knowing we threw everything away for a future we could get this close to and still never reach because we were too stubborn."

"We will sacrifice ourselves if necessary," Beldan said. "But that's not the idea, of course. The idea is to broadcast the threat in the hope that it will force Moses to back off, or at least deal reasonably with us."

Sandy shook her head. "Won't work. We're already committed to you, and we have every intention of staying in power long enough to turn things over to people who'll treat you fairly. There's a good chance Moses won't even try his coup until we're down, so any promise he makes now is meaningless. No, Beldan, we have one problem now. Get down. Everything else we work out however we can—afterward."

Beldan stared silently for a while, then turned away. "I guess it will have to do," he murmured. "For now."

He left.

Sandy turned to Jonel with a sigh. "So . . . aside from that, how do we stand? Are we going to get most of them moved in time?"

"We'll get them all," said Jonel. "But it'll be tight."

Sandy nodded. "And the local governments into new, secret quarters?"

"Most of them are already moving."

"With good defenses on both those and the pilot stations?"

"As good as we can manage. We'll soon know if that's good enough."

Sandy was silent, thinking over one of the last things she had said to Beldan. "How soon? What do you think, Jonel—are they going to strike before, during, or after?"

"I wish I knew. Not before; I feel pretty sure of that. There's nothing in it for them. But beyond that . . . I can think of two ways they might figure it. One is that they don't dare act during the descent for fear of jeopardizing the flight itself."

"And the other?"

"That it's the best of all times—because we wouldn't dare strike back, for the same reason."

Sandy and Jonel, with Scott and eight-year-old Karen, were the last to move. The last couple of days brought the hectic preparations to a nerve-wracking climax, and then—with an odd feeling of letdown despite the sinister undercurrents that remained—it was time.

Sandy cast one last glance around the room, ironically reminded of a person leaving home on vacation, back when such things were possible. She laughed nervously. "Are we forgetting anything?"

"I don't think so." Jonel smiled and touched her hand. "Let's go."

We're leaving so much, she thought. But she turned out the light—as if it mattered—and pulled the door shut. Scott walked silently beside them, his lean face full of uncertainty, through the short branch tunnel toward their waiting car. Karen bounded ahead of them—footsteps and chatter echoing off the walls, strawberry blond hair flinging the dim yellow light back in transient sparks—full of the eagerness Sandy kept trying to convince herself she still felt. She thought ruefully of how little time she and Jonel had had to spend with their granddaughter, and was grateful that Karen had so far kept as much zest for life as she had. *She'll take to a new world better than most of her elders*, Sandy thought, *if they'll give her a chance.*

And therein lies such hope as we have.

Jonel opened the door of the tunnel bug and let Karen climb into the back seat, followed by Scott. He and Sandy took the front. It was tight; even with the things of state already sent ahead, personal items that wouldn't fit in the trunk spilled over into the passenger compartment. Jonel tilted the joystick and with a quiet hum the car slid away from the platform and into the Titusville tunnel.

I hope we don't meet anybody, Sandy thought as they sped through the deserted tunnel, occasionally passing a terminal where a dozen public cars sat silent and empty. At every turn she half feared that the headlight, boring through the blackness and ricocheting off walls, would spot a pedestrian or another moving bug. Then the car would act automatically on the warning that anyone in the tunnels today would be shot on sight—and the victim might well be innocent and unsuspecting. She didn't think she could stand that. She certainly didn't want Karen to see it.

She felt deep relief when Jonel's dizzying succession of sharp turns past flashing junction signs brought them into Titusville. They veered into an unmarked side tunnel, turned twice more, and stopped by a blank door.

"Everybody out," said Jonel. "Briskly."

• • •

The room they filed into, through a short vestibule, was of fair size, but none too large to be shared for an extended period by four humans and two Kyyra. It was familiar to Sandy, but not familiar enough. She hadn't made it over for copilot training nearly as often as she had intended. But Jonel had done better, and with any luck even that would prove to have been unnecessary.

Thick green drapes formed the left wall, broken at two points by the ends of thin metal partitions. Much of the right wall was devoted to a big, curved console jammed with tiny controls and indicators, all labeled with Kyyra symbols—except one small English group at the right end. A screen near the middle showed Clark's World. Qabrim sat in a massive and elaborate swivel chair at the center of the console; another, similar but smaller, stood empty next to his. Beldan stood looking over Qabrim's shoulder at something on the panel. They were conversing in their own language, but broke off when the humans came in.

There were greetings—painfully stiff and formal—and introductions, since Qabrim did not know Scott and Karen. Those things taken care of, Beldan came right to the point. "We're all here. Is there any reason to delay longer?"

Jonel shook his head. "I can't think of any."

Beldan spoke a few musical syllables to Qabrim. Qabrim replied tersely, then turned his whole attention to the console and touched things. Beldan took his pipe out of his robe and began playing meditatively. *Their tunes have changed,* Sandy observed. *Is it just styles changing with time, or something deeper that came with the loss of the Coordinator? After all these years, they're still alien, in a lot of ways.*

Other sounds died out, leaving Beldan's haunting melody alone. Even Karen was quiet, for once, intently watching Qabrim's every move. Sandy tried to picture the unseen changes he was producing—the tunnel through which they had come sealing off, forever shutting off the old spaceport and the entire past that it belonged to....

This should be a joyous occasion, she thought. *I've looked forward to it for more than half my life.*

So why can't I feel more that way?

That was all too easy to answer.

Beldan pulled a cord and the green drapes parted to reveal three alcoves with beds—a slightly undersized double in the middle, opposite the console, a pair of stacked bunks in the left end compartment, a single in the right. He stretched out on that one, gathering several straps to assemble a padded harness around himself. "Better strap in," he said. "There should be no need, but if anything should go wrong, it's most likely to happen near the beginning or end."

Sandy and Jonel lay down side by side on the wide middle bunk, under a low, padded ceiling. As she figured out how to connect her harness, she heard Scott and Karen talking softly in the compartment to her left, trying to reassure each other as Scott made sure Karen was securely strapped in. And she saw Qabrim strapping himself into the padded control seat.

"Thirty seconds," he said. He and Beldan exchanged several of their own syllables. Sandy felt muscles tense throughout her body, and consciously relaxed them.

After a while she imagined she felt a quivering, but it was too faint to be sure. There was no noise; the Kyyra, in defiance of what humans had not long ago considered natural law, were too efficient for that. But under and around Titusville, delicate tendrils of exhaustless annihilation, drawn out from the dying drive reaction under Qabrim's remote control, should be embracing the city, creeping toward the surface, severing it from the Earth and sealing the edge.

And meanwhile lifting gently from below, lifting the severed slab skyward while holding it intact and undistorted against all its natural instabilities.

It still made Sandy nervous to think about it. But it was no longer academic. She felt her weight building up, pressing her more and more firmly into the bed. In a few minutes, she estimated that it tripled or quadrupled. That left her still below "normal," but enough above anything in recent memory to be uncomfortable at first. But consciousness of its significance overcame any discomfort. *It means*, she thought with delight, *we're airborne—or whatever I should call it. We must be miles up. Dozens, maybe even hundreds.*

We made it!

So far.

She grinned and squeezed Jonel's hand. He squeezed back. Beldan started piping. Karen asked, "Will we get much heavier?"

"I don't know." Scott's voice was strained.

Qabrim was unfastening his harness. "Not too much, Karen," he said. "I'm easing it up toward what it'll be after we land, but it'll be so gradual you can relax. Walk around or sleep if you like. It'll be hours before anything exciting happens."

I wish I could believe that, Sandy thought wryly as she unstrapped and stood up. But she refused to dwell on it. It felt too good to know they were on their way down.

She poked her head around the end of the partition to see Karen easing herself off the top bunk and onto the ladder with a mildly comical mixture of caution and haste. She grinned at Sandy. "We're really doing it, aren't we? And all the others, too."

"As far as I know." *It must be quite a sight*, Sandy thought. *Five thousand cities rising like a flock of frightened birds from the surface of one planet, to migrate in a few hours to another. Too bad we can't watch.* "How does it feel to have weight?"

"Different." Karen wrinkled her nose slightly as she stepped off the ladder and tried to jump. "I miss being bouncy. And I think I'll get tired at first, even after all that exercise. But I'll get used to it. Just wait till I can go outside every day."

"That's the spirit." Karen went off. Sandy looked down at Scott, still lying on the lower bunk with his eyes closed. "How about you, Scott?"

"I think I'll stay here and rest," he murmured.

She looked at him for quite a while. This depression he had been in lately was not good. She had hoped that the excitement of journey's end would snap him out of it.

But she decided not to say any more just now.

Half an hour later, Karen tugged at her sleeve and whispered, "Grandma, can I talk to you a minute? It's Daddy. I'm worried about him."

Sandy sat down with her on the double bed. *So am I*, she thought. "What's the problem?"

"I thought he'd be as excited as I am, but he just lies there and grunts when I talk to him. And he yelled at me. What's wrong?"

"Hm-m-m. Well, Karen, maybe he's just tired. Things have been pretty hectic lately."

"He didn't act just tired."

"Sometimes it's hard to tell. Remember, this is going to be a big change for him. Most people are a little afraid of change, even if it's supposed to make things better. And they tend to get more afraid as they get older."

"You're older than Daddy."

"True. But I remember Before. He doesn't." Sandy chuckled and lifted the curtain of soft hair away from Karen's ear to whisper, "Besides, don't tell anybody, but I'm a little afraid, too."

"Really?"

"Really. Aren't you?"

Karen studied her grandmother's face with an intent frown for several seconds. Then she broke into a grin with a certain amount of relief in it. "Uh-huh. But don't you tell anybody either."

"My lips are sealed. Now, I'll talk to your Daddy. But don't you worry about him. O.K.?"

"O.K."

Sandy stepped around the partition to where Scott still lay, breathing slowly. "Awake?" she asked.

He opened his eyes but didn't look at her. "Uh-huh."

She sat down on the edge of the bunk. "Karen's worried about you. I told her I'd talk to you."

"I heard. Not much privacy in here."

"True. Are you feeling O.K.?"

Scott nodded. "Yes. I'm sorry I snapped at her. But she was getting on my nerves." He propped himself up on an elbow and looked at Sandy as if he urgently needed to defend himself. "Look, Mom, I know my attitude hasn't been what you'd like lately. I hope you understand why."

"I think I do."

"I had as much enthusiasm for the trip as anybody when I was young—"

"You're still young, Scott. You're not even thirty."

"I don't feel young. But, O.K. . . . when I was younger. When I was little. I thought it was something great, then—us and the Kyyra working together to save ourselves from extinction and find a place where we could build lives like you had on Earth Before. Anybody'd feel that, being around you and Dad and Henry and Beldan all the time—"

Well . . . almost anybody, Sandy thought, remembering Greg.

"—but I'm not so sure any more. One thing after another has chipped away at my faith until there's not much left. Forced marriage . . . work draft and cannibal crews . . . Greg . . . Alycia's first miscarriage . . . what finally happened to her just when we thought we had a real marriage . . . all the things going wrong now. . . .

"It's got hard to keep believing—either that we'll succeed, or that it'll be worth it. I've tried to keep up a good front, for Karen. She'll do better if she can start with a positive attitude. But me? Now that it's happening and there's nothing I can do but wait, I keep thinking about the problems, and she keeps chattering about how great it's going to be. It just got to me."

This time Sandy did reach out to rub his head and shoulders. "You've just had too much time to think," she said. "When you get outside and take your future into your own hands, you'll be all right." Her tone shifted slightly. "But you'd better do something about Karen. She's worried about more than you, though she doesn't know it. You're making her afraid there's something about what we're doing that's so scary you're afraid to tell her."

"I'll talk to her." Scott sat up. For a moment he sat silent, a little like Rodin's *Thinker*, but closer to action. Watching him, Sandy became vaguely aware of an extra voice out in the main room, but it didn't quite register.

Until Jonel glanced her way and said, "Better come out here, Sandy. Somebody on the radio wants to talk to both of us."

She straightened up abruptly. Now she recognized the voice. Moses was making his move.

"The time," the too-familiar baritone said smoothly, "is at hand. By the time we're on the ground, control will be out of your hands and safely in ours. It will go easier for everybody if you cooperate now. And encourage everyone under you to do the same."

He paused. When neither Jonel nor Sandy said anything, he resumed just as smoothly. "At this moment, our agents are within minutes of seizing each of the landing cities. I strongly urge every government to surrender now, so violence will not be necessary. Needless to say, that includes you in Titusville."

Sandy checked an indicator on the government communication set at the end of the main console. The transmission was not scrambled. They would have to assume everyone on Earth was listening.

"Your claim seems a bit premature," Jonel said evenly. "You

mean your agents are within minutes of *trying* to seize the cities. That's not the same as success. We anticipated this, of course. The cities are prepared to defend themselves." If Moses thought they wouldn't try, he had misjudged. An inflight attack was one possibility they had definitely anticipated, and plans were ready for it. But they would be limited in what they could do. . . .

"Need I point out," said Moses, "that we are at a rather critical stage of things? Any attempt to resist will pose a threat to safe descent and landing—and lives. Is that what you want? More slaughter of the people you claim to protect?"

"Evidently it's what you want," said Jonel. "No resistance will be necessary unless you strike first. It hardly seems necessary to point out that the one sure way to avoid those risks is for you to call off your dogs before they bite anybody."

"Unfortunately, that also means passing up our one good chance to make sure we end your so-called emergency rule. No, Mr. Turabian, we can't afford that. So the responsibility for safety must be yours. You've said repeatedly that you plan to abdicate once we're down. Why not do it now?"

"We didn't say," said Sandy, "we'd hand it over to a new dictator."

"That's harsh, Mrs. Turabian. I don't intend to keep it. All I want to do is give it back to the people."

"We know that's what we mean to do. We don't know about you."

"I could have said the same thing," said Moses. "Interesting, isn't it, that we both say we want the same thing, but neither of us dares trust the other. Tell me, can you give us some proof? Some sign of good faith that will let us feel really confident that you mean what you say?"

"Can you?"

"Stalemate. So we fall back on the old historical standby— brute force. How gauche."

"You don't have to," said Jonel. "If you really care as much as you say about people, you won't."

"And we don't both want the same things." Sandy added. "How about the Kyyra aid question? If your intentions are so good, why have you paved your way by appealing to the worst side of people? At least we haven't done that."

"Haven't you?" Moses asked quietly, and Sandy cringed. She was almost relieved when he went on, more rapidly, "We're wasting time. You had your chance, Mr. and Mrs. Turabian. Whatever happens now is on your hands. It's a pity you're willing to jeopardize the cities. But so be it. I'll see you soon."

"Our guards," said Jonel, "are ready for you. And remember that anything that jeopardizes Titusville jeopardizes you and your plans as well."

"Your guards," said Moses, "are some of us. I repeat, we'll see you soon." A tiny light went out on the panel, showing that Moses' carrier wave had vanished. The call was over.

Sandy looked at Jonel, and at Karen, standing with a worried look by the foot of Scott's bed. "Do you think," she almost whispered, "that could be true about our guards?"

Jonel shrugged. "It's not impossible. We'll find out soon enough, I suspect."

That particular possibility seemed increasingly remote as hours went by without visitors. But there was no shortage of tension. Not only the nagging uncertainty of when Moses would strike and with what result, but many things—the frantic preparations, the early rising for the trip to Titusville, the steady tug of almost a full gee, the problems between humans and Kyyra—all had taken their toll. Everyone was edgy. Beldan had withdrawn so far he spoke only such few words as he must. Scott was not much better, though for different reasons. Karen didn't become quiet, but she did become wary of irritating the others, and her cheerful anticipation was increasingly eroded by nervous apprehension.

It was just as well that the same things which made people jumpy had also made them tired. The trip down would last many hours, so everyone—except Qabrim—tried to sleep, and often only one or two were up at a time. It bothered Sandy that Qabrim had to stay awake and at the helm for the whole time, but neither she nor Jonel had learned enough to try replacing him. Even tired, he would do far better.

For her, the hours passed in a fitful alternation of catnaps and pacing, algae snacks and screen-watching. Always, when she woke, she went first to stand beside Qabrim or sit in the copilot's chair and look at the view, watching the disk grow until it overflowed the screen and gave way to details like continents and seas. Between those times, as she tried to sleep, there was a tossing, shifting, unceasing procession of dreams and half-dreams. The dreams were full of openness and freedom, of bright blues and wispy clouds and feathery breezes. There was more of the Christmas Eve imagery, and occasional snatches of the "Songs of Old and New Earth" she had long ago written and sung for Scott and Greg.

And all of it harshly tempered by the impending threat. As the hours went by, there was less sleeping and more pacing as unnerving reports came in to emphasize that Moses wasn't bluffing. The first three calls came less than an hour after his call to Titusville. They were not distress calls, exactly— Ahmadabad and Bratislava and Lusaka couldn't possibly have expected anybody to come to their aid. They merely told the world they were under attack, and the nature of the broadcasts was such that the whole, chillingly swift takeover was heard in real time.

Such reports came more and more frequently. The raiders were not always successful; a fair number of cities eliminated them. But too many did not. And some did even worse. The one that really shook Sandy and Jonel was Krung Thep.

"Guerrillas have pentrated the control center," a voice said in thickly accented English. "They're scuffling—"

Noises: steps, furniture, voices speaking agitated Thai, explosive sounds, two shrieks. . . .

The original voice, becoming shrill: "The pilot's unconscious. There's no one at the controls!"

Beldan leaned on the console as if stunned. Sandy's skin tingled. Karen stared with wide eyes. "What'll happen to them?" she whispered.

Qabrim twiddled something on a remote part of his panel. His face twisted into a Kyyra expression that Sandy thought was related to a frown. "They're close to the ground . . . going down fast . . . nobody's doing anything. . . ."

"Can't you help?"

"No. I have all I can handle here, and no connection to them." He stared intently at the panel. "They're spinning. . . ."

The next five minutes were agony. A couple of other reports intervened, but Sandy hardly heard them. But she heard Qabrim when he looked suddenly down and murmured, "They've hit. The quake must have been considerable. I can't imagine any survivors."

He and Beldan let their faces go alien and began to pipe. Sandy lay down on her cot, feeling sick.

It wasn't long before Kiev reported that it was surrendering without a struggle. "Nothing," its spokesman said, "can be worth another Krung Thep. We surrender. We implore the world government to do the same, and make surrender the policy for all governments to follow...."

Jonel looked at Sandy. "We can't do it, of course."

"Can't we?" She pondered, more doubtful than she could imagined herself a few hours ago. "No, we can't." But her voice sounded weak in her own ears.

There were other Krung Theps—at least three or four—and there were other Kievs. The decision was not easy—Sandy preferred to leave this one mostly to Jonel—but they held out. Cities would still use their own judgment about when, if at all, to surrender. For Titusville it would be an extreme last resort.

Sandy was lying down next to Jonel, with the end getting near and the horizon on the screen almost straight, when the buffeting started. Not a regular quake like the ones everyone was used to, but a faint, irregular series of bumps that seemed to come from outside. She fought down the urge to sit suddenly upright. "What's that, Qabrim?"

"Only a little turbulence. We're getting down into the atmosphere. I'd suggest strapping in for the rest of the trip. I'm broadcasting a warning." He had already followed his own advice, and was now putting on a rugged helmet that almost matched his smooth head.

He must think it could get pretty rough, Sandy thought as she reassembled her harness. *Well, I guess it should. Even if it wasn't before we got here, we ought to stir it up a bit.*

The significance of Qabrim's key word washed over her in a sudden refreshing flood, momentarily sweeping everything else away. Her face broke into the first broad smile of pure exhilaration she could remember in many months.

Atmosphere. Air. That buffeting meant it was really out there—the sky, the breezes, the chance for some semblance of the life she and Jonel had been planning over half a lifetime ago and had to defer until now.

And now it was coming. Christmas morning was actually coming.

She looked at the clock over the console.

Only three more hours.

Three hours is a long time to be strapped in. For most of the first two, the turbulence wasn't too bad. Several times Karen whined that she didn't need to be strapped down, and tried to wheedle permission to get up. Each time Scott convinced her she mustn't, though he was obviously not very convinced himself. They grew audibly jumpier as the hours crept by. But a city does not fly gracefully, even with Kyyra technology, and the process could not be hurried.

By the end of the second hour, nobody was asking to get up. It grew so rough near the ground that Sandy found herself clinching her fists and gasping with some of the more startling jolts. *Did they know it would be this bad?* she wondered. But she didn't ask. From behind, at least, Qabrim seemed content. She wished she could see his face, and the screen that by now must show hills and valleys skimming by not far below....

And still Moses did not come.

The warning voice broke quite suddenly from the comset. "They're here," it squawked curtly, barely recognizable as Murdoch, commander of the guards outside. "Looks like six or seven—"

His voice choked off abruptly in a confused burst of muffled shots and shouts. Sandy's whole body stiffened; her hand and Jonel's found each other at the same instant and held tight. Karen whimpered, "What do we—"

But there was no time to answer, or even to finish, for the activity on the radio had already collapsed into silence. Hurried footsteps sounded outside and, with a crash, the door flew open. Two men strode in.

And everyone inside was still strapped down and vulnerable.

The newcomers lurched and staggered with the pitching of the room. The one in front, a redhead as chunky as the gun he held, looked about twenty-five, but even more prematurely aged than Scott. His eyes darted nervously around the room. Sandy lay very still. The other man, skinny and with dishwater-blond hair starting to gray and restricted almost entirely to his temples, was older and more self-assured.

The redhead yelled, "Nobody move!"

The graying blond looked unhurriedly around, somehow maintaining an air of confidence despite his undignified struggle to stay on his feet. "He's right, you know," he said with a slight smile, "even if his manners are a bit unrefined. This is my colleague, Griffith. I am Moses."

He finished surveying the room under Griffith's protective eye, and sat down in the copilot's chair and strapped in. "That's better." He swiveled around to scan the bunks. "You'd better strap in, too, Griffith. There. Next to Mrs. Turabian."

"You can't," Sandy hissed. "That's taken."

"An odd claim for one in your position to make," Moses smiled. "It can easily be vacated—"

"It's all right, Sandy." Jonel unstrapped and stood up. "Don't argue with them." Griffith edged past him and lay down next to Sandy, his gun never wavering. Jonel sat down on the floor next to Sandy's side of the bed, bracing himself between it and the wall.

"I apologize for the inconvenience," Moses said, "but there aren't enough places. Forces us to make priority decisions. Obviously Griffith and I need protection; we can't risk key members of the new government before it's even well established. We can't gamble with the aliens; we need them to get us down. And I have an old-fashioned regard for women and children. Don't worry, Mrs. Turabian. Your husband can take care of himself."

Qabrim faced Moses with a mixture of humanly recognizable contempt and something chillingly alien. "But I can't do my job with you sitting there."

"Oh, yes, you can. And I want to keep an eye on you to make sure. I stay right here."

Beldan's voice came abruptly from his bunk. "No. Let me remind you who has whom over a barrel, Moses. You two have one minute to get out of this room. Or we don't go down."

"What?"

Qabrim started to say something and Beldan cut him off roughly with a quick burst in Kyyra. Sandy frowned. "But, Beldan—"

"I've thought it over, Sandy. If the alternative is to let—"

Qabrim tried again; Beldan cut him off even more savagely. Sandy began to fear that he wasn't bluffing. "But it's not worth—"

"On the contrary. The price is really surprisingly small—"

Quite abruptly, the buffeting became much more violent. Incoherent noises came from Scott and Karen; Jonel bounced and grunted. Sandy felt her body strain upward against the harness, then suddenly downward into the bed. She felt a sudden chill as she saw that Qabrim no longer looked calm. He, too, was tossed about in his seat, straining at his straps. His hands darted rapidly over the controls. "Qabrim," she made herself ask, "is—"

"Squall line," he spat out, stretching across the panel. He spouted Kyyra at Beldan; Beldan replied the same way. Several fast exchanges shot between them.

"You'll speak English in here!" Moses ordered. "None of that—"

Qabrim turned just enough to glare at him. "You want down in one piece? Then we'll talk how we talk best. There isn't time for anything else." He switched his speech back to Kyyra and his whole attention back to the console.

But too late. The room lurched with a new kind of violence. Things shook; an odd sound between a groan and a rumble came from somewhere outside. Three or four shocks hit in rapid succession. Qabrim yelped something frantic in his own language. His hands darted toward widely separated parts of the panel, twisting things violently.

Part of Sandy knew, even then, but she asked reflexively. "What—"

"Separation." He didn't wait for the whole question. "Thunderstorms can be violent, too. And this fool distracted me. We've lost a piece. . . ." His arms and fingers writhed, his voice rose tightly. "I don't know if I can handle it."

Jonel was already trying to stand up, but the room was pitching so he lost his balance and hurtled across the room. He caught himself with outstretched arms and fell loosely. He didn't try to stand up. He crawled to the console and pulled himself up to his knees. "Do you move or do I sit on your lap?" he grunted to Moses.

"Sit," Moses grunted back. Jonel did.

Qabrim quickly traced an outline on the panel. "This group," he said. Then, with obvious relief, he gave his full attention to another set.

For a few seconds Jonel tried to work that way, but the position quickly proved too awkward. He stood up, carefully and precariously, swaying like a sailor in a storm. Planting his feet wide and bracing one leg against the console and one against Moses, he managed to stay upright as his fingers played over the controls.

But not easily, Sandy noted tensely. *And he's favoring one leg. Did he hurt it when he fell?*

If he can hold out till we're past the storms....

For a few seconds, the violence lessened slightly. Then, as if it had been gathering force, came a blow that seemed to momentarily upend the whole room. Suddenly Jonel's feet were not on the floor. He was flipped into the air, back down, his head swung so far back that Sandy caught an inverted glimpse of his startled face as he flew toward the partition at her left. For a sickening instant, she heard a sound like knuckles cracking. But that hardly had time to register before his head hit the partition, hard, and he dropped limply to the floor. Beyond the partition, she heard Karen's rising wail: *"Grandpa!"*

And then sobs.

The important part of Sandy felt the same way. But the part that was momentarily in charge had no time for that. Jonel had hardly hit the still-tossing floor before she was out of her harness and rolling off the bed. She had better luck than Jonel in crawling to the console; she tried not to look at the blood trickling from his head as she passed him.

"What do I do?" she asked as she pulled herself up at the console. Qabrim showed her. She did it. It was even harder than she had expected, but with her whole being focused on the task, she managed. Gradually, during an eternity that the clock called four minutes, the battering subsided. Not completely, but back to levels they had lived with before they hit the squall line.

Qabrim relaxed very slightly. "You'd better strap in, Mrs. Turabian."

"Can you do it alone?" she asked, concentrating on an indicator dot that kept wanting to spiral outward. "Or am I actually helping?"

"You're helping. But—"

"Then I stay." Sandy concentrated grimly on holding her indicators somewhere near center. She heard Scott moving around behind her, where Jonel lay, but she didn't look back. She did allow herself one glance at the screen, showing a fluffy plain of what looked like treetops sliding along just below them, almost a blur, but slowing. She looked back at her controls. Her fingers tried to shake, but she couldn't allow that. "Better strap in, Scott."

"But—"

"I don't want to hear it. If you can do anything in fifteen seconds, do it. Otherwise strap in."

He didn't speak. But he moved back to his bunk in much less than fifteen seconds.

The steady motion in the screen had almost stopped, but the image wobbled. The turbulence grew worse again, and the controls harder to handle.

"Very little drive left," Qabrim explained brusquely. "Has to end just as we touch down, so it doesn't spread into what we land on—"

And then came the first impact, hard enough to throw Sandy to the floor. "Don't try to get up," Qabrim snapped. His hands flew over the console as the whole room shook convulsively. Sandy obeyed, lying flat on her stomach and shielding her head with her arms. The shaking continued for many seconds as the bottom of Titusville flattened several square miles of alien forest and adjusted itself to the irregularities of the ground beneath. A series of sharp shocks sent pieces of ceiling and wall crashing down, but no large ones hit Sandy.

And then, with a final apologetic shudder, it died.

In the hush that followed, Sandy went limp, finally able to admit she was exhausted. *We're down*, she thought, dazed, but she didn't really make the connection with reality until she heard Qabrim say, "Well done, Mrs. Turabian. We've arrived."

She opened her eyes to look across the floor at Jonel, still lying motionless, and everything she hadn't been able to let herself feel before came welling up. With hot, wet eyes she looked questioningly up at Scott, who was unstrapping himself with a blankly grim expression.

"I couldn't do anything," he said.

She nodded dully and crawled to Jonel, allowing herself a minute to convince herself it was true, and to think the farewell she was too late to deliver.

A shadow moved across the floor and steps came alongside her. Moses knelt next to her, his face pale and somber, as if this one incident had for the first time shown him the tragic side of what he was doing. "I'm sorry it had to turn out this way, Mrs. Turabian," he said, very quietly. "But I saw no alternative. When you declined either to surrender or to provide convincing assurance—"

"Shut up," she said acidly, turning on him. "You have a good tongue, but—"

"Please, Mrs. Turabian." He closed his eyes. "This is painful enough without that. My intentions were completely honorable. It's unfortunate—"

"There's nothing more dangerous than good intentions in bad hands. It's painful for you, you say? You want sympathy from me? You should have thought of that before. A long time before." She glared at him. "So just what have you won, anyway? Titusville."

He drew himself up, rebuffed, reasserting himself. "No, Mrs. Turabian—much more than Titusville. Everything. You must have heard reports on the way down. We have most of the cities. The others are just a matter of time."

She shrugged. "So somebody has each city. But how do you propose to bind them together? How are you going to administer it all? Except for the other chunk of Titusville, the nearest human city is ninety miles off. There's a Kyyra site a little closer—only eighty miles. Those distances are typical. All across untouched, unexplored wilderness. No roads, no maps, no airports or planes or railroads. And just full of animals and hazards you know nothing about. How are you going to control even the next city, much less all of them?"

"We're already linked by radio, of course. And after—"

"Hah! So you can give orders. But what's to make them obey, once they realize you have no way to enforce them? You can't slap knuckles by radio, and you can't govern without slapping knuckles. Gradually—and it won't take long—your puppets will drift away and become free agents. And there won't be a thing you can do about it."

Moses smiled and sneered in one motion. "No way to enforce? Come, Mrs. Turabian, let's not be naive. Why do you think I personally took Titusville? Because this is now the center of the world government which has always tied it all together. And—"

"And you plan to use our administrative machinery? Of course, Moses. We've always known that. But we've also known it doesn't exist."

For the first time, his face registered shock. "What?"

"It doesn't exist. It did, when we were on Earth. But it depended on the communication and transportation systems we'd build there. Clark's World is as unexplored and roadless for us as it is for you. For all practical purposes, every town is on its own now—especially if you keep what you've taken."

"But . . . you're lying. All your threats about how you would deal with takeover attempts—"

"Propaganda. I'm not lying now, but we were then. Because we knew you—and others—were listening."

"But it wasn't just what you said. Our spies captured detailed plans, things never intended for public consumption—"

"But planted. We knew you were a tough audience, Moses. We had to make the show worthy of you."

He studied her face as if trying to convince himself she was serious. Finally he said, "But if that's true—why did you struggle at all? It would have been so much simpler—"

"To voluntarily let your puppets take over from well-established and experienced governments? To let you treat the Kyyra the unspeakable way you've promised?" She paused. "And it's not quite true that there was no way to get goods and services from one site to another. We would have had a network. A weak one, but better than nothing."

His anger flared. "Make up your mind, Mrs. Turabian. Is there a network or isn't there? And if there is, why can't we use it?"

"The Kyyra have ships and shuttles," she said quietly. "Not many, but some. That's all there is. And they won't deal with you—or vice versa."

Moses shifted his gaze to Beldan. With obvious effort, he squeezed distaste out of his face, leaving nothing. "Suppose," he said tightly, "I could find a way to modify my stand on aid. Isn't it conceivable that you could—"

"No," said Beldan. "Never with you. With Sandy, gladly." He started to play his pipe.

"Then we'll make it on our own," Moses muttered. "We're a tough breed, now, those of us who've made it this far." His voice rose furiously, aimed at Beldan. "And we'll see that you get no help, just as I promised. Nothing. Not even the pilots you were counting on to go back as teachers."

Beldan's eyes jerked. Sandy, though appalled by the threat, asked quietly, "What reason could you possibly have for that except personal vindictiveness? Is that one of your honorable intentions, Moses?"

He forced a smile. "I'm honor-bound, Mrs. Turabian. I promised no help for the Kyyra. I have to keep my promises, don't I?" His expression changed abruptly. "And yes, there's a personal element, too. If it hadn't been for them, we'd never have had to destroy our own planet and leave our own galaxy. I could have had a normal life. And I'm just old enough, Mrs. Turabian, that I do remember a little of Old Earth."

"But it wasn't them," Sandy said. "It was their ancestors. You can't blame them for what their ancestors did. The ones we know—if it hadn't been for them, you wouldn't be alive now. Doesn't that count for anything?"

"They owed us that. Now their debt's paid and we're even. A race that can do something like that is never to be trusted again. They're lucky that withholding help is all we're doing."

"I think you'll reconsider even that. I won't waste any more time talking ethics to you. But I know you care about self-preservation. Remember those miles? Sometimes, to keep alive, we're going to *have* to get from one place to another. Some of the things growing out there are food, and some are poison. Do you know which are which? The Kyyra have ships and food converters. If we ever hope to use them, we're going to need their good will. Our one-way dependence on them may be over, Moses, but our *mutual* dependence is just beginning. You lay a hand on even one Kyyra pilot, and you'll regret it to your dying day—which may be a lot sooner than you'd planned."

Moses was shaking visibly now, and his face looked as if he had something bitter in his mouth that he couldn't spit out. For almost a minute he pondered the hollowness of his victory before he said sullenly, "I may try to keep that option open. Just in case."

Sandy relaxed slightly. "A wise choice. And while you're keeping options open—I'm here if you need me. Meanwhile . . . you claim to be a humane man. I've come all the way here to see a new world, and I don't see anything else I can do in here. Are you going to let me go outside and look?"

He considered for quite a while, and it struck Sandy that he looked as drained as she felt. "You can go," he said at last. "Griffith, you go along. No need to stay too close, but keep an eye on her."

The light was almost blinding at first; it had been years since she had seen so much. As soon as she emerged from the tunnel she stood very straight to breathe deeply and look all around. A few other people had already come out, but she hardly noticed them. There was too much else to see and hear and smell.

And feel.

The break was not far away. She scrambled across the jumbled gray and brown ground and in half a minute stood at the edge of a not quite sheer drop. The landing had shattered the weakened edge so that it now fell away as a steep boulder slope—not quite too steep to climb—to the level forest a few hundred feet below.

A few miles to the southeast, with snowcapped mountains far beyond it, the other piece of Titusville stood as an isolated, barren plateau. Sandy felt an abrupt, odd pang of sorrow for the native things that had been crushed by the landing cities. *We'll be gentler, later,* she told them silently. *I hope.*

She sat down on the warm ground at the edge to pull herself together and drink in the reality of being on a planet. Warm, light breezes caressed first one cheek and then the other. Soft sounds drifted up from below, of wind in foliage and uncounted kinds of unfamiliar animal life. She looked down at the green carpet—not quite any green she knew, but lush and richly textured in the late afternoon light—and saw that some of the animals had been attracted to the base of the slab and were prowling around it, looking up. She couldn't tell much about their shapes, but several looked more than large enough to be potentially dangerous. But they showed no inclination to climb up, so she dismissed them as an immediate threat. She closed her eyes, listening to their distant hoots and whistles and breathing in the smells.

Most were unfamiliar, but pervading them all, to her surprise and delight, was the same clean smell of approaching rain she remembered from Old Earth. Smells are strange things, seldom remembered as consciously as sights and sounds, but if they ever recur, evoking associations as no other sense can. This one brought back an overwhelming flood of vivid memories of times spent in mountains and woods and shores in a faraway galaxy. For a moment Sandy let those wash over her, savoring them. Then she opened her eyes again to the new reality of Clark's World.

Is it wrong, she asked herself, *to be overjoyed at the same time I'm afraid and more grief-stricken than I've ever been before? I don't think so. Jonel would understand.*

It's going to rain, she thought suddenly. *How soon?* A few dark cloud shadows drifted over the green, but mostly the sky overhead was clear turquoise. But off to the West, and seemingly stretching out over the blue-gray sea to the south, she saw the line of storms that had killed Jonel. The big gray cloud masses were moving this way with visible speed, and the nearest were not far off. A soft, lazy roll of thunder drifted to her ears.

She stood up. Two big leathery-winged things, emerald green with iridescent purple splotches, swooped close, circled with wild giggles faintly suggestive of bass loons, and flew off. A drab crescent "moon," the corpse of Earth, peeked fleetingly through a hole in the clouds.

Two voices, thin in the open air, called her name.

"Mom!"

"Grandma!"

She looked to see Scott and Karen coming toward her from the tunnel exit. Scott's face was nearly blank; Karen was uncharacteristically quiet, but wide-eyed. They said few words, of no particular import. For a few minutes the three of them huddled together as Scott and Karen drank in new sensations. Then Karen asked Scott, "Can I look around a little?"

"O.K.," he said. "But don't go far, and don't get too close to the edge."

He sat down on a hummock, and Sandy on another next to him, gazing into herself and out to the west. In those few minutes, the gray clouds had claimed more of the sky, blotting out the dead Earth and the new sun. Thunder rolled around the horizon, closer than before, but weaker, as if the storms were running out of steam. After a while Scott asked quietly, "Well, Mom, do you still think it was worth it?"

She still heard the bitterness in his voice, and it hurt. But the urge to lash out at him lasted less than a second. *He'll be all right,* she reminded herself. "How can you doubt it?" she asked gently, and she answered herself before he could. *To him, this is all new and frightening. All that it means to me, it doesn't to him. Yet.*

"Greg," he said tonelessly. "Alycia. Dad. Moses. The Kyyra. Need I go on?"

"No." She looked at him. Her voice became less gentle. "You maybe thought all our problems would magically be over when we got here? Problems are never over, Scott—but people cut down the ones they can and build lives among the rest. Everything you say is true, and it's just the beginning. There'll be anarchy at first, and petty tyrants and civil wars, and famines and winters and droughts and stupid, fatal mistakes. And guilt. Nothing will ever wipe out the fact that we wiped out billions of human lives and uncountable nonhuman ones coming here, that we destroyed a planet's whole ecology more than a decade before it had to die. Nothing will ever make that right or good."

She thought of a dolphin she had once been privileged to know, and had to wait before she could continue. "But if we hadn't done that, it all would have died anyway. All of it—not just almost all. We wouldn't be here. We *are* here, Scott, and that's what's going to count in the long run. We kept some of Earth's life going, and there's no reason for it to stop now. The problems we have now are trifles; they're things people have been living with since people began. But never before have they had to look straight in the face of sure death for everything on Earth and say, 'We won't accept it. Some of us are going to keep going and rebuild something worth having, even if we have to go two million light-years to do it.' That's what we've done, Scott. And you wonder if it was worthwhile?"

He looked at her for a long time, as if he'd just seen something incredible in her face that he had never before realized was there. Finally he said, "You really believe in it, don't you? Even now."

She nodded stiffly. "Somebody has to. The future's there, if we want it enough." She paused, pondered briefly, and added, "It always is, you know."

He didn't say anything else. He sat pensively for a few more minutes, then stood up silently, motioned to Karen, and escorted her slowly back to the tunnel. But Sandy knew they'd be back.

She stretched, relaxed, looked out and up, slowly regaining a kind of peace she had not known for decades—a peace that was seriously marred, for her, only by the fact that Jonel was not here to share it. "You'd like it," she whispered, as if he could hear. "It's beautiful."

The storm was catching up with them. The dark gray now covered the sky, the air had cooled, and it was starting to sprinkle in big round drops that splattered on and around her, mingling with her tears and washing them away.

For a moment she was almost disappointed. She had wanted to watch the sunset.

But there would be plenty of nights for sunsets. For now, raindrops were all she could want.